CALL NURSE MILLIE

It's 1945 and, as the troops begin to return home, the inhabitants of London attempt to put their lives back together. For 25-year-old Millie, a qualified nurse and midwife, the jubilation at the end of the war is short-lived as she tends to the needs of the East End community around her. But while Millie witnesses tragedy and brutality in her job, she also finds strength and kindness. And when misfortune befalls her own family, it is the enduring spirit of the community that shows Millie that even the toughest of circumstances can be overcome.

CALL NURSE MILLIE

CALL NURSE MILLIE

by

Jean Fullerton

Magna Large Print Books
Long Preston, North Yorkshire,
BD23 4ND, England.

British Library Cataloguing in Publication Data.

Fullerton, Jean
    Call Nurse Millie.

    A catalogue record of this book is
    available from the British Library

    ISBN   978-0-7505-3797-1

First published in Great Britain by Orion Books,
an imprint of The Orion Publishing Group Ltd., 2013

Copyright © Jean Fullerton 2013

Cover illustration by arrangement with mirrorpix

The moral right of Jean Fullerton to be identified as the author of this
work has been asserted in accordance with the Copyright, Designs
and Patents Act, 1988

Published in Large Print 2013 by arrangement with
Orion Publishing Group

Magna Large Print is an imprint of Library Magna Books Ltd.

Printed and bound in Great Britain by
T.J. (International) Ltd., Cornwall, PL28 8RW

To my longest standing and best friend Dee

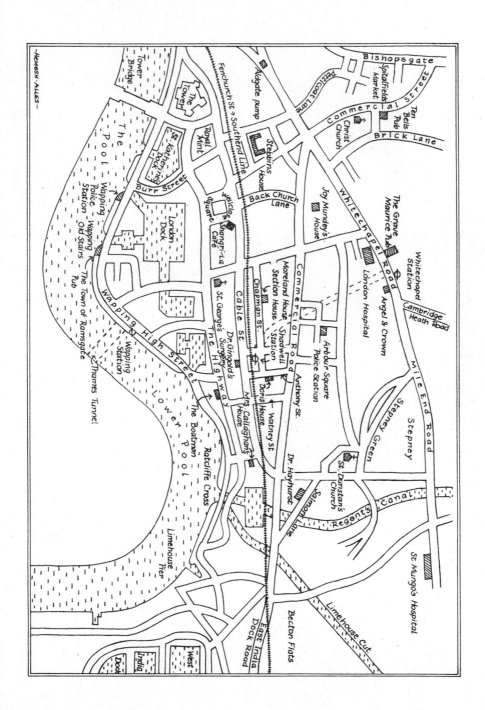

Chapter One

Millie Sullivan pushed an escaped curl of auburn hair from her eyes with the back of her hand. She wished she'd put on her cotton petticoat under her navy blue uniform instead of the rayon one. Although the milk float was only just rolling along the street, it was already sweltering hot.

With a practised hand Millie wrapped the new-born infant in a warm towel. 'There we go, young lady, say hello to your ma.'

She handed the child to the woman propped up in the bed. Mo Driscoll, already mother to four lively boys, took the baby.

'Thank you, Sister,' she said, tucking her daughter into the crook of her arm and gazing down at the baby. 'Isn't she beautiful?'

'She's an angel,' Mo's mother, standing on the other side of the bed, replied. 'And a welcome change.' She looked at Millie. 'I'll clear up, Sister. You look done in.'

'I am, but thankfully it's my last night on call.' Millie handed a parcel of newspaper containing soiled gauze to the older woman. 'Could you pop these on the fire?'

'To be sure.' She took the packet and threw it in the zinc bucket alongside the dirty linen. 'That superintendent works you nurses too hard. You should try and put your feet up when you get back.'

Millie smiled. Chance would be a fine thing. She plopped her instruments into the small galli-pot half-filled with Dettol, took off her gloves and glanced at her watch. Eight-thirty a.m.! Thank goodness.

She'd be back by the time Miss Summers gave out the day's work. Also, as Annie Fletcher, the trainee Queen's Nurse student assigned to Millie, was laid up with tonsillitis, Millie had given a couple of Annie's morning insulin injection visits to Gladys to do, and she wanted to make sure she'd done them.

'Do you know what you're going to call her?' Millie asked Mo, washing her hands in the bowl balanced on the rickety bedside table.

'Colleen, after me mum,' she replied.

Mother and daughter exchanged an affection-ate look and Millie glanced at her watch again.

She ought to get on, as she'd promised her own mum that she'd pop home in time for Churchill's announcement at three p.m. Her parents, Doris and Arthur, only lived a short bus ride away in Bow but, as Millie had two newborns to check plus a handful of pregnant women to see before she swapped her midwifery bag for her district one for her afternoon visits, it would be a close-run thing.

Millie packed the four small enamel dressing-bowls inside each other, then stowed them in her case between her scissors and the bottle of Det-tol. She snapped the clasp shut.

'I'll call back tomorrow, but if there's any prob-lem just ring Munroe House to get the on-call nurse,' Millie said, squeezing down the side of

14

the bed towards the door.

Like so many others in East London, the Driscolls' home was just the two downstairs rooms in an old terraced house that Hitler's bombs had somehow missed.

Colleen took the manila envelope tucked into the side of the dressing-table mirror and passed it to Millie. Millie opened it and took out two crumpled ten-shilling notes, popping them into the side pocket of her bag. I'll write it in when I get back to the clinic, she thought.

Leaving Mo in the care of her mother, Millie stepped out of the front door and looked up at the clear blue sky. Harris Street was filled with people milling around and chatting to each other. Women, their hair bound up in scarves knotted at the front and wearing sleeveless, wrap-around aprons, sat outside their houses.

They were already sewing coloured bunting in anticipation of the Prime Minister's broadcast. Most of the doors had been thrown open and the strains of 'Don't Sit Under the Apple Tree' filled the street, with the voices of the women singing along. They had clearly been about their chores since early that morning, as the doorsteps were already scrubbed white. Bedroom windows had been flung open and the curtains fluttering in the wind added to the festive mood. At the far end of the street a dozen or so boys were playing cricket with an upturned orange box as a wicket, while their sisters bobbed up and down the chalked squares of a hopscotch game.

Millie tilted her face to the sun. She closed her

15

eyes for a moment to enjoy the dappled shadow on her eyelids and the warmth on her cheeks.

'Has Mo had her nipper, Sister?' asked a woman who was beating out her doormat on the side of a house.

'About an hour ago,' Millie replied.

'What did she have?' asked the woman, setting out the newspapers on the rack outside the corner shop.

'You'd better ask Mr Driscoll.' Millie heaved her black leather Gladstone bag into the basket on the front of her bicycle. 'But I will say, you'll see some frilly baby clothes on the washing line from now on,' she added, unlocking the chain threaded around the lamp-post and through her front wheel.

Everyone laughed.

An old woman with iron curlers in her hair looked out of a front window. 'She'll need to keep her strength up, so I'll pop her over a drop of stew, Sister.'

'I'm sure she'll appreciate that,' Millie replied.

'Well, God bless the mite,' called a woman who was polishing her windows with newspaper. 'And, sure, isn't this the best of days to be born on?'

'It will be when old Churchill tells us it's all over,' shouted a man lounging under a lamp-post with two others. 'I mean, Hitler's been dead a week, so that must be an end to it. Hey, Sister! Do you think the Driscolls will call her Clementine after the old boy's missus?'

Millie laughed and grabbed the handlebars. 'I wouldn't count on it.'

She noticed the woman leaning on the windowsill at the far end of the street, a young boy playing with a model tank beside her. Millie wheeled her bike towards them.

'Jonnie looks a lot better, Mrs Brown,' she said, stopping in front of the pair. 'Has his cough gone?'

Mrs Brown nodded and looked down lovingly at her son. 'He's almost back to his old self, thanks to you, Sister. If it hadn't been for you showing me how to sponge him to keep the fever down, I don't know that he'd still be with us.'

Millie ruffled the boy's hair. 'I'm sure it was having his mum sitting by his bedside day and night that got him through the measles.'

Jonnie looked up. 'Do you want to come to our party later, miss? There's going to be jelly and blancmange and pilchards and everything.'

Millie laughed. 'Not together, I hope! I'd love to, but I'm going to see my mum and dad.'

He turned back to his tank and vroomed it along the pavement.

Millie said goodbye to his mother, scooted her old boneshaker into motion and then climbed on to the seat. She pressed down on the pedals to build up speed and then, checking the traffic, swung left on to the Highway and headed for Munroe House Nurses' Home to have breakfast and restock her bag before starting her postnatal rounds.

The breeze caught a couple of stray wisps of hair from beneath Millie's broad-brimmed hat and fluttered them against her cheeks. It also carried the sour odour of the river, half a mile away. As if sensing the joy in the air, the sparrows hopped merrily over the charred beams of the bombed-out houses. It was the most wonderful of days. From today there would be no more sirens warning of enemy aircraft or the eerie silence after a Doodlebug's engine cut out and fell to earth. No, the dark days were over and baby Driscoll couldn't have picked a more perfect day to enter the world!

Millie pushed on, ringing her bell, waving at the beat officer seeing schoolchildren across the road and smiling at the people passing by on their way to work.

Finally, after twenty minutes of weaving between the lorries and a handful of old-fashioned horse-drawn wagons hauling goods from the docks, Millie pedalled through the back gates of the nurses' home.

Munroe House, where Millie and thirty other nurses employed by the St George's and St Dunstan's District Nursing Association lived and worked, was a large, four-storeyed Victorian house situated at the Limehouse end of Commercial Road, just past St Martha's and St Mungo's Catholic Church.

It had once housed a family and an army of servants within its high-ceilinged rooms, and it had been bequeathed to the Association after the Great War. Standing on one pedal, Millie swung herself off the bike and guided it towards the bike stand by the old stable walls. She wedged the front wheel into a vacant slot, grabbed her bag and made her way to the back door.

Pushing open the door, she headed for the refectory. The room where the nurses ate their meals was once the family parlour. Its lofty, ornate ceiling was cream in colour and had been painted so often that what had once been delicate crafted grapes now looked like clumps of potatoes. The room had been redecorated with apricot-coloured flowers and green foliage on a mushroom-hued background just before the outbreak of war, but it had now faded into gloomy shades of brown. There were two long, scrubbed tables that could accommodate at least a dozen nurses around each. Luckily, as all thirty nurses were never in the house at any one time, there was always a place free.

Half-a-dozen nurses at the far end of one of the tables looked up and acknowledged Millie, then returned to their breakfast.

Connie Byrne, sitting at the table by the kitchen, raised her head and smiled. In contrast to Millie's dark looks, Connie was a strawberry blonde with high cheekbones and golden-green eyes. She was just an inch or two taller than Millie's five foot four, but as she and Millie had the same slender figure, the two girls extended their meagre wartime wardrobes by swapping clothes.

Each of the nurses employed by the St George's and St Dunstan's District Nursing Association and who had completed the Queen's Nurse training were allocated to a set geographical area. They were the nursing Sisters who planned the care of the local patients, but they often had a nursing assistant to help them in day-to-day patient care. Connie had the patch next to Millie's. She covered the close-packed houses east along the Highway to Ratcliffe Cross, while Millie took the west section, including the Chapman Estate, and the dingy end of Cable Street.

'I hope you haven't polished off all the grub,' Millie said, walking over to the breakfast table and pouring a cup of tea from the oversized enamel teapot. 'Some of us have been up for hours and already done a day's work.'

Cradling the cup in her capable fingers, Connie grinned. 'I thought I heard the phone ring. What time was it?'

'Just after six.' Millie sat next to her and put her bag on the floor beneath the chair. She took a slice of toast from the rack.

Connie passed her the butter dish. 'It's axle grease, I'm afraid.'

'What, already? Miss Summers could have only given Cook this week's ration book two days ago.' Millie eyed the solid block of marge. 'I'll make do.'

'Who was it?' Connie asked, as Millie reached for the pot of damson jam.

'Mrs Driscoll,' Millie replied, digging her knife into the ruby jelly. 'A girl.'

Millie glanced at the large wall clock.

'Don't worry,' Connie said. 'You've got time to finish your breakfast before allocation.'

'It's just that, you know ... being six nurses down.' Millie forced a smile.

'You take too much on yourself,' Connie said, taking a sip of tea.

'Someone has to. Anything from your Charlie?'

Connie shook her head. 'I can't believe it's almost a year since I got his last letter, but the Army post is simply shocking, and his mother's heard nothing either. I expect he's too busy rounding up the last of Mussolini's thugs to write, but I'm sure

20

I'll hear something soon.'

Millie put her hand over her pal's, and squeezed. 'Don't worry. The top brass will be kicking him home soon enough.'

Beattie Topping, their friend who covered the Stepney area, came over.

'Morning, girls,' she said, pinning the last few strands of light brown hair away from her face as she sat down opposite them. 'Some of us are going to ask for permission to go up West later for the celebrations. Why don't you come?'

Millie poured a cup of tea for Beattie. 'Who's us?'

'Me, Eva, Joyce and some of the other girls. We're going up to the Palace to see if the King and Queen come out on the balcony. It's going to be a party and no mistake.'

'Do you think the Old Girl will give us all a pass?' Connie asked.

'I don't see how she can say no, as long as there's someone here to answer the phone. It's not every day we win a war.' She looked sheepishly at Millie. 'We thought perhaps you wouldn't mind asking her.'

'I will, but you'll have to go without me,' Millie replied. 'I promised Mum and Dad I'd join them to listen to the Prime Minister's broadcast.'

Connie elbowed her. 'You can be back here for eight and we can all catch the tube together. Come on. Let's put our glad rags on and dance until dawn with the rest of London. After dodging bombs for six years, don't we deserve a bit of fun?'

'I should say.' Beattie winked. 'There'll be hundreds of our brave boys looking for a girl to swing

21

on their arm. It's nothing less than your patriotic duty not to disappoint them.'

Millie laughed. 'Well, if it's for king and country, how could I refuse? Let me know how many of you want a pass and I'll ask Miss Summers after allocations.'

The door swung open and Gladys Potter strolled in. She went to the mirror over the fireplace, took her hat off and patted the rolls on either side of her head back into place.

'Have you given Mrs Rogers her insulin?' Millie asked.

'You asked me to, didn't you?' Gladys replied, fingering through the flattened curls of her fringe without glancing around.

'What about Mr Gordon?'

'I'll do him on my way to Turner Street when I go out,' she replied.

'But he can't have his breakfast until you've been.'

Gladys swung around. 'Look, I've already done three of my own patients plus yours, so he'll have to wait!' She turned to the mirror, pressing her lips together to redistribute the red lipstick she wasn't supposed to wear on duty.

'What is it with her?' asked Beattie in a low voice.

'Don't take no notice. Me and Millie were in the same nursing set as her at the London and she was a cow even then,' said Connie quietly.

'One night Old Iron Knickers, the matron, found an American airman that Gladys was knocking around with in the linen room at the nurses' home,' Millie explained in a whisper. 'If it

22

wasn't for the war Gladys would have been kicked out on the spot. She wasn't, but she had to do three months of nights on the men's ortho-paedic ward as punishment, and then had to report to matron every night at six o'clock, eight o'clock and ten for another three.'

'What's that got to do with you?' asked Sally.

'Gladys thinks it was me who told matron,' Millie replied. 'I didn't, but...' she shrugged.

The grandfather clock in the hall started to chime.

Connie swallowed the last of her tea. 'We'd better go through.'

Millie stood up and the three women left the refectory to make their way to the treatment room at the far end of the corridor.

There was no sign of Miss Summers, so Millie slid around to her place in the chair near the top of the central table. Connie and Beattie followed.

The room at the hub of Munroe House had been the morning room once used by the lady of the house, and it was large enough to accom-modate an examination couch, a sizable table and a dozen straight-backed chairs. Pinned on the pale cream wall surrounding the nurses were posters advising people to use a handkerchief when they sneezed, and not to spit, and reminding children that Dr Carrot was their best friend. A floor-to-ceiling cupboard stood against the opposite wall, while the blackboard that listed the names of the nurses allocated to the clinic each day was hooked behind the door. The equipment ready to be loaned out to patients, such as china bedpans and bed cradles that kept

23

blankets off patients' legs, was stored between the empty wine racks in the cellar below. As always, the acidic smell of iodine mingled with Dettol and hung heavy in the air.

Other nurses filed in, Gladys being the last, perching on a chair with her legs crossed and a blasé expression on her face.

As the second hand of the large clock fixed above the door ticked by, the nurses waited. After a few moments the chattering started.

'Perhaps someone should go and see what's keeping her,' Gladys said, looking across at Millie as the noise in the room grew louder.

Millie stood up and went towards the door but as she got there it opened and Miss Summers walked in. Millie's heart sank. Not only had the superintendent misbuttoned the front of her uniform, but she was wearing one black shoe and one brown.

Miss Summers' watery eyes ran over Millie as she tried to focus. 'What are you doing, Sullivan?'

'Coming to find you, Miss Summers,' Millie replied, catching a faint whiff of gin.

'But I'm here,' replied Miss Summers as she tottered past Millie. 'Now, for today's allocations,' she said, planting her generous rear on the chair. She opened the enormous bound book and the nurses sat with their notebooks and pencils poised.

The superintendent stared at the ledger with a baffled expression on her face.

'Excuse me, Miss Summers.' Millie reached across and turned the book the right way up.

There was a titter from the far end of the table.

Miss Summers took her old spectacles from her

top pocket, wedged them on the tip of her nose and peered at the page in front of her.

'Dr Murray asks that someone call in to talk about a patient in Sydney Street, so that would be you, Nurse Barrett,' she said looking over the rim of her spectacles.

'Excuse me, Superintendent, but Nurse Scott is the Whitechapel East nurse,' Millie said, nodding at Sally Scott sitting on the other side of the table.

Miss Summers shot her an irritated look. 'That's what I said. Nurse Scott will visit.' She looked down at the neat columns of copperplate writing and mumbled her way through the remaining telephoned requests. 'And if all that were not enough, those pen-pushers at the Public Health Department are on to us again about visiting the schools. Don't they know there's a war on?' Miss Summers scowled at the sheet as if it were responsible for the lack of nurses.

'Not any more there ain't,' Gladys muttered to her two friends sitting either side of her.

Millie leaned forward. 'Would you like me to organise the school visits, Miss Summers?'

The superintendent raised her head. A Kirby grip broke loose and a strand of grey hair flopped over her right eye. 'Please don't interrupt me, Sullivan.'

'Sorry, Miss Summers,' Millie said.

Miss Summers glanced at the book again. 'Sullivan, I want you to arrange the school visits.'

Sally and Beattie gave Millie a sympathetic look. The phone sitting on the table outside in the hall rang.

'Mrs Jupp?' asked Beattie.

25

Connie shook her head. 'Mrs Williams. She was due two weeks ago.'

Millie stood up. 'I'll get it.'

She squeezed her way behind the nurses alongside her and went into the hall. The metallic ring of the black telephone echoed around the tiled hall and up the stairwell.

Millie picked up the receiver. 'Good morning. Munroe House. How can I help you?'

'This is Doctor Hurst from St Andrew's Hospital. I'd like to speak to one of your nurses, a Miss Sullivan, if I may,' a male voice said.

'Speaking.' There was a pause. 'Miss Sullivan speaking,' she repeated.

'I'm sorry. I didn't think I would get through to you directly. I'm afraid your father has been admitted to Bromley Ward in St Andrew's. Your mother is at his bedside but I think she will need you with her soon.'

Heels tapped across the polished floor and wheels squeaked as the nurses pushed the black trolley to the far end of Bromley Ward. The large ward clock set above the nurses' station by the door ticked out the minutes. The clatter of a bucket and a faint smell of disinfectant told Millie the ward orderly was mopping up a spillage somewhere. Millie couldn't see any of this because screens had been drawn around her father's bed.

Arthur Sullivan lay still with his eyes closed and, as a bed bath was a nurse's first duty when a patient was admitted, newly washed and with his hair combed. Millie ran her eyes over the blue counterpane and wondered how many of them

26

she must have thrown over, smoothed flat and tucked in during her seven years of nursing.

His barrel chest still rose and fell with unhurried regularity, but already Millie could hear the rattle in the back of his throat. Despite his droopy right eye and slack mouth, Arthur looked younger than his fifty-two years and now much more like the father she remembered hoisting her on his shoulders at Southend so she could see the Punch and Judy show at the end of the pier. Millie squeezed her father's nicotine-stained fingers as images of him holding nails between his lips as he made a cradle for her best doll filled her mind. She hooked her fingers around her father's wrist to feel his pulse. It was thready, with an occasionally missed beat.

Millie looked across at her mother Doris keeping vigil on the other side of the bed.

Whereas her father's years had mysteriously slipped away, Doris looked every day of her forty-seven years. Somewhere between discovering her husband collapsed and climbing into the back of the ambulance, she'd remembered to shrug on a summer coat, but she was still wearing her tartan slippers. Her drained, colourless complexion matched perfectly the faded candy-striped curtains behind her.

'He only went out to pull a couple of carrots,' Doris muttered, without taking her eyes from her husband. 'I didn't think anything of it when he didn't come in. I just thought he was chatting to Peggy next door; you know, her with the bad knee and the Jack Russell, but when I noticed his bacon and eggs getting cold on the table I went out to see,' the tears welled up in her pale eyes, 'and that's when I found him just lying there, like that, among the beans and cabbages, staring up at the sky.' Doris pulled a handkerchief out of her pocket. 'If only I'd gone out straight away I could have called the ambulance sooner and...' she blew her nose.

'I don't think it would have made any difference,' Millie said gently.

The screen behind her mother moved and a young man dressed in a white coat stepped through. With his brown hair, round-rimmed glasses and smooth cheeks he looked no more than twelve, but the stethoscope hanging around his neck marked him out as the junior houseman.

'I'm Mr Sullivan's daughter,' Millie said, standing up and walking around to stand beside her mother.

'Good day. I'm Dr Hurst. I telephoned you earlier,' he said.

'Do you know what's wrong with my Arthur?' Doris asked.

The doctor picked up the clipboard hanging on the end of the bed and glanced at it. 'We've done some tests and I can tell you that Mr Sullivan has suffered a stroke.'

The colour drained from her mother's face. 'But how? Arthur's as strong as an ox and he's never had a day on the sick in his life.'

The doctor glanced over the chart again. 'Your husband has suffered a cerebral haemorrhage in the motor part of his brain and, more seriously, his medulla oblongata.'

Her mother looked blankly at Millie.

28

'Dad's had a bleed into the part of his brain that takes care of his breathing and heartbeat,' Millie said woodenly.

'But he will get better, won't he?' Doris asked anxiously. 'I mean, George Duffy at number four had a stroke last November and now he's as fit as a fiddle.'

'Vascular accidents are by their very nature unpredictable, Mrs Sullivan,' the young doctor said in a ponderous tone. 'But I feel confident in my assessment that, due to the extent of the vascular involvement, your husband will not recover from this episode.'

'You mean he won't be able to walk or talk or something?'

Millie took her mother's hand. 'The doctor means there's nothing they can do, Mum, and it's just a matter of time.'

Doris stared blankly at her for a moment, and then covered her mouth with her hands.

The doctor returned the chart to the end of the bed. 'I'll let you have a few moments alone,' he said, before leaving through the screens.

Millie returned to her seat on the other side of the bed and she and her mother sat in silence for a moment, and then Doris straightened the collar of her husband's pyjamas.

'You're a daft old bugger, so you are, Arthur,' she said, softly. 'My mother always said you were a man born the wrong way around. Only you could have stroke on the day it's all over.' She took her husband's hand again. 'How am I going to cope without you?'

'You've still got me, Mum,' Millie replied, as

pain tightened in her chest.

Doris nodded. 'I know. I know. But me and your dad have known each other almost thirty years.'

'Quick, turn it on so everyone can hear,' a woman called from the other side of the screens. There were some crackling sounds as someone turned the tuning dial, and then a blast of music from a military band.

The music stopped and the plummy voice of the announcer spoke. 'This is the BBC. We are now going over live to the Cabinet Room at Ten Downing Street where the Prime Minister will address the nation.'

A buzz of excitement went around the ward just as a small trickle of spit slipped out from the corner of Arthur Sullivan's slack lips. Millie wiped it away with a gauze square.

'Yesterday morning at two forty-one a.m.,' the unmistakeable voice of Winston Churchill said, 'at General Eisenhower's headquarters...'

Arthur gurgled and stopped breathing. His skin blanched and the birthmark over his left eye mottled as his circulation ceased.

'Arthur!' Doris whispered, clutching his lifeless hand.

As Churchill announced unconditional surrender of the German state, Millie rose and placed her hands over her mother's.

'He's gone, Mum,' she said quietly after a while.

Her mother lifted her husband's hand to her cheek and kissed it. With a lingering look at her father, Millie moved the screen aside and stepped out.

'We may allow ourselves a brief period of rejoicing...' Millie heard the Prime Minister say, and a cheer went up. The matron in her frilly starched cap, nurses in green candy-striped uniforms and patients in dressing gowns and slippers shook hands and hugged each other.

One of the nurses spotted Millie and came over. 'Isn't it marvellous?' she asked, her round face shining with joy. 'I can hardly believe that it's all finally over.'

'My father's just gone,' Millie said flatly.

The young nurse became serious instantly. 'I'll tell the doctor.'

She hurried to Dr Hurst, who was sharing a drink with the ward orderly. She spoke to him and they came over. Millie followed them back behind the screens. Her mother was as she'd left her, clutching her husband's hand and gazing aimlessly at the clouds passing by outside the window.

Millie put her arm around her shoulders. 'Shall we let the doctor have a bit of room?'

'Yes, of course,' Doris said, standing up and stepping aside.

The doctor placed his stethoscope on Arthur's chest for a couple of seconds and then slung it around his neck.

'I'm sorry,' he said.

Doris nodded. 'Thank you, doctor. I'm very grateful for all you've done and I'm sure my Arthur would say the same if...' She wiped her nose with her handkerchief, and then sat down next to the bed again.

'If you could let us have a few moments,' Millie

said, as her mother started to sob noiselessly.

The doctor left. On the other side of the screen people chatted and laughed while the BBC orchestra played dance music.

'I should have come yesterday instead of covering Mavis's evening round,' Millie said quietly, staring down at her father.

Doris looked up. 'Don't be silly, dear. You've got an important job and people rely on you.'

'That's true, but even so.'

The screens parted and the nurse slipped through the gap. 'I'm very sorry for your loss, Mrs Sullivan. Is there anything you'd like? A cup of tea perhaps?'

'Thank you, and I understand you've a lot to do, so we'd better get on.' Doris stood up.

The nurse looked dismayed. 'No, no, Mrs Sullivan. There's no rush. Stay as long as you like.'

Doris smiled. 'You're a good girl for saying it, but my daughter's a nurse so I know what it's like.' She hooked her handbag over her arm. 'She's a Queen's Nurse and works on the district now. Top of her class at the London she was, too.'

The nurse smiled politely.

'You've been very kind,' Millie said. 'Can I collect my father's property and death certificate tomorrow?'

'I'm not sure,' replied the nurse. 'Now the Prime Minister's announced a two-day holiday, I don't know if the almoner will be in. Perhaps if you telephone.'

'I will.' Millie looked at her mother.

Doris leaned over her husband and gave him a peck on the cheek. 'Goodbye,' she whispered, then pushed the screens aside and hurried out.

Millie went after her into the long corridor just as her mother disappeared down the stairs. Submerging every nursing instinct, Millie ran down the stone stairs to the ground floor and caught up with her mother outside the main door.

'Perhaps you should go and sit with him for a while, Mum. The nurses won't mind.'

Doris shook her head. 'After twenty-seven years as man and wife there's not much me and your dad haven't said, and he knows.'

Millie slipped her arm through her mother's. 'Well then, let's find a taxi and get you home.'

'Don't be silly, dear. It's only four stops on the bus and your dad would think I'd had a win on the horses spending money like that.' Tears welled up in her mother's eyes.

Millie forced a smile. 'I think Dad would understand,' Millie led her mother towards the main road, 'and especially if he could see what you've got on your feet.'

'Don't worry, Millie,' Connie's voice said down the telephone. 'I'll sort out your round and divide it between me, Eva and Beattie. You just look after your mum.'

'I owe you,' Millie replied.

'Don't be daft. It's the least we could do and, Millie, all the girls are really sorry about your dad.'

The lump in Millie's throat grew. 'Thanks. I'll see you Thursday.' She put the receiver down and looked through the glass of the telephone box. On the other side of the street there was a crowd outside the pub waving Union Jacks and singing. The saloon door swung open and an upright piano was dragged into the street.

Millie watched them from the silence of the telephone box as they manoeuvred the piano on to the pavement, and then she took a couple of pennies from her purse. She put them on the shelf above the tatty telephone directories and picked up the receiver again. She dialled her Aunt Ruby's telephone number.

It rang a few times before being picked up.

'Ilford 5174,' a woman's voice at the other end said, almost drowned out by the music and laughter in the background.

The pips went and Millie pressed the coin into the slot. 'Hello, Aunt Ruby, it's me, Millie.'

'Millie! What do you want?' her aunt replied sharply. 'I hope you're not ringing to tell me you won't be coming to clean tomorrow.'

'No, you've got the wrong Millie. I'm not your charlady – I'm your niece,' Millie shouted, putting her finger in her other ear to cut out a chorus of 'Roll Out the Barrel' from the street.

'Yes, I know we're at peace, but that's no reason to let standards slip,' Ruby replied.

'Aunt Ruby! It's me, Millie.'

'Oh, Amelia. Just a moment,' the sound became muffled. 'Antony darling, be a sweetie and close the door.' The noise stopped and Ruby took her hand from the mouthpiece. 'I thought you would have rung immediately after Mr Churchill's rousing speech, not three hours later. Still, I expect you're out enjoying yourself. We're just having an impromptu, red, white and blue party.

You know, just a few friends for cocktails. More in keeping with the occasion than a street party, don't you think?'

Millie took a deep breath. 'Aunt Ruby, I have some bad news.' Millie fed the telephone a few more coins and recounted the events of the after-noon in a quivery voice.

There was a silence for a few seconds and then Ruby spoke. 'Oh, Amelia.'

'I'm sorry to tell you like this, but the station sergeant at Ilford police station didn't think there would be an officer free to send around to you until tomorrow. I'd have jumped on the bus myself but I can't leave Mum.'

'I should think not. How is she?'

'It's been such a shock that I don't think it's sunk in yet.'

'And I'm sorry. Your father was a good man. You haven't contacted Bill, Martha or Edie, have you?'

'No. I thought I'd tell you first.'

'Good. Bill doesn't open the door after five, and if the police turned up at Martha's door she'd have one of her wobbly heads for a week. You'd better let me break the news to my brother and sister. And don't expect that Edie will be able to come down for the funeral, not with her legs.'

'I haven't even thought so far ahead,' Millie replied. 'The superintendent has given me com-passionate leave for a couple of days but I'll have to go back on Thursday, and so I wondered if you would come and help us make the arrange-ments.'

'Of course I will. After all, your mother will be

35

too upset to make sure the funeral is organised properly. I'm at the hairdressers at ten but I'll come down after.'

'Thank you, Aunt Ruby. I'll see you tomorrow.'

'Amelia dear, just one thing. You said your father collapsed in the vegetable patch. Was he gardening?'

'No. He just popped out to pull a few carrots before going off to work.'

Ruby sighed. 'Thank goodness for that. At least the neighbours saw him stretchered out properly dressed in a shirt and collar. I'll be down for lunch but don't go to any fuss. Perhaps a bit of fish, if you have it, but nothing special – just a little plate of something, there's a dear. Goodbye.'

She hung up.

Millie replaced the receiver and pressed button B, collected her unused coins and slipped them in her pocket. She pushed open the door of the telephone box and stepped outside.

The street party was in full swing now, with people laughing and dancing. Someone had strung bunting across from house to house and around the lamp-posts; it fluttered above tables laden with sandwiches and cakes from precious ration stores. There were a couple of uniformed servicemen sporting a giggly young woman on each arm, and from time to time an old timer in a cloth cap would slap the soldiers on the shoulder and toast their health.

Millie skirted around the revelries and headed for her mother's house at the end of the cul-de-sac. Pulling the string attached to the front door to lift the latch, she walked into the silent house.

36

Her mother was sitting in her chair beside the fireplace, staring at the picture on the table beside her. It was the one of Millie's mother and father sitting in deckchairs on the beach at Jaywick the previous year. They each had an ice cream in their hands and a happy smile on their faces. The lump returned to Millie's throat.

Doris looked around when her daughter walked in.

'What did Ruby say?'

'She'll be here by dinnertime.'

Chapter Two

Millie splashed water over her face a couple of times, then leaned on the sides of the hand basin and raised her head to look in the small mirror above. After a quick assessment of her pasty complexion and red-rimmed eyes, she concluded that if she'd been a patient she would have ordered herself straight to bed. She picked up the towel hanging beside the sink and dabbed her face dry. Stretching her eyes wide to relieve their puffiness, she picked up her jar of Pond's cream and smoothed it over her neck and face. It wouldn't get rid of the dark shadows, but it made her feel half human.

As a senior nurse, Millie had one of the original bedchambers on the third floor, overlooking the old orchard. Well, half of it, anyhow, because the room had been divided down the middle some time before, so the ornate plasterwork cornices on the ceiling stopped abruptly against the wall behind her bed. Even though her single wardrobe, chest of drawers and desk had no more than a couple of inches between them, Millie couldn't complain, as her bedroom was more spacious than the nurses' lodgings in the servants' rooms on the floor above.

She curled around to check her stocking seams were straight, then picked up her petticoat draped over the back of the chair and slipped it over her head. There was a knock at the door.

'It's not locked,' Millie said, taking a clean uniform from her wardrobe.

The door opened and Connie came in. 'Someone said you were back.'

'Yes, I caught the bus first thing. I knocked on your door but you'd already gone on your rounds.'

'I was covering the early calls and I've just popped back to get a bedpan for my next patient. We weren't expecting you back until tomorrow,' she said, sitting on Millie's bed.

'I know but now the Sheriff has arrived I–'

'The Sheriff?' interrupted Connie, looking puzzled.

'Sorry. My Aunt Ruby,' Millie replied. 'We call her that because she tries to lay down the law. I think the whole family, my mum included, breathed a sigh of relief when she moved to Ilford three years ago. It's an hour's bus ride away, so she can't just pop in at whim any more, although to be truthful she's been a great help in the last couple of days. All the same, she and I have already had words about who should be invited to Dad's...'

The word caught, and a tear rolled down Millie's cheek. She brushed it away. 'I'm sorry.'

Connie came over and put her arm around her friend's shoulders. 'There, there. It's only natural. You have to let it out.'

'I know.' Millie pulled out her handkerchief and blew her nose. 'But after all the sights we've seen in the past six years you'd think I'd be stronger.'

Connie squeezed her. 'Don't be daft.' She let Millie go and sat on the bed. 'When's the funeral?'

'We haven't sorted it out yet. Because of the celebrations and two days' holiday, the funeral directors have been shut. I rang them this morning though, and we have an appointment at four-thirty tomorrow afternoon.'

Millie rubbed her forehead to ease the throbbing.

'You've got one of your heads starting, haven't you?' Connie asked.

Millie nodded.

Connie stood up. 'I'll fetch you some aspirin.'

'It's all right. I'm going down to the treatment room. I tell you, what with arguing with my aunt, and the street party that went on outside until dawn, I don't reckon I've had more than a few hours' sleep in the past two days.' Millie sighed. 'I'll let Miss Summers know I'll be out tomorrow afternoon for a few hours after my round. I hope she won't grumble.'

'I don't see how she can when you're not supposed to be here anyway,' Connie pulled out a Kirby grip and repositioned it. 'I ought to get on or I'll have Mr Ottershaw complaining.' She opened the door. 'I'd like to come to the funeral, if you don't mind.'

'I should say not. In fact, I'd be very grateful if you would. You can hold me back if my aunt starts up.'

Connie left. Millie stared at the door for a second, then straightened the starched collar of her uniform in the mirror and followed her friend out.

Running her hand lightly over the polished wooden banister, Millie made her way down the sweeping staircase to the hall. She could hear the cook, Mrs White, accompanying Bing Crosby as he sang 'If I Had My Way' on the radio while one of the maids swept the rug in the nurses' sitting room. Millie headed for the superintendent's room at the far end of the hallway. She raised her hand to knock but then noticed it was ajar. She pushed it open.

'Excuse me, Miss Sum–'

Millie's mouth dropped open as she saw that instead of the senior nurse sitting behind her desk, it was Alfie-boy, the cook's son. As always, he was dressed in a suit that, with its boxed shoulders, long-line jacket and baggy trousers, could only have been described as sharp. He jumped up as she walked in.

'Oh! It's you, Millie.' The corners of his mouth lifted, taking his pencil-thin moustache with them. '*Sorry*, Miss Sullivan.'

'What are you doing in here?' Millie asked, giving him a cool look.

Alfie-boy grabbed the kitchen order book. 'Me ma asked me to fetch 'er this,' he said holding it aloft.

Millie noticed the desk drawer was open. 'Then what are you doing?'

'I'm so sorry to hear about your old pa, truly I am.' He slipped the book in his pocket and nudged the desk drawer shut with his knee. 'It don't seem right somehow that after dodging incendiary bombs, Doodlebugs and houses falling on his head the poor old bugger should drop dead in his own yard,' he said, sauntering around the table.

41

The corners of Millie's eyes pinched again. 'Thank you, it was quite a shock.'

Alfie-boy stopped just in front of her and a combination of Old Spice and brilliantine wafted up. 'I bet it was. I tell you what.' He looked over his shoulder. 'I've got some nylons in the car straight from an American NAAFI. I've just sold Gladys a couple of pairs, but they'll look ten times better on your pins. Special price. Half a crown! You can't say fairer than that, can you?'

'Perhaps another time.'

He shoved his hands in his pockets. 'Suit yourself.' He strolled past her to the door, then turned. 'But if you change your mind, just give us the wink, sweetheart.'

Millie stared after him as he left the room, then put Alfie-boy out of her mind.

She went around to the other side of the desk and opened the message book to write the superintendent a message. She was just about to take the pen from the inkwell and write under the last entry when the top drawer caught her eye.

She inched the drawer open.

'Sullivan!'

Millie jumped and the drawer slammed shut.

Miss Summers stood on the other side of the table. Her jowls wobbled ever so slightly as her piggy eyes glared at Millie.

'Sullivan.' The superintendent's mouth curled, but it wasn't a smile. 'What on earth are you doing delving in my drawers?'

Sitting in Mooney's funeral parlour and monumental masons, Millie stifled a yawn and tried to

42

concentrate. In keeping with the solemnity of its business, the reception area was predominantly grey and purple with the odd streak of black. Ebenezer Mooney, the founder of the establishment, whose black-and-white photo had looked down on grieving relatives for half a century, seemed to be wearing the same grave expression as his descendant, who was now taking down Arthur Sullivan's particulars. The yawn crept up again and Millie stretched her eyes to hold it at bay.

The midwives' on-call telephone in the hall had woken her at four a.m., and when her alarm rang two hours later she was still wide awake. Millie had managed to stave off her bone-weariness while cycling on her morning round, but now that she was enfolded in the soft upholstery of the comfy old sofa, sleep was beginning to steal over her. She blinked and looked at her mother sitting beside her.

Although Doris had dabbed face powder on her cheeks, it couldn't disguise the ashen pallor or cover the deep shadows beneath her eyes. In spite of the warm weather, she'd taken her black winter coat out of mothballs to wear over her grey dress. Millie's eyes drifted past her mother and on to her aunt sitting on a much less comfortable button-back Chesterfield.

Aunt Ruby's tight features were set in a solemn expression, with her Crimson Kiss mouth pulled down at the corners. In contrast to Millie's mother's modest attire, Ruby wore a box-shouldered Prince of Wales check suit, complete with Astrakhan collar and cuffs, which fitted snugly over her modest bosom. A Robin-Hood-style hat with a feather on one side topped off the ensemble, and her newly permed light-brown hair flicked up in curls around her ears. She was, as the locals liked to put it, well-preserved.

Millie's gaze returned to Mr Mooney on the other side of the desk as he dotted an 'I'.

'So, Mrs Sullivan, you require *three* hearses and the *Regal* coffin,' the funeral director said, peering over his glasses at Millie's mother.

'That is correct,' Aunt Ruby cut in. 'My brother-in-law's funeral must be dignified, but in keeping with his position. Did I mention he was a master plumber?'

'Twice,' answered Mr Moody. 'And I'm sure he would be heartened by your consideration, but you do understand that the Regal is solid walnut and, with the shortages and the like, will cost thirty guineas, plus another forty for the hearses, not to mention the usual crematorium expenses.'

Ruby's eyes narrowed. 'If we wanted a penny-pinched affair we would have gone to the Co-operative Society.'

Mr Mooney wrung his hands deferentially. 'Yes, of course.'

'Oh dear, seventy guineas,' Doris said. 'That does seem quite a bit.'

'Perhaps we should consider the stained-pine casket,' replied Millie. 'And make do with just two hea–'

'No matter how you tart them up,' Aunt Ruby insisted, 'pine coffins look what they are – cheap. And mourners can't be expected to catch the bus to the City of London crematorium, can they?'

44

'I suppose not,' agreed Millie. 'But what do you think, Mum?'

'I think we'll have the Regal, but I'm sure we can manage with just two hearses,' said Doris.

'Very good,' said the undertaker. 'Now, if I can move on to the formalities. Have you the death certificate?'

Millie opened her handbag and produced the document she'd collected from the almoner on her way to her mother's home that afternoon.

The undertaker looked it over and then placed it in the file. 'Will your own minister be conducting the service?'

Doris nodded. 'Reverend Norbert called last night to give his condolences, and my daughter will telephone him once we have finalised the arrangements,' she said in a quavery voice.

'Good, good. I think that is everything for now. I will drop you a letter of confirmation.' Mr Moody peered over his glasses.

Doris rose to her feet and so did everyone else.

The undertaker came around the desk to open the front door. 'Good day, Mrs Sullivan. And may I once again give you my deepest condolences for your most grievous loss?' he said in a professional tone.

'Thank you, you've been most kind,' Doris replied.

Millie slipped her arm through her mother's and guided her out of the dour parlour.

It was already just after five, and so the rush hour had already begun. Buses and cars streamed eastwards, taking City workers over the Bow Bridge to the leafy suburbs of Stratford, Forest

Gate and West Ham.

As the funeral director's door closed behind them, Doris pulled a handkerchief from her pocket. 'I still can't believe my Arthur's gone,' she said, dabbing her eyes. 'I don't know how I'm going to get by without him.'

Millie hugged her. 'I know, Mum. But we'll see it through together.'

'Yes, chin up, Doris,' said Ruby who had followed them out. She took out a cigarette and lit it. 'Can you see a cab?'

'I don't think we need a taxi, Aunt Ruby. After all, it's only a five-minute walk,' Doris said.

Ruby snapped the cigarette case shut. 'I suppose so; and a walk might help put a bit of colour back in your cheeks, dear. And it will give us a chance to discuss the catering on the way.'

'Catering!' groaned Millie.

Ruby looked puzzled. 'Of course. We'll have to put on a spread. I thought I'd ask that woman from the baker's who did a nice table for your neighbour when her husband died, Doris. Of course, we'll want something more than Spam and pilchards, and I wonder if we could get some salmon. It would have to be tinned, but leave that to me.' Ruby winked. 'I have some contacts.'

'That sounds all well and fine,' Millie said, stepping back for a woman pushing a pram with a toddler sitting on top. 'But surely between us we could put together ourselves a couple of plate-loads of sandwiches.'

Her aunt looked aghast. 'A couple of plates of sandwiches! After all he's done for you, you want to send your father out of this world with a

46

couple of plates of sandwiches?'

Millie's eyes narrowed. 'What I'm trying to make you understand, Aunt Ruby, is that until we know about Dad's pension, Mum will have to watch the pennies.'

A couple of women, dressed in wraparound overalls and with curlers under their hairnets, pushed past them.

Ruby stepped closer to Millie. 'Perhaps it would be better to talk about this when we get home,' she said in a low voice.

'I'm afraid I have to get back to Munroe House,' Millie said. 'I've a couple of maternity visits to do and then the dressings to get ready for tomorrow.'

'But we haven't decided on the service yet,' her aunt said.

Doris let go of Millie's arm. 'Millie has a very important job, Ruby. People rely on her, and we can choose the hymns tomorrow when the vicar calls,' Doris said firmly.

Ruby flicked her half-smoked cigarette on to the pavement and crushed it under her foot. 'Well, Amelia, we wouldn't want to hold you up, and if you hurry you might catch that bus.' She nodded toward a number twenty-five trundling down the road towards them.

'Will you be all right, if I make tracks, Mum?' Millie asked.

'Of course I will,' Doris replied. 'You can't keep your patients waiting.'

'I'll be up as soon as I've finished my morning round tomorrow.' Millie hugged her mother and tenderly kissed her cheek.

She kissed her aunt hastily and dashed to the

47

kerb just as the bus drew to a halt. Millie grabbed the upright rail and jumped on to the backboard.

'See you tomorrow, Mum,' she called, hanging on with one hand and waving with the other as the bus picked up speed. 'You, too, Aunt Ruby.'

'Yes, see you then, Amelia, and don't worry,' Ruby called back cheerily. 'I'll make sure the buffet will be the talk of the neighbourhood!'

There was the usual collection of deep-bodied prams lined up outside the Watney Street Practice as Millie brought her bicycle to a halt and hopped off. She leaned it against the wall, retrieved her bag and went through the open front door.

The nurses from Munroe House dealt with at least a dozen doctors from various practices, and although they all had patients scattered throughout the area, it was the responsibility of the nurse covering the street where the surgery was situated to pick up all the messages.

Despite the dozens of feet trudging in and out of the old house each day, Dr Gingold's surgery, situated halfway down the market in one of the old terraced houses, had the appearance of a dwelling that someone had locked the door on fifty years before and hadn't visited since.

The waiting room had once been the front parlour, and at first glance the wallpaper appeared to be just vertical stripes of brown and not so brown, although if closely inspected it was possible to make out the delicate green and russet foliage that intertwined towards the ceiling.

The grate in the cast-iron fireplace that had

once housed a roaring fire and been the focal point of the room was now empty except for the odd cigarette packet or sweet wrapper discarded in the gathered dust. Above it, on the mantelshelf where proud family pictures might have stood, were dog-eared signs telling you that 'Coughs and Sneezes Spread Diseases'. The handful of people sitting on a collection of rickety chairs looked up as Millie walked in.

'Morning,' she said, giving them all a cheery smile.

There was a corporate murmur by way of a greeting. Millie spotted Lilly Crowther, the daughter of one of her regulars, sitting at the side of the fireplace with a red-faced infant on her lap.

'Has the doctor got someone in there?' she asked, stepping away from a man with a particularly wet-sounding cough.

'Peggy Keen,' Lilly replied. 'She went in ages ago. I hope she's out soon, as I've got to get my groceries yet and there's already a queue outside Lipton's. There'll be all hell to pay if my old man don't have a bit of meat on his plate tonight.'

'Bloody shocking, isn't it?' agreed a woman wearing wax cherries on the brim of her hat. 'I had to queue for three hours yesterday just for a scrawny rabbit. I thought things would ease up a bit after VE day, but they're getting worse, if anything.'

There was a rumble of agreement. Millie smiled politely.

'Peggy's in for her lumbago, nurse,' said a large-bosomed woman with curlers in her hair at the far end of the room. 'She's been a martyr to it.

49

Has been for years.'

'I hope she's sure it's the lumbago,' said Lilly, ''cos my cousin's husband had a touch of that but it went straight to his kidneys. Nearly done for 'im, it did.'

The door opened and Peggy Keen came out.

'What did the doctor say, Peg?' asked the woman with the curlers.

'Said I should lay flat for an hour or two each afternoon to stretch my spine.' She pulled a face. 'Fat chance of that happening with my lot.'

'What you need is a mustard plaster to draw out all the ache,' an old man in the corner chipped in. 'Soon sort you out. Always did for my old da, and he lived to be eighty-five.'

Peggy brightened. 'I'll try that. Good thing I dropped by.'

'Next!' called a woman's voice from the end of the hallway. A young lad with a face full of erupting spots began to rise.

'I just need to talk to the doctor quickly,' Millie said, scooting out before he could answer. She headed towards the door at the far end and knocked.

'Come!'

Millie went in. The smell of disinfectant and surgical spirit mingled together made her nose tingle.

Rachel Gingold sat at her desk with her head bowed, scribbling in a set of buff-coloured notes with a stout fountain pen.

Dr Rachel, as she was known to everyone, had fled her Polish homeland just a step in front of the Nazis invading it. After landing in Dover with

50

only a smattering of English, she took just three months to be admitted to the General Medical Council, and then she turned her back on several lucrative offers of private practice and opted instead to settle in East London. Despite the six-pence cost of a consultation, her waiting room was always full.

As always, Dr Rachel's unruly salt-and-pepper hair was scrunched up into a topknot and secured by several tortoiseshell combs. She wore a muted blue-grey suit with a drop waist that would have been fashionable twenty years before, some knitted stockings and a pair of serviceable brogues with a buckle on the side.

She looked up. 'Ah, Nurse Sullivan, just let me finish this. And sit, sit!'

Millie sat on the edge of the chair next to the desk and looked around.

The consulting room was, in fact, the parlour with a door knocked through to the kitchen beyond. There was a tall bookcase crammed with books of different bindings and size, on top of which were shoved still more. An examination couch with a clean cotton draw-sheet along its length and a lamp at the foot end sat under the window, alongside which stood a stainless-steel trolley with instruments laid out side by side like the best cutlery at Christmas. But the room was dominated by the roll-top desk, which took up most of the back wall. It was thick-legged, un-adorned and polished almost black by countless maids applying beeswax to it over the years. Although designed so that the lattice shutter could be pulled down, this was now impossible because

51

of the piles of papers, letters, notes and ripped-out pages of medical journals.

After a few moments Dr Gingold scratched her signature and looked up expectantly.

'And what can I do for you, Sister?'

Millie pulled her notebook out from the side pocket of her bag. 'You left instructions to call in.'

'Did I?'

'Something about a new patient you want me to visit.'

Dr Gingold threw her hands in the air. '*Oi*, of course, of course.' She shuffled through the chaos of papers in front of her. 'I tell you, Nurse Sullivan, sometimes I think my brain,' she tapped her head, 'is turning to strudel. Ah, here we are.' She held a sheet at arm's length in front of her with one hand, while locating her glasses hanging around her neck with the other.

She wedged them on her nose. 'Here we are. Mr Dawkins in Cable Street needs an enema. And Mrs Gyver's ulcer is weeping again and there's three new maternity cases.' Dr Gingold looked over her glasses. 'I'm sure there'll be one or two of those over the next few months.'

Millie smiled. 'I'm sure.'

'Mrs Tuttle and Mrs Cohen are multigravidas and so shouldn't need your attention urgently, but Mrs Kemp has already had three miscarriages all around the five-months mark, so although she's only just missed two periods, I'd like you to keep a special eye on her this time.'

'Yes, doctor,' Millie replied, scribbling the names in her book.

Dr Gingold sifted through the papers again and handed Millie half a sheet of paper. 'I've jotted down their addresses.'

Millie folded it away and closed her notebook. 'I'm sorry to ask, but will it be all right if I visit her on Thursday, as I have my father's funeral this afternoon?'

A look of genuine sympathy spread across the doctor's finely lined face. 'Certainly, my dear *młoda damo*. I was so sorry to hear your sad news.' The doctor shook her head and tutted. 'So young to lose a parent. And how is your poor mother taking it?'

'Oh, you know. Bearing up.'

Doctor Gingold reached over and patted Millie's hand. 'And she has you to love and support her.'

Millie forced a smile. 'Yes. And her sister's staying until next week so that helps, but...'

Doctor Gingold studied the young Sister closely. 'But?'

'It's so unfair,' Millie blurted out.

The front door banged against the wall and boots tramped along the hallway into the waiting room.

Millie stood up. 'I'm so sorry, you've got patients to see and I'm taking up your time,' she said, knowing that as a nurse she should keep her personal feelings under control. 'I'll pop in on Friday to give you my full report.' She picked up her bag and started to rise.

Doctor Gingold reached out and grasped Millie's hand in a surprisingly strong grip. 'Death is never fair to those left behind.'

It was almost nine o'clock in the evening by the time Millie dragged herself back into Munroe House. Good use was being made of the regulation four inches of water in the bath, as Eva's tuneful tones singing 'The Boogie-Woogie Bugle Boy from Company B' drifted through the bathroom door.

Millie knocked. 'Can you give us a shout when you're done?'

'Will do,' Eva called back. 'How are you, love?'

'Oh, you know,' replied Millie. 'I'll be in Connie's room.'

She walked on to her friend's room at the end of the hall and knocked.

'Come in.'

Millie walked in. Connie was kneeling in front of her chest with the lower drawer pulled out.

'Sorting out your bottom drawer again?' Millie said, kicking off her shoes and flopping on to Connie's bed.

'Do you think it's too frilly?' Connie replied, holding up an anti-macassar.

'No, it's fine. Any news?' Millie asked.

Connie shook her head. 'No, not yet.'

'I'm sure there'll be a letter any day now,' Millie said, looking sympathetically at her.

'I blooming hope so, or I'll have a few words to say when I do see him.' Connie shoved the chair-protector back into the drawer and slammed it closed. 'I know Charlie isn't one to put pen to paper, but now he's just hanging around in some army camp in Italy I thought he could have at least sent me a note.' She glanced at Millie. 'I'm sorry to be rattling on when you've got so much

54

more on your plate. How did the funeral go?'

'Very well, I think,' replied Millie. 'It seemed like half of Bow turned up to pay their respects, the vicar gave a good address, and the women from the baker's put on a decent spread, including salmon. And despite my aunt nagging on about needing three hearses, everyone got to the crematorium on time in two, even my Aunt Edie and her knees.'

Connie looked uneasy. 'And how was your aunt?'

'Well, apart from sniffing every time she spotted someone in brown shoes, and constantly saying that the vicar was going on too long, she was her usual self. Talking to the people who she considered important and ignoring those who weren't.'

'What about your mum?' asked Connie.

'She sobbed at the graveside, as you'd expect,' replied Millie. 'But other than that, she held up remarkably well. She was almost chirpy at the gathering, talking to everyone and thanking them for coming, but I expect it'll hit her properly when Aunt Ruby goes home and things get back to normal.'

'Isn't that always the way?' said Connie.

Millie nodded as tears gathered on her lower lids. 'Why do people always have to tell you that you should be thankful they never suffered?' Millie burst out. 'As if it makes them being dead better somehow.' One large tear escaped and rolled down Millie's cheek. 'It isn't fair.'

Connie stretched over and held her hand. 'Of course it's not.'

There was a knock. 'Bathroom's free,' Eva called through the door.

'Thanks,' called Connie. 'Now come on,' she said, helping Millie to swing her legs off the bed. 'A long soak is just what you need to let you unwind, and you'd better nab the bathroom before someone else jumps in. And while you're having a soak I'll make us both an Ovaltine.'

Millie walked slowly to her own room, stripped off her uniform, put on her dressing gown and collected the rest of her things from the wash stand. She padded along the corridor to the bathroom.

Rivulets of condensation trickled down the window and the cork floormat still bore the mark of where Eva had stood. Millie turned on the taps and scooped out a handful of gentian violet crystals and threw them into the swirling water.

Hanging up her dressing gown on the back of the door, Millie tested the water with her toe and then sank into the bath. The water settled around her hips. The regulation four inches of water barely covered her legs, but Connie was right, the soothing warmth would help untie the knots of tension in her shoulders and back.

Millie settled back and closed her eyes. Her mind drifted off to the events of the day, her mother's polite fortitude at facing the future as a widow, then drifted on to Connie's preparation for her new life with Charlie: one woman at the start of her journey as a wife, and the other at the end. Millie turned her thoughts to herself.

There had been William Wilcox, whom she'd known since school, but that had fizzled out when she started as a pupil nurse. She'd walked out once or twice with some of the doctors at the hospital, but as they often regarded the nurses' home as a sort of in-house harem these young doctors were never going to last. Of course, there were a few servicemen she'd met during the war in the makeshift NAAFIs and ballrooms throughout London, but they were shipped in and out so fast it was difficult to keep track. Still, no matter, thought Millie. Now the upheaval of war was over, perhaps she would meet someone like Connie's Charlie and settle down.

Chapter Three

Millie pulled the last two metal boxes of gauze squares out of Munroe House's main oven then carried them across the hall and into the treatment room opposite. She placed them alongside the others on the long wooden bench by the sink to cool ready for her and her student Annie Fletcher's morning rounds. Placing her hands in the small of her back, Millie stretched to relieve the knots that a day's worth of bending and lifting had put there.

It had taken her almost an hour and a half to cut the dressings into the required four-inch squares and pack them in tins ready to be baked sterile in the oven.

Of course, the nurses only baked enough for new patients. The nearest and dearest of those visited regularly by the Association would be expected to sterilise the dressings needed for their loved ones and prepare the room for their visiting nurse before her arrival. As Millie surveyed the two dozen undecorated tins on the bench, she couldn't help imagining the dozens of others tucked in alongside the hot-pots and roasting tins all over the area.

She locked the cupboard and went to the deep oblong pans filled with Dettol on the ceramic draining board in which their scissors, probes and ear syringes were soaking. Satisfied they were still submerged sufficiently, carefully Millie wiped down the stainless-steel dressing trolley and stacked the buckets underneath. As she finished, Annie walked in.

Like Millie herself, Annie had been rigorously interviewed by the Association's committee before being accepted as a novice Queen's Nurse and she was now halfway through her six months of training. Although at first glance Annie was so slightly built that she could have been mistaken for a tall child, she was in fact twenty-four and a qualified nurse and midwife. With bright blonde curls, doe-like eyes and a gentle smile, she was already a great favourite with Millie's patients.

'I've tidied the equipment cupboard and I've scrubbed the bedpan Mrs Wendover returned and left it soaking in the tub,' she said.

'Thank you, Nurse Fletcher,' Millie said, replacing her bottle of surgical spirit and buckling it firmly in place in her bag.

When Millie had undertaken her Queen's Nurse training before the war, it was possible to work alongside a fellow nurse for years before knowing their Christian name, as many matrons forbade the nurses in their charge to address each other so informally. Although the war had loosened up some of the old ways, the Association's nurses were still addressed by their formal titles unless they were off duty.

'I have to go out in half an hour, but Nurse Scott is going to do my early evening visits, so you can assist her until I get back after supper,' Millie said, slipping her payment book into the side pocket of her case.

'Yes, Sister,' Annie said. 'Do you think Cook will be back by then?'

'I've no idea,' Millie replied. 'Goodness knows where she's got to this morning. There's been no word as to what's happened, as far as I know. But I'm afraid if she doesn't turn up we will have to make our own supper.'

Annie shrugged. 'I don't mind, as long as it's more than a bit of bread and scrape.'

Millie laughed. 'I'm sure we can do better than that. You could make an invalid broth or junket. You'll be tested on both of these for your oral exam, and so you might as well get some practice in.'

The treatment door opened and they looked around. Mrs Harper, the chairwoman of the Association, wearing an immaculate suit and a fur stole with a fox head at both ends, stood in the doorway. Behind her, sporting a tweed coat and a close-fitting hat over her Toni-waved grey curls, stood Mrs Roper, the treasurer. Both regarded Millie bleakly.

'Good afternoon, Mrs Harper. Mrs Roper,' Millie said, rising to her feet and nudging Annie to do the same.

'Sister Sullivan,' Mrs Harper replied, tightly. 'Would you come with me, please?'

'Of course,' Millie turned to Annie. 'Make a start on rolling the clean bandages until I return.'

'Yes, Sister,' Annie replied, looking nervously at the two well turned-out women in the doorway.

Millie followed them into the hall and towards Miss Summers' office. Beattie and Eva, the Jamaica Street nurse, stood halfway up the stairs.

They looked questioningly at Millie. She shrugged. Without knocking, Mrs Harper stormed into the superintendent's room.

Miss Summers, who was slouched in the chair behind her desk with her hands across her bosom and her eyes closed, jumped up.

'What?'

She saw who was standing in the doorway and blanched. 'Mrs Harper and Mrs Roper,' Miss Summers said, searching the desk for her glasses. 'What? What a pleasant surprise. May I offer you some tea?'

Mrs Harper closed the door firmly. 'No, thank you. I'm afraid there's nothing pleasurable about our visit, Miss Summers. In fact, I can say without doubt that this is the most shameful matter I have ever had to deal with in all my fifteen years as chairwoman of the Association.'

'And I also,' Mrs Roper chipped in, glaring at the superintendent.

Miss Summers' eyes flickered on to Millie. 'Well, if it is such a delicate matter perhaps we should discuss it in private.'

Millie stepped back, but Mrs Harper raised a hand. 'I wish Nurse Sullivan to remain.'

'Very well,' Miss Summers replied, begrudgingly. 'Won't you take a seat?'

Mrs Harper drew herself up to her full height and looked down her hooked nose at the woman behind the desk.

'This morning at five minutes past eight my breakfast was interrupted by a Detective Chief Inspector Mills, a criminal investigation officer from Arbour Square Police Station,' she said in a ponderous tone. 'He informed me that following a lengthy undercover investigation into black-market profiteering and rationing fraud he had arrested one Alfred White, who I believe is the son of your cook.'

Miss Summers' lips pulled into two thin lines. 'I'm not surprised. I always said he had a shifty look about him.'

'The Chief Inspector's search of Alfred's house,' Mrs Harper continued, 'turned up some very interesting items.'

'I'm sure it did, but what has that to do with the Association?'

'It concerns the St George's and St Dunstan's District Nursing Association,' Mrs Roper said, 'because amongst the American nylons and stolen chocolate bars, the police found tins of corned beef, powdered eggs and butter, which were later identified as coming from the larder in Munroe House. Mrs White was also arrested and she confessed to passing almost a quarter of the food purchased by the Association each week to feed the nurses on to her son to sell.'

Miss Summers opened and shut her mouth like a goldfish swimming around in a bowl. 'Food?'

Mrs Roper's eyes narrowed. 'The police also found ration books allocated to the nurses of Munroe House.'

'Ration books!'

Mrs Harper leaned over the table. 'Yes, ration books, Superintendent. Ration books that you are responsible for.'

The colour drained from Miss Summers' face. 'I don't understand.' She fumbled around her top drawer. 'I have them here. See.' She flourished a handful of ration books. 'I give them to Cook on a Friday and once she's bought the week's provisions she gives them straight back. The rest of the time they are in my charge.'

Mrs Roper took the books from her.

'How many nurses are there in Munroe House, Nurse Sullivan?' she asked.

'Thirty-seven,' replied Millie.

Mrs Roper counted the ration books. 'So if you include the two maids and yourself I should be holding forty books in my hand, whereas in fact there are only twenty-six.'

'Twenty-six!'

'I am bound to tell you, Miss Summers,' Mrs Harper said in her best committee voice, 'in accordance with the articles of association and the rules of affiliation to the Queen's Nursing Institute, I called an emergency meeting of the Association's committee at lunchtime and laid the whole matter before them. It was decided unanimously that you should be removed as superintendent with immediate effect.'

Miss Summers' jowls quivered. 'I'm dismissed?'

Mrs Roper folded her arms. 'You are. The committee voted, very generously in my opinion, under the circumstances, to give you a week's wages. You have until this evening to pack what you need.' Mrs Harper stepped forward and loomed over the superintendent. 'The committee has had misgivings about your fitness to hold the post of superintendent for some time, but none of us imagined that even you could be blind to such goings on.'

63

Miss Summers stared dumbly for a moment, then her face flushed red. 'But I've done nothing wrong. And how was I to know Mrs White was stealing food? It's not my job to watch her about her business. And as to her son taking a couple of ration books – well, I wouldn't be surprised if he hadn't put one of the nurses up to it.' Her close-set eyes flickered over Millie. 'Now, come to think of it, only a few days ago I caught Sullivan searching through my desk.'

'I was *not* searching your desk, Miss Summers, I came looking for you,' Millie replied, feeling her neck grow warm.

Mrs Harper waved aside the superintendent's words. 'There's no point trying to implicate others in your guilt, Miss Summers. It is clear from the evidence the police have obtained that you have been grossly negligent in your duties in Munroe House and have betrayed the trust of the committee placed in you. As I say, you have until the end of the day to leave.'

Miss Summers stared at them in disbelief for a few moments, then struggled to her feet. 'I'll not sit here and listen to you ... you ... pair of jumped-up busybodies blacken my good name.' She sidled around the desk and glared angrily up at the two women. 'And as to being dismissed – I resign!'

She shoved her way between her visitors and marched out of the room, slamming the door behind her.

Millie stared after her for a moment and then looked in shock at the other two women. 'I had no idea.'

'Nor did anyone.' Mrs Harper looked Millie over. 'Although I don't suppose we'll be able to keep the scandal out of the local newspaper, the committee is relying on your complete discretion about the conversation that has just taken place.'

'Of course,' replied Millie.

Mrs Roper picked up the ledgers from Miss Summers' desk. 'I shall be taking the accounts for a few days so the auditors can scrutinise them, but they should be back by the end of the week so you can enter the weekly fees. The committee will contact the grocer and butcher so they can send their bills direct to the committee until this mess has been sorted out, and we will advertise for a new cook. But I'm afraid you will have to shift for yourselves for a week or so.'

'I'm sure we can do that,' Millie said.

'Of course, replacing Miss Summers will take a little longer, but I'm sure Munroe House and the district will function quite well until we do.'

'We will all do our very best,' Millie replied.

Mrs Harper smiled. 'I know you will.' She straightened her hat and repositioned her fur stole. 'Good day to you, Nurse Sullivan.'

She turned to leave, with Mrs Roper close on her heels.

'Excuse me,' Millie said, as they reached the door.

They looked at her.

'I'm sorry, but who will be undertaking Miss Summers' duties until the new superintendent arrives?'

Mrs Harper's sandy-coloured eyebrows rose. 'My dear Nurse Sullivan, you will, of course.'

Millie plopped her surgical tweezers into the Dettol solution and turned her head. 'If you could just drop your trousers, Mr Fallow, we can make a start.'

A smile burst over Bert Fallow's round face. 'Now that's an offer I haven't had for a long time.'

'Oi, Bert, don't you let me hear you cheeking the Sister,' his wife's voice called from the kitchen.

'Course not, Vi,' he shouted back.

He winked at Millie and she smiled.

'It's all right, Mrs Fallow,' she called back.

Bert Fallow was the landlord of the Boatman public house, which sat halfway up Coleman's Street. In its day the narrow passageway that ran between New Gravel Lane and Wapping Wall must have been a pretty forbidding place, and, although virtually the whole street had been blown away during the Blitz, the Boatman had somehow come through unscathed and now stood like the last tooth in an old man's mouth, alone and proud.

Although the Prospect of Whitby and the Town of Ramsgate might claim to be the oldest pubs in the area, judging by the low-slung beams in the bar and the cramped living conditions at the rear, Millie would lay a pound to a penny that the Boatman could give them both a few years.

Vi, who really ran the pub, came into the room with a cigarette hanging from her red lips, wiping her hands on a teacloth. Unlike Bert, who seemed to be about to burst out of his clothes, Vi

66

Fallow was stick-thin, with cheekbones that looked as if they could break through the surface at any moment.

'Come on then, Bert. Sister's not got all day,' she said, ash fluttering over her pink cardigan as she spoke.

Bert stood up and unbuttoned his trousers. 'I don't see what the fuss is all about – it's a bit sore, that's all.'

Vi gave him a ferocious glare from under her mascaraed eyelashes. Bert dropped his trousers to reveal his baggy grey pants then sat back in the chair. Ferreting up the gaping leg of his underwear he unstrapped his false leg and held it aloft.

'There!' he said raising the stump of what had once been his left leg. The fleshy top was oozing blood and pus, while the scar was blistered.

Vi slapped her husband on the shoulder. 'Look at the mess you've made of it.'

Millie bent forward to inspect where the leather socket and buckle had rubbed the skin raw.

'I have to agree with your wife,' Millie said. 'What on earth have you been doing?'

Bert opened his mouth to speak but Vi got in first.

'I'll tell you what he's been doing, Sister. Campaigning, that's what.' She belted Bert again, affectionately. 'Silly old bugger.'

'I didn't know you were interested in politics,' said Millie, starting to unpack her equipment.

'I am. And this,' he shook his prosthesis, sending the leather straps and laces flapping around, 'is why. Shot off on No Man's Land to win half a

67

league of land that Jerry took back a week later, and all at the say-so of some inbred aristocrat whose grandmother slept with the bloody Prince of Wales.' His face took on a rapt expression. 'It's time for the working class to tear their freedom from the grasp of "them".'

Millie laughed. 'You sound just like my dad.'

Bert's eyes sparkled. 'Is he a Labour man?'

'Through and through,' Millie replied, thinking of the many times he'd taken her to Speakers' Corner on a Sunday afternoon.

'Then I'm sure he'll be out there fighting for a Labour victory too,' Bert replied.

Millie didn't answer. The last thing a good nurse did was to burden her patient with her own problems.

'And let me tell you, we're going to win.' Bert raised his fist and shook it westwards, roughly in the direction of Westminster. 'Yes, we're going to oust those Tory parasites in parliament who have grown fat on the sweat of oth–'

'Here we go again.' Vi rolled her eyes.

'Others,' continued Bert, glaring at his wife. 'For the honest working man of this country has been ground under the capitalist heel. But no more.' He clenched his fist and pounded it into his other palm. 'Our comrades in the Soviet Union have the right idea about dealing with the nobility.'

'Oi,' interjected Vi, 'I hope you're not talking about our King and Queen. 'Cos I've warned you before, Albert Fallow, I won't hear a word against them two under my roof. Do you hear? Not one word!'

'All right, all right, woman, perhaps not.'

'And those darling little girls? Are you going to do what the Soviets did to the Tsar and his family, too?'

Bert shifted in his seat. 'Of course not. I didn't mean anything by it.'

'I tell you, Sister, when I heard Princess Elizabeth on the wireless say, "Come on, Margaret, and goodnight, children," I cried. Straight up, I did.'

'Yes, it was very touching,' said Millie, reaching into her bag for her bottle of iodine.

'For Gawd's sake, Vi,' bellowed Bert, getting red in the face. 'I'm not talking about our own royal family.'

Vi folded her arms decisively. 'Well, I'm glad to hear it or you'd be washing your own clothes and cooking your own dinners from now on if you are.'

'I'm talking about Churchill and his crew, the Tories,' Bert forced out through rigid lips. 'It's them that want to put the masses back into the shackles of poverty and unemployment. But we won't let them. The working man of this country won the war and now we're going to win the peace, and you're going to be part of it too, Sister.'

'Me?'

'Of course you! When us proletariat have kicked the bloody landed-gentry out of office it will all be different. There'll be no need of soup kitchens under Labour; and they're committed to introducing a new health system, so that anyone can see a doctor if they need him, and not only if they can pay him.'

'That's all well and good,' Millie said, pulling

69

on her rubber gloves, 'but until then I'll have to dress your wound each day, and I'm afraid it will cost you three and six a week.'

Vi whacked her husband for the third time. 'Now, see what a lot of trouble you've put the Sister to.'

'And you'll have to stay off of it as much as possible,' said Millie.

'Did you 'ear that, Bert?' Vi snatched up her husband's false leg. 'The oppressed masses will have to start the revolution without you, Karl Marx, because if Sister is going to take the trouble to visit you every day, then I'm not having you waste her time.' Vi marched off towards the bar. 'And if you try and get it back, Bert, it'll be the worse for you,' was Vi's parting shot as she left the room.

Bert stared after his wife for a moment, and then turned to Millie. 'Tell her to fetch me leg back, Sister. She'll listen to you,' he begged.

'I will, but only if you promise me you'll stay off your leg. Because if you don't, you'd better hope that whoever wins the election brings in the new health service pretty quick. If you rub that wound down to the bone, you and your stump will be one of the first patients.'

'Goodness,' Doris said to Millie, reaching into the wardrobe and pulling out an old-fashioned double-breasted suit. 'I remember when your father bought this.'

Ruby laughed at her sister. 'I recall thinking that when Arthur turned up wearing it at Edie's twenty-first he looked like James Cagney getting

70

ready to rob a bank.'

They were in Millie's mother's bedroom, supposedly sorting out her father's clothes. But there was yet to be a garment laid on the sateen quilted eiderdown to be got rid of. Although she was helping mother and daughter, Ruby was dressed as if she was going to a WI meeting, in a fluted skirt and jacket, and with a jaunty silk scarf tied loosely around her throat.

Doris smiled. 'I suppose he did.' Her eyes travelled over the garment. 'Arthur wore this when he took me up West just after we were married. And right dapper he looked in it, too.' She smoothed her hand up the front of the jacket and fingered the lapel. 'He always had a rose in the buttonhole and the sweet smell would drift up as we danced.'

'Why don't you give it to the church for the nearly new rail at the church summer bazaar?' said Ruby, reaching to take it.

Doris clung on to it. 'Oh, I couldn't part with it, Ruby.'

'It would do someone a good turn,' Millie said patiently.

Her mother shook her head and put it back into the wardrobe with the other four suits she 'couldn't bear to part with'.

'I had to do the same when my Bernard died, God rest his soul, so I know how hard it is, Doris,' Ruby coaxed. 'But you'll have to start to move on.'

Doris hugged the suit to her. 'I will, but not with this.'

'All right, Mum,' Millie said soothingly, as she

71

and Ruby exchanged a look. She went over to the chest and pulled the top drawer open. 'What about letting some of Dad's old jumpers go? They'd help some poor family out, wouldn't they?'

Her mother walked over and ran her hand over the Fair Isle jumper she'd knitted for her husband and then pushed the drawer closed. 'No one will want them this time of year. I'll send them along to the Christmas sale.'

Doris pottered over to her dressing table, rearranged the comb and hairbrush and straightened the lace doily. 'Well, I think we've done enough for now. Shall we have a cup of tea?'

Without waiting for a reply, she hurried out the room.

Ruby sighed and looked at her watch. 'It's almost three. Antony will be here any moment so we might as well have a cuppa as I don't think we're going to get much more done this afternoon.'

She walked out of the bedroom and followed her sister downstairs.

Millie listened to her footsteps and looked around at the familiar room, and then went downstairs too.

Steam was already escaping from the kettle spout when she reached the kitchen and the opening bars of the *Workers' Playtime* signature tune were playing.

'I don't know why they still say, "It's coming from somewhere in Britain",' said Doris just as Millie walked in. 'Because the Germans aren't listening anymore.'

'I suppose it's habit,' Ruby said. She looked at

72

her watch again. 'Antony should be here by now.' She gave a worried glance towards the front door. 'I'm just going to pop my head out to see if I can spot him.'

She left the kitchen.

'She seems very keen on this one, doesn't she?' Millie said, taking the cups and saucers from the glass-fronted kitchen dresser and setting them on the table.

Her mother nodded.

'Do you want me to pay these for you, Mum?' Millie asked, pointing to the handful of un-opened bills on the table.

Her mother stirred the teapot and set the strainer on the first cup. 'I'll do them tomorrow when I go out.'

'It's no trouble,' Millie said, pulling out a chair and sitting down at the kitchen table.

'Don't be silly, dear. You've got enough to do.' Doris poured the tea.

Millie picked up her tea and glanced out of the window. 'Who mowed the grass?' she asked, blowing across the top of her cup.

'Your father, of course, who else?' Doris replied. 'He did it yesterday just before it rained. Freda said he wouldn't mind and she sent him around when he got in from work.'

'You mean Mr Wood from number fifteen cut the grass?' Millie said.

'That's right, dear. Biscuit?' Her mother prized off the lid and held out the tin. 'I got you four ounces of bourbons in Sainsbury's just as you asked me to this morning. As if I'd forget.'

'They're Dad's favourites, not mine, Mum,'

Millie said, staring at the half-a-dozen biscuits at the bottom of the tin.

Her mother looked bewildered for a moment, and then something flickered in her eyes and her face crumpled.

'What am I to do?' she sobbed, covering her face with her hands and slumping on to the chair.

'It's all right, Mum.' Millie stood up and went around the table to her mother. 'It's perfectly normal to forget Dad's not here anymore,' she said, hugging her around the shoulders. 'But you'll adjust to it in time.'

'You're right.' Doris wiped her cheeks. 'I can't give in.'

'That's right,' said Millie encouragingly. 'Why don't we have this cup of tea and then have another go at sorting out Dad's clothes?'

Ruby strolled back into the kitchen with Tony close behind her.

Millie had been a little surprised when she met her aunt's latest admirer, as barrel-chested and brawny types weren't the sort Ruby usually went for. But Tony Harris had a good-natured way about him, and although by his own admission he hadn't been inside a school since he was eight, he had an obvious instinct for business, which meant that, aside from his building firm, he had his fingers in a variety of money-making pies.

'Afternoon, ladies,' he said, with a broad wink. 'Sorry I'm late. I got stuck behind a Labour Party lorry crawling along the Mile End Road.'

Ruby's red lips pulled tight. 'I don't know why the Prime Minister is allowing Bolsheviks to parade about the streets in broad daylight.'

'They're allowed to, Aunt Ruby, because it's a general election and isn't that what we've been fighting for these last six years?' laughed Millie.

'You might have been, dear,' Ruby replied tartly. 'But as dear Winston said himself, these Socialists are just like the Gestapo and are thoroughly un-British.'

Tony sat down at the kitchen table.

'Well, thank goodness you've arrived, Tony,' Doris said putting a cup of tea in front of him. 'Poor Ruby's been beside herself with worry. Hasn't she, Millie?'

'Oh, yes,' said Millie, giving her aunt an innocent look. 'I'm sure she was just about to ring around the hospitals to see if you'd been in an accident.'

Tony grinned. 'Is that right, sweetheart? You've been fretting for me?'

Ruby's neck flushed. 'I just thought you might have had a puncture or something. And of course we don't want to be late for the Conservative Club's meeting about the victory celebrations tonight.'

'How can they plan the celebrations?' asked Millie. 'The election's not until next week, and even then the overseas votes won't be in for weeks.'

Ruby waved a dismissive hand. 'Winston's bound to win. All the papers say so. And then all this talk about welfare and common good will be forgotten and England will go back to how it used to be.'

Sitting behind the superintendent's desk, Millie counted out twenty shillings to make a pound, and slipped the silver coins into the stiff paper bank pouch and folded it in on itself. She rested it against the row of similar bundles on the left of the desk. Jabbing her pen in the inkwell, she wrote the amount beneath the last entry of this week's receipts, then drew a large tick at the bottom of Eva's weekly record book and closed it. She put it on the completed pile, yawned and took another from the dozen or so books still to be logged.

As always, it would be a close-run thing between the money actually collected by the nurses and the money the Association treasurer expected to receive. Most patients made it a matter of personal pride to pay the Association's nurses for their care, even if it meant scrimping on another area of household expenditure. The treasurer and the board were sympathetic to cases of real hardship and would often write off a nursing debt in cases of infant, maternal or child death or for the very elderly without relatives, but there were always a few notorious non-payers. Although their often inventive reasons why they didn't have a shilling for the nurse could raise a smile, it was a drain nevertheless on the Association's meagre finances.

Of course, since the Labour party's landslide victory the month before, there had been a lot of talk in the papers about the new government bringing in the national health service, intended as a system where no one would have to pay to see a doctor or go to hospital. But, unfortunately, until the government actually put their plans into action for free health care, it was Millie's job as the acting superintendent to chase up outstanding payments.

And so once the accounts were finished, she'd have to make a start on the strongly worded letters requesting the immediate settlement of outstanding bills, a task she hated.

There was a light tap on the door.

'Come in.'

The door opened and Frances Groves, the Whitehorse Road nurse, walked in carrying a tea tray.

At twenty-three, Frances was one of the youngest nurses working for the Association. A slim redhead, she only just stretched to five foot two in her regulation lace-up shoes, but with a kindly nature and her happy, open expression, Frances was treasured by all her patients.

Millie looked surprised. 'Is it that time already?'

'Oh, it's almost four, but as Lilly's still peeling potatoes I said I'd bring in your tea,' Frances said.

Although Mrs Archer had wasted no time in engaging a new cook for Munroe House, unfortunately she wasn't due to arrive for another four weeks, and so, along with all her usual duties, Millie had had to spend time devising a cooking rota between the nurses.

She ran her hands over her face and massaged her brow.

'You look tired,' Frances said as she set the tray down.

Millie forced a smile. 'It's just a bit hectic around here at the moment; you know how it is.' She poured a cup of tea and spooned half a teaspoon from the precious sugar bowl, and then took a sip. 'But this is just what I need to pick me up and help me finish off these accounts. Thank you.'

Millie put the cup down and reached for the next ledger.

Frances shifted from one foot to the other. 'I know you're busy and I wouldn't ask if it weren't important, but may I have a word with you, Sister?'

'Well, I'm only halfway through the end-of-week accounts, and I still have the lotion order to complete before I start my put-to-bed–'

'Please, Sister.'

Millie pushed aside her mental list of things still to be done, and smiled. 'Why don't you take a seat? And please call me Millie.'

Frances glanced around and giggled. 'I don't like to. Not with you being the superintendent and sitting behind Miss Summers' desk and the like. But if you're sure.'

Millie nodded. 'It will give me an excuse to have a break from all this paperwork. I think I'm actually going cross-eyed, so please tell me what's on your mind.'

Frances took a deep breath. 'Well, it's like this. I got a letter from my Tommy this morning saying that although he's still in France, as his unit is only a few miles from the coast, they are going to be one of the first to be demobbed.'

Millie laughed. 'I bet you can't wait. After all, how many days were you married before he was shipped out? Ten?'

'Thirteen,' Frances replied. 'And that was over two years ago. I've had nothing but letters to keep me warm since. If you know what I mean.'

Millie suppressed a smile.

Frances blushed and looked briefly at her hands and then back to Millie. 'The thing is, Miss ... Millie. Me and Tommy agreed as soon as he got back that we'd settle down proper. You know, find a home and start a family. He's already written to his old foreman at Ford and they've offered him his old job back on the assembly line, so as soon as Jimmy gets his papers we'll be looking for a house in Dagenham. There are rumours the new government is going to build council houses near the main works and we're going to put our names down for one.'

'Dagenham!'

Frances bit her lip. 'I'm sorry, especially with you run off your feet, and of course we've got to find a place first and so it won't be for a month or two. But I'll be gone quite soon, I'm afraid. After everything we've been through Tommy reckons we're due a bit of happiness.'

Although she felt sad, Millie forced a warm smile. 'And I couldn't agree more. And when hasn't there been too much work and not enough nurses?'

'Not any time I can remember,' replied Frances, visibly relieved.

'Exactly,' continued Millie. 'And I've heard Dagenham is very nice. Full of houses with gardens and trees. The perfect place, in fact, to raise a family.'

Frances beamed at her. 'That's what he said.' She stood up. 'Well, thanks for your time, Miss Sullivan,' she giggled. 'I mean Millie. But I'd better let you get on before your tea gets cold.'

'Thank you, and it's a sin to waste a good cuppa.' Millie picked up her cup and took another sip. 'Would you just pass me the rota from the peg before you leave?'

'Of course.' Frances unhooked the clipboard and handed it to Millie.

As the door closed Millie's eyes drifted on to the two envelopes sitting in her in-tray. One was from Rosie Adams, saying she was going to join her brother in Canada; and the other was from Win Jones, informing the Association that she would be leaving at the end of the month to marry her fiancé.

Millie sighed, then picked up the sheet with the allocations for the month pencilled in neat columns and reached for her eraser.

Millie stepped out from behind the screen, and the women sitting in the treatment room turned. Although she'd only unlocked the surgery door twenty minutes before, as usual the weekly Munroe House antenatal clinic was packed.

She and Annie had set out chairs on one side of the room, the examination couch on the other, and then they had divided one from the other with a portable screen. It was supposed to provide privacy, but the fabric was so threadbare that a not too dirty window would have been more effective.

'Mrs Riley,' Millie called above the chatter.

Dot Riley took a last drag from the roll-up dangling out of the corner of her mouth, then pinched it out and slipped it in her pocket. She lifted the toddler off her lap, heaved herself to her

80

feet and waddled towards Millie. Two little girls standing alongside in faded hand-me-downs followed their mother.

'Good afternoon,' Millie said, as she pulled the panel across behind her patient.

Mrs Riley collapsed on to the examination couch and it creaked under her weight.

Millie smiled at the three little girls who had lined up in height order.

'Now, will you be good girls and stand there,' Millie shuffled them back against the glass-fronted instrument cupboard, 'while I have a chat with your mum?'

The two older ones, Lizzy and Cathy, nodded solemnly, while their baby sister Mary explored her right nostril with her index finger.

Millie turned back to their mother. 'And how are you today?'

'Well, I can tell you straight, Sister, I'm bejiggered.'

'I'm not surprised,' Millie replied, reaching out and stopping Lizzy from grabbing the kidney bowl from the dressing trolley. 'You've got more on your plate than most.'

'Too right. I'm just right glad the other girls are at school; it's bloody Fred Karno's army when they're not. I blame himself. My Paddy. He's only got to hang his trousers over the end of the bed and I'm up the stick.'

'And all of them are a credit to you,' said Millie. 'Now if you could just lie on the couch.'

Annie helped Mrs Riley to lift her legs and then deftly caught Mary before she disappeared back into the waiting area.

The two nurses took up their places either side of the woman sprawled on the examination couch.

Millie smiled politely. 'This is Nurse Fletcher. She's training to become a Queen's Nurse. She's going to examine you.'

'Right you are,' Mrs Riley shuffled further down, setting her stomach wobbling like a blancmange.

She lifted her top to reveal a grey vest secured at one shoulder by a safety pin. She pulled down the top of her skirt to expose similarly washed-out knickers.

Millie scanned down the front page of her patient's notes. 'Mrs Riley is a thirty-four-year-old multigravida–'

Annie looked astonished. 'Thirty-four!'

Millie glared at her pupil.

Mrs Riley shrugged with acceptance. 'That's all right; I've had a 'ard life.'

'And this is her thirteenth pregnancy,' continued Millie.

'And every one o' them a girl!' boasted Mrs Riley.

Millie looked across at her pupil. 'What do we do first?'

'Measure pubic bone to navel and then to fundus.'

'Very well.' Millie took out her tape measure and handed it to her pupil.

Annie ran it down from Mrs Riley's sternum to navel and then on to her pubic bone.

'Twenty and twenty-four.'

Millie wrote it in the notes and compared it

with last month's measurement.

'Are you sure of your dates, Mrs Riley?' Millie asked, as her fingers searched. 'You seem a lot further on.'

'I am. He came 'ome fully how's yer father after an 'ome win last September, and I didn't have the heart to tell him no.'

'But what about before that?' asked Annie.

'There weren't no before-that since her.' Mrs Riley nodded at thirteen–month-old Mary sitting on the floor.

Millie looked across at Annie. 'Well, Nurse Fletcher, perhaps you'd like to examine Mrs Riley and tell me what you feel?'

The noise on the other side of the screen suddenly hushed as the women in the waiting room strained to hear.

Annie palpated Mrs Riley's generous folds in an attempt to find the baby hidden beneath. 'I think the back is lying on the right side.' She felt down the left side. 'And I'm pretty certain the feet are up here.' She stretched her right hand across the expanse of Dot's lower abdomen. 'I can't seem to find the head.'

A mutter went around on the other side of the screen.

'They can't find the head.'

'I'm not surprised,' someone said in a loud whisper.

'They can't be a day over twenty apiece,' hissed another.

'But they've studied. You know, read a lot of books and such.'

'Well then, they should know where the 'ead is

then, shouldn't they?' chipped in a third.

There was a snigger.

'Let me try.' Millie placed her hand across Mrs Riley's pubic bone and pressed gently. As potatoes were part of every meal Mrs Riley put on the table, five years of rationing had had a minimal effect on her figure, and so Millie wasn't surprised her pupil couldn't locate the baby's head. In truth, she could barely distinguish one part of the baby from another herself.

As she worked her way down her patient's right side trying to get an idea of what was where, she had an uneasy feeling. She glanced at Mrs Riley's feet and then her chart. Her ankles weren't swollen and her blood pressure was fine. Perhaps the baby was misaligned? Breech, or even lying across – that might account for not finding the baby's head where she expected it to be. Trying not to look alarmed, Millie gently worked her way around. Suddenly her hand encompassed a distinct roundness. She let out a sign of relief.

'Here we are.' She rocked the baby's head gently in the pelvis to make sure.

'They've got the 'ead,' someone whispered again.

'Well, fank Gawd for that,' replied another voice.

Then Annie finished her own examination and stood back.

Millie tucked the notes in the box file. 'Well, Mrs Riley, I think I can safely say the baby is head down and in just the right place. I'd also go as far as to predict that your husband will be calling Munroe House in about two months.'

'I know,' Dot said, pulling down her blouse.

'Mrs Callaghan told me that last week.'

'Did she now?' Millie replied, tight-lipped.

'Who's Mrs Callaghan?' asked Annie.

'Well, you must be new around here if you don't know Bridget Callaghan.' Dot Riley chuckled. 'I reckon she's delivered more babies than you've had hot dinners. She said that everything was just as it should be, but she didn't mind if you looked me over too.'

'That's good of her,' said Millie flatly.

Dot smiled, revealing a set of uneven, tobacco-stained teeth. 'Now, Sister, don't take it the wrong way. You and your nurses are real angels, so you are, but Mrs C's one of the old-time midwives. I'd say Bridget must have helped see half the babies in the area take their first breath and she knows more about winkling out an awkward baby than all that's written in books.'

'But this isn't the old times now, Mrs Riley,' Millie said, trying to sound professional. 'And childbirth is much safer when we apply modern scientific methods to it.'

Mrs Riley patted Millie's hand. 'You're right of course, Sister. But,' Mrs Riley crossed herself, 'praise Mary, Mrs C told me that after twelve runs at it I'm finally carrying a boy.'

'I suppose she dangled a wedding ring over your stomach.'

Mrs Riley rolled her eyes. 'I'm surprised you believe in that old wives' tale, Sister. No, Mrs C could see it clear as day.' She grabbed her pendulous breasts and thrust them at Millie. 'Look. My right titty's bigger than the left.'

Annie turned and tidied the trolley, her shoulders shaking, while Millie stared.

Mrs Riley released her breasts so they could settle back on to her waistband.

Millie repositioned Mrs Riley's clothing. 'Well, everything seems in order for now, but I would like to see you again in four weeks,' she said, helping the pregnant woman to her feet.

Mrs Riley took out the half-smoked cigarette and stuck it in her mouth. 'If you like, ducks. But there's no need as Mrs Callaghan's keeping an eye on me.'

Millie gave her a tight smile. 'I'd still like to see you myself, Mrs Riley, if you don't mind.'

Mrs Riley shrugged.

An enamel kidney bowl clattered on the floor and Mrs Riley swiped the back of her hand across her daughter Mary's head.

''Ow many times do I have to tell you to leave things alone or I'll get the policeman to take you away,' she growled at the toddler as she grabbed her hand and dragged her out.

Annie closed the curtain behind her and turned to Millie. 'Who is this Mrs Callaghan?' she whispered as she stripped the soiled draw-sheet off the couch and replaced it with a clean one.

'Before the Nursing Association put properly trained midwives into the area, babies were delivered by the mother's own female relatives – you know, mothers, aunts or sisters – or sometimes by local women who were sort of folk midwives,' replied Millie in a low voice. 'Mrs Callaghan fancies herself as one of these old-style midwives, but she is really a busybodying old bat.'

Annie looked puzzled. 'I still don't see why you're so bothered by some old woman's silly superstitions.'

'I wouldn't be,' replied Millie, wiping the Pinard foetal stethoscope with Dettol-soaked gauze so that it was ready for the next patient, 'if all she did was predict the sex or the baby's hair colour. She's safe enough with a straightforward delivery, I grant. But in almost every first or difficult birth she assists with the mother gets post-delivery fever or a nasty tear underneath.'

Annie winced. 'For goodness sake, why on earth do women go to her?'

'Because most of our mothers were delivered by Mrs Callaghan themselves,' Millie replied. 'And their mothers think she's some sort of wise woman who can do no wrong.'

'Can't you tell the doctors and get them to do something?' asked Annie.

Millie pulled the next patient's notes out. 'I have, and most of them encourage women to use our services. But I'm afraid to say, Annie, that around here old habits die hard, and so for now we just have to hope she doesn't end up killing someone.'

Chapter Four

Connie took the tickets the girl in the kiosk pushed through the small window and made her way through the crowds in the Regency's foyer. Outside a banner had been slung across the 1930s Art Deco frontage saying 'Celebrate VJ day in style'.

'Come on, the band's started and we won't get a table if we don't hurry,' Connie called as she headed for the cloakroom.

Through the scrolled-gilt double doors that led to the hall, the sound of the band's brass section belting out 'Little Brown Jug' drifted through.

Beattie laughed and plunged into the throng after her friend. She craned her neck around. 'Come on, Millie, or you'll lose us.'

In truth, Millie wouldn't have minded because after a long day balancing her time between her visits, the Association's paperwork and another rather difficult telephone conversation with Aunt Ruby, she would rather have taken a cup of hot cocoa to bed than hop around a dancefloor. However, it was VJ day, and Connie and Beattie had insisted that Millie put on her glad rags, telling her she needed to cheer herself up, about which they were probably right. So, pulling out her newest dress, Millie had curled her hair and carefully applied a coating of Cherry Kiss to her lips.

Now, Millie watched her friends jostling in the

throng for a moment, then sighed and, resting her hand lightly on the polished wooden handrail, slowly walked down the carpeted steps to join them. After exchanging her coat for a ticket and checking her make-up while squashed alongside a dozen girls doing the same in the Ladies, Millie followed Connie and Beattie through the crowded bar and on to the dancefloor proper.

Connie stood on tiptoe and scanned around over the heads of the dancers. 'All the tables are gone.'

'Never mind,' said Beattie. 'We can squeeze in by that pillar.'

'That'll do,' Connie replied, raising her voice over the music. 'With a bit of luck we won't be doing much sitting down. I'll get us all a gin and it.'

She elbowed her way to the bar.

Beattie slipped her arm around Millie's waist and squeezed. 'Come on, girl, shake a leg, or someone will pinch our spot,' she said softly, guiding her around the dancers and towards the ornate corner pillar.

The music changed tempo and the dancers clasped hands, jumping and swinging back and forth in an exuberant jitterbug.

Connie returned with their drinks.

'There you go,' she said, handing them around. 'Cheers.'

Millie took a sip.

Beattie raised her glass. 'To our Millie, the new superintendent.'

'To Millie,' echoed Connie.

'Thanks. But don't count your chickens,' Millie

said. 'There's certain to be other candidates who will be applying.'

'But none'll be a patch on you,' Beattie said, tapping her toe in time with the beat. 'Well, the band's not Tommy Dorsey's, but they're not bad.'

'Excuse us, ladies,' a male voice said.

Millie turned to find three smartly dressed young men standing behind her.

The tall chap in the middle with dark hair smiled. 'Me and my mates were wondering if the three prettiest girls in the hall would let us take them for a turn around the floor.'

Beattie scoffed. 'How many times have you used that old line before?'

'Hundreds,' laughed his blond friend. 'And it works every time.'

'Well, girls, how can we say no to such flattery?' Connie laughed. She hooked her arm in Millie's. 'Can we, Millie?' she asked, looking encouragingly at her.

Millie forced aside her gloomy mood and smiled. 'No, we can't.'

The tallest young man offered his arm and Millie allowed him to lead her on to the dance-floor for a quickstep. They chatted as he guided her around the floor under the twinkling glitter-ball, but when the dance finished she made her excuses and returned to her drink. Tucking herself next to the column, Millie watched high-spirited couples quickstep past her.

Connie had changed partners and was now dancing with a slimly built chap in a brown suit, while Beattie was chatting to someone at the front of the stage. Another young man asked Millie to

90

take to the floor but she declined.

Connie came back breathless, with her eyes sparkling. 'What was yours like?'

'So-so,' Millie replied. 'He's a trackman in the shunting yard at Stratford. Yours?'

Connie laughed. 'Two left feet.'

The music stopped and the leader announced a ten-minute interval.

Millie finished the last of her drink. 'Look, Connie, I've had a great time but I think I might head back.'

Connie looked as if she were about to protest, but whatever she was about to say remained unspoken. Her eyes focused on something just over Millie's right shoulder, and then a canny smile lifted one corner of her mouth.

'Trust me, Millie, if you have half the sense you were born with and your eyes set straight in your head, you won't be rushing to go anywhere for a while.'

Millie turned and her eyes widened.

A man stood on the other side of the dancefloor looking unflinchingly across at her. He was at least six foot, if not an inch or two taller and although, like most men in the hall, he wore a dark, off-the-peg suit, it sat as if especially tailored to draw attention to his broad shoulders. The trousers, too, fitted just snugly enough to emphasise the shape of his legs. His angular face was clean shaven and his black hair had more than a hint of curl in it.

As her gaze met his, Millie was mightily pleased she'd chanced a pair of nylons rather than paint her legs with the permanganate mixture from the clinic.

'It seems you have an admirer, Millie,' Connie murmured.

Millie couldn't answer.

The band filed back on to the stage and took up their positions. The leader snapped his fingers three times and the horn section blasted out the opening chords of 'In the Mood'. The man finished his drink, put his glass down and, without taking his eyes from her, sauntered across the dancefloor towards Millie.

He stopped in front of her and his smoky green eyes rested on her face.

'Good evening, Miss. Would you like to dance?' He held out his hand.

Millie took it. 'I'd love to,' she replied as his fingers closed over hers.

He drew Millie to him, slipped his arm around her waist and held her decisively. Millie rested her other hand lightly on his shoulder, feeling the hardness of the muscles beneath.

His firm lips lifted in a smile and he guided her into a space amongst the dancers and then, with the smallest pressure on her hand and back, swirled her around in a quickstep.

'Do you come here often?' he asked, confidently stepping sideways on the downbeat and swinging her around.

'Once or twice a month,' Millie replied, enjoying the sensation of his hand in the small of her back. 'It's a good band.'

He glanced towards the stage. 'They're not Tommy Dorsey's, but they're not bad.'

Millie laughed.

'What's so funny?' he asked, sidestepping nimbly

to avoid another couple.

'That's exactly what my friend Beattie said,' Millie replied, as her feet and mood took flight.

He laughed a deep, rolling laugh. 'I'm Alex Nolan.'

'And I'm Millie Sullivan.' Millie looked impressed. 'Nolan? Any relation to Nolan & Sons Shipping at Limehouse?'

'My gran said we were, but it must be way back because I haven't got their money.' He smiled as a shaft of light illuminated his face, showing in a flash the deep green of his eyes. 'Are you from around here?'

'Bow,' Millie replied, briefly looking at his blunt chin at her eye level. 'And you?'

'Canning Town, but I'm in digs with a couple of mates,' he replied.

'What do you do?'

'Bit of this and that,' he replied, throwing in a double step.

Millie matched his move. 'Sounds dodgy.'

He smiled enigmatically. 'And you?'

'That and this,' she replied, with a wry smile. 'And I'm sharing digs with my friends, too.'

He laughed again. They back-stepped to avoid Connie and a chap with curly hair barging into them.

'Your friend's having fun,' he said. 'I haven't seen her with the same partner twice.'

Millie looked surprised. 'How do you know she's my friend?'

'I spotted you as soon as you walked in, and the two girls you were with,' Alex replied, looking down at her.

'She won't dance with anyone more than once because she's engaged,' Millie explained, as his fingers tightened around her hand. 'Her fellow's being demobbed in a few weeks and they're getting married, so I expect she won't be dancing with anyone but him from then on.'

'And is that why you've only had one dance, because of your fellow?' The corner of Alex's lips lifted.

Millie raised an eyebrow. 'Who says I have one?'

'I can't believe you haven't.' Alex's gaze ran slowly over her face. 'Not a good-looking woman like you.'

Something in the way he said 'woman' sent a shiver up Millie's spine, but she kept her expression cool. 'You're not backward in coming forward, are you?'

'I'm just saying it like I see it,' he said in a low tone.

Millie's cheeks grew warm. 'I'm not walking out with anyone at the moment because I'm choosy.'

His eyes changed subtly, and he smiled.

Millie broke from his gaze and breathed in the tangy smell of his aftershave.

Alex's arm tightened as he whirled her in a last, extravagant sidestep as the orchestra rounded up the last chords. He brought her to a halt and released her. They stared at each other.

'Thank you,' he said, 'I can't remember the last time I enjoyed a turn around the dancefloor so much.'

'Me neither,' replied Millie.

The dancers applauded the band and Alex walked Millie back to where Connie and Beattie were waiting.

'Thank you again,' he said, as Millie joined her friends. 'And I'm glad you're choosy.'

'Why?'

'Because you chose me, Millie.'

Alex turned and strode away. Millie watched him, wondering if he would approach one of the many girls at the end of the dancefloor, but he didn't. Instead he headed for the bar where he joined a couple of other men and ordered a pint.

'Goodness,' said Beattie. 'I didn't know they made 'em like that anymore.'

'Nor did I,' Millie said, watching Alex sip the froth off his beer.

'And he could give Fred Astaire a bit of a run for his money,' Connie added.

'Perhaps he could,' agreed Millie, remembering his sure hand at her waist. 'But in my opinion, Alex Nolan thinks a mite too much of himself.'

Millie put the pen back in the inkwell on the writing bureau and pinched the inside corners of her eyes. She rested her head back and looked around the nurses' sitting room.

The room was located on the first floor, directly above the treatment room. And like the rest of the house, it was long overdue a fresh coat of paint. The carpet, a red and gold one with a deep fringe, was of good quality although the constant passage of feet back and forth had worn some areas down to the canvas backing. The furniture was a hotch-potch of styles and ages, from upright wheel-backed chairs that creaked when you sat on them to the rounded pre-war sofas. A large portrait of the founder of the association, Miss Robina Munroe, a kindly looking woman in a tartan crinoline and bonnet, hung above the stone fireplace while pastel sketches of rural scenes, complete with milkmaids and cattle, graced the other walls.

Although it was almost dark, after six years of the blackout, the novelty of watching the sunset without someone shouting 'put that light out' meant that the heavy drapes in the sitting room were still tied back. And, as it was Sunday night, almost every nurse in the home was there, other than the handful of girls who attended Evensong.

Thankfully the room was spacious enough to accommodate the variety of activities. At the far end Gladys and three of her friends, Marge, Nancy and Trudy, were practising the latest dance steps to an up-tempo band tune. They whirled and swung to the beat, but every now and again the tempo slowed so one of them dashed over to crank the handle of the old gramophone again.

Beattie, Joyce and a few others were sitting around the hearth, chatting as they darned their thick work stockings or repaired frayed seams. Sally had commandeered the old winged chair and had her nose in a book, while Eva, Mavis and two others played whist.

Millie picked up the letter and read it through again. The door opened and Connie walked in with a magazine under her arm. As usual, Connie had been around to her mother's house for Sunday tea.

Like her, Connie was a local girl although, unlike Millie, her family still lived just off Old Gravel Lane in the heart of the old docks. She had three brothers, four sisters, and a dozen assorted nieces and nephews, along with umpteen cousins dotted around from Limehouse Basin to Canning Town.

Connie spotted Millie and hurried over.

'How's your family?' Millie asked.

'Oh you know, loud and quarrelsome,' Connie replied, pulling up a chair beside Millie. 'But I picked this up from my Doreen.' She unfurled a copy of *Woman* magazine and opened it at the centre. 'It's got a special wedding section. Aren't they gorgeous?'

Millie gazed down at the display of wedding dresses. 'They are, and a lot of coupons.'

'I've been saving mine for a year and so I should have enough. If not, I can a trim the skirt in a bit. There's a pattern I've seen in Woolworths that's very like this one,' she tapped her finger on a boxed-shoulder dress with a sweetheart neckline. 'Will you help me make it?'

'Of course.'

'Although I doubt I'll be able to afford a veil like that one,' Connie said, studying the sweeping lace of the picture.

Millie gripped her friend's hand. 'Perhaps not, but you'll look so ravishing that Charlie will be speechless when he sees you walking down the aisle.'

Connie's shoulders sagged. 'If he ever does.'

'Still no news?'

Connie shook her head. 'I nipped over to see his mum on the way back to see if she'd heard anything.'

'Had she?'

'I don't know. There was no one home.' Connie closed the magazine with a sigh. 'I'll pop in on her again in the morning, if I get the chance.' She glanced at the letter in Millie's hand. 'How's it going?'

Millie scanned the sheet of paper again. 'I've rewritten it four times so far and I'm still not happy with it. I listed my qualifications and my experience, but I don't suppose they are any different from anyone else applying for the position of superintendent.'

'You've emphasised the fact you've already been doing the job for the past couple of months, haven't you?' Connie asked.

'I have, and that I've seen two student nurses through their Queen's Nurse training.'

'Well, that should do it. Plus Father Gilbert's reference, which must carry some weight, as he's Munroe House's parish priest,' Connie said.

Millie chewed her lower lip. 'I suppose. I just wish I had a better idea what the Association committee are looking for.'

'Well, whatever it is, I'm sure you've got it,' Connie replied. 'When's the application got to be in?'

'Friday,' Millie replied.

'Application?'

Millie and Connie looked up quickly.

Gladys stood over them. 'Don't tell us you're going to apply for old Summers' job?' she said, raising her voice.

Someone took the needle off the record mid-trombone solo. Sally raised her head and Beattie and Joyce looked over, their sewing needles poised in mid-air.

98

'Why shouldn't she?' Connie asked. 'Millie's been doing the job in all but name for years.'

Millie regarded Gladys coolly. 'Are you applying for it, then?'

'Not bloody likely,' Gladys replied. 'All that, "Yes, Mrs Harper, and no, Mrs Harper and three bags full, Mrs Harper." And all that sitting around on your backside all day – it ain't real nursing, is it?'

A wry smile twisted Millie's lips. 'If that's the case, I'm surprised your letter of application isn't sitting on Mrs Harper's desk already. After all, you've spent half your day sitting on your backside in the treatment room instead of visiting your patients.'

Gladys's face flushed. 'I graft as hard as anyone here, you included, Millie Sullivan.'

'You do, Gladys,' Sally called across. 'Work hard at avoiding it.'

Everyone laughed.

Gladys glared at Millie for a moment, then strode over to her friends, who were hovering by the gramophone.

'It's getting too stuffy in here – let's go down to the Boatman and have a G and T in the snug,' she said, snatching her cardigan from the chair and marching towards the door.

Marge, Nancy and Trudy exchanged a couple of nervous glances but followed her out anyway.

'Don't forget you've to be in at ten,' Millie called after them.

Gladys spun around and jabbed her painted fingernail at Millie. 'I'll come in when I please, Millie Sullivan, because you ain't the bloody superintendent yet.'

Just as another crack of lightning cut across the sky, Millie pushed open the front door of Munroe House and stepped into the hallway. Taking off her hat, she shook it out, removed her sodden coat and hooked it on the stand.

'Is that you, Millie?'

Millie looked up as Sally leaned over the first-floor banister. 'Yes. What's the problem?' she replied, as rainwater dripped on to the polished wood of the floor.

'It's Mr Riley. Phoned about an hour ago to say his wife got pains,' Sally replied, scooting her fair hair out of her eyes. 'Joyce offered to go, but I told her not to bother as you'd be back any moment. Where have you been?'

'Trying to get Mrs Fenton back in bed,' Millie replied, climbing the stairs towards her. 'It took me half an hour of banging on doors to get the neighbours to help me get her off the floor and back on her feet. Then I had to wait a quarter of an hour because Shadwell Bridge was up; and all that in a downpour that would float the Ark.'

'Do you want me to make you a cuppa while you get changed?' Sally asked.

Millie shook her head. 'Thanks, but I'd better get straight over there. She's not due for another few weeks, so it's probably just practice pain.'

Sally rolled her eyes. 'You'd think after twelve children she'd know the difference.'

'Maybe,' Millie grinned. 'You can make me a cocoa when I get back.'

'You're on. I'll give Connie and Beattie a knock

100

and see if they want to join us. And take my coat – you'll catch your death if you go out in yours.'

Millie went to her room, changed into her mid-wife's uniform and then went back downstairs and searched out Sally's coat amongst the others. Thankfully, although the thunder rumbled still overhead, setting dogs barking, the worst of the storm had passed and within a few moments she was pedalling her bike down Commercial Road towards Star Court where the Rileys lived.

She chained her bicycle to the lamp-post and took her bag out of the basket. Number ten Star Court had once been a grand affair four storeys high, but now it was home to seven families. Whenever Millie called there always seemed to be cabbage boiling and a child crying some-where. All fourteen Rileys lived in the three downstairs rooms.

Millie slipped down the arched alley that ran between numbers ten and twelve and pushed open the back gate. Walking through the back yard, she breathed through her mouth as she passed the communal toilet at the end.

Millie knocked on the back door and Nora, the Rileys' second daughter, opened it. Millie followed the twelve-year-old through into the family's main living area. This was a bare room with a few sticks of dilapidated furniture and a threadbare curtain strung across the window. There was an old stove against one wall with a couple of blackened pots on it, and a sink sitting on bricks with a single cold-water tap.

All the children, except the youngest, Mary, were sitting around the table as they ate from bowls containing grey-looking stew. Mary was tied to a chair alongside her eldest sister Dotty, who fed her while she ate her own supper.

'Where's your father?' Millie asked.

''E's gone down the Ship. He says to fetch him when it's all over,' Nora informed her as she squeezed back into her place. 'Ma's in the back room. Mrs Callaghan's wiv 'er.'

Millie's hand tightened around the handle of her bag. 'I'll go through, then.'

She sidestepped around the children hunched over their supper at the table and opened the adjoining door.

Mrs Riley was sitting up in bed with a baby in her arms.

Millie's gaze travelled past her patient and on to the woman on the other side of the room. Mrs Callaghan stood no more than five foot high and was probably somewhere near the same dimension around her middle. However, her substantial bosom, rolling hips and solid thighs channelled downwards to a pair of tiny feet, giving her the silhouette of a spinning top. She was dressed as usual in the sleeveless, faded, patterned overall worn by most of the women in the area, with her frizzy grey hair covered by a scarf tied in a knot at the front. And although her piercing black eyes were so deeply hooded that the lids almost obscured her vision, she missed nothing.

Mrs Callaghan gave Millie a patronising look. 'Nice of you to turn up, but you shouldn't have troubled yourself.'

Millie smiled professionally at Mrs Riley. 'Sorry I took so long getting here, Mrs Riley.'

Mrs Riley grinned. 'Don't worry yourself, ducks. Mrs Callaghan 'as done the necessary.'

'And it's a boy,' added Mrs Callaghan smugly. 'Just like I said.'

Millie put her bag down at the end of the bed. 'Now that I'm here, perhaps you'd let me have a little look to make sure everything is as it should be.'

'I shouldn't bother,' Mrs Callaghan replied, as Millie took off her coat. 'The afterbirth's out in one piece. It's in the gazunder if you want to see it.'

Going over to the side table, Millie peered into the chamber pot at the liver-coloured mass covered in blood. She looked up. 'That seems in order.'

Millie opened her bag and pulled out her fisherman's scales and net sack. She arranged them on the bed and stretched out her arms. 'If you let me have the baby I'll weigh him.'

Mrs Riley gave her the child and then reached for her tobacco tin. She pulled out one she'd rolled earlier.

'Six pounds two ounces,' Mrs Callaghan said, handing her patient a box of matches.

Millie unwrapped the child and laid him in the middle of the netting and looked him over. He was a good pink colour, alert and the cord was tied off neatly with a silk thread. He gripped her finger and, when she stroked his cheek, his head turned towards it.

'Have you put him to the breast, Mrs Riley?'

'As soon as he popped out,' Mrs Callaghan answered.

'Yet, and got a suck like his old man, 'e has, too,' Mrs Riley chuckled, snorting smoke out of her nose.

'And you want to keep him there to stop the next one arriving too soon,' said Mrs Callaghan.

'There is some truth to that old wives' tale, Mrs Callaghan,' said Millie. 'But there are now more modern methods of family planning, Mrs Riley. You could–'

'Gawd love us, girl,' Mrs Callaghan laughed. 'We had French letters long before you were a twinkle in yer father's eye, girl. And other things that you've never heard of, like the Irishman's back yard.'

Mrs Riley sniggered and winked at Millie.

'I was actually talking about Dutch caps and gels that interfere with the sperm and prevent it reaching the mother's egg.' Millie smiled coolly at her adversary. 'But I wouldn't expect you to know much about them.'

The old woman's heavy jowls flushed.

'Well, thank you for your consideration, Sister, but as I told you before, now I've given my Paddy 'is boy I'm shutting up shop.'

Millie turned her attention back to the infant and fastened the loops at the corner of the net on to the hook. She gently lifted him until he was clear of the bed.

'Six pounds two ounces,' Millie said in a clipped tone as she watched the needle hover on the gauge.

'I bet the vicar won't let you go in for the "guess the weight of the cake" competition at the church bazaar, Bridget,' chuckled Mrs Riley.

104

Mrs Callaghan preened herself. 'It's just experience, that's all.' She smiled at Millie. 'Something you can't learn in a book.'

Millie lowered the child to the bed and lifted him out of the net. 'There you go, young man,' she said cheerily to the newborn infant. Something warm trickled down the front of her uniform.

The two women laughed. Millie looked down to see an arc of clear yellow urine shooting straight from the baby's penis squarely on to her chest.

Mrs Callaghan lumbered around to Millie's side of the bed. 'Here, give him to me,' she said, taking him from Millie.

Using a couple of squares of gauze from her bag, Millie dabbed the front of her dress. Then, without bothering to pack it properly, she bundled her equipment back into her case and snapped it shut.

Millie stood up. 'Well, congratulations Mrs Riley, you have a lovely boy. I'll be in tomorrow to see how you're getting on.'

'Thank you,' said Mrs Riley, struggling to keep a straight face.

Millie picked up her bag. 'Good day to you, Mrs Callaghan.'

The old woman wiped a tear from her eye. 'And to you, Sister.'

Feeling their eyes burning into her back, Millie picked up her coat and left the room to the sounds of uncontrollable laughter as she closed the door.

As the hall clock struck eight o'clock, Millie

crossed through the second from last scribbled message in the daybook and looked up. The dozen nurses, dressed in their navy uniforms with their bags under their chairs, were sitting around the treatment-room table, notepads in hand, taking the daily handover. The distinct smell of carbolic filled the air from the syringes, hypodermics and scissors soaking in the kidney bowls and enamel dishes on the workbench under the window. Alongside them sealed white paper bags of baked dressings sat ready for the nurses to collect on their way out.

'So if you could drop in to the almoner at St George's Hospital on your way through, Nurse Pattison, I'd be grateful,' Millie said to her friend at the other end of the table.

Joyce made a note in her pocket book.

Millie's stomach rumbled and she realised she hadn't had breakfast. That was the third morning in a row, but what could she do? Although the morning work officially started at seven-thirty, she could only keep on top of the mountain of Association paperwork by doing an hour in the office before everyone else stirred. And then, of course, she still had her patients to visit.

Millie put thoughts of toast and jam aside. 'Now, before we finish, there's one other matter we need to discuss,' she said, as the nurses started to collect themselves together. 'The students.'

'What have they been moaning about now?' asked Trudy.

'Nothing,' replied Millie. 'Although I wouldn't blame them if they were. They've got plenty to complain about.'

'Such as?' asked Gladys, folding her arms.

'The fact that Doreen and Joan are only twelve weeks away from their final exams and haven't been out with any of us for well over a month,' Millie replied.

'There's been a war on,' said Marge, one of Gladys's followers.

'Well, there isn't any more, and it's not going to look good if the QN examiner arrives and our students can't even put a room in nursing order, is it?' Everyone except Gladys and her two friends shook their heads. Millie's shoulders relaxed a little. 'Well then, I've decided—'

Gladys pulled a face, and Trudy and Marge sniggered.

'—that to make sure the students' report books are completed properly and they are given every chance to practise their skills, I am going to make one experienced nurse responsible for a particular student.'

Gladys snorted. 'Well, I'm not being saddled with that dimwit Annie.'

'Me neither,' replied Trudy and Marge in unison.

'Annie Fletcher is an intelligent young woman,' Millie said, feeling her temper rise, 'and has the makings of an excellent district nurse.'

'That's if her own shadow doesn't frighten her to death first,' Trudy commented.

'She very young, that's all,' Millie said, looking pointedly at Gladys. 'She just needs a bit more confidence, which isn't helped by people taking the mickey out of her. However, I've decided to oversee Annie myself. Beattie will look after Joan, and Eva will oversee Pat, while you, Gladys, will keep an eye on Doreen.'

Gladys's mouth turned down and she rolled her eyes. 'My daily round takes me long enough as it is without trailing a student around with me.'

Millie glared at her. 'I'm not saying you have to take her every day – in fact, all the students are perfectly fine as they are, visiting patients and reporting back, but I just want them supported so they can pass their exams. After all, it costs the Association eighty pounds to train them, plus their wages and board and lodging.'

Gladys laughed. 'Oh, now I see what it's all about.'

'What?'

'You trying to wangle the superintendent's job by sucking up to the Association.'

'Don't be ridiculous, Gladys,' cut in Beattie. 'And I agree with Millie. The four of them have had a rough time of it. I mean, Miss Summers didn't know who they were half the time, let alone organise their training properly.'

'And you're the one always moaning about how short-staffed we are, and now you've got a chance to do something about it, you're still complaining,' Eva told Gladys.

'And if they all fail, the Queen's Nurse Institute might refuse to register the Association's students next year and then we'd all be working double shifts,' Millie said, looking hard at Gladys. 'Is that what you want?'

Gladys's gaze wavered. 'Of course not. All I'm saying is why don't you leave things as they are and let the new superintendent worry about it?'

108

'That wouldn't be right,' Millie said. 'And besides, it might be another two months before the new superintendent is in the post and by then it will be too late.' She smiled. 'One of the perks of being in charge is being able make sure the students are looked after properly.' She closed the message book. 'Now, lastly, Dr Hayhurst left a message for someone to call in at the surgery. He doesn't say where the patient lives, so is anyone passing Salmon Lane?'

The room fell silent.

'Surely someone can pop in,' she said.

'Afraid I've got visits at the Aldgate end of the patch this morning,' Joyce said, picking up her bag and making ready to go.

Sally stood up and put on her hat. 'And I'm down to Hermitage Walk.'

'Eva?'

'At the Highway School searching for nits.'

'Beattie?'

'St Katherine's clinic with Dr Tyler.'

Millie looked at Connie. 'Could you?'

'You know I would, Millie, but I've got a half-day, remember? I'm looking at wedding fabric.' Connie's chair scraped on the floor as she stood up. She smiled apologetically. 'Sorry.'

Millie's eyes rested on Gladys at the far end of the table.

'Not a chance,' she said, slowly rising to her feet and straightening the seam in her stocking.

Millie glanced at the nurses beating a hasty retreat and none of them met her eye.

She pressed her lips together. 'It seems I'll have to go, then.'

Gladys's top lip curled. 'Just consider Dr Hayhurst as another one of the perks of being in charge.'

Finding a space between the prams, Millie parked her bike outside the Salmon Lane surgery and, as the railings had all been taken for the war effort, chained it to the boot scrape set in the wall. As Millie looked up at the brass plate with Dr Hayhurst's medical credentials and the surgery opening times etched on it, the anxiety that she'd kept at bay on her twenty-minute ride rose to the surface again. She squashed it down and lifted her bag determinedly from the basket.

Like most of the surgeries in the area, Dr Hayhurst's was the ground floor of an old Georgian town house and was well maintained, with window boxes on the windowsills above. Unlike most of his colleagues, he didn't live above the shop, so to speak, but made the half-hour journey in his Morris Oxford each day from his smart semi-detached in Forest Gate. His surgery was wedged incongruously between the Jack and Jill pie and eel shop and Finbow's hardware shop.

Pushing open the black-painted door, Millie stepped inside. Trying to maintain her unruffled appearance, she strolled into the waiting room. Despite the lack of decorating supplies for the past six years, Dr Hayhurst's waiting room always had a fresh coat of paint each year. The net curtains at the window were clean and gathered evenly, while the chairs were of a uniform make and set neatly back against the walls. Around the wall, in polished mahogany frames, hung various certificates and diplomas decorated with heraldic symbols and splodges of red wax, although the object that drew the eye was a portrait above the marble fireplace of the man himself, dressed in formal evening-wear and standing at the bottom of a sweeping staircase like a benevolent lord of the manor. He also had one other outlandish, almost unheard of thing in the surgery: a receptionist.

Miss Jarvis, sitting behind the desk at the far end of the room, raised her head and patted her brown curls as Millie approached.

'Doctor Hayhurst asked for someone to call,' Millie said to the stylish-looking young woman.

'I know.' Miss Jarvis stood up, adjusted her skirt and then picked up a pile of notes. 'I would have thought you would have been here sooner.'

'I didn't think it was an urgent call. Is it?' Millie asked, as she watched the secretary wriggle over to the filing cabinet.

'Not really but you know how busy Dr Hayhurst is.' She pulled out the top drawer, filing the notes.

'I could come back,' Millie replied.

Miss Jarvis slammed the filing cabinet shut and clip-clopped back to her desk. 'No, now you're here you might as well go in. But don't take too long – he has a very urgent appointment in an hour and can't be late.'

The telephone rang and she picked up the receiver.

'Dr Hayhurst's surgery. How may I help you?' she said, in a plummy voice. Her red lips widened into a smile. 'Oh, Mr Shottington, how are you?'

111

There was a pause. 'And Mrs Shottington?' Another pause. 'Of course, I quite understand and don't worry.' She waved Millie towards the door. 'I'll tell him you'll meet him in the club house at two.'

Millie made her way down the hall to the office at the back of the house. She stopped outside the door. She stared at it for a moment then took a long breath and knocked.

'Come in.'

Millie walked in.

Dr Hayhurst was bent over a putting iron, lining up a shot.

'The notes are done,' he said without looking around. 'Also, ring my wife, Pamela, and tell her I'm having dinner with Algie, there's a good girl.' He tapped the golf ball into the cup turned on its side at the other end of the room.

'Dr Hayhurst,' Millie said, in her best professional tone.

He looked around and a lascivious smile spread slowly across his face. 'Well, hello, nursey.'

Reginald Hayhurst was probably in his early forties. He was dressed in a snugly fitting Harris Tweed suit and mustard waistcoat, across which a gold chain dangled. He stood a little under six foot and with a slim build, dark brown hair and a square chin, he had the look of a matinée idol. But then handsome is as handsome does, and this was never truer than in Hello-nursey Hayhurst's case.

He dropped the iron into the golf caddy alongside his desk and balanced a buttock on the desk's edge.

'So I'm favoured with a visit from the delect-

112

able Sister Sullivan? Lucky me.'

Millie smiled pleasantly. 'You left a message for someone to call in.'

'And here you are.' He stretched out and picked up a note from his desk. 'I want one of your nurses to visit a couple of patients. Here.' He held it out.

Millie forced herself to walk towards him. She reached out to take the paper but he moved it away.

'I must say, you're looking in very good shape today, Sister Sullivan.' His eyes moved up to her breasts.

A prickle of anxiety started between Millie's shoulder blades but somehow she managed to hide it.

Keeping her expression cool, Millie reached across him.

Dr Hayhurst, spreading his legs a little wider, moved the paper out of reach again, forcing her to step closer. A waft of expensive aftershave tickled her nose as the buttons of her uniform brushed against his lapels. Millie forced herself to look at him. They stared at each other for a moment, then Millie snatched the note and stepped away.

Dr Hayhurst studied her for a second and then pulled the putter out of the golf bag again.

Millie ran her eyes over the paper, hoping Dr Hayhurst couldn't see it tremble in her hand. 'Can you tell me about Mrs Stubbs?'

'Well, she's as batty as a fruit cake, for a start,' he said, strolling to the end of the room and setting the teacup straight. 'But I want you to have a look at her legs.'

'Can you be a little more specific?'

113

He shrugged. 'Ulcerated, I think.'

'Haven't you examined them?' Millie asked.

He smiled. 'Just see what you think and then slap on a dressing.'

'Yes, doctor. And Mr Tyler's treatment?'

Dr Hayhurst picked up the golf ball and plopped it on the floor in front of him. 'Soap-and-water enema twice a week until his bowels are back to normal. And plenty of carbolic. Bloody idiot called me out twice last week with stomach cramps, so I want him cleared out until his colon resembles a storm drain.'

'Of course, doctor.' Millie sighed inwardly. 'And Mrs Yates?'

'Pop in and see what you can do. I've left a prescription for a pick-me-up at the pharmacist, so take that around with you. She's as old as the hills and just as deaf, so just jolly her along.' He tapped the ball. It rolled across the room and pinged against the cup.

Millie folded her note and slipped it into the side of her bag. 'Is there anything else I can do for you?'

Dr Hayhurst regarded her levelly, and Millie felt her cheeks grow warm.

'Have you any other patients you'd like a nurse to visit?' she asked firmly.

'Not at present,' he replied.

Millie snapped her bag shut and managed a brittle smile. 'Then I'd better get on. I have the afternoon dressing clinic starting in an hour.'

She marched to the door but Dr Hayhurst got there first. He stood in front of her for a moment, and then opened it.

Millie let out a breath and walked forward. As she came abreast of him he put his hand up and on to the doorframe, blocking her path.

'Oh, and make sure you get the money for my tonic out of Mrs Yates.' He patted her bottom. 'There's a good girl.'

Chapter Five

Millie watched as Annie unwound the last strip of bandage around Mr Pugh's head, exposing the improvised dressing over his left eye.

'You were lucky – we were just about to close the clinic doors at four,' Millie said, as Annie discarded the dirty bandage into the enamel bucket beside the dressing trolley.

She and Annie had spent the last two-and-a-half hours working in the treatment room and had dressed at least a dozen wounds, lanced three boils, and syringed two pairs of ears, not to mention removing splinters from nail beds, grit from eyes and an earring from a lad's nasal passage. And they weren't yet finished, as there were three buckets of dressings to burn, and equipment to boil and then soak in Dettol. If they were lucky perhaps, they could snatch a quick cuppa before starting the evening round.

Annie reached for the blood-stiffened gauze covering the wound.

'Don't remove it just yet,' Millie said. She leaned forward and inspected the skin surrounding the eye socket.

Mr Pugh, a solidly built individual with one straggly hedge of hair across his brow and grey tufts spiking out of his ears and nose, looked up at her with his good eye.

'Tell me straight, Sister,' he asked, with just a

tremor in his gravelly voice, 'is it bad?'

Millie smiled reassuringly. 'I'll let you know when I've had a proper look.' She turned to Annie. 'Now, what do we do first?'

'Find out all about the patient and what caused the injury,' Annie replied, her bright blue eyes wide with enthusiasm.

'And?'

The student nurse took a new record card from the stationery rack. 'Record it in the patient's notes.'

'Off you go, then.'

A bouncy curl escaped from under Annie's cap as she pulled up a chair beside Mr Pugh and noted down his details.

Contrary to Gladys' assertion, Annie was probably the brightest Queen's nurse student the Association had employed for many years, Millie felt. She had a gentle way about her, a ready smile and wouldn't be hurried when dealing with a patient, which is how it should be. However, as the youngest of the four trainees, she was prone to shyness and lacked self-confidence, traits which Millie was determined to remedy before Annie stood in front of the QN examiner in November.

'And can you tell me exactly what happened?' Annie asked, looking intently at her patient.

'We was just getting ready to release the pressure in the sugar vat when the piggin' gasket blew,' Mr Pugh replied. 'Caught me right in the moosh. And bugger me, did it burn!' He gave Millie an apologetic look. 'Pardon my French, Sister.'

'Doesn't the sugar refinery supply you with a hood and goggles?' Millie asked, noting that the

117

blistering extended beyond his grizzled hairline.

'There's a couple knocking about somewhere but Gawd, I'd be a right laughing stock if I strolled on to the floor togged up like a right nancy-boy.'

Millie looked at Annie. 'What shall we do next?'

'Soften the dressing with the water and remove it.'

Millie nodded. Annie picked up the beaker of cooled, boiled water and gently dripped it over the stiff dressing. Mr Pugh drew in a sharp breath between his teeth and grimaced.

'I'm sorry,' Annie said.

He slapped his leg a couple of times and blew out hard. 'Don't mind me, girl.' He pulled out a hip flask and took a large swig. 'You just do what you have to.'

Millie picked up the forceps and, as gently as she could, peeled the gauze away. A look of horror flashed across Annie's face as Millie discarded the dressing.

The scalding sugar had removed the skin from temple to cheekbone, exposing the raw flesh beneath and blistering the surrounding area. Although there were pinpricks of blood from the superficial capillaries, intense heat had sealed the large blood vessels and shrivelled his eyelashes. There was also a dirty residue of something oily over the whole area.

'Well, Sister, what do you think?'

'I think you were very lucky not to lose your eye, but that the scorching temperature of the sugar has killed any bugs and so the wound probably won't get infected,' Millie said. She circled her finger around the area. 'But what's all

118

this black muck?'

'Axle grease,' Mr Pugh replied. 'My mate, he squirted it on 'cos we didn't have no butter.'

Millie sighed. 'Well, you'd better take another couple of swills of that hip flask, as we'll have to remove it before we can put a dressing on.'

Under the factory grime the colour drained from Mr Pugh's face and he knocked back the last drop of spirit.

Millie and Annie washed their hands, donned their rubber gloves and masks and, while Mr Pugh sat rigid in the chair, staring fixedly ahead, they teased and swabbed off the thick lubricant from the raw flesh. Finally, after twenty minutes, the wound-bed was clean.

'Now it's just the final dressing,' she said to Mr Pugh, who by now had beads of perspiration dotted across his brow.

Mr Pugh let out a long breath and his shoulders slumped. 'Thank Gawd for that.'

'And you'll have to go to your doctor so he can take a look at it,' Millie added as Annie collected a clean dressing pack.

She unpacked it and then set out the gauze, galley pots and a tube of cream.

'Now, I'm going to let you do the dressing by yourself,' Millie said to Annie, 'so I can sign it off in your record book.'

There was a brief knock on the door. Millie looked around as Beattie walked into the treatment room.

'I'm sorry, Sister Sullivan,' she said. 'There's a phone call for you. It's a Mrs Dixon. It sounds urgent.'

Millie's heart gave an uncomfortable thump and she turned to Annie. 'You carry on here. I'll only be a moment.'

'Very good, Sister,' Annie said, smearing ointment on a tongue depressor, ready to apply it to the burn.

Millie stripped off her gloves and hurried out of the room after her friend.

'I'm sorry to call you out, Millie,' Beattie said, as they reached the hall. 'But your aunt wouldn't take no for an answer.'

At that moment Gladys walked out of the sitting room wearing her best dress and with her hair newly curled and tucked.

'Your aunt?' she said, innocently. 'Don't tell me you're taking a personal phonecall while you're on duty, Acting Superintendent Sullivan!'

'It's an emergency,' Beattie snapped.

Gladys's face twisted into a sharp smile as she looked at Millie. 'Of course it is. I suppose it's another one of those perks you were on about earlier.'

Millie picked up the receiver and cupped her hand over the mouthpiece. 'Don't let me keep you, Gladys.'

Gladys gave her a hard look, then spun around and strode down the hall.

Millie removed her hand and put the handset to her ear. 'Hello.'

'Amelia, is that you?'

'Yes, Aunt Ruby, what's wrong?'

'It's your mother.'

'She's not ill, is she?' Millie asked, as a horrible sensation of déjà vu swept over her.

'No, no,' replied Aunt Ruby impatiently. 'But you have to come straight away.'

'But I'm in the middle of a dressing clinic and–'

'Amelia! Your mother needs you,' Aunt Ruby's strident tone bellowed down the earpiece.

'I'll have to find someone to cover me and I'll be there as soon as I can,' Millie said, as anxiety clutched at her chest.

'Be as quick as you can.'

Her aunt hung up and Millie put the phone down.

'What's wrong?' asked Beattie.

'She wouldn't say. Just that I had to come straight away.' She looked at Beattie. 'Annie's treating the last patient, so do you think you could see that she finishes?'

'Of course.' Beattie waved her off. 'You just do what you have to and I'll finish up.'

'But there's the evening round,' Millie replied.

'Just leave it to me,' Beattie said, taking her by the elbow and guiding her away from the treatment room. 'I'll get the girls to take one each and that should cover it.'

Millie bit her lower lip. 'I suppose Annie could start with the eye drops and insulins, and if I go on my bike with my case I can catch you up later.'

'You just go and sort out what you need to, and we'll hold the fort until you get back. Now off you go.' Beattie shooed Millie away.

Millie hurried to the stairs and took them two at a time, grabbed her handbag and nurse's case, and then dashed back downstairs. As she reached the bottom step Gladys stepped out from the storeroom and gave Millie, and then the telephone, a pointed look.

Millie ignored Gladys and tried to appear un-ruffled as she headed towards the back door.

The muscles in Millie's legs ached as she swung off the Mile End Road and into Harley Grove. She'd cycled the three miles from Munroe House to her mother's road in record time and with growing panic.

She skidded to a halt and pushed the bicycle through the side gate. Leaving it propped up against the wall, she sped around to the back door. She found her mother and aunt in the kitchen, sitting across the table from each other but staring in opposite directions.

Ruby, dressed in a muted-blue boxed-shoulder suit with a matching hat, looked around as she walked in. 'Thank goodness you're here.'

'What's happened, Mum?' Millie asked, sitting on the chair beside her mother.

Her mother looked pointedly at her sister. 'Nothing that Ruby needed to call you away from work about.'

Ruby stubbed out her half-smoked cigarette. 'Tell her, Doris. Tell your daughter what you've done or, should I say, what you haven't done.'

Doris glared at her sister. 'I don't know why you're making such a fuss, Ruby,' Doris said coolly. 'It's only a couple of bills.'

Ruby snatched up a pile of papers from the table in front of her. 'I'd call this more than a couple, wouldn't you? If I hadn't come by and found the coalman hammering on the door for his money, goodness knows how long it would have been before bailiffs were on the doorstep.'

Millie looked incredulously at her mother. 'I've never known you be even a day late paying anything.'

'I haven't had time, that's all,' her mother replied, looking at a point just above Millie's head.

'That's because you're spending all day running around after the whole street and joining every blooming club and society going,' Ruby cut in. 'What have you signed up for this week?'

'Only the church's New Mothers' Club,' Doris replied. 'And why shouldn't I help out a neighbour, Ruby? When Arthur was alive I had a routine, you know. Getting him off to work, doing the housework and then getting his dinner for when he came home. Now I wake up alone with nothing to look forward to except climbing into an empty bed at the end of it. I'm just trying to keep myself busy.'

Ruby gave her sister a dubious look. 'Luckily I had the money to pay Maguire's, but of course now all the neighbours know our business.'

'For goodness sake!' Millie rolled her eyes.

'Our family have always paid their way,' Ruby said, taking out another cigarette and lighting it. 'Our mother would have gone hungry before having a tradesman knock twice for their money.'

'Except when the rent man or tally came by, and you, Bill, Martha, Edie and Mum had to huddle silently under the table.'

Two splashes of red showed under Aunt Ruby's powdered cheeks. 'Yes, well, Amelia, that was in the old days and times were hard then.'

Millie took the bills from her Aunt's hand. 'I'll

123

pop round and pay these first thing tomorrow and that will solve the problem.'

Ruby picked up a headed letter. 'It won't solve this.'

Millie took the letter. It was from Glasson and Sons, the landlord who owned all the houses in her mother's street and a number of other streets in Bow.

A cold hand of dread clutched around her heart as Millie scanned down the badly typed letter.

Millie snatched up her mac. 'Get your hat and coat on, Mum, we're going to sort this out right now.'

Huddled under an umbrella and dodging between the puddles, Millie and her mother took just over twenty minutes to walk from Harley Grove to the estate office for Glasson and Sons, which was situated at the back of a hardware shop at the Old Ford end of Roman Road.

The yard had once been a coal merchant's, as evidenced by the black stains on the back wall. The old house in the corner had been converted into an office. Now it stood alone in the street, as a bombing raid had obliterated the row of Edwardian terraces and now stout beams embedded in the debris next door propped up a side wall.

Without pausing, Millie shoved open the door and marched up the steep stairs to the office. A young woman sitting in front of a typewriter at the top of the stairs looked up as Millie came in.

'Can I help you?' she asked in a clipped tone.

'I'm Miss Sullivan, and this is my mother who lives at number twenty-four Harley Grove. We've come to see Mr Wright,' Millie said, walking towards a half-glazed door through which she could see a figure moving about in the room beyond. 'Is he in?'

The girl jumped up and barred her way. 'Mr Wright is in the office but I'm not sure if he is able to see you.'

Her mother tugged gently at Millie's arm. 'Perhaps we should have made an appointment.'

Millie smiled at the receptionist. 'Make an appointment to see one of Dad's oldest friends, Lenny?' she said at the top of her voice. 'I'm sure if the man who stood in your front parlour after Dad's funeral not two months ago, and told us if there was anything he could do to help–'

The office door flew open and Lenny Wright stood large in the frame. He was some ten years younger than Millie's father and he wore a chalk-striped suit which, had the lapels been an inch wider and the turn-ups a fraction deeper, would have been considered flash. The two-tone shoes and extravagant Windsor knot of his tie added to the spivvishness of his appearance. When he saw Millie and her mother a flush of embarrassment spread up from his tight collar.

'I'm sorry, Mr Wright,' the secretary said nervously.

'That's all right, Vera.' His eyes flickered briefly over Millie and her mother. 'You'd better come in.'

Millie stood aside to let her mother go into the office and then followed behind, giving Lenny a chilly look as she passed.

He shut the door. 'I suppose you've come about

the letter.'

'Of course we have,' Millie replied, struggling to hold on to her temper.

Lenny pulled out a chair for Doris. 'Perhaps you'd like to sit, Mrs Sullivan.'

Millie's mother sat down. Lenny pulled out the second one, but Millie glared at him. He beat a hasty retreat back behind his desk.

'Now, what is it you want me to explain?' he asked in an even tone.

'You can explain why you've put my mother's rent up to five shillings a week! That's almost double.' She dragged the letter from her pocket and flourished it at him.

'There's no point getting angry with me, Millie Sullivan,' he said, the flush spreading up to his cheeks. 'Mr Glasson's put everyone's rents up, not just yours, Doris,' he said, looking sympathetically at her.

'But I thought you was my Arthur's friend,' Millie's mother replied softly.

'I am, I am,' he replied. 'But this is not about friendship. It's about business. Look, Mrs Sullivan, it's simple a case of supply and demand. Viz, everyone wants a roof over their heads; but as half of London is rubble, the rents have gone up.'

'What happened to "all pulling together"?' Millie asked tartly.

Lenny looked at her steadily. 'The war's over now, Millie, and Mr Glasson has a perfect right to get the maximum from his investments.'

Millie looked coolly at the rent collector. 'How do you think my mum will be able to pay five shillings a week on Dad's pension?'

126

Lenny shrugged and raised his hands, palm upwards. 'I know. But the truth is, Mrs Sullivan, there are six rooms in your house and only you living in a couple of them.'

'But it's my home,' Doris said, looking as if she were about to cry.

'But we could house three families easily in that house.' He leaned across the table. 'Think of those poor little kiddies, Doris. Hugging their teddies and crying became they ain't got nowhere to live.'

'And no doubt Mr Glasson is going to charge them three shillings apiece for the privilege,' Millie said, not even trying to keep the sarcasm from her tone.

Lenny shifted in his chair. 'Five, actually, as naturally the boss has to allow for the kiddies' breakages.'

'But couldn't you speak to Mr Glasson, Lenny?' Doris said, clutching her handbag tighter. 'If you explained that I've never been in arrears and that I'm finding it a bit of a struggle at the moment, perhaps he'll understand. After all, you and my Arthur have known each other since you were in short trousers.'

Lenny shrugged. 'I know, and there ain't a day that passes without me wishing I could slip down the Ship and have a swift half with my mate Arthur. But I'm sorry, Doris, business is business.'

Millie hooked her arm through her mother's and helped her to her feet. 'We're wasting our time here, Mum. Let's go.'

Her mother looked up at Millie. 'But what am I to do?'

127

'Don't worry, Mum. We'll think of something,' Millie said.

Lenny smiled benevolently. 'I tell you what, Doris, I've got a room for the same money going in a house in Canning Town. It backs on to the Cut so there can be a bit of a whiff at low tide, but the family downstairs are clean.'

Millie froze for an instant as she fought with the urge to slap the duplicitous expression off Lenny Wright's heavy face.

'Come on, Mum,' she said gently, guiding her mother across the room.

Millie paused at the door and looked back at Lenny sitting behind the desk. 'You might pretend that hiking up rents so high it forces people on to the street is business, but to my mind,' she jabbed her finger at him, 'you and that crook Glasson are nothing more than profiteers.'

Chapter Six

Millie adjusted the hem of her uniform for the fifth time in as many minutes and then stared back at the heavy oak door at the far end of the corridor behind which the interviews for Munroe House's superintendent were taking place.

Her stomach fluttered and her pulse raced again. Millie took a long slow breath and tried to run through the St George's and St Dunstan's District Nursing Association's statement of intent, but she couldn't remember the first line.

Millie was sitting, or rather was perched, on a long bench on the first-floor landing of St George's Hospital just off the Highway. It was where the Association held their committee meetings. Although St George's had been afforded the title of hospital fifteen years ago, and every nook and cranny had been painted in the regulation green and cream, the old building couldn't quite shake off its workhouse past.

Millie looked down and studied the polished toes of her shoes for a moment, then brushed off a minute speck of dirt from her sleeve.

She'd received a letter a week ago from Mrs Harper telling her that she was one of two candidates for the post and in view of the fact she had her morning work to complete, she was to present herself for interview at three p.m. It was now ten minutes past.

A handle rattled, but instead of the large oak door to the boardroom opening, the one opposite, with 'In-Patients' Department' painted in brown letters on the glass panel, did and a young man with a shaving rash who was dressed in an oversized suit emerged. Clutching a half-dozen files to his chest, he hurried past Millie towards the stairs, his heels echoing on the tiled floor.

She gazed up at the gilt-edged portraits of the past patrons of the hospital, wearing old-fashioned morning suits and grave expressions. She was just about to count the roses on the plaster cornices when the boardroom door swung open and a woman walked out.

She was probably ten or so years older than Millie. Slim, with neatly trimmed ash-blonde hair swept back from her face and curled around her ears. She wore a well-fitted navy suit with a belted jacket, a straight skirt, which sat snugly on her hips, and simple, if somewhat high-heeled, court shoes. A pill-box hat with a veil hovering around it sat at a jaunty angle on her head and even at this distance it was clear she was wearing lipstick, which made Millie feel a whole lot better. After all, surely the committee wasn't going to look favourably on someone who attended an interview for a superintendent's post dressed as if they were going out for the evening.

The woman caught sight of Millie and her pale blue eyes scrutinised her for a moment, then she hooked her handbag in the crook of her arm and, without a second glance, strode past Millie to the stairs.

The boardroom door opened again and Mrs

Overton, the Association's secretary, stepped out.

'Miss Sullivan.'

Millie gripped her nurse's bag firmly and rose to her feet.

'If you would follow me, please.'

With her heart beating wildly in her chest, Millie walked into the wood-panelled boardroom.

The secretary motioned for Millie to take a seat and resumed hers behind the polished committee table. Millie sat in the lone chair and put her bag on the floor. She pressed her knees and ankles together, rested her hands on her lap and looked at the five people facing her.

Mrs Harper, flanked by Mrs Fletcher, sat on the left, while Mrs Archer sat on the right next to Mrs Overton. Sprawled in the middle, like a pin-striped rooster in a hen house, sat the Association's president, Mr Algernon Shottington, the surgical consultant from the London Hospital.

He was dressed, as one would expect the number-one abdominal and chest surgeon to be, in an impeccable tailored suit, with a floral waistcoat beneath, a bow tie at the front of his starched wing-collared shirt, and at his wrists cufflinks with his initials engraved.

Millie was surprised to see Mr Shottington, because he rarely took part in any of the Association's day-to-day business. He shuffled through the papers in front of him, and then looked up at Millie.

'Miss Sullivan,' he said, his full lips lifting into a smile. 'Thank you for coming. I'm sorry if we kept you waiting.'

'Not at all,' replied Millie, hearing a faint tremor

in her voice.

He smiled affably at her. 'I think you know everyone here.'

'Yes, I do.'

'Good.' He gave the four middle-aged women around him a syrupy smile. 'Because, as much as I am pleased to be the thorn amongst such fine-looking roses, I do have a hospital to run, so shall we proceed, ladies?'

'Certainly, Mr Shottington,' Mrs Overton said breathlessly.

Mrs Fletcher batted stubby eyelashes. 'Of course, Mr Shottington.'

Mrs Archer twirled her pencil in her greying hair. 'By all means, Mr Shottington.'

'After you've been so good as to give up your time to help us, Mr Shottington, it's the least we can do,' simpered Mrs Harper, heaving her expansive bosom with a sigh.

Mr Shottington inclined his head graciously. Then he took out his monocle and jammed it under his right brow. He lifted Millie's application letter and scanned it.

'Very impressive,' he said, looking at her over the top.

'Thank you, sir,' Millie replied, relaxing a little.

He glanced at Mrs Harper. 'I see you've given Miss Sullivan a glowing reference, as has my colleague Dr Gingold, and also a certain Father Gilbert?' He looked questioningly at Mrs Harper.

'He's the rector of St Edmund's in Sutton Street,' she explained. 'Munroe House is in his parish.'

'Excellent,' Mr Shottington replied, scanning

132

Millie's letter again.

'We are most fortunate to have a nurse of your calibre working for the Association,' Mrs Harper continued, and her colleagues murmured agreement.

'I'm sure we are, my dear lady,' Mr Shottington replied. 'But we will have to ask some questions.'

'Yes, of course,' Mrs Harper agreed, nodding so rapidly the feathers in her hat couldn't keep up.

Mr Shottington put Millie's application letter down and looked at her closely.

He quizzed her about the proper storage of cresol, acetic acid and potassium bromide, and the various ointments used for skin complaints. Mrs Harper then asked how Millie would assess a patient's ability to pay the fees before, finally, Mrs Palmer enquired how she thought she might assist the Association in fundraising, all of which Millie answered without hesitation.

'Well, I must say, Mrs Harper, that fulsome as your reference is, it doesn't do this young lady justice,' Mr Shottington said. 'Would that the Sisters on my wards in the London were of her calibre.'

Millie felt herself blush. 'It's good of you to say so.'

'She has been an absolute brick since the unfortunate incident concerning the ration books,' Mrs Harper said, smiling encouragingly at her.

'So I've heard.' Mr Shottington wove one set of chubby fingers through the other and rested them on his silk waistcoat. 'Just a couple more questions, if I may?'

Millie nodded and ran through the correct proportions of chlorinated lime to boric acid for cleaning wounds, and then the regulations for the administration of morphine under the 1920 Dangerous Drugs Act.

'I believe that your father has recently died,' said Mr Shottington.

'Yes, yes, he did. Nearly four months ago,' Millie replied, feeling the familiar lump form in her throat.

'I'm very sorry to hear that,' Mr Shottington said, his expression the epitome of compassion. 'Have you brothers and sisters?'

'No. I'm an only child.'

'An only child, eh?' Mr Shottington shook his head dolefully. 'Then perhaps you should reconsider your application.'

Millie heart thumped uncomfortably in her chest. 'I don't see what my recent bereavement has to do with my application.'

Mr Shottington looked aghast. 'Do you not?'

'No, I–'

'Well then, let me tell you, Miss Sullivan,' Mr Shottington boomed, his thick eyebrows pulling together tightly. 'Being the superintendent is a great responsibility and very demanding, and even more so if this new socialist government tries to force this hare-brained scheme of a free service on us all. I'd have to be absolutely sure you had your priorities in the correct order, and that your duty to the many patients served by the Association would always come uppermost, before we could consider you for the post, wouldn't we, ladies? And would this really be possible for you now?'

The women on either side of him looked uneasy, but they nodded nonetheless.

Millie looked Mr Shottington squarely in the eye. 'I can assure you, Mr Shottington, I would never shirk my responsibility to my patients.'

Mr Shottington looked as if he was about to add something else but Mrs Harper spoke first.

'Thank you for your reassurance, Miss Sullivan,' she said firmly. 'And, based on your past record, I am certain you would not.'

Mr Shottington's eyes narrowed and he gave the women beside him a firm look, although soon his affable expression returned.

'I would be less than a gentleman to argue with you, dear ladies,' he said, giving the chairwoman a beguiling smile.

The committee members breathed a communal sigh of relief.

'There is one other question.' Mr Shottington leaned forward and his piggy eyes studied Millie boldly. 'You're a pretty little thing, Miss Sullivan, and what's to say that some lucky lad just returning home from giving the Germans a damn good thrashing won't whisk you down the aisle and have you in the family way before Christmas?'

Millie's mouth dropped open. 'But I don't even have a young man.'

A crafty smile crept across Mr Shottington's face. 'Come on, Miss Sullivan. Don't try to tell me you're not looking out for the chance to get a ring on your finger. And when you do, then where will we be? Looking for another superintendent, that's where.'

Millie pulled her shoulders back. 'I cannot say that if I met the right man I wouldn't like to get married one day. But I can assure you at this present time and for the foreseeable future I have no plans to do so,' she said in a clear voice that rang around the cavernous room.

There was a long silence. Millie stared unwaveringly at Mr Shottington, and finally a congenial smile spread across his fleshy face.

'I'm obliged to you for clarifying the point, Miss Sullivan.' He spread his hands out in front of him on the table. 'And now, if there are no other questions,' he said, continuing before anyone could respond, 'I'll thank you for your time. You'll get a letter in a few days telling you of our decision. Thank you.'

He gave her a smile that didn't reach his eyes.

Millie picked up her nurse's bag and stood up. 'Thank you for your time, Mr Shottington, and you, too, Mrs Harper.'

The chairwoman of the Association gave her an apologetic smile. Millie turned and walked out. As she closed the door a sense of despondency settled on her shoulders and she heartily wished she'd not already eaten this week's tiny ration of chocolate.

The clock in the hall struck nine-thirty in the evening as Millie spooned in a heaped tablespoon of cocoa into her favourite mug and then whipped the saucepan off the heat before the boiling milk bubbled over. She poured it into the cup and then added a spoonful of sugar from her rations. She folded the top of the bag and put it back in the cupboard alongside the other nurses' rations, and then shut the door.

Thankfully, since new cook Mrs Pierce had put on her apron, lumpy potatoes and tasteless stew were a thing of the past. Now, each night two pots of soaking oats were always set ready on the back gas rings ready for the porridge for the next morning's breakfast, while the cups, saucers and plates were neatly stacked along the sideboard ready for use.

Millie lifted the ridged net cover from a plate of scones and took one and then, cradling her mug of cocoa, she made her way past the two gleaming enamel ovens to the kitchen door.

In the nurses' lounge someone, probably Eva, was tinkling 'When the Red, Red Robin' on the old upright piano while a couple of voices sung along. With a headache threatening to take hold any second, Millie decided to head for the office to drink her cocoa.

As the last few rays of daylight were still streaking into the room, Millie left the curtains open and sat at the desk. Her eyes rested on the account books that she'd have to start tomorrow if she was to have any hope of getting them to Mrs Harper by the end of the month.

Millie rested her head on the buttoned leather back of the chair and stared up. After studying the curls of foliage around the plaster ceiling rose for a moment or two she sat up and took a sip of her drink. There was a knock at the door.

'Come in,' Millie called wearily, praying it wasn't yet another nurse tendering her notice to get married.

The door opened and Connie's head appeared around the edge. 'There you are, Millie. You missed supper.'

'I had it with my Mum and only got back half

137

an hour ago.'

'Well, never mind.' Connie bounced across to the desk. 'You'll never guess what.'

Millie smiled. 'Charlie's coming home?'

'Yes.' Connie hugged herself and pirouetted. 'And at last we'll be wed.'

'I didn't see a letter for you this morning,' Millie said.

She'd gone through the post twice looking for a letter from the Association. Mrs Harper had said two weeks and it had been that yesterday.

'No, there wasn't, but I bumped into my old school friend Fran, and her chap's in the same regiment as Charlie and so she told me they're arriving home at London Bridge on the three-thirty train from Hastings on the twenty-ninth of September.'

'That's only two weeks away,' Millie said.

'I know.'

Millie gave her friend a puzzled look. 'I'm surprised he didn't let you know.'

'So am I, and I'll have a sharp word or two to say about that when I see him, I can tell you.' Connie frowned. 'I thought his Ma looked a bit shifty when I saw her in the market last week. Knowing him, I bet he told her to keep it under her hat so he could give me a shock by pitching up on the doorstep. But he'll be the one shocked when that train pulls in, 'cause I'm going to meet it.' Connie dragged up a chair alongside Millie and plonked herself down. 'Thank goodness I got the fabric for the dress last week. We'll have to get it cut out this week to get it ready in time: And then there's the church to arrange. It will have to

138

be by special licence, of course, but they are easy enough to arrange, as nearly everyone's in a hurry to get hitched these days.' She clutched Millie's arm. 'And you will come with me to meet Charlie, won't you?'

'I don't know,' Millie replied. 'I'd've thought that after all this time you'd want him all to yourself.'

Connie shook her head and set her soft waves bouncing. 'I'm too nervous. It's been almost four years since I've seen him and it's going to be a bit strange, and so I'd feel better if you were with me. Say you'll come. Please.' Her eyes twinkled. 'You are my chief bridesmaid, after all.'

Millie laughed. 'All right. Even though I'll be the biggest gooseberry that ever lived, I'll come.'

Connie jumped up and hugged her. 'Thank you.' She sat down again, rested an elbow on the desk, cupped her chin and peered at Millie. 'You look a bit peaky. Are you all right?'

'I'm fine,' Millie said, mustering a smile from somewhere. 'I've just got these to do, that's all.' She swept her hand across the mounting pile of account books and nurses' receipts. But after a small pause, Millie told Connie about the visit to Glasson's rent office and how it had been preying on her mind since.

'Bloody crooks,' Connie said after Millie had finished. 'It's happening all over. It seems if the Luftwaffe hasn't managed to put you on the streets, some thieving landlord will finish the job. Is there no way your ma can afford the increase?'

Millie shook her head. 'After we got home and I'd calmed down, I spent an hour going back and forth over her budget. No matter how I added it

139

up, she'll never be able to afford the rent from what she gets on Dad's pension. She's talked about finding a job, but she gave up work when she and Dad married, and with demobbed men taking all the jobs at the moment there isn't much chance of her getting something that will pay more than five shillings a week anyhow. I am going to make up the difference in the rent for a couple of weeks until she finds somewhere, but that can't go on for ever.'

'How is she in herself?' Connie said.

'Surprisingly perky about the whole thing,' Millie replied. 'She's talking about the "Dunkirk spirit" and keeping her chin up.'

'That's good,' said Connie.

'I'm not sure to be honest, as she just doesn't seem quite right. And although she says she is, I still don't think she's sleeping properly. I know grief can work its way through each person in different ways, but I am concerned.' Millie sighed.

Connie put her hand over her friend's, and squeezed. 'I think you're worrying over nothing. Have you thought of trying to find her a place around here? Then you'll only be around the corner. My dad's done a bit of decorating on the Chapman Estate recently and said there's been a lot of people there upping sticks and moving out east to Plaistow and Forest Gate. Dad had a word with Mr Ansell, the governor, a couple of weeks ago, and got him to let me and Charlie put our names down for one of those old cottages in Anthony Street, or at least we will be once Charlie is home. Why don't you pop around to the estate office in the morning and see if there's another one coming up for rent?'

'I could.' Millie's face lit up. 'And in fact I know Mr Ansell as I delivered his third baby just after Christmas.'

'Well, there you go,' Connie said, patting her hand.

'I don't expect he'll be able to offer me anything like the house in Harley Grove though,' Millie said, thinking of the well-proportioned rooms and long garden of the old Regency terrace.

'Not on the Chapman, I grant. But it is close by to here, and there is a rumour that the estate is one of the first marked out for being knocked down by the council, and then your mum would be top of the list for a brand new council house. I hope this rumour is true, because I'd like to move away from the docks before we start a family.'

'Perhaps you're right, Connie,' Millie replied. 'Leaving Harley Grove is going to be a wrench for Mum, but it might turn out to be a good thing in the long run. And at least if she were only around the corner I could keep a closer eye on her.'

Connie laughed. 'And so can I, when me and her are neighbours.'

Nevertheless Millie found the worries to do with her mother hard to shake off, and feeling as if the weight of the world were sitting heavily on her shoulders, the next afternoon she pedalled to Greenbank for a quick visit to remove some stitches from a child's forehead before returning to Munroe House. Millie stowed her bike in a rack and then, taking her bag from the basket, made her way through the back door and into the

141

hall. The smell of a tasty lamb stew seeped under the kitchen door and started Millie's stomach rumbling.

The morning post was on the hall table. She checked it and, finding no letter for her, she continued towards the office. She opened the door and saw Mrs Harper sitting in the chair by the window. She rose as Millie walked in.

'Good morning, Nurse Sullivan,' Mrs Harper said, giving Millie a fragile smile.

'Good morning, Mrs Harper,' Millie replied, trying to hide her surprise. 'I hope you haven't been waiting long.'

'Only half an hour, but Mrs Pierce kindly made me a cup of tea.' Her eyes flickered briefly on to the empty cup on the small occasional table beside the chair.

'I'm sorry to keep you waiting,' Millie said.

'Not at all, but I'm glad you're back a little early from your morning round, as I was hoping to have a word with you before lunch.' Mrs Harper forced another tight smile. 'Please sit down.' She indicated the chair opposite the one she'd just vacated.

Millie sat down and put her bag under the chair. The chairwoman resumed her seat by perching awkwardly on the front.

'I must apologise for not sending you a letter with the outcome of the interview before now, but there was a great deal of discussion between the members of the panel.' Mrs Harper's mouth pulled into a tight line. 'That is, Mrs Fletcher, Mrs Overton and myself agreed that it would be unfair for you to be told of the decision in an impersonal letter. Therefore, as chairwoman of the

142

St George's and St Dunstan's District Nursing Association, it falls on me to inform you that, after much deliberation and with great regret, we are unable to offer you the post of superintendent of Munroe House.'

The blood pounded in Millie's ears.

'I'm very sorry,' Mrs Harper hastily continued. 'And I know that on paper you have all the attributes and experience that we could possibly ask for, but we had to be advised by the professional member of the panel.'

Millie gasped. 'Mr Shottington objected to my appointment?'

'I'm afraid so. I know it's not–'

'But why?' Millie interrupted.

Above the frothy lace of Mrs Harper's blouse a flush spread up her neck. She cleared her throat. 'Firstly, he was concerned that you would put your mother's care before your duty to patients.'

Millie looked dismayed. 'But I thought I assured you otherwise.'

'Mr Shottington was still concerned, it would seem,' Mrs Harper replied sharply. 'And...'

'And? Mrs Harper?' Millie asked, staring forthrightly at the woman opposite.

The chairwoman held her gaze for a moment, then lowered her eyes. 'Then there is the matter of your age and the likelihood of you getting married.'

'But I'm not even courting.'

Mrs Harper forced herself to look at Millie's upset face. 'We understand that. But Mr Shottington is certain that a young woman like yourself would soon be thinking of settling down, especially now the war's over.'

There was an uncomfortable silence.

'So who has got the job?' Millie asked after a few moments.

'A Miss Dutton.'

'And where does she come from?'

'Well, she worked for the Epping and Harlow Nursing Association a few years back but she moved to London in 1936 to take up the post of surgical sister on the Chalfont Ward at Barts.'

'So she's had little experience of nursing out in the city, has not managed a district nursing team and has spent the last nine years as a hospital nurse,' Millie said tersely.

Mrs Harper frowned. 'I must confess, Mrs Overton and I were a little concerned on that point, but Mr Shottington assured us that what Miss Dutton appears to lack in experience, she makes up for in capability and dedication.'

'He knows her?'

'Only in passing. She was a ward sister in the Brompton when he was there a couple of years ago, but he had no idea she was applying for the post.' Mrs Harper looked ill at ease again. 'I'm sorry, Miss Sullivan. I know you must be disappointed. But Mr Shottington is the Association's president, and it's because of his links with the medical committee, maternity advisory body and the welfare board at the council that we have been able to secure sufficient funding these past few years. Added to which he is a highly esteemed consultant, and so we have to bow to his superior knowledge in such matters.'

There was another embarrassing silence and

then Millie stood up.

'It was very kind of you to come in person to tell me the panel's decision,' she said, politely.

Mrs Harper rose to her feet. 'Well, it was the least I could do under the circumstances,' she said, pulling on her gloves and hooking her handbag over her arm. 'I know it's a disappointment but I'm sure you and Miss Dutton will get on famously once you get to know each other. You may have seen her. She was the young lady interviewed immediately before you.'

'So, if you could take a fresh mackintosh around to Mrs Simpson in Redman's Road, Sally, I'd be grateful,' Millie said, crossing through the last item on the list. 'But remind her to place a couple of layers of newspaper on it before she covers it with the sheet or else the urine will soak through in no time and crack the rubber. I've noted it in the loan book already.'

'I will,' Sally replied.

Millie shut the book and placed her hands on the top. She cast her eyes around at the dozen nurses squashed around the table.

'There is one other matter I would like to mention before you go off on your rounds.' Millie took a deep breath. 'Mrs Harper, the chairwoman of the Association, came here yesterday to inform me that the board has appointed a new superintendent. A Miss Dutton.'

She'd told Connie and Beattie the news last night over cocoa and they gave her a supportive look as a ripple of surprise travelled around the table.

145

'So you didn't get the job, then,' sneered Gladys.

Millie gave her a chilly glance. 'No, I didn't.'

'And it's a bloody disgrace, too,' snapped Connie.

'So it is,' agreed Beattie.

Marge, sitting next to Gladys, gave Millie's friends a scornful look. 'You two would say that, wouldn't you?'

'Well, it is,' cut in Eva. 'Even you have to admit, Gladys, that Millie has all the experience necessary to run Munroe House.'

Gladys shifted in her chair. 'Well, obviously the board didn't think so, did they? Or they wouldn't have given this Dutton woman the job.'

'Miss Dutton is a very experienced nurse,' Millie interjected, 'and comes highly recommended.'

'You must be disappointed, though,' said Gladys.

'Well, naturally,' Millie replied. 'If I hadn't wanted the job, I wouldn't have applied for it. But I didn't get it and that's an end to the matter.' She forced a professional smile. 'And I'm sure that when Miss Dutton arrives in a month's time we will all do our utmost to make her welcome. Now, if there's nothing more?' She looked around the table. 'We'll do morning prayers and then you can get on your way.'

The nurses around the table clasped their hands together and lowered their heads. Millie prayed for all the Association's patients and for the nurses caring for them, and then they all joined in the Lord's Prayer.

There was a scrape of chairs as the nurses rose and left the treatment room. Millie watched

146

them file through the door for a moment, and then closed the book.

Connie pulled up the seat beside her and put her hand over Millie's. 'Are you still upset?'

'No, I'm not upset any more, Connie, I'm blooming-well fuming,' Millie said, as her anger bubbled over again. 'Not only is it so ruddy unfair, I could have really done with the extra five shillings a week as I haven't found Mum anywhere else to live yet.'

'Nothing going on the Chapman's yet?' asked Connie.

Millie shook her head. 'I've popped in to see Mr Ansell twice in the last week but there was still nothing. I even applied at the Greenbody Trust, but the only thing they could offer me was a third-floor flat in Stebbins House and I couldn't let her live in there.'

Connie looked horrified. 'I should say not. The police only patrol that end of Cable Street in daylight and even then in threes or fours.' She gently touched Millie's shoulder. 'Come on, chin up, Millie.'

Grasping her bag from under the chair, Millie stood up and walked to the white enamel dresser. She plonked her case on the surface. Connie followed her over.

'Still, there's no point crying over spilt milk,' Millie said, opening the glass-fronted cupboard and retrieving a tin of baked gauze from the top shelf. 'Mr Shottington decided himself that Miss Dutton was the better candidate. And that's an end to it.'

Chapter Seven

Beattie's eyes glowed as she watched the dancers bob around to a jive. 'I've never seen the Regency so packed on a Tuesday night.'

Connie nodded. 'I know. I had my toe crushed twice during the last dance. You can hardly move on the floor.'

'And so many men,' added Sally, smiling at a good-looking young chap sauntering by.

'And all of them dressed by the same tailor,' Millie added, nodding at a group of the men in demob suits standing around the bar.

Eva wove her way through the crowded dancefloor carrying a tray of drinks.

'There you go, girls,' she said, putting it on the small table they had claimed as their own.

Beattie and Sally reached for their drinks, but before they could take a sip both of them and Eva were whisked away and on to the dancefloor.

Millie looked at Connie, who was mouthing the words to the perennial favourite, 'Little Brown Jug', while tapping her toes to the beat.

'Are you nervous?'

Connie stopped singing. 'About tomorrow? A bit, but I'm sure Charlie will be happy with the arrangements for the wedding. Of course, I need to organise the flowers and cake and make sure he has a decent suit to wear.'

Millie's eyebrows rose. 'Cake?'

'Bread pudding with a cardboard replica over it, but it'll look just like the real thing in the photographs,' Connie said.

'What time's the train again?' asked Millie, stepping aside to let a couple through to the dancefloor.

'Three-thirty, but I want to be there early,' Connie replied. 'Oh, Millie, I'm so excited. Thanks for coming with me.'

'Don't be silly,' Millie replied with a smile. 'That's what chief bridesmaids are for, aren't they?'

She took a sip of her gin and tonic and cast her gaze slowly over the dancers.

'He's not here yet,' said Connie.

'Who?'

Connie grinned. 'You know who.'

Millie tried to maintain her innocent expression but couldn't quite manage it. 'Well, I suppose I was just wondering if I might see Alex Nolan tonight.'

Connie was just about to answer when the band stopped. Most of the couples stayed on the floor. The band struck up the opening bars of 'In the Mood' and a young man with a short back and sides and an ill-fitting jacket stepped in front of Millie.

'Would you like to dance with a man who helped defeat Hitler, Miss?' he asked, giving her a cheeky grin.

'Well, that's very kind but–'

'She's already spoken for,' cut in Connie. 'But I will.'

Before Millie could protest, Connie stepped

149

forward and soon she and her new dance partner were pirouetting around the hall.

Millie took another sip of her drink and swayed to the rhythm.

'Hello there, Millie Sullivan,' a deep voice said. 'Are you waiting for me?'

Millie turned and found herself looking up into the expressive face of Alex Nolan.

He was dressed in the same understated but elegant manner as the first time she met him, in a navy single-breasted suit, fresh white shirt and a diagonally striped tie looped into a Windsor knot at his throat. Before she could tell it not to, her heart did a little double beat.

'Oh, hello,' replied Millie, smiling politely. 'It's Alan, isn't it?'

'Archibald. Archibald Peaseswiftly.' He chuckled. 'Surely you remember?'

Millie laughed. He took her drink and put it on the table. 'Come on, they're playing our tune.'

He grabbed her hand, guided her on to the dancefloor and then, holding her firmly in his arms, twirled her into a foxtrot. This time he added in popular sidesteps and variations, guiding Millie, as before, with a gentle pressure of his hand to send her whatever way he wanted, or tightening around her waist to draw her close. With her hand on his shoulder and feeling his legs brush against hers as they danced, Millie gave herself over to the pleasure of rhythm and the presence of a strong man.

With a final strain from the orchestra and a final elegant whirl from Alex, Millie came to a halt. She clapped, but instead of walking her back to the table, Alex took her hand and pulled her gently towards him, slipping his arm around her waist again and stepping her off on the first beat of the next dance.

'I might have promised the next waltz to someone else,' she said, as they settled into a steady one-two-three tempo.

His eyes twinkled. 'I know, but I'm not ready to let you go just yet,' he said, holding her against him for half a beat and then stepping backwards.

They glided around for another few minutes before the music stopped. The musicians put aside their instruments as someone brought them a tray loaded with beer for their refreshment break.

Alex flicked a stray lock of black hair off his forehead. 'Let me buy you a drink.'

He led her from the dancefloor and towards the crowded bar.

'What would you like?' he asked as they were enveloped in the crush to get drinks before the second half of the programme started.

'A shandy, please,' Millie replied, finding herself very close to him.

She expected him to urge her to have something stronger, as most men did, but instead he gave her a boyish smile. 'One shandy coming up.'

He turned and as he tried to catch the barmaid's eye, Millie studied his profile, unable to stop herself noting the firm shape of his mouth and how his sideburn bristles stopped in an orderly line below his cheekbones. Their drinks arrived and Alex handed over a couple of coins.

'Shall we squeeze ourselves into the corner over

there?' he asked, lifting their drinks above his head to avoid them being knocked.

Millie nodded and headed for the booth on the far side of the bar. There was a couple tucked at one end so she slipped into the seat on the other end. Alex pulled up a stool and sat alongside, his knees grazing against hers.

'I see you've come with the same group of friends,' he said, sipping the head off his pint.

'Yes, we work together,' Millie replied. 'Are you alone?'

He shook his head. 'My chums are over there.'

He indicated a handful of hefty individuals dressed in dark-coloured suits lounging against the corner of the bar. They stood with their hands in their pockets and backs to the wall, studying the crowd. Some of the men waiting to order drinks were giving them a wide berth. When they saw Alex looking their way, they raised their glasses.

The bandleader announced the next dance and the drinkers in the bar started to make their way towards the dancefloor.

'Let's sit this one out,' Alex suggested.

Millie smiled. 'I don't mind, but if they strike up for a rumba ... well!'

Alex laughed and took another mouthful of beer. 'I'm glad I spotted you tonight.'

'Are you?' Millie asked, feeling a little glow of pleasure.

His eyes studied her face. 'I am. In fact, I've looked out for you for the past three weeks. And I was beginning to wonder if I was ever going to see you again.'

'We were planning to come last week, but we've had two girls leave this month and the rest of us have had to do double shifts for a fortnight.' Millie smiled. 'You know, when duty calls.'

Alex gave a faint smile. 'It's the same where I am. Has been for six months.'

'So you haven't just been demobbed?' said Millie with some surprise.

He shook his head. 'Kicked out a year ago,' he said with a grin. 'Just before all the fun at Monte Casino.'

'You were in Italy!'

He nodded. 'Eighth Army.'

'Sorry, Alex,' a man's voice cut in.

Millie looked up to see one of the men from the bar, a squat chap with close-cropped hair and a broken nose, looming over them.

Alex gave him a testy look. 'Miss Sullivan, let me introduce Georgie Tugman.'

'Evening miss,' Georgie said, without looking at Millie. 'Alex, you're needed.'

'Can't it wait?'

Georgie glanced nervously at the door to the lobby. ''Fraid not. There's trouble with the manager. Sorry.'

Alex sent Georgie another hard look, before smiling at Millie. 'I'm sorry, Millie, but I won't be long. Please save me that rumba.'

He threw back his pint and stood up. 'This had better be important,' he said to Georgie as he strode away.

Millie finished off her drink and then she decided to powder her nose before rejoining her friends. Although the thought of swaying to a

Latin beat in Alex's arms sent tingles up her spine, she couldn't just sit like a wallflower in the bar waiting for him to come back. If Alex wanted that rumba, he'd have to find her.

The Ladies was brimming over with women re-applying their lipstick and redrawing the smudged line drawn on the back of their legs with an eye-brow pencil. Millie did what she had to, but when she left the Ladies the press of people outside blocked her path back to the hall. Someone had opened the fire door to let some air into the stuffy ballroom. She had her ticket in her pocket so if she nipped out into the side alley she could walk around to the front door to get back in.

As she went outside she saw a group of men and a couple of women at the other end of the alley. The two women wore floral dresses that fluttered around their knees and, judging by the way they were staggering about in their high shoes, they'd been drinking something a lot stronger than shandy. They were flailing their arms around and swearing at the men who were trying to usher them along the alleyway towards the main street. Suddenly one of the women broke free and, after ducking unsteadily to avoid recapture, threw her arms around one of the men. He stepped back into the light and something akin to ice water flooded over Millie. Illuminated in the pool of light from the lamp-post stood Alex with his arm – the arm that had guided Millie so skilfully around the dancefloor – encircling the floozy's waist.

'Hello, sweetheart,' she slurred, draping herself around Alex and smoothing his lapel. 'Fancy

154

seeing you here.'

Alex caught her hand and put her from him. 'I told you what would happen if I caught you hanging around and making trouble, Rose.'

She fell sideways but managed to keep on her feet. 'I didn't know you would be here tonight, boss.' She blew him a kiss. Don't be too hard on your little–' He took hold of her arm. 'Oww!' she squealed.

Alex handed her over to Georgie, who was standing behind him. 'The night boys should be outside by now, so if you lot don't mind making sure these two beauties get a ride back to the shop, I'm on a promise of a rumba.'

Alex and his tough-looking friends escorted the two drunken women along the Regency's side passage towards the main street. The alley felt very silent.

Millie stood motionless as the scene she'd just witnessed replayed over and over in her mind. The heady thrill of Alex Nolan's hand resting lightly on her hip and the smooth coolness of his palm against hers stole over her, but Millie cut it short.

On a promise of a rumba! She should think not. Indeed certainly not, especially now that she had seen how Alex Nolan treated his old girl-friends.

Connie's cup stopped halfway to her mouth and her jaw dropped. 'No!'

'It's true,' replied Millie, ignoring the niggle of disappointment in the pit of her stomach. 'I saw it with my own eyes.'

155

She and Connie were squashed in the window table of the station tea room. The place was packed, as the whole of London seemed to be meeting a loved one from a train that afternoon.

'But he seems so nice. You know, normal. Handsome too,' Connie said. 'Are you sure he's a crook?'

'It's the only explanation. He's surrounded by a bunch of men with broken noses and hands like shovels. Rose, the woman who threw her arms around his neck, called him "boss", and she and her friend wouldn't have looked out of place touting for custom along Cable Street. And he told them, the thugs with him, to tell the "night boys", presumably some other gang members, to take the women back to the "shop".'

'You think he was talking about a brothel?'

A wry smile lifted the corners of Millie's mouth. 'I don't think he meant the greengrocer's. And then he had the cheek to tell his heavies he was on a promise.'

Connie's blue eyes opened wide in shook. 'Oh, Millie, he didn't persuade you to...'

'Promise of a dance, Connie. Of a dance,' Millie said sharply. 'What do you take me for?'

'Well, I've known girls do what they shouldn't, and for uglier men,' Connie replied.

Millie frowned. 'I wish you wouldn't keep going on about how handsome he is. It wouldn't make any difference if Alex Nolan looked like Tyrone Power.'

'Actually, now you mention it, he does have the same dark Irish look about him,' Connie said.

'Has he?' replied Millie. 'I can't say I've noticed

156

his thick black hair or his deep green eyes, but even if I had, now I know what he's really about, I won't be letting him lead me out on to the dancefloor – or anywhere else, for that matter.'

'Well, it's lucky you found out sooner rather than later,' said Connie in her nurse-knows-best voice.

'Yes, isn't it?' replied Millie, flatly.

Connie patted Millie on the shoulder. 'Cheer up. There's plenty more fish in the sea.' She glanced at the wall clock. 'Oh, is that the time? We'd better go.' She snatched up the bill. 'My treat.'

If the teashop was crowded, then the main concourse was positively heaving with people all pushing and shoving to get to the right platform. Although the loudspeakers above their head were blaring out the arrivals, Millie could barely hear what was said above the din.

'What platform does it say?' asked Connie.

'Five.' Millie replied, at last finding the Hastings train listed on the Arrivals board above.

Connie grabbed her arm. 'Oh, quick. I don't want to be late,' she said, hurrying her along to the platform gate.

When they got there Connie opened her handbag and pulled out her compact. She flipped it open and powdered her nose and cheeks, then she reapplied her lipstick, before tucking the compact away again.

Connie straightened her skirt. 'Is this all right? I'm not too sure about the colour. Maybe I should have worn the blue one.'

'It looks just fine,' Millie assured her. 'And I'm

sure that after four years Charlie won't even notice the colour.'

Connie nodded. 'You're right.' Her gaze flickered down the platform. 'It's coming!' she shouted, jumping up and down on the spot. 'Charlie's train's coming.'

Millie pressed against the metal rail and watched the train puff into the station and grind to a halt just before the buffers.

Connie gripped her hand. 'Oh, Millie, I can't believe he's actually here.'

'It might be best if I wait by the newspaper stand,' Millie said, as the carriage doors started banging open.

'No, don't be daft. Charlie won't mind.' Connie laughed. 'And I can't wait to see the look on his face when he sees me.'

Connie stood on tiptoe. 'There he is. Charlie!' she screamed after a while, pushing through the gate and dashing down the platform.

Millie peered through the smoke and steam and spotted Charlie Ross's tall frame emerge from a carriage at the rear of the train.

She set off down the platform at a leisurely pace, not wanting to intrude on the lovers' reunion. But instead of throwing his kit bag over his shoulder and coming towards them, Charlie had turned to help someone.

Connie had seen it too and stopped, allowing Millie to catch her up. For a moment Millie thought the person was a child, but as she stepped down from the train Millie realised that Connie's fiancé was assisting a slender young woman with long, jet-black hair and tanned skin. Well, that was

158

to say, she was slender, except for her middle, which Millie's experienced eye put at six months gone.

Charlie slipped his arm around the woman and kissed her. He threw his kit bag over his shoulder and took the small suitcase from her. She held his arm and they walked towards the platform gate.

The colour drained from Connie's face. 'Charlie!'

He stopped dead. 'Connie! What are you doing here?'

'What the bloody hell do you think I'm doing here, Charlie Ross? And,' Connie looked the woman beside him slowly up and down, 'who the bloody hell is this?'

Charlie took a deep breath. 'Calm down, Connie. This is Maria and–'

'We married,' the young woman cut in, her dark eyes flashing angrily at Connie. She stepped forward and touched her chest. 'At Army base. I Mrs Ross, Carlo's wife.'

'Wife!' screamed Connie.

Maria smoothed her hand over her swollen stomach. 'And I have 'is bambino here,' she said, smiling lovingly up at Charlie.

'Let me handle this, ducks,' replied Charlie, with an adoring glance at his wife.

Millie put her arm around her friend's shoulder. 'Let's go, Connie,' she said, calmly.

Connie shrugged her off excitedly. 'But you wrote and told me, Charlie, that we were to be married as soon as you came back. I've booked the church and everything.'

He looked at her incredulously. 'For goodness

sake, Connie, that was two years ago. And I'm sorry, Connie. I really am, but,' he smiled dotingly at Maria, 'I fell in love. And knowing the way things sometimes 'appen I thought you would have found some other bloke too, as it's been such a long time and I never wrote for ages.'

Millie put her arm around Connie's shoulders again. 'Come away, Connie,' she urged, much more firmly.

This time Connie nodded, and Millie led her back down the platform.

Balancing a tray in one hand, Millie knocked lightly on Connie's door with the other.

'Only me,' she called, opening it slowly.

Connie was exactly where Millie had left her twenty minutes before, sitting red-eyed and crossed-legged in the middle of her bed with her wedding dress across her lap.

'I've made us a nice cup of tea,' Millie said, closing the door quietly.

Connie nodded without any enthusiasm. Millie closed the door with her foot and placed the tray on her dressing table.

Connie ran her hands over the beading around the neckline. 'It's so beautiful.'

'It is,' agreed Millie, handing her friend a mug. 'Let me hang it back in the wardrobe in case it gets tea on it.'

'It doesn't matter,' Connie replied, 'because I'm never going to wear it now.'

'Even so, it would be shame to ruin it,' Millie replied, taking it from her and slipping it on a hanger.

She opened the wardrobe door and hung it alongside Connie's uniforms and her going-away outfit. Millie closed the door and noticed that the picture frame that had stood on Connie's bedside cabinet for the past six years was now empty of Charlie's once beloved photograph. This was now ripped in two, lying in the waste paper bin alongside a bundle of his old letters.

Connie looked bleakly at Millie. 'How could he do it?' she wondered for the tenth time since they left London Bridge station.

'I don't suppose he meant to,' Millie said, sitting on the bed next to her friend.

Connie looked askance. 'You don't get married by accident.'

'No,' replied Millie in a measured tone. 'But these sorts of things happen to men during a war.'

'In films, but not to ordinary blokes like my Charlie.' Connie's face crumpled. 'But he's not my Charlie any more, is he? He's her bloody *Carlo*.'

Connie started crying again quietly. Millie reached across to her dressing table and gave her friend a fresh handkerchief.

Connie blew her nose noisily. 'I'll never forgive him.'

'Of course you won't.'

'Even if he were to crawl here on his bended knees and begged me to marry him, I wouldn't. And when I think of all the men I've turned down,' Connie went on, wiping her nose again. 'Do you remember that big American who came from Indiana, or was it Idaho?'

'Illinois.'

Connie snapped her fingers. 'That's him. Pleaded with me, he did, to "be his gal", but I said no.' Her brows pulled together tightly. 'I bloody wouldn't have if I'd known my sodding fiancé was making *bambinos* with that skinny Eyetie.' Connie took a handkerchief from her sleeve and blew her nose. 'I tell you, Millie, I've been a right bloody fool.'

'No you haven't,' Millie replied, squeezing her again.

'It will be the talk of every street corner tomorrow.'

'And forgotten by Saturday.' Millie smiled fondly at her friend.

'And what about my family?'

'They'll rally around you, tell you that they always knew he was a rotter, and then they'll hate Charlie Ross to a man.'

Connie gave a pained laugh. 'They will, won't they?' she said, rubbing her cheeks with her hands.

'To a man.'

'I'll have to let the vicar know, too.' Connie's shoulders sagged. 'And I'd better drop in at the Chapman's estate office so they can,' her lower lip started to wobble once more 'let the house go,' she wailed, covering her face with her hands.

Millie shuffled up and put her arm around Connie as she sobbed.

After a couple of minutes Connie lifted her head. 'I was going to make it a snug little home. With lace curtains and all,' she said, wiping her eyes.

Millie's heart thumped in her chest. 'Connie.'

Connie looked up. 'Yes.'

162

Millie smiled. 'I understand how very upset you are and I hope you don't think I'm being selfish in asking but...'

'But what?'

Millie took a deep breath. 'Could I come to Chapman's yard with you tomorrow?'

Millie pulled the key with a buff luggage label tied to it out of her pocket and jiggled it in the lock. She opened the door to number seventy-one Anthony Street and stood back. 'In you go, Mum, and see what you think.'

The one-up one-down house they stood in front of was probably over two hundred years old. It had a dull brown front door with a half-circle of glass at the top and vertical letter box and knocker, both of which showed signs of rust. There was one casement window facing on to the street, and where the pavement stones had been laid over the original earth walkway, the holes of the foundation's air brick were only just at street level.

Her mother stepped into the twelve-by-twelve-foot room that was the cottage's main living area and looked around. 'It's a little smaller than I imagined.'

'It's almost the same size as the front room at home,' Millie replied, forcing a bright expression on to her face. 'All the window panes are in one piece and the fire surround can't be more than ten years old.'

Her mother glanced around at the faded, old-fashioned wallpaper peeling off the walls, cracked paintwork and bare floorboards, and didn't deign

163

to answer.

Millie went to the windows. 'And the curtains in the front room would fit, so that's something you haven't got to worry about, Mum.'

'That's true,' her mother agreed.

'And we could hang a few pictures up along here,' Millie said, tapping the wood panelling that encased the stairs.

Her mother rattled the door at the end. 'And is the back room through here?'

'That's the door to the stairs, Mum. I did tell you there was only one downstairs room.' Millie forced the old door open. 'It will keep the warmth in during the winter. Save on coal.'

Her mother peered up the narrow set of stairs that lead to the upper floor and gave Millie a wan smile.

'Shall we go and look at the upstairs?' Millie asked, standing back so her mother could climb the stairs.

It didn't take long, as the room above was a replica in size and condition of the one below. She and her mother studied the four walls and one window in silence for a moment before returning to the parlour.

'And this is the kitchen.' Millie guided her mother through into the minute scullery at the back.

She squeezed in behind her. 'Mr Ansell has promised to replace the cooker if you take the place,' she said, as her mother looked in horror at the antique gas appliance in the corner coated with a thick layer of dirt. 'And your new kitchen cabinet would easily fit in the corner.' She rested her hand on the deep butler sink under the window. 'And a bit of bleach and elbow grease will soon bring the sparkle back to this.'

Doris looked in. 'I'm sure you're right.'

Millie kicked some mouse droppings under the sink. 'Do you want to look outside?'

She threw back the top and bottom bolts and they stepped out into the tiny triangular back-yard with a toilet and coalhole along one side.

Doris stared blankly ahead at the moss-covered rear wall as Millie's heart sank.

'I know it might not be what you had in mind, Mum, but what with the bombing and the troops arriving back on every train, it's the only place going for love or money nearby that you won't have to share. But the main reason I want you to take the place is because Munroe House is only a stone's throw away and so I can pop in every day to make sure you're all right.'

Her mother looked concerned. 'I wouldn't want you to get into trouble.'

'No, I mean when I'm not on duty,' Millie replied. She put her hand on her mother's arm. 'I know it's a bit musty at the moment, but it just needs a good airing. After all, no one's lived in it for two months. I've already spoken to Aunt Ruby and she says that Tony will come and do any little repairs needed; and Beattie, Sally and Eva have volunteered to give me a hand with the decor-ating.'

'I thought your friend Eva lived here,' her mother said, looking puzzled.

'No, Mum, that was Connie,' Millie replied, patiently, 'and she didn't live here, she was

165

moving in when she got married. Don't you remember she had to call off the wedding? And that I went to the estate office with her a week ago when she had to let the house go, so I could put your name down for the place before anyone else did?'

In fact, contrary to Millie thinking she might be annoyed, Connie was keen to help Millie secure the house for her mother. Connie had put Charlie on the rent book and wanted to cancel it before he got wind of it and decided to move his new wife there instead.

'Oh, yes, I remember now.' Her mother frowned. 'I'm sorry Millie – I don't seem to be able to concentrate these days. It seems so strange not to have Dad around as he used to take care of so much. And sometimes if I'm dozing in the chair, it feels like he's sitting opposite in his. Daft isn't it? I relied on him so much.'

'No of course not, as I feel like you too sometimes. It's just the upheaval since he died that's upsetting us at the moment. It's quite natural, but once the move is out of the way you'll settle down again, I'm sure,' Millie reassured her mother.

'I'm sure you're right,' Doris said with a heavy sigh. 'But I don't know where I'm going to put everything.'

'You know that you won't be able to bring everything from the old house, don't you, Mum?' Millie said, as a twinge of guilt tugged at her. 'But we have two weeks before you move, so you have time to decide what to bring. And didn't Aunt Ruby say she would keep a few bits for you in their spare room?'

'I know,' Doris's lower lip trembled and she closed her eyes. 'But I just wish Arthur was here, Millie.'

A lump caught in Millie's throat.

She put her arm around her mother. 'So do I, Mum. But he's not, I'm afraid, and so we just have to get on with it. And he wouldn't want you to be unhappy after he'd gone, remember.'

Doris mustered a faint smile. 'Stay calm and carry on, and all that.'

'That's the ticket,' replied Millie. 'I know you don't want to move, Mum, but after I've paid my living-in allowance I just haven't got enough to make up the shortfall in the rent, and you can't pay it out of your savings for ever, or you'll have nothing to fall back on if anything unexpected happens.'

Doris sighed. 'I know, dear. And as Ruby's always saying, there's no point moaning about things, you just have to get on with it. And I'm sure that once we've given the place a good freshen-up it will be quite jolly. I could replant your dad's favourite roses in tubs out here.'

'That's the spirit,' said Millie. 'So you'll take it?'

Her mother nodded, and then she took Millie's hand and kissed it. 'You're a good girl, so you are, and Dad would say the same if he were here.'

Chapter Eight

Millie was the last person to arrive in the sitting room in Munroe House. Almost every nurse working for the Association was squashed into the parlour. Many of them, like Millie, were in their uniforms, having just finished their morning rounds, but even some of the girls who were on a day off were there. Gladys and her cronies were huddled in the corner, and they looked up as Millie walked in. Gladys said something that made the other two giggle.

Giving them a frosty look, Millie slipped into a chair behind Connie and Beattie.

'Where have you been?' hissed Connie. 'Miss Dutton will be here at any moment.'

'I was held up at Mrs Crump's. The yard pump handle was stuck, so I had to fetch two buckets of water from the Red Lion,' Millie replied, straightening the seams in her stockings.

She'd pressed her newest uniform twice and spent half an hour polishing her shoes last night in preparation for meeting the new superintendent.

'Your hair looks nice,' Connie said, casting her gaze over Millie's head.

Millie patted the thick roll of hair just above her collar. 'I thought I'd try a new style.'

Connie winked. 'I'm sure Alex Nolan will like it too.'

Millie glared at her and was about repeat once again how she didn't care if he did or if he didn't, when the door opened. Mrs Archer strode in, followed by the woman Millie had last seen trit-trotting down the corridor in St George's hospital two long months ago.

Instead of the tailored suit she'd worn for the interview, Miss Dutton was now more properly dressed in a new navy uniform. Her pale hair was almost hidden beneath a frilly nurse's cap. Her cool blue eyes and slightly flushed cheeks were now devoid of make-up. She followed the Association's chairwoman stiffly to the empty chair at the far end of the room. Mrs Archer indicated for Miss Dutton to take a seat and she sat down, pressing her knees together and tugging her skirt over them. Mrs Archer took position beside Miss Dutton and glanced at the clock on the mantel-shelf, which showed ten minutes to midday.

'I think I can just about say good morning to you all.'

The nurses laughed and Mrs Archer beamed at them with rosy-cheeked goodwill.

'As Mrs Pierce will be ringing the bell for dinner soon, I think I had better get on with things.' Mrs Archer turned to the woman beside her. 'I'd like formally to introduce St George's and St Dunstan's District Nursing Association's new super-intendent, Miss Dutton. And I'm sure you'd like to welcome her in the usual way.'

The nurses clapped, and Miss Dutton acknow-ledged it by raising the corners of her mouth a quarter of an inch.

'Miss Dutton has a vast amount of experience

169

we will all be able to learn from, and she comes highly recommended,' continued the chairwoman. 'And I'm sure you'll all do your very best to help her settle in.' She cast her eyes around. 'Perhaps you could help Miss Dutton by introducing yourselves and telling her the area you are responsible for.' She looked at Sally. 'If you wouldn't mind getting the ball rolling, Nurse Scott, and do please stand up so Miss Dutton can see you.'

One by one the nurses stood up and said their name and work area, and then it was Millie's turn.

Unfolding her legs, Millie rose to her feet. 'Sister Sullivan,' she said in a clear voice, aware of the sudden hush in the room. 'I cover Wapping's maternity and district nurse patients. And welcome to Munroe House.'

There was a flicker of recognition and Miss Dutton gave a small nod.

'Nurse Sullivan has been holding the fort since the last superintendent left and has done a splendid job,' Mrs Harper's cheery voice cut in.

Miss Dutton raised an almost invisible eyebrow. 'I'm sure she has.'

'Nurse Sullivan has reorganised the training of the Association's four students and even managed to simplify the weekly accounting procedure,' continued the chairwoman. 'I'm sure she will be only too happy to help you make sense of the way Munroe House functions, won't you, Nurse Sullivan?'

Millie smiled tightly. 'Of course.'

The two women regarded each other for a

moment and then Millie resumed her seat.

The chair in front of Millie creaked as Connie leaned back. 'She recognises you, then,' she said out of the side of her mouth.

Miss Dutton stood up.

'Thank you, for your warm welcome, Mrs Archer,' she said, shooting a quick look at the woman beside her, and then around the room, 'and to you all. I'm very pleased to have been appointed as the new superintendent for Munroe House. I know that the St George's and St Dunstan's District Nursing Association was founded by Miss Robina Munroe, who worked with Florence Nightingale in the Crimea almost a hundred years ago and that my predecessor clung to the deep-rooted tradition of the last century. But nursing, as with everything else, has to change and so the Association must put aside the old and embrace the new. And if we do, I'm sure we will all get on splendidly.'

'So she's going to reorganise everything,' said Connie in a low voice.

Beattie nodded as Millie's mouth pulled into a grim line.

Mrs Archer spoke again to Miss Dutton. 'And our president assures us that you are the person who will do that.'

'Mr Shottington?' whispered Beattie. 'What's he got to do with it?'

Millie moved sideways so she was hidden from view behind Connie. 'Apparently she was a ward sister at the Brompton when he was there.'

Beattie rolled her eyes.

'Miss Dutton will be living in Miss Summers'

old quarters until the two rooms above the stables are refurbished,' Mrs Harper concluded.

A murmur of surprise went around the room.

'But what about the telephone?' asked Millie. 'Miss Dutton won't be able to hear it ring at night from across the courtyard.'

Several nurses nodded. A splash of colour spread up Miss Dutton's neck and she looked uneasy.

'I know the superintendent has always lived in the main house to ensure out-of-hours calls are answered,' Mrs Archer replied. 'However, the president felt that in future the night telephone should be the responsibility of the nurse on call, and not the superintendent anymore.'

'I'm surprised at Mr Shottington taking such an interest,' said Connie under her breath.

'I'm surprised he knows where the super-intendent lives,' replied Millie. 'I can't remember the last time he stepped across the threshold.'

'And I thought the Association was strapped for cash, so where's the money coming from?' added Beattie.

The hum in the room grew louder.

'I agree with Mr Shottington,' proclaimed Gladys in a loud voice. 'The superintendent has enough to do without being woken up every time the phone rings during the night.' She smiled artlessly at Miss Dutton. 'Welcome to Munroe House, Miss Dutton, and I'd be pleased to help you settle in any way I can.'

Stan Rodger, who lived next door to Millie's mother in Harley Grove, turned his Hillman Minx into Anthony Street just as the midday factory hooters sounded to signal the dinner break. He pulled up behind a van with the words 'Harris & Co Builders' emblazoned on it, belonging to Ruby's gentleman friend, Tony. The lorry was almost empty now, and two men were manhandling the sideboard down from the vehicle.

The front door to number seventy-one was open and it wasn't the only one, as her mother's new neighbours were out in force, keeping an eye on the proceedings.

'Here we are, all safe and sound,' said Stan, as he put the handbrake on.

'I can't thank you enough for bringing me and Mum down,' Millie said from the back seat.

Doris lifted her handbag on to her knee. 'Will you let me give you something for your trouble?'

'No I won't, Doris,' Stan replied firmly. 'Not after all you and your Arthur have done for me and Lena over the years.'

'That's very kind of you, Stan,' Doris said, resting her hand on his arm. 'I'd like to offer you a cup of tea but I'm not sure I know where the teapot is.'

Stan smiled. 'Don't be daft. Me and Lena will come down when you've settled in.'

Millie opened the door and climbed out of the cramped back seat as Stan helped Doris out of the front. As Stan drove off, Aunt Ruby's head popped out of the front door of number seventy-one.

Although she was allegedly 'helping' with the move, Aunt Ruby was still dressed in a pair of tailored slacks and a beaded jumper. Her only concession to the task was the scarf wrapped over her hair and secured at the front.

She spotted them and frowned. 'Oh, there you are, Doris. I was beginning to think you'd got lost.'

'Sorry,' said Millie, guiding her mother between several tea chests still waiting on the pavement. 'They've cordoned off Ben Jonson Road, as there's an unexploded bomb down by the gas works.'

Ruby's red lips pulled tight. 'Well, I suppose that can't be helped, although we've almost done it all by now.'

Millie and her mother followed Ruby through the door and into the downstairs room. Millie had spent yesterday giving the house a final wash and brush up, and as the van's first trip of the day from Bow to Stepney had brought the two best carpets from Harley Grove, one of them was already unrolled on the new lino in the lounge.

'Tony got the men to take the bedroom furniture up as soon as they offloaded it. The bed's been fixed together and I've made it up. The suitcases and boxes with your clothes in need unpacking, Doris. Once they've finished upstairs, I'll get Anthony to bring in the sofa and the other bits.' Ruby said, squeezing around a tea chest full of family knick-knacks and photos in the middle of the room.

'That's very good of you and Tony, Ruby,' Doris said. 'I don't know how me and Millie would have managed if you hadn't pitched in.'

'Don't be daft, that's what sisters do, Doris,' Ruby replied.

One of the men came in carrying an upright

174

lamp, complete with shade, and the three women stepped back to let him pass.

'Is there anything you want me to do?' asked Millie.

'You can put the kettle on,' chipped in Tony, as he emerged from the door to the upstairs. 'Me and the boys would murder for a cup of tea.'

Millie smiled. 'One round of tea coming up.'

'I'll help,' Doris said, following her. 'I should start setting the kitchen in order.'

'I haven't got around to unpacking the boxes under the window,' Ruby called after them. 'So you'll have to search around in them to find the cups.'

Millie went through to the kitchen and filled the kettle from the single, cold-water tap and then set it on the sparkling New World gas cooker, complete with an integrated plate-warmer.

While her mother tidied the crockery and cutlery away in the kitchen dresser, Millie made tea. Everyone stopped to drink their cuppa, and then Tony and his men started bringing in the remaining downstairs furniture while Ruby hung the curtains.

'Well, I think that's it,' said Tony not long afterwards, popping down the old gramophone on the occasional table in the corner.

'Thank you, Tony,' said Doris, coming in from the kitchen. 'I just said to Ruby that I don't know what we would have done today without you and Ruby.'

'That's all right, Doris,' he replied, giving her a friendly smile. 'That's what families are for. Ain't it, Ruby?'

'Family first, that was what our mum used to say,' Ruby agreed. She looked at her watch. 'I have a meeting at the church later about the Bishop's visit and I have to be there. Do you think you two can manage now if Anthony and I go?'

'Of course, there are only a couple of boxes left to unpack,' said Millie.

Ruby hugged Doris, kissing the air beside her cheek. 'I'll see you for dinner then on Sunday.'

She picked up her handbag from the sideboard, and she and Tony left.

Doris collected the used cups. 'Do you want another cuppa?'

'That's a good idea,' said Millie, pleased to see a little more colour in her mother's cheeks. 'I'll just wave them off, and then pop around the corner to get us some fish and chips for dinner.'

Outside, Ruby was repairing her lipstick in the van's wing mirror as Tony secured the tarpaulin on the back.

'I am grateful, Aunt Ruby, for all you and Tony have done,' Millie said.

'I know you are, and we're only too pleased to help.' Ruby glanced around up and down the street. 'But I thought you would have found somewhere a bit more suitable for your mother.'

'Haven't you read about the shortage of housing?' Millie reminded her aunt.

Ruby took a cigarette out and lit it. 'The press always exaggerate these things, don't they? I'm sure the housing situation can't be as bad as they make out.'

'Tell that to the families that I sometimes see

who are living in factories and those still tucking their children into bed on tube platforms each night,' Millie replied. 'I only got this house because my friend had to give it up. And at least mum hasn't got to share. I know that it might not look like it just now, but she's one of the lucky ones.'

'I suppose we have to be thankful for small mercies. But even if you couldn't get anything nicer, surely you could have found something in a better area? I mean – the people! The curtains started twitching the moment Anthony turned into the street, and I haven't seen a man yet wearing a jacket or tie. I had hoped when you were overlooked for the superintendent post you would have–'

'Thanks, Aunt Ruby, but I know you are in a hurry,' Millie said firmly, pulling open the passenger door of the van. Ruby's neck flushed. She hesitated for a couple of seconds and then climbed in.

Tony turned on the engine and the lorry spluttered into life.

Ruby sat rigidly looking ahead for a moment and then she wound down the window. 'I'm only trying to help, Amelia.'

'I know, Aunt Ruby – and we do appreciate all you have done.'

With a cheery wave, Tony released the handbrake and turned the steering wheel.

'And I wasn't overlooked,' Millie shouted, once the van had pulled away.

Millie stowed her bike on the rack just as St

Martha's and St Mungo's clock struck 10 p.m. Lifting her bag from the front basket, she picked her way through the puddles in the yard to the back door of Munroe House. She ducked inside and stamped on the coconut mat, showering the black and white hall tiles with rainwater. As she took off her mac and shook it out, the door to the treatment room opened and Connie's head popped out.

'My goodness,' she said, coming out and hurrying toward Millie. 'I didn't think you'd be back for hours.'

'Neither did I,' replied Millie, hanging her coat up on a spare hook. 'But when I got to Mrs Tyler's, the baby was already saying hello to the world, thanks to blooming Mrs Callaghan.'

Connie smiled sympathetically. 'Come with me and I'll make you a cocoa.'

Millie put her sodden felt hat on the table and followed her friend into the warm kitchen at the end of the corridor.

Putting her bag on the floor, Millie sat on one of the tall stools, while Connie relit the gas under the pot-bellied kettle.

'I tell you straight, Connie, the last thing I needed tonight was to cycle three miles in the pouring rain, only to have Mrs Callaghan's fat face smirking at me when I arrived. I don't know how she does it. It's as if she smells a woman going into labour.'

Connie smiled. 'Perhaps she's got a crystal ball.'

Millie gave a hard laugh. 'She probably keeps it with her cauldron and broomstick! But, still, that's the third time in as many months she's

178

delivered a baby before I arrived.'

'Only because they were quick and straight-forward births,' Connie replied, collecting a bottle of milk from the refrigerator. 'I dread to think what would happen if a baby was misaligned.' She lifted the whistling kettle off the heat. 'Never mind. This will make you feel better.'

She passed a mug to Millie, who looked glumly at the frothy chocolate-coloured liquid.

'Cheer up,' Connie said, sitting down on the other side of the table. 'It's your last night on call, and then you're off until Monday. And Harry Fontaine's band is playing all week at the Astoria, which means we're set to trip the light fantastic on Saturday. And who knows?' Connie took an innocent sip of her drink. 'Perhaps Alex Nolan will be there.'

Before Millie could tell her friend for the ump-teenth time that she wasn't interested in Alex Nolan, the telephone rang.

Connie put her hand on Millie's arm. 'I'll answer it.'

She left the room and Millie blew the heat from the top of her mug, wondering whether anyone at this moment was making Alex a night-time drink. She shoved the thought away and drank her cocoa. The telephone bell ceased and Connie's muffled voice drifted through from the other side of the door. After a few moments the door opened again and Connie walked back in.

Millie looked up. 'Another visit request?'

'I'm afraid so,' replied Connie.

'Where?'

'Arbour Square police station.'

Millie's eyebrows rose in surprise. 'Surely they need the divisional surgeon, not a nurse.'

'They don't want a nurse.' Connie's lips twisted into a wry smile. 'They have a woman in the cells who urgently needs a midwife. The station sergeant sounded frantic.'

'I bet he did.' Millie swallowed the last few mouthfuls in her mug and picked up her bag. 'It's probably a false alarm, but I'll have to go and find out what's happening.'

'Well, you can be sure of one thing,' Connie said.

'What?'

'With her husband playing hide and seek with the local Old Bill most of the time, at least you won't find Mrs Callaghan opening the door to you down at the nick.'

Thankfully, by the time Millie pedalled out through the back gates of Munroe House for the second time that night, the storm had moved on and could now be heard rumbling over the Royal Docks to the east. The police station was only a quarter of a mile away, and so within a few minutes of leaving the nurses' home she was leaning her bike against the railings outside the police station.

Picking up her bag, Millie climbed the couple of steps to the main entrance and pushed open one of the heavy oak doors. The police station was a hundred years old and had the standard green tiles halfway up the walls and polished wooden flooring. The main reception was on Millie's right, behind which was the front office. There was an

180

opaque glass screen shielding the police car-radio operator from view.

There were a couple of people at the station desk, but when the sergeant spotted Millie he broke off immediately and lifted the hinged part of the desk.

'Thank goodness, you're here, Sister. I'm Sergeant Hanson,' he said, looking visibly relieved and grabbing her elbow. 'This way.'

He tore open the door leading into the police station proper.

'I haven't locked my bike yet,' Millie said, as he ushered her in.

'Wallace!'

A slender young constable with a protuberant Adam's apple and a shaving rash appeared around the corner.

'Take the Sister's cycle around to the yard,' the sergeant barked as he guided Millie along the corridor toward the set of stairs at the end.

'So you've got a pregnant prisoner?' Millie asked as they made their way up the stone steps to the women's cells on the first floor.

He nodded. 'But it was only when Mrs West, the matron, did the strip search that we found out she was up the duff. She says there's no need to bother you, but I'd be happier if you'd take a look.'

As they reached the top of the stairs, Sergeant Hanson knocked on the solid brown door in front of them. The small inspection hole opened and a woman's face appeared.

'I've got the midwife, Matron,' Sergeant Hanson said.

The woman rolled her eyes. 'All this fuss.'

The trap snapped shut and the door unlocked. Millie stepped in. The women's custody suite had four cells running off the main room. There was a desk in one corner on which a tray with an untouched meal sat alongside a pile of files. A combination of boiled cabbage, unwashed bodies and badly flushing toilets floated in the air.

Mrs West, the matron designated to care for the detained women, was in her late fifties, with tightly pulled-back grey hair and a hard-bitten expression. With a dark uniform, white cap and laced-up shoes, she could almost have been taken for a ward sister as she stood beside the desk, were it not for the bunch of heavy keys and small truncheon hanging from her belt. She looked sourly at Millie.

'What's happening?' Millie asked as the sergeant closed the door behind them.

'Nothing, but now you're here I suppose you'd better have a shufty.'

Clutching her bag tightly, Millie followed the matron towards the cell on the right.

Someone banged furiously on the iron door to Millie's right. 'When am I going to get some grub?' bellowed a woman's voice from behind it.

'When I'm good and ready,' yelled the matron, grabbing the truncheon and smashing it on the cell door. 'Now, unless you want me to come in and belt you one, shut up, Elsie!'

'The girl says she's in labour,' the custody sergeant said to Millie.

'I keep telling you, George,' the matron cut in, 'she's telling porky pies.'

'If I could see my patient,' Millie said, looking intently at the older woman.

They walked on to the door at the far end. The matron fumbled with her keys for a moment, then selected one and stuck it in the lock.

'You've locked a woman in labour in a cell!' Millie asked, unable to hide her alarm.

'She's been arrested, ain't she?' replied the matron, pushing the door open.

Millie went in.

A petite young woman with a black plait travelling down to her hips knelt on the floor. Her voluminous floral skirt spread around her and she stared blankly at the grey tiles of the wall while untying knots in the fringes of her shawl. She was breathing heavily, but made no sound.

'I'm Sister Sullivan. The sergeant called me because he thinks you might need my help,' Millie said, kneeling beside her.

The girl looked at Millie with wild black eyes. 'Go away!' she spat out through rigid teeth. 'I do alone. Without you. Without her!' She shot a venomous look at the matron.

'Bloody gyppos,' muttered the matron, which earned her another caustic look from the young prisoner.

Beads of perspiration sprang out on the girl's forehead and her nostrils flared.

Millie slipped her arm around her slender shoulder. 'I'm here to help, but I need to examine you.'

The girl looked suspiciously at Millie. 'You police like her?' Her eyes flashed at the matron.

Millie shook her head. 'I'm not police. I'm a midwife.'

183

The young woman studied her for a moment, then gasped and her knuckles whitened as she gripped the wooden bench. Millie helped her to her feet and then on to the bench. The girl rested back on the grey pillow and slowly stretched her legs, keeping her hands protectively over her stomach.

'What's your name?'

'Angelica.'

'Is this your first baby, Angelica?'

Angelica nodded.

'How long have you had pains?' Millie asked, running her gaze over the woman's face, checking her pallor for anaemia and sniffing her breath for diabetes.

'Since midday,' she whispered as another contraction gathered. 'I was on my way home when one of his dogs,' she glared at the sergeant and ran her thumb up her chin sharply towards him, 'picked me up.'

'He saw you looting on a bombsite,' said the sergeant testily.

'He saw me pulling up a few greens for the pot. I was doing no ha–' Angelica gripped her stomach and drew up her legs. 'The baby, 'e is coming.'

The matron tutted loudly and rolled her eyes again. 'What a performance.'

Millie glanced over her shoulder at the two standing in the doorway. 'Would you leave, please?' she said firmly.

The matron looked as if she was about to protest, but the sergeant pulled her back and half-closed the door.

Angelica gripped Millie's hand. 'Please, you are

a good woman, make them take me to my family.'

'I think it might be a little late for that.' Millie lifted the girl's skirt and found two ribbons tied around her waist.

'Quick, undo them,' Angelica said, her hand frantically plucking at the knots.

Millie looked puzzled. 'They're not in the way.'

'If you don't, the cord will wrap around the baby's neck.'

Millie untied them and then pulled down the girl's surprisingly clean knickers. As she removed them, Angelica spread her knees to reveal a triangle of damp pubic hair with a bulging vulva at the centre.

Millie covered the girl's hips with her flowery skirt. 'Sergeant!'

Sergeant Hanson's head appeared around the cell door.

'Call an ambulance and put these,' Millie snapped open her case and handed him her pack of instruments, 'in boiling water for five minutes and then bring as many towels as you have. Now!'

The policeman disappeared and Millie turned back to her patient. She moved her skirt again then opened the pack and dragged on her sterile gloves. Gently she slipped her two fingers inside the young woman and immediately felt the unruptured water sac bulging through the open neck of the womb. Millie extracted her hand and Angelica grasped it.

'My baby?'

Millie gave what she hoped was a reassuring smile. 'Everything's fine,' she replied, trying not

185

to dwell on the possible complications that could occur delivering a first baby, let alone in a cold, bare police cell. 'I think the baby will be here very soon, but I need you to do exactly what I say when the next pain comes. Will you?'

Angelica's eyes grew wide again but she pressed her lips together and nodded. Millie positioned herself between the girl's legs and held her hands ready. The young woman's stomach clenched again and she drew in her breath.

'Raise your chin and blow out!' instructed Millie, glancing at her watch to check the timing.

Angelica strained but forced herself to look up. Millie held her breath as another contraction pushed Angelica's baby almost into the world. Just as the young woman relaxed with the contraction subsiding, water gushed from her, soaking the lower part of Millie's skirt and the mattress beneath. Millie examined the mother again and relief flooded over her as she felt the baby's neck without a tangle of umbilical cord around it.

She grinned at the young girl. 'Your baby's fine and now push with the next pain.'

A spark of determination flashed in Angelica's eyes, then she bore down. The head, with a mass of curly black hair, squeezed through almost instantly with the minimum of damage. Millie eased the shoulder out then lifted the baby.

Sergeant Hanson appeared in the doorway with a bundle of towels in his hand. 'The ambulan–'

'Quick, spread one out,' Millie said, holding the baby aloft.

The officer placed one over Angelica's legs and Millie wrapped the child and placed it, still attached by the cord, into his mother's arms. The afterbirth slipped out almost immediately and Millie wrapped it into another towel for the hospital doctor to check.

'What are you going to call him?' Millie asked, covering the girl's private parts as two ambulance men walked in carrying a stretcher.

Angelica covered the baby's face with her hand. 'I can't tell you until he's baptised, so the spirits are confused and can't harm him.'

Millie smiled. 'Well, in that case, hello sweetheart, and welcome to the world.' She turned to Angelica. 'These two nice chaps will take you to hospital so the doctor can make sure you and the baby are all right. And I'll call by and see you next week when you're discharged.'

Millie stood up and her knees cracked. The ambulance men lifted Angelica and her new son gently on to the stretcher, but she grabbed Millie's arm. 'May the Virgin reward you.'

Millie straightened her soggy skirt and smiled. The ambulance men took up the strain and carried Angelica out to the waiting ambulance.

'I need you to write a statement, sister,' Sergeant Hanson said to Millie as she started to pack away her case. 'It can wait until tomorrow if you like.'

Millie shook her head. 'I've got to write my own notes so I might as well do both at once.'

The officer grinned. 'Then let me buy you a cuppa in the canteen. The night duty will be taking over in quarter of an hour but I'll tell the night sergeant you're up there and he'll make sure you get home all right.'

187

Mrs West was standing in the lobby when Millie emerged from the cell.

'Thank you for your help, Matron.' Millie smiled and casually glanced at the blood-soaked mattress and amniotic fluid on the cell floor. 'And it shouldn't take you too long to set things back in order.'

Upstairs Sergeant Hanson settled Millie in the corner with a steaming mug of tea while she wrote the report in her on-call notebook. The last few officers of the late shift trickled out as she finished off her brief statement of the events for the police.

The canteen assistant behind the tea bar was just brewing up another pot when the door opened.

'Right, lads. Get yourself out and about and around the ground,' a deep male voice shouted from the corridor. 'And don't forget, I'm too busy having tea at the palace this week to visit you ugly lot in hospital, so keep out of trouble.'

There was a chorus of male laughter.

'I'll see you on your points later,' he continued. 'Don't be late.'

'Right you are, Sarge,' someone called.

'Not if I see you first,' shouted another.

The sound of tramping feet echoed around the stairwell as the night patrol made their way down.

The door flew open, and Alex Nolan strode into the canteen.

Millie's heart skipped at least a dozen beats. If he looked good in a well-fitting suit, he looked unbelievably handsome in a police uniform.

He saw her and stopped dead. 'Millie?'

She nodded, unable to speak.

188

A smile spread across his angular face. 'And for once old Hanson wasn't telling a whopper when he said there was a pretty little nurse sitting in the canteen. Give us a cuppa, Dolly,' he called to the canteen woman.

'Right you are, Sergeant,' Dolly called back, pouring him one and stirring in two sugars.

Alex picked up his mug and took a sip then ambled towards her. He stopped in front of the table and pulled out the chair opposite. 'Mind if I join you?'

Millie shook her head and stared up into Alex Nolan's dark green eyes.

Millie hooked her mac over the coat peg, popped her hat on top and made her way slowly upstairs. She knocked on Connie's door.

There was a pause and then a faint, 'Come in.'

Millie pushed open the door and popped her head around.

'Are you awake?' Millie asked, already in the room.

'I am now,' Connie yawned. She scraped her hair out of her eyes and turned on her bedside lamp. 'What time is it?'

'Just after eleven-thirty,' Millie answered, closing the door quietly.

'Eleven-thirty!'

'I know it's a bit late, but I wanted to tell you about what happened at the police station,' Millie said.

'I'm guessing by your jolly smile it went all right.'

Millie nodded as she pulled Connie's pink

189

boudoir chair out from her dressing table and over to the bed. 'Yes. It was one of the gypsy girls from the encampment on Beckton Flats.' Millie told her about the delivery. 'And I wouldn't like to meet the matron alone at night in a dark alley. Right spiteful cow she—'

'Aren't they all,' Connie cut in, turning the light off. 'But could you save the rest until morning? We have to be up at six.'

Connie pulled the cover over and snuggled down.

'And Alex Nolan was there,' Millie said, as her heart gave a double beat just at the sound of his name.

Connie sat up and switched the lamp back on. 'Alex Nolan?' she said, looking fully at Millie. 'Was he under arrest?'

Millie shook her head and laughed. 'No, it turns out he's the section sergeant on B Relief.'

Connie's eyes nearly popped out of her head. 'He's a policeman!'

'And you could have knocked me down with a feather when the canteen door opened and he strolled in,' said Millie.

'I bet! What does he look like in uniform?'

The image of Alex standing in the middle of the room looking at her flashed into Millie's mind.

'All right,' she replied. 'Well, perhaps a bit more than all right. But I felt so embarrassed. You know, thinking he was a rogue when actually he's the complete opposite.'

'Oh, I wouldn't go that far,' said Connie, raising an eyebrow. 'I've seen the glint in his eyes when he looks at you.'

A little coil of excitement wriggled in Millie's stomach. 'Don't be silly,' she replied, trying to remain composed.

'So what did he say when you told him you had him down as Wapping's answer to Al Capone?' Connie asked.

'Funnily enough I didn't mention it,' Millie joked, feeling ridiculously foolish again. 'He only had time for a quick cup of tea before he had to leave on patrol, and I had to get back too, and so there wasn't time.' Millie straightened an imaginary crease in her uniform. 'Perhaps I'll drop it into the conversation when we go out next week.'

Connie's mouth dropped. 'You're going out with him? When?'

'Saturday,' Millie said, finally letting the grin escape that she'd suppressed all the way back from the police station.

'Where's he taking you?'

'They've brought some of the paintings back from storage, so he suggested the Portrait Gallery, and then we're going on for a meal somewhere,' Millie said, already feeling excited at the prospect. 'It's worked out quite well as I'm on my weekend off and he finishes his month of nights on Tuesday and so, as he put it himself, he should be back in the land of the living by then.'

'Well, you be careful,' replied Connie. 'You know what men are like. All lovey-dovey and sweet kisses until some other woman wiggles by.'

'For goodness sake, Connie, we're just visiting an art gallery.'

Connie looked unrepentant. 'I know, but I'm just saying.'

'Anyhow, it will be a nice afternoon away from underneath Miss Dutton's prying nose, if nothing else,' replied Millie.

'And speaking of the new superintendent,' said Connie, reaching for the lamp again, 'I, for one, don't want to suffer her bad temper for being late for report in the morning.'

'Me neither,' said Millie, standing up. 'Give me a knock if I'm not stirring, will you?'

Connie nodded and switched off the light. Millie crept out. Although there was a small night-light on the landing, the house was silent. Avoiding the creaky floorboards, Millie tiptoed along the corridor to her own room.

Inside, the moonlight was streaking into the room through the open curtains, so Millie didn't bother to switch on the light. She undressed, hung her clothes up and then slipped into bed. She closed her eyes and an image of Alex Nolan flashed into her head, allowing her to run through her conversation with him word for word and smile by smile.

Chapter Nine

Millie shoved the front wheels of her bike over a clod of earth, cracking the thin surface-ice and silently swore under her breath. She'd had to get off the bike way back where the grassland changed to marsh, about half a mile away. Stopping to catch her breath, Millie peered through the fog across the vast expanse of Beckton Flats to where a handful of round-topped caravans stood. She could make out three horses and a half-grown foal munching the coarse shrubland on one side, a pile of scrap metal on the other and a ring of stone containing a small fire in the middle. Despite the poor visibility, Millie could see the colourful painting on the sides of the wooden homes and the washing strung between.

Blowing on her gloveless hands, Millie took a firm grip on her handlebars and pushed on. Thanks to an unexploded bomb being discovered just north of Albert Docks, she'd already had to cycle an extra mile along West India Dock Road and with three visits yet to do from her morning list, she'd be lucky if she got back to Munroe House before dinner was finished.

Thankfully she'd swapped her afternoon duty at the resettlement clinic with Eva in order that she could take her mother shopping in Stratford. But whereas they'd planned to be there for two p.m., now they'd be lucky to make it much before three-thirty.

A couple of bedraggled-looking dogs announced her arrival, their breath visible in the frosty air. Half a dozen women and what looked like twice the number of children climbed down from the wagons. The women, many of whom were little more than children themselves, had the same dark features as Angelica, and were dressed in similar dark skirts and shapeless jackets as she had worn at the police station. Most of the women had shawls around their heads, pulled modestly forward to shield their faces. The children in bedraggled clothes and oversized boots huddled around their mothers' skirts and watched Millie with large, solemn eyes.

'Hello,' Millie called cheerfully. 'I'm Sister Sullivan. Is Angelica here?'

The women exchanged glances but didn't answer.

Millie pushed her cycle further into the settlement. 'I've just come to make sure that both she and the baby are all right. That's all.'

The door of the caravan at the back of the camp opened and an old woman stepped out. With her coffee-coloured complexion and snow-white hair, she made a striking picture standing on the front board of a travellers' wagon. Although she was dressed in black, her headdress was made of lace, unlike the other women's.

Millie smiled at her. 'Perhaps you can help me. The hospital telephoned to say Angelica's family had taken her home. I'm the midwife who was with her yesterday in the police station.'

The old woman studied Millie for a few

194

seconds longer and then beckoned her forward.

Millie leaned her cycle against a handcart and, picking her bag from the basket, she walked towards the caravan. As she climbed up the wooden stairs on to the platform, the old woman stepped in front of her.

'I am Mrs Killick, the mother of this family. Why do you seek my granddaughter?' the old woman asked. 'Do you think because she is not in your noisy, unfriendly hospital some harm has come to her?'

Millie smiled calmly. 'Not at all. I'm sure she's very well cared for indeed. It's just that it is usual for mothers to remain in hospital for two weeks after delivery to make sure everything is all right, and so I'd like to have a quick look at her to set my own mind at rest.'

'Eve didn't lie abed for fourteen days when she had Cain and Abel,' Mrs Killick said.

'No, but then neither of them were born in a cold and dirty police cell,' Millie replied. 'And although our Lord was born in a stable, I'd still like to check Angelica and her baby are well.'

The old woman considered her for a moment, then lifted the heavy curtain covering the doorway. 'Follow me.'

The interior was lit by an old-fashioned oil lamp hanging from an ornate iron hook and, as her eyes adjusted to the light, Millie found herself standing on a rag rug in the middle of the living area of the wagon. There was a pot-bellied stove chained against one wall and a set of drawers and a Dutch dresser against the other, on which a number of pretty china bowls and plates were displayed. A floral curtain hung from the roof to the floor at the far end which, Millie guessed, hid the family's sleeping quarters from view. There was a warm herby aroma, giving the atmosphere a rich earthy feel.

'You've never been inside a vardo before?' the old woman asked.

'No,' said Millie, who had stopped to look with interest at the array of polished copper pans hooked over the stove in size order. 'It's bigger than I imagined.'

The old woman walked to the far end of the caravan and moved the curtain aside. Angelica lay in a cabin-like bed supported by half-a-dozen pillows, snug under a worn patchwork quilt with her baby beside her.

Millie smiled at her. 'Hello again,' she said, putting down her bag. 'And how are you?'

'A little sore,' Angelica replied.

'I'm not surprised,' Millie replied. 'You only had a baby less than twenty-four hours ago. What about your son?'

Angelica looked lovingly at the sleeping infant beside her. 'He's the most perfect baby.'

'Is he feeding well?'

The old woman's wrinkled face lifted in an indulgent smile. 'He'd be chewing a bone if we gave it him.'

'It's sore, but he latches on straight away,' said Angelica. 'My cousin, who had a boy a month ago, is feeding him until I have something.'

'Good,' replied Millie, trying not to show her surprise. 'Can I take a look at him?'

Angelica lifted him up and gave him to Millie.

196

The infant stretched and pulled a face but didn't wake.

'Goodness, he's a good weight,' Millie said, tucking him in the crook of her arm.

Mrs Killick leaned forward and eased the knitted blanket covering the baby's face down a little. 'He's a fair darling little lad.'

Millie laid him on to the bed and then pulled out the mesh sling from her bag and slipped it under the baby. She then reached in for the sprung fisherman's scales, fastened the sling with the baby inside on the end hook and raised it up.

'Six pounds seven ounces,' Millie said, as the baby rotated slowly in the sling.

She rested him back on the bed and the old woman scooped him out and cradled him to her chest. Millie turned to Angelica. 'Is it all right if I examine you?'

Angelica looked at her grandmother, who nodded. The young girl rolled down the covers and shuffled down. Millie opened her bag and set out her equipment on the shelf just above Angelica's head. As quickly as she could, she set her thermometer to soak while she palpated Angelica's stomach, checked her breasts and colour of the discharge on her pad. Then she shook out the thermometer and placed it under her tongue.

'So, do you find everything as it should be?' asked Mrs Killick.

Millie smiled at her. 'I do. It all seems to be settling back into place, as it should. I think the milk will come in tomorrow. And that little chap,' she nodded at the sleeping baby, 'didn't give his mother so much as a scratch, and so I'd say she'd

197

be back to normal in a month or two.'

Mrs Killick beamed at her granddaughter. 'Thaddeus will be pleased you'll be able to breed again so soon, Angelica.'

'It was a figure of speech. It would be better if Angelica waited at least a year before she became pregnant again as most doctors agree it is better for children to be spaced.' Millie delved into the side pocket of her bag and pulled out some Ministry of Health leaflets. 'There are lots of reliable methods you can use to plan your family.'

Angelica looked puzzled. 'But you know it's a woman's job to give her man sons.'

'And you have,' said Millie, trying to give her the pamphlets. 'But it's better if you can have a gap between them, and you're only a babe yourself. There's condoms and gels you can use to–'

'It is not our way,' cut in Angelica, thrusting the brochures back at Millie.

'If a woman's old enough to bleed, she's old enough to be a mother.' The old woman pulled the covers up over her granddaughter again and turned to Millie. 'I thank you for what you've done, Sister, but we won't keep you longer.' She folded her arms.

Millie gave an inward sigh and packed away her instruments. 'I'll pop back again at the end of the week just to check on Angelica and the lad again, if you don't mind.'

The old woman gave a noncommittal smile.

Millie snapped the clasp shut and stood up; Mrs Killick held back the curtain for her to leave. Millie picked up her bag but as she ducked her head under the curtain the old woman spoke.

'Why did you unknot Angelica's sashes?' she asked, her coal-black eyes scrutinising Millie's face.

'Because it was important to her,' Millie replied.

'You are an honourable woman, Sister.'

'Why thank–'

Mrs Killick grasped Millie's hand and turned it over. 'You will be blessed with two daughters and a son with the green eyes of his father.'

A ripple of excitement ran through Millie but she damped it down. 'I'll see you in a few days,' she said, taking her hand back.

The old woman watched her as she walked down the few steps and collected her bike from where she left it. She turned and looked at Mrs Killick standing on the front board of the caravan. Millie waved and a flicker of emotion passed over the old woman's face, then she smiled.

'Goodbye, Sister,' she called back.

Alex leaned back as the waitress set a fresh tray of tea on the table in front of them. 'So, where were you brought up?'

They had already occupied the corner table of the sumptuously decorated Lyons corner house in Shaftesbury Avenue for an hour and, ignoring the disapproving looks from the Nippy who was looking to clear the table, had just ordered another pot of tea. The place was packed with couples like themselves having a day out in London.

'Bow,' replied Millie. 'We lived in Harley Grove just down from the station and around the corner from Coburn Girls' School, where I went.'

Alex raised an eyebrow. 'A grammar-school girl, eh? I thought you looked brainy.'

Millie laughed and poured their fourth cup of tea. 'What school did you go to?'

'The Highway. That's to say, it was the school I was sent to. Whether I was ever there is another matter.' He shovelled in two spoonfuls of sugar and stirred vigorously. 'What about your folks? What do they do?'

Millie gave him a brief account of her family to date.

'I'm sorry about your father,' he said when she'd finished. 'That's bad going like that, just as it's all over.'

'That's what everyone says,' Millie replied.

'What about your mother? How's she coping?' he asked. Millie forced a smile. 'Oh, soldiering on. You know. What about your folks?'

'Well, I don't rightly know what my old man did.' A wry smile twisted his lips. 'I doubt my mum did either, as a month after I was born he disappeared for good, so we moved in with my gran in Fenton Street. Do you know it?'

Millie nodded. 'I should do – it's on my patch and I have a couple of patients there.'

'Well, we lived at the far end, opposite the fish and chip shop. I have a sister, Minnie, fifteen years older than me, who moved to her little plot on Dunton when the bombs started falling. She's got three kids and a work-shy husband. I pop down to see her now and again. I've another, Beryl, two years younger, who moved to Canada with her husband before the war. She's got a boy. There was a brother, Frank, squeezed between the two girls. He was in the merchant Navy, but his ship was part of an Atlantic convoy and was lost at sea.'

'I'm sorry,' Millie said.

Alex shrugged. 'We've all lost someone. He went to sea when he was fourteen, and I was six, and as he only came back every couple of years it's a bit difficult to miss him.'

'And your mum?'

'Died, just after Frank left. Influenza, according to the death certificate.'

'So your gran brought you up.'

Alex smiled and Millie felt the warmth of it. 'She did, God bless her. Minnie was already gone and Beryl married, and so Gran just had me. She had a firm hand, mind you, but I dare say I needed it and although she didn't have two ha'pennies to rub together, I never went hungry.' A look of pain flitted across his face. 'She was one of those caught in the Bethnal Green Station stampede. She was visiting my Aunt Kit in Roman Road when the raid started. They took shelter in the station and got caught in the panic. The coroner recorded suffocation as the cause of death for both of them.'

'My goodness,' said Millie. 'I read about the disaster in the papers and I thought it must be Bethnal Green Station, but that's all I know.'

'Well, you know as much as me. I thought I might find something out now, but the council are still very hush-hush about it. So you see, other than Minnie and her bunch, I'm on my tod. Just as well really, with the odd hours I do as a copper.'

'Actually, Alex, you'll never guess what I thought you did for a living,' Millie said.

201

'What?' He picked up his tea.

She gave a little laugh. 'I thought you were a boss of a criminal gang.'

Alex spluttered and the two women on the table next to them looked over disapprovingly. 'Stone the crows!'

'Well, it's a natural mistake,' Millie said, taking a sip of tea to hide her embarrassment.

'What, 'cause of the way I talk?' he asked, studying her across the table.

'No,' laughed Millie. 'Because of what you said to the two floozies outside the Regency and because every time I saw you there were half-a-dozen men who looked like heavyweight boxers standing behind you.'

Alex smiled. 'I suppose old Georgie Tugman looks more like a villain than a copper, but even so...' His eyes twinkled with amusement.

'All right, Mr Clever,' Millie said. 'What did you think I was? A shop girl or a secretary, I suppose?'

Alex studied her face. 'I knew exactly what you were the moment I took you in my arms,' he said in a thoughtful tone.

Millie's heart gave a little flutter.

'Ginger Rogers' dancing teacher, of course.'

Millie laughed.

'But I suppose I could have been a crook – most of my pals were.' He popped the last piece of cake in his mouth.

'So why are you a policeman instead? And how come you know so much about art?' Millie asked, noting the shape of his hand as he held the cup.

'The answer's the same for both: the war,' Alex

replied. 'It was the best thing that happened to me. In thirty-eight I was just another fella standing by the dock gates waiting for a mean-mouthed foreman to give me a day's work. A year later I'm a fully trained gunner driving across the desert looking up at a full moon rising over the sand dunes, meeting a Bedouin caravan slowly winding its way across the horizon, and listening to the spring breeze rustling through palm trees in an oasis.'

'You make it sound romantic, like something out of an old Rudolph Valentino film. What about the fighting?' Millie asked.

'There was plenty of that.' Alex leaned back. 'We went back and forth across the same bit of bloody sand a couple of times fighting Rommel, and it's no fun being pounded by 'eavy artillery day and night. But there were plenty of laughs too.' His smile widened. 'Like the time Jock, who was in charge of the shells, used some local vegetable in our dinner and turned the whole lot purple, dumplings and all. We even saw Mount Etna go up when we were bobbing about off Sicily. Like a massive Roman candle, it were. Lit up the whole troopship.'

'And art?' Millie asked.

'That was thanks to this.' He stretched out the leg shielded by the table and pulled up his left trouser leg.

Millie looked down at his muscular leg with a white scar running lengthways and cutting a path through the soft hair.

'Oh my goodness,' she said. 'You're lucky you didn't lose the leg.'

'That's what the surgeon said,' Alex replied,

203

shaking his clothing down.

'Is that why you said you were kicked out of the Army?' Millie asked.

He nodded. 'I was in hospital in Malta for four months, on morphine for half of them, but once I came around I had to find something to do. I was never into books at school but when you're stuck staring at the wall for days on end you have to find summink to take the edge off the boredom or you'll go bonkers, so I started working my way through the hospital's little library. Light stuff at first, a bit of Dickens and then I moved on to Walter Scott and Sherlock Holmes. I read everything, including *Pride and Prejudice*.'

Millie sighed. 'I love that book! Me and Connie listened to the whole series on the wireless a couple of months back.'

Alex raised an eyebrow. 'Yer, well. I can't say it did much for me. But anyway a bit later they shipped a new chap into the bed next to me. It turned out he was a professor of art at a university up north. There was a set of big picture books in the hospital library about the Old Masters – you know, Michelangelo, Titian, Rubens – so once he was back on his feet the Prof would set himself in the day room a couple of times a week and, using one of the books, would give us a talk. It was cheaper than playing cards, so I gave it a whirl.' A serious-minded expression flitted across his face for a second then the rakish smile returned. 'And of course I thought it might one day help me get a grammar school girl to come on a second date.'

Millie rested her chin on her hand and gazed across at him. 'What makes you think you needed the help?'

Millie and Annie shuffled along the bench to let two latecomers sit down. Every available chair in the treatment room was occupied by the nurses – in fact, some were doubled up, half on and half off a seat.

Millie glanced up at the clock as several nurses around the table yawned. Seven twenty-eight. She cast her eyes around and mentally checked off who was there and who wasn't. The door opened and the chattering ceased as Miss Dutton walked in.

She cast her pale blue eyes over them. 'Good morning, nurses.'

'Good morning, Superintendent,' they said in unison.

She pulled out the chair at the head of the table and sat down. She clasped her hands together on top of the leather-bound report book. 'Shall we pray?'

The nurses folded their hands in their laps and lowered their heads.

'Dear Lord, we...'

As Miss Dutton's voice droned out the familiar words, Millie's thoughts rested on her father, mother, aunt Ruby, Connie, Annie and the rest of the nurses in Munroe House and, lastly, on herself. She echoed 'Amen' and looked up.

Miss Dutton opened the large ledger and the nurses took out their notepads and pens.

'The first item on today's list is for Nurse Scott,' she said, looking at Sally. 'Dr Hayhurst has asked that you call in on Mrs Dooley in Jute Street to check her legs.'

Sally nodded and scribbled it in her pad.

Miss Dutton's lips pulled together a little as she regarded Sally's bowed head, but after a pause she continued on with the list.

'Finally, Turner Street School would like the nurse to call on Wednesday instead of Tuesday as the next week they are having the inspectors in,' she concluded.

The nurses tucked their report books in their bags and made ready to leave.

'There are a couple of other matters before you go,' Miss Dutton said, weaving her fingers together and resting her hands on the ledger.

The nurses sat down again.

'Since becoming superintendent a month ago, I have been carrying out a thorough review of the way Munroe House and provision of nursing and maternity services are run,' Miss Dutton said in a clipped voice. She smiled frostily. 'I was given to understand that the previous superintendent was – how can I put this delicately – a little lax and the nursing services were well below an acceptable standard. But I was pleasantly surprised to find the contrary to be true. Although I have applied the standards used in Barts Hospital, I cannot find any fault with the day-to-day running of Munroe House. In fact, the clinic is surprisingly efficient. The ordering of dressings, the equipment loans records and cleanliness of the treatment room and instruments are comparable with the best hospital standards. Even the students' training is well organised and I am confident that all four of the Association's students will pass with flying colours.'

The nurses in the room visibly relaxed and smiled at each other.

'That's because Nurse Sullivan has been in charge since Miss Summers left,' piped up Annie, beaming at Millie.

There was a murmur of agreement, and Connie and Beattie gave Millie the thumbs-up.

Miss Dutton's composure slipped a little. 'I'm sure Nurse Sullivan did her best but I'm afraid there are some things I found which I can only describe as deplorable.'

Millie bristled. 'What things?'

'The lack of respect for my position for one,' said Miss Dutton. 'In future, when I walk into the room for handover, you are to rise.'

The nurses around the table stared at her in disbelief.

'Furthermore, when I give you an order you are to respond, "Yes, Superintendent." Do you understand?'

'Yes, Superintendent,' the nurses replied un-enthusiastically.

Miss Dutton turned her beady eyes on to Annie. 'In my day, Nurse Whoever-you-are, a proba-tionary nurse would know her place and only speak to a senior nurse when spoken to, and,' she gave Millie a glacial look, 'one thing I noticed you haven't done as acting superintendent, Sullivan, is the weekly room inspection.'

Millie held her gaze. 'That's because they haven't been done in any Nursing Association nurses' home that I know of since before the war and because they are an unnecessary intrusion into a nurse's private life.'

Miss Dutton's lips pulled even tighter. 'The war's over now and while others might be content to let standards slip, I am not. I will be inspecting each room weekly and fines will be imposed for rooms I deem to be below an acceptable standard. And, finally, there is a request from the council's welfare department for two nurses to help with screening returning servicemen for any health issues. It's between two and four each afternoon at the town hall. I'll devise a rota and post it on the noticeboard. It starts next week.' The corners of her mouth lifted. 'I'm sure all of you will be delighted to assist our valiant soldiers return to civilian life.'

The nurses glanced at each other nervously and then looked at Millie.

'Of course, we're happy to do what we can to help the boys coming back, Superintendent,' Millie said, in as level a tone as she could manage, 'but if we have to do an extra clinic in the middle of the afternoon, then on some days nurses will be working from eight o'clock in the morning until nine with only an hour at lunch and the same for supper. Do you think that's fair?'

Miss Dutton turned her flint-like eyes on Millie. 'Do you think it's fair that men who have fought for their country should just be discharged on to the streets?'

'Of course not, but–'

'Are you arguing with me, Sullivan?' asked Miss Dutton, her flint-like eyes boring into Millie.

'I am merely asking if nurses will now be required to work an eleven-hour day,' Millie replied coolly.

208

Miss Dutton looked away. 'Temporarily, until we recruit more nurses.' She closed the report book with a thump and stood up. She cast her gaze around the table and the nurses rose to their feet.

'And that's all I have to say at present about the changes I'm introducing, except to tell you I will be looking at ways of improving the days-off rota soon. Good day.' She tucked the report book under her arm and walked out.

The chairs scraped as nurses started to pick up their bags and make their way to breakfast. Connie and Beattie threaded their way through their colleagues to join Millie.

'Eleven-hour days and room inspection,' said Connie, rolling her eyes.

'And yes Superintendent, no Superintendent, three bags full Superintendent,' added Beattie, pulling a face. 'I'm surprised she didn't want us to salute her as well.'

'But the eleven-hour days are only until we get more staff, aren't they?' Annie asked as the four of them made their way towards the door.

'What Miss Dutton doesn't say, Annie,' said Millie ruefully, 'is that with a national shortage of trained nurses, hundreds leaving to get married and this Association paying at least two-and-six a week less than most of the others in London, where she's going to find them?'

The shop assistant behind the counter of the Co-operative store in Stratford had managed to keep her the-customer-is-always-right expression on her face for almost thirty minutes, but after bringing out the fourth set of bedding for Ruby to inspect, it was beginning to slip. As it was Tuesday afternoon the drapery department wasn't all that busy, but there were enough customers milling around to keep the sales staff occupied cutting lengths of curtaining or showing the latest line in tablecloths.

'What do you think, Doris?' Ruby asked, holding the sheet up to the light.

'It looks the same as the last one to me,' Millie's mother replied.

Ruby pulled a face. 'I thought the weave of the previous one was a little tighter but now I'm not sure. I don't want to waste coupons on something that will be threadbare in a year's time.'

As her mother and Ruby debated the weave, hemming and suitability of the bed linen, Millie stifled a yawn and forced her eyes to stay open. She had hoped to put her feet up before going out on her evening round but as it was almost three and they weren't nearly finished shopping, there was very little chance of that happening now.

Ruby's voice cut through the fog. 'Well, if you have nothing better, then this will have to do. I have to have something new to put on the guest beds for Christmas.' She flicked the sheet towards the assistant, who refolded it.

'That will be nine shillings and thruppence, please, Madam,' she said, totting up the cost on her pad. 'Have you a divvy number?'

'3062,' replied Ruby, handing over a ten-shilling note and her coupon book.

The assistant pulled a pair of scissors out of the pocket and snipped off the required number of coupons, and then popped the money, the top sheet of the bill and the coupons into a brass container, the size of a can of corned beef. Putting it in the mesh cradle above her head, she pulled the chain and the tin flew across the room on a taut wire above their heads and to the cashier sitting in a raised booth at the other side of the room. She rang up the amount on a large ornate till then sent the cassette back. The assistant caught it, took the change and the signed receipt out, and handed it to Ruby.

'Thank you, madam, and we hope to see you at the Co-operative store again soon,' she said in a tone that indicated otherwise.

Ruby tucked the brown-paper package under her arm. 'Not until you have better-quality stock in, you won't.' She turned to Millie and Doris. 'Time for tea, don't you think?'

They found a table by the window in the café at the front of the shop overlooking the Broadway. Setting their shopping on one chair, Millie, Ruby and Doris took the other three around the table. The Latino sounds of Edmundo Ros and his Rumba Band drifted over the restaurant from a domed Bakelite radio behind the till. Millie and her mother picked up an afternoon tea menu from the silver rack and cast their eye over it.

The waitress, a young brunette wearing a uniform at least two sizes too big, came over.

'Tea for three and a selection of cakes, please, and don't dawdle,' Ruby said. 'I have to catch the four-ten Green Line back to Ilford.'

The waitress scribbled it down and went off to get their order. Millie and her mother put the tea

211

menus back where they'd found them. Ruby opened her bag and took out her cigarettes.

'I thought you were going to buy some new linen, Doris,' Ruby said, lighting up.

Millie's mother shook her head. 'The old ones will do for a bit longer if I turn them sides to middle.'

The waitress arrived with the tea. Ruby rested her cigarette on the side of the ashtray and balanced the tea strainer on the first cup. 'Yes, well, if you're not using your coupons, I'll buy them off you. I could do with some new curtains for the bedrooms.'

'I would, but I've already given them to Millie for her bottom drawer,' Doris replied.

Ruby handed Doris her tea. 'I'm sure Amelia is very grateful, Doris, but you'll be in a pickle if you used all your coupons and find you need some new towels or pillow cases. Maybe it would be better to wait until she has a young man.'

'Millie's got a young man, Ruby,' Doris said, looking gleefully at her sister.

'Mum!' Millie said.

One of Ruby's finely plucked eyebrows rose. 'Amelia, why didn't you tell me?'

Millie's cheeks felt suddenly warm. 'There's nothing to tell, really. He–'

'He's a policeman at Arbour Square,' Doris said, leaning across the table towards her sister. 'And they met at the Regency.'

A nostalgic expression transfixed Ruby's face. 'Ah, the Regency,' she sighed. 'That's where I met Bernard. I remember it as clear as if it were yesterday. He'd only just come back from France and was still in his uniform. He looked so handsome. Of course, in those days we did real dancing, not like all this jitter-hopping and lindy-bugs nonsense they do nowadays.'

Ruby paused, as she always did when she mentioned her husband, who'd died leaving her a very nice nest egg and a corporation pension. She looked at Millie and her crimson lips twitched.

'So, your young man is a constable.'

'He's a sergeant actually, Aunt Ruby,' Millie said. 'And he was in the Desert Rats and fought at El Alamein and then in Sicily although, as we've only been out on a couple of dates, I don't think it's fair to call him my young man.'

Ruby nodded approvingly. 'I can't say it's before time. I'd been married five years and your mother had already had you by the time we were your age, Amelia. And if you want to keep this one, I'd advise you to always wear something nice, flowery – you know, feminine. Men like to have a pretty girl on their arm to show off. I'm only saying as I wouldn't want to see you left on the shelf.'

'Honestly,' Millie laughed, 'you're talking as if I'm thirty-five, not twenty-five. I've got years before I qualify as an old maid.'

'Perhaps, but you don't want to leave it too late. Doris! What on earth?'

Millie looked at her mother. Tears were streaming down her cheeks and her shoulders were shaking.

'Mum, what's wrong?' Millie asked, putting her hand over her mother's.

'It's th-th-this song,' she sobbed. 'Your dad

used to whistle it around the house all the time.'

Ruby unclipped her handbag and handed her sister a handkerchief.

Doris blew her nose. 'I'm sorry. Sometimes in the morning there is a moment just before I wake up when I think Arthur's still beside me and I'm happy. But then I realise he's not, and then the black cloud presses down on me again.' Her shoulders shook as she dissolved into tears again.

Ruby patted her sister's arm. 'I know it's hard, dear. But Arthur's been gone almost eight months now, and you know you can't keep bursting into tears at the drop of a hat like this. It's not good for you.'

Doris dabbed her eyes. 'You're right, Ruby, and I shouldn't give into it. And besides things are looking up and I've got some news of my own. I've got a job,' she said merrily. 'It's just in a shop but I am pleased.'

'That's marvellous, Mum,' said Millie.

'I agree. Just what you need to get you out and about,' said Ruby, taking out another cigarette and lighting it. 'After all, all the tears in the world won't bring dear Arthur back.'

Chapter Ten

Millie and Alex laughed at the quick retort from the speaker balanced precariously on a box. Like the crowd around them, they had stopped on their afternoon stroll in Hyde Park to lend an ear to the handful of orators putting the world to rights at Speakers' Corner.

The soapbox politician bowed to his audience and they started to drift away. Alex slipped his arm around Millie.

'They've unbricked Selfridges' window and put up a Christmas display. Do you want to stroll down and take a look?' he asked. 'Then we can really push the boat out and have a posh cup of tea in their café.'

'That's sounds perfect,' Millie replied, smiling up at Alex.

The frosty air had put a sparkle in his eyes and ruffled his hair in a way that made her want to run her fingers through it.

He tucked her hand into the crook of his arm. As they reached the three-arched monument, Alex pulled her into one of the cavities.

'Come here,' he said, gathering her to him.

A tingle of anticipation ran through Millie as he lowered his mouth on to hers. She curled herself into him and enjoyed the thrilling combination of his lips, arms and body. Millie's hands ran up his chest and around his neck. Alex shifted position.

215

One hand reached up and fixed her head while the other tightened. His legs and hips pressed against hers and she only just stopped herself from returning the gesture. They clung together for a long moment, then he released her lips. They strolled on and joined the Christmas shoppers in Oxford Street.

Although Selfridges still retained some of its scars from the direct hit the year before, it had done its best to get into the Christmas spirit. Its window displays weren't as extravagant as the ones Millie remembered as a child, but the sparkling Christmas trees, nodding reindeer and elves decked out in red and green, making toys for Santa's dash across the skies, certainly had children pressing their noses to the glass.

They stood gazing at it for a few minutes and then Alex hooked her arm in his again. 'I'd say it's time for that cuppa.'

As there were dozens of people waiting to travel up in the store's newly restored lifts, Millie and Alex decided to walk the three floors to the improvised tearoom. He guided her to a table on the far side of the room. The waitress came over and took their order.

'They've done the old place up just fine,' Alex said, helping Millie into her seat.

'You've been here before?'

'Course,' he said, pulling his chair in. 'I bring all my girlfriends here. Are you jealous?'

'No,' replied Millie primly.

Alex leaned back and stretched his long legs under the table. 'Not even a little bit?'

'Perhaps just a little.'

He grinned. 'Well, let me set your mind at rest, sweetheart. There's only you.'

'I know,' Millie replied, with an amused smile hovering over her lips. 'Who else would put up with your cheek?'

Alex laughed a deep rumbling laugh that rolled over her like a warm blanket. Their tea arrived. Millie poured it out and gave Alex his.

'Do you know, at one time tea was so expensive that it was kept under lock and key and often cost more per pound than a coachman's weekly wage,' Alex said as he stirred in his sugar.

Millie laughed. 'Is there no end to your talents, Mr Nolan? Art at the National, the development of steam power at the Science Museum, and now the history of tea?'

'I told you I learned about painting in Malta,' Alex replied.

'But it isn't just who painted them you know, but about the politics and history of the period, too,' said Millie.

He shrugged. 'I read a lot.'

'I try to as well, but even so,' she tilted her head. 'I'm really surprised your school didn't put you in for a scholarship to Raines or Coopers.'

A wry smiled lifted the corner of Alex's mouth. 'They did, but I was too young and stupid to understand what I was being offered, and by the time I realised what I'd thrown away, it was too late.'

Alex regarded her for a moment or two and then shifted forward. 'Remember I told you about the professor in the hospital and the art books?'

Millie nodded.

'Well, boredom was only half the reason why I started educating myself. Bob Hartley was the other. He and I joined on the same day in 1939 and a more mismatched couple of buggers you couldn't have found, Millie.' Alex laughed softly. 'Me scraping the doorframes at six-two and him only an inch or two taller than you. He was at university when hostilities started but joined up straight away. I used to rib him about always having his nose in a book, but he told me I had brains too and ought to make something more of myself. We came through the desert without a scratch, but our luck ran out when we hit a land-mine on the road to Monte Casino. Bob copped it instantly – I doubt he even knew. The jeep rolled and snapped my leg in three places. But waking up in hospital still alive made me realise that I'd been given a second chance, and I swore then I wasn't going to waste it this time. In fact – now don't laugh,' Alex gave Millie an oddly boyish smile, 'I signed up for a correspondence course with the University of London external programme, and when I finish my Higher School Certificate next summer I'll be able to apply to university.'

'My goodness, Alex,' Millie said. 'Why would I laugh?'

'Well, you know, a common bloke like me studying for a degree,' he replied.

Millie smiled. 'There's *nothing* common about you, Alex, and I'm actually very impressed. I don't know anyone with a Higher Certificate, let alone a degree. What are you going to study?'

218

Alex's relaxed smile returned. 'I fancy doing modern history,' he said. 'I'll have to do it the same way, as I can't afford to actually go to university, but once I've got a degree I'll be able to jump up the ranks to superintendent, if not higher, more quickly. I thought I might even buy myself a house somewhere nice like Forest Gate or East Ham.'

Millie looked astonished.

The expression in his eyes changed subtly. 'Of course, Millie, I don't want to live there alone,' he said pointedly.

Millie stared across the table at him. Alex held her gaze. The clock in the corner chimed four.

Alex broke the tension with a smile, and knocked back the last of his tea. 'I ought to get you back.'

The sun had set by the time they emerged on to the street. They strolled arm in arm towards Bond Street, but as they reached Butlins' main office Alex grabbed Millie's hand.

'Come on.'

They passed the windows containing tableaux of happy holidaymakers playing tennis and splashing in open-air swimming pools to the huge board with a strong man wearing an old-fashioned bathing suit and carrying a curvy young bathing belle, complete with frilly knickers and mob cap, under his arm. Both had oval holes instead of faces. The board had 'Butlins Holiday Camp' emblazed across the bottom.

'How much?' Alex asked the photographer waiting unobtrusively nearby, ready to snap prospective customers.

'One and six,' he replied, setting his camera in place.

'Quick, Millie,' Alex said, walking her around to the back of the screen.

'I feel daft,' she said, but looked through the gap nonetheless.

Alex did the same, slipping his arm around her waist as they stood there. The photographer took position and looked through his viewfinder.

'Cheese!' Alex tickled her, Millie giggled and there was a flash of light.

'He's going to send it to the section house,' Alex said, when he returned from paying the photographer. He put his arm around Millie. 'And when I look at it I'll remember how a hard-nut elementary school geezer like me managed to impress a smart grammar-school young lady like you.'

Millie stamped her feet on the thick coconut matting by the back door to shake the mud and ice from her shoes. She was frozen to the bone and her fingers were numb from gripping the handlebars, which was worrying, as it was only the middle of December. She hung her coat and hat on the peg. Putting down her bag, she rested on the radiator to get the warmth back into her legs and hands.

The door to the refectory opened and Beattie's head popped out.

'Thank goodness you're back early,' she said, walking down the hall towards Millie.

'Why?'

'Charlie Ross's wife had her baby last night.'

220

'Where's Connie?' asked Millie.

'In the treatment room.'

Connie was at the sink scrubbing a pair of forceps vigorously under the running water. She looked up as Millie walked in.

'Have you heard?' she asked, looking at Millie with red-rimmed eyes.

'Beattie just told me,' Millie replied, closing the door and going to her friend.

'Sally was called out to her last night. She was waiting for the right moment to tell me but Gladys got in first and gave me the happy tidings over breakfast. I bet it made her day,' Connie said bitterly.

Millie put her arm around her friend. 'Oh, Connie.'

Connie sniffed. 'Sally said he was dark like *her* but with Charlie's eyes. She also said the house smelt of garlic and that there was a big plaster Madonna and a bottle of holy water on the mantel.' She gave a hard laugh. 'I'm sure that will please Charlie's mother no end, seeing she's a strict Methodist.'

Millie hugged her. 'You're better off without him.'

'I know.' Connie pulled out a handkerchief and wiped her eyes. 'It just doesn't feel like that at the moment.'

'You just need a bit more time. That's all.'

'You're probably right.' Connie glanced up at the clock. 'You're back early.'

Millie dropped her arm. 'I cycled all the way to Beckton Flats, only to find the gypsies have moved on, so I've just had a futile journey of six miles along the Canning Town Road against an icy wind blowing up the Thames.'

'Well, it'll be dinner in half an hour, so you can help me put these instruments in this infernal contraption,' she said, tapping their new steriliser with the forceps.

Millie eyed the square metal box on little stubby legs that had been installed two weeks ago. 'It's funny how we've been asking for an autoclave for years and have been repeatedly told no, and then Miss Dutton asks for one and it turns up the next week.'

'I suppose we should be thankful for that, at least,' said Connie. 'But it doesn't stop her being a bloody witch. Did you hear she didn't believe that Eva was really sick and got her out of bed to go out on her rounds this morning?'

'But she had a temperature last night,' replied Millie.

'Miss Dutton took it again this morning and pronounced her fit for work. She'll be lucky if she doesn't have double pneumonia by Friday.'

The door opened and Miss Dutton walked in. Millie and Connie stood up straight.

The superintendent's lips pulled together. 'Sister Sullivan, shouldn't you be out on your rounds?'

'I finished early,' Millie replied.

'And so you thought you would loiter around chatting until dinner,' Miss Dutton said.

'I thought I'd pick up a bedpan for Mrs Finn and deliver it this afternoon instead of tomorrow now that I have some spare time this morning,' Millie replied.

Miss Dutton's gaze flickered between Millie and Connie. 'Then why are you in here wasting time with Sister Byrne?'

Millie gave her a cool look. 'Because I care about the nurses who live in Munroe House and if one of them is upset or sick I try to comfort them. That is, after all, what nurses do, isn't it, Miss Dutton?'

The superintendent's neck flushed and her eyes narrowed as she glared at Millie. 'A nurse's first duty is to her patients, Sister Sullivan, and if you want to continue working for the Association then you and Sister Byrne had better remember that.' She turned and opened the door. 'And your case is cluttering up the hall. You'd better move it before I report you to the committee for not taking proper care of it.' She slammed out.

Connie looked anxiously at Millie. 'She wouldn't sack us, would she?'

'No, of course not,' replied Millie, with far more conviction that she felt.

Millie walked over to the loans cupboard and lifted a china slipper-pan down from the shelf. 'I'd better whip this around to Mrs F before the gong goes. I'll see you in a while.'

Millie tucked the bedpan under her arm and walked back into the hall. She put on her coat and hat and picked up her case. Someone opened the front door and a blast of wind and rain blew down the hall. A meaty smell of stew that had seeped out of the kitchen drifted into Millie nose and her stomach rumbled. Ignoring it, Millie wrapped her scarf tightly around her neck then steeled herself to face another two miles' cycle.

'Right,' said Millie, putting down a cup of cocoa in front of Annie, who was sitting opposite her. 'Let's go through a few cases.'

It was almost nine o'clock and while their fellow nurses were gathered around the radio for *Variety Band Box*, Millie and Annie were sitting at the table in the treatment room with the third edition of the *Hand Book for Queen's Nurses*, the current *Faber's Nurse's Pocket Encyclopaedia Diary and Guide* and *Nursing and Diseases for Sick Children*, along with the past six volumes of *Queen's Nurses' Magazine*.

Annie took a sip of her cocoa as Millie settled herself in the chair.

'I'll read the list of patients out to you and give you time to make a few notes. Then I'll ask you some questions exactly as the examining matron will do in the real exam. Do you understand?'

Annie nodded.

Millie scanned down her preparation notes. 'You have six patients on your morning list, Nurse Fletcher. Mrs White, who has just delivered her second baby two days ago. Mrs Green, who is a diabetic and needs insulin. Mr Brown, who has pneumonia and has been prescribed penicillin. Mrs Black, who is bed-bound and incontinent. Master Blue, who is seven years old and recovering from whooping cough. And then, lastly, Mr Pink, who has been sent home from hospital after having abdominal surgery to repair a stomach ulcer.'

Annie scribbled in her notebook. Millie looked up at the clock and watched the second hand go around the dial twice then spoke.

'Firstly, Nurse Fletcher, I would like you to tell me which order would you visit your patients, and why?'

Annie pulled her shoulders back and looked at Millie. 'I would visit Mrs Green first, as she will not be able to have her breakfast until I have given her insulin. Then I would visit Mrs White, as maternity and miscarriage cases are a priority. I would then go back to the clinic to change my uniform and bag before doing my general nursing.'

'Why is that?' asked Millie.

'To reduce the risk of infection,' answered Annie.

'Continue, Nurse Fletcher,' said Millie in a ponderous tone.

'Then I would visit Mr Pink because he has just been discharged from hospital and will be anxious waiting for the nurse. And also, as he has a surgical wound, it will need twice-daily dressings, so an early visit and a mid-afternoon visit would reduce the chances of his dressing leaking. After that I would visit Mr Brown to give—'

'Wouldn't it be better to visit Mr Brown before Mr Pink, Nurse Fletcher? After all, an injection would take only twenty minutes, whereas you might be with Mr Pink for over an hour.'

Annie twisted her pen in her hand. 'Err ... well, perhaps I...'

'Annie!' cut in Millie. 'You can't afford to dither. If the examiners question your decisions, you must have an answer ready. But if you go blank, don't um and ah: put on a face like you're considering the question until the answer comes to you. Now, take a deep breath and explain to me

225

about Mr Brown.'

'Sorry.' Annie sat upright again. 'Although penicillin has to be given twice a day, Mr Brown has a contagious infection and should be seen after Mr Pink to prevent cross-infection. As long as there is sufficient time between each dose, then Mr Brown will have no ill effects from being seen a little later.'

Millie nodded approvingly. 'And a sufficient time would be...?'

'Eight to ten hours, which means that Mr Brown's second injection would have to be given during the evening visits. After Mr Brown I would...' she ran through the rest of the fictitious patients, putting them in the correct clinical order.

'What would you do if you noticed Mrs White's baby had a sticky eye?'

'I would call the doctor out straight away in case the child has contracted syphilis...'

Millie stared at her hard.

'I ... I mean gonorrhoea,' stammered Annie. 'Because if it goes untreated, the disease could cause blindness.'

'Good,' Millie said, smiling reassuringly. 'Now, if I might ask you a little more about Master Blue. He is out of the danger period, but isn't making as speedy a recovery as he should because he has lost his appetite. What would you do?'

'I would try to encourage him to eat by making beef tea or an egg or milk jelly to tempt him.'

'Can you tell me how to make those particular invalid foods?'

Annie explained the two recipes fully, including adding extra vitamins and advising the child's mother to obtain extra rations from the local food office.

'Very good. Now please tell me who provides the midwifery services and under which parliamentary act?'

Annie smiled. 'Under the Midwifery Act of 1936 the local authority has a statutory duty to provide domiciliary midwifery services and to charge patients according to their circumstances,' she said, quoting the *Hand Book for Queen's Nurses* almost word for word.

Millie glanced at the last few questions. 'I'd like to finish off by asking you about the midwifery service.'

Annie looked attentive.

'Firstly, what constitutes a premature baby?'

'If a baby is less than five pounds or twenty inches in length,' Annie replied, without hesitation.

'And how would you advise a mother to feed a premature baby?'

'Breast-feeding is best for all babies,' answered Annie. 'And if the baby is too weak to suck, then the milk can be drawn off and given to the infant using a sterile feeding bottle.'

'And if the mother is too ill to feed or loses her milk?'

'Then the doctor will usually decide the regime, but if he leaves it to the midwife then the standard practice is either one part to sixteen sweetened condensed milk to water or one part to twenty-six full-cream dried milk.' She clasped her hand over her mouth. 'No ... no ... it's the other way around. Or is it? Or is it one to eight

227

and one to sixteen? No, that's after seven days.' Her mouth dropped open and she stared terror-stricken at Millie. 'I can't remember. I ...' her face crumpled. 'I'm going to fail, I know I am.'

Millie reached over and closed her hand over Annie's. 'No, you're not!'

'I am,' sobbed Annie. 'It's only a week until I have to face the board and I can't even remember the right constituents of artificial feeding.'

'You passed your hospital finals with very good marks,' Millie said.

'I don't know how. I hadn't slept for a week worrying about them and when I turned the paper over I panicked so much I couldn't understand a word of what was written for a good fifteen minutes. Doing the Queen's Nurses' written exams will be bad enough, but facing three examiners firing questions at me sounds much worse.' Annie slumped in her chair.

Millie shook her. 'Yes, you will, Annie Fletcher, because you are one of the best student QNs the St George's and St Dunstan's District Nursing Association has ever had.'

Annie brushed away her tears with the heel of her hand. 'Am I?'

'You are, and you know I wouldn't say it if it wasn't true.' Millie squeezed her hand. 'But what you have to do is to start believing in yourself. Now come on, finish your cocoa and we'll go through a few more questions before lights out.'

Chapter Eleven

Millie left Dr Gingold's surgery and unchained her bike. After negotiating her way through the men with pneumatic drills digging up the pavement, she hopped on her cycle and pedalled slowly westwards, turning into Wellclose Square.

The tall, four-storey houses in the square that were almost two hundred years old had once been home to wealthy ship and dock owners. In their day each would have had an army of servants living in the attic rooms, and a coach and pair in hand stabled at the back.

The carriages, horses and servants had long departed and in their place were drunks, cheap doss-houses and seedy cafés whose names changed after each police raid, although the clientele remained the same. The pimps and girls were asleep now, so at midday, in her nurse's uniform, Millie was quite safe to use the square as a cut-through to the Highway. It was a different matter after dark, when the area became little more than an open-air brothel, with couples using memorials in the Danish church in the middle as impromptu couches.

Whizzing past the dilapidated old Wilton's Music Hall on the north side of the square, Millie swung left and on to the Highway, then past the bombed-out shell of St George's Church on her left and rolled to a halt outside Letterman's chemist.

She got off her bike and was just about to go into the chemist's when a woman's voice screamed, 'Nurse!'

Millie looked around. A woman in a tight skirt and jumper, and with bleached hair piled high and red lips, waved frantically, and ran toward her on dangerously high heels across the road.

'Oh, Miss, it's Gina. You 'ave to come, and quick about it,' she said, puffing to a stop in front of Millie.

'You won't need your bike,' the woman said, as Millie started to unchain it. 'It's only in the square. I'm Olive, by the way.'

They crossed Wellclose Square to the Shangri-La Café in the corner. It was the ground floor of one of the tall Georgian houses and had a blacked-out front window and a scruffy door with a painting of a pagoda, a couple of geishas and the name of the shop in garish gold lettering.

Olive looked nervously at Millie. 'We have to walk through the main part to get to the stairs, Sister, and well, it might be best if you keep your eyes down, as Mikal – he runs the place – can be a bit funny.'

She pushed open the door and walked in. Clutching her bag tightly in her hand, Millie followed.

The smell of tobacco and cheap booze hit Millie as soon as she entered. The main area of the café had been the front parlour of the house, but there were no traces of cosy domesticity in the room now. Lino, not carpet, covered the floor, and at the far end was a homemade counter with a greasy individual in a dirty shirt leaning on it. All around the room were crudely made tables and chairs with men in rough clothes sitting at them.

Although it was not yet noon, all the men had either glasses of spirit or bottles of beer in their hands. Sitting at the table alongside them or lounging by the counter were half a dozen young women dressed only in flimsy underslips with no brassieres, girdles or knickers beneath, and stockings held up by elastic garters. Because of the muted light in the room and the panstick and rouge on the girls' faces, it was difficult to be sure, but most of the girls couldn't have been much older than twenty.

A couple of the men looked across and leered. Millie averted her eyes and followed Olive through the room and up an uncarpeted staircase. As she turned on to the landing at the top a door opened and a heavily built African man lumbered out, buttoning up his trousers as he pushed past her. Millie glanced into the room and saw an iron-framed bed that had a faded candlewick bedspread crumpled on it, a bottle of beer and two glasses on a table. Crouched over a bucket in the corner was a young redhead in the same state of undress as the women below, washing between her legs with a grubby flannel.

'These are the visitors' rooms,' Olive explained. 'We sleep above.'

Millie followed Olive up to the top of the house to what once had been the servants' quarters.

'Gina's in here,' said Olive, pushing open the last door. Millie went in.

Although this room, like the one below, was sparsely furnished, with two old iron beds pushed against opposite walls, the magazine pictures of flowers and animals pinned to the walls, and the brightly coloured fabric threaded across the window on a piece of string gave the room a touchingly childlike feel.

'It's all right, Gina, my love, I have the nurse to see you,' Olive said, going to the bed on the far side of the room and bending over the woman lying on it.

Millie went over and put her bag down.

Gina turned her head and looked up at Millie. Her enormous eyes shimmered with fever.

'Hello, Gina,' Millie said, casting her gaze over the beads of sweat glistening on coffee-coloured skin. 'I've come to see what's wrong with you. Have you pain anywhere?'

Gina slid her hand on to her lower stomach and mouthed something but no sound came out. Her focus wavered and eyes rolled upwards. Millie took her hand and felt the young woman's racing pulse.

'How long as she been like this?' Millie asked, putting the back of her hand on Gina's forehead.

'She has been a bit off-colour for a day or so but yesterday night she started burning up,' Olive answered. Her gaze flickered uncertainly over Millie's face. 'She had a bit of trouble.'

Millie pulled back the bedcovers and drew back as the smell of gangrene wafted up. She cast her eyes quickly over Gina's thin, febrile body under the threadbare nightdress. Millie lifted up the girl's gown. Stale blood mingled with yellowy discharge streaked down the inside of Gina's thighs, forming a brown stain on the sheet beneath.

Millie stood up. 'When did she have the abortion?'

Olive looked anxious. 'Abortion? I don't know anything about that.'

The door burst open and a bony old woman with frizzy orange hair, a jagged scar down her right cheek and wearing a dressing gown with ostrich feathers around the edge walked in.

'Who the fuck are you?' she asked, glaring at Millie.

'Did you do this?' Millie replied, pointing at the woman on the bed.

'Do what?' she asked nonchalantly.

'Perform an abortion on this woman.'

The madam blanched for a second, then rounded on Olive. 'Did you tell er that?'

Fear flashed into Olive's eyes. 'I said no such thing, Margie. Honest.'

The commotion had brought three or four other women out of their rooms and they now stood looking in.

Margie turned back to Millie. 'See, it's just 'er monthlies, that's all, and she'll be as right as rain tomorrow.'

Millie pulled the cover off Gina. 'She'll likely be dead tomorrow unless she gets to hospital.'

'Oh Jesus! Mary, Mother of God,' Olive wailed, crossing herself and sinking to her knees beside the bed.

'There's no time for that,' Millie said firmly. 'Fetch some cold water and start washing your friend down with this,' Millie snatched the frayed towel from the back of the chair and handed it to Olive.

233

Olive ran out of the room. Millie went to the window and, after a bit of jigging, pushed it up. 'It should keep her temperature down until the ambulance arrives.'

Margie forced a laugh. 'Mikal won't allow no ambulance buggers up here.'

'What won't Mikal allow?'

Millie looked up. A tall man who, had he been dressed in a flowing Bedouin robe instead of a zoot suit, would have been the epitome of an Arab sheikh, stood in the doorway.

He half turned his head. 'Get back to work.'

The women outside the room scurried away as both Olive and Margie shrunk into the corner.

'Who are you?' he asked, as his eyes ran slowly over Millie.

'I'm the district nurse for this area, and Olive asked me to see her friend who wasn't well.'

'Well, you've seen her,' he replied, grabbing Millie's arm painfully. 'Now, out.' He propelled her towards the door.

Millie snatched her arm back and went over to the bed. 'This woman needs an ambulance – now!'

Mikal regarded Millie levelly for a moment. 'Margie!'

'Yes, Mikal,' Margie replied, looking nervously up at him.

'Give Gina a couple of aspirin. And get her,' he jabbed his finger at Millie, 'out before she loses us custom.'

He turned to go, but Millie stepped in front of him. 'Can't you see she's very ill?' she said, pointing at the woman lying on the bed. 'She's got septicaemia.'

Mikal laughed. 'Septa what?'

'Blood poisoning caused by her recent abortion,' replied Millie. 'If she doesn't get medical treatment she will die.'

Olive crossed herself again. 'Oh, Jesus, Mary, Mother of God, if I'd have known I–'

Mikal shot Olive a razor-sharp look and instantly she stopped talking.

He looked innocently at Millie. 'Abortion? What is this you say? We don't know nothing about any such a thing, do we, Margie?'

Margie laughed nervously. 'Course not, Mikal. We ain't got nuffink to do wiv anyfink like that, but I can't answer to what these girls get up to when my bleedin' back's turned.'

Millie went back to Gina and put her hand on her forehead again. The chill from the open window had stopped her temperature rising any further, but she was still burning and now her eyes were blank. If Millie didn't get her to casualty soon, it would be too late. She stood up.

'Look, I'm not interested in who she went to see or who helped her get rid of her baby. What I'm concerned with is saving her life,' Millie said.

Mikal strolled over and glanced dispassionately at Gina. 'You, nursey,' he said, smiling and moving his hand across Millie's breasts as he lifted up her Queen's Nurse Badge, 'you fix her.'

'I've just told you, she needs to be seen by a doctor,' Millie answered as firmly as she could. 'Now, either you let me call the ambulance or I walk out of this house and straight to Leman Street police station.'

He glared hatefully at Millie, and then an artless

smile, full of teeth and goodwill, spread across his face. 'Of course, nursey,' he said, stepping back and sweeping a bow. 'Anything you say, nursey.'

Millie turned to Olive. 'Get that water and sponge her down till I get back.'

Olive nodded and Millie picked up her bag.

Mikal grabbed Millie's arm again. 'Tell them to use the back stairs. And don't show your face again.' He threw her aside and strode out of the room.

Millie walked down the same polished corridor she'd passed up and down as a student nurse so often, now heading towards Truman Ward. She side-stepped to let an orderly pushing a theatre trolley and a student nurse caring for the un-conscious patient on it pass, and then she pushed open the heavy oak door to the ward.

Inside was the familiar hum of quietly spoken voices punctuated by the squeak of metal wheels as a nurse pushed a patient in a wheelchair towards the communal day-room at the far end of the long ward. The ward sister, who was giving out medication from the mobile enamelled drug cabinet, looked up from her task as the door clicked shut behind Millie.

She closed the lid and bustled towards Millie, the lace of her nurse's cap flapping around her scraped-back grey hair with each step.

'Can I help you?' she said, taking in Millie's navy uniform, Queen's Nurse badge and Glad-stone bag in one quick sweep.

Millie smiled. 'Good morning, Sister Truman,' she said, addressing her in the traditional way. 'I know it's not visiting time but, if it's not too inconvenient could I pop in quickly and see Miss Gina Pereira, the young girl who was brought in from Wellclose Square yesterday.'

The ward sister's mouth pulled tight. 'I'm expecting Mr Corfield, the consultant, to arrive any time.'

'I'd be most grateful if you would, as I'm the nurse who called the ambulance,' explained Millie.

The ward sister looked her over again. 'Very well,' she said, grudgingly.

She marched down the middle of the ward and Millie followed. She stopped at the end of the last bed.

Millie looked down at Gina who now, with her hair combed neatly either side of her face and devoid of her make-up, looked little more than a child.

She was pale with dark circles under her eyes but she didn't appear feverish. There was an inverted glass bottle half full of glucose suspended from a stand beside the bed. This dripped via a thin rubber tube into the needle in the back of her right hand, which was bandaged to a splint.

'How is she?' Millie asked.

'As well as can be expected,' the sister replied flatly. 'She hasn't woken up properly yet, so it still could go either way.'

Millie's gaze drifted back to Gina, whose head barely made a dent in the pillow. 'Poor girl.'

The sister tutted. 'Wicked girl, more like. I wouldn't waste my sympathy.'

Millie looked aghast.

'Excuse me, Sister,' a cultured voice said. 'I've just seen Mr Corfield going into Booth Ward.'

Millie turned. Standing behind her was a tall nurse who was probably a year or two younger than herself. The lilac-striped uniform complemented her fair colouring perfectly and her air of calm composure was further emphasised by her broad forehead and neatly swept back hair. As she was in the middle of her morning work, she'd removed the long detachable sleeves from her uniform. She looked serenely at them and although her eyes were ice blue, there was nothing cold in their expression.

Alarm flashed across the ward sister's ruddy face. 'Bother. I haven't got the notes in order yet.' Her sharp eyes flickered over the blonde nurse. 'You should have told me sooner, Villiers.'

'My apologies, Sister,' Nurse Villiers replied, without a trace of remorse. 'Shall I take over?'

'Yes, and then make sure the patients are tidy and sitting on their beds, as Mr Corfield requires.' She glanced at Millie. 'And don't you be too long.'

'No, Sister.'

Sister Truman marched off.

Nurse Villiers turned to Millie and smiled pleasantly. 'I take it you're the district nurse who called the ambulance for Gina.'

'Yes, her friend Olive stopped me on my rounds and took me to her,' Millie replied.

'And I also hear tell that you marched into a brothel and did battle with the pimp,' Nurse Villiers said, the cultured tone of her voice making the word pimp sound oddly comical.

'Well it wasn't quite like that, but I did have to

insist quite firmly that Gina went to hospital,' replied Millie.

Nurse Villiers' eyes lit up with admiration. 'How terribly brave of you.'

'Not really.' Millie laughed. 'To tell the truth, I was quaking in my boots, but I had to because...'

'If you hadn't, she would have died,' Nurse Villiers said.

Millie's gaze returned to the sick young woman in the bed. 'How is she really?'

Nurse Villiers took Gina's hand gently and looked down at her. 'Alas, she is still very poorly and it might be a few days before we know for certain. But she is young and with God's blessing she will recover.'

Millie raised an eyebrow. 'So you don't subscribe to the ward sister's view about shoving girls like Gina out of sight.'

'I certainly do not.' Nurse Villiers' fine brows drew together. 'If our Lord himself looked with compassion on women such as Gina, should we not follow his example?'

'Well, yes we should,' replied Millie. 'Unfortunately most people think that girls like Gina choose to go on the streets, whereas in my experience young women are often tricked into prostitution by...'

'...loathsome scoundrels such as the one you confronted yesterday,' Nurse Villiers finished.

'Exactly.'

Millie stared at Nurse Villiers for a moment, then glanced at her watch. 'I ought to get on. I've still got three patients to see before dinnertime. Will you please tell Sister Truman I said thank you for letting me pop in.'

'Of course,' Nurse Villiers replied. 'And if you telephone about this time tomorrow I will tell you how Gina is progressing.'

'That's very kind of you.'

Millie turned to walk back up the ward and Nurse Villiers fell into step next to her.

'It's all right – I can see myself out,' Millie said, glancing past the younger nurse to where the ward sister was dashing back and forth across the ward. 'I don't want to hold you up any further, not with the consultant due any moment.'

A quirky smile lifted the corner of Nurse Villiers' mouth. 'I must confess, Sister Sullivan, that when I said I saw Mr Corfield going into Booth Ward I should have added that just as he reached the door he was called back to theatre, so I fear he may be some time.' She opened the door. 'It's been a pleasure to meet you, Sister Sullivan.'

Millie grinned. 'And, Nurse Villiers, it's been a pleasure to meet you, too. I hope we run into each other again sometime.'

Millie swung herself around the bottom of the stairs as the grandfather clock in the hall chimed six-thirty. Millie yawned. It wasn't surprising she was weary. She hadn't got in until midnight. Forcing her eyes open to clear them of sleep, Millie made her way into the refectory. As Christmas was only two weeks away, Millie had been delegated to approach Miss Dutton about the arrangements. She'd begrudgingly given them a couple of pounds out of the petty cash so they could order a tree and now, thanks to two hours' hard work the day before, the bare refectory had jolly coloured paperchains strung across it, with Chinese lanterns made from cardboard and painted tissue dangling between.

Beattie and Connie were already sitting at the end of the table, so Millie collected her porridge and toast from the breakfast sideboard and joined them. Beattie poured her a mug of tea and pushed it over.

Millie yawned again and her two friends exchanged an amused look.

'So, how is Alex?' Beattie asked as Millie stirred in her sugar. Although she tried to stop it, a smile spread across Millie's face.

'Wonderful,' she sighed, thinking Saturday couldn't come fast enough.

He'd been on lates all week and although she'd met him for a quick coffee in the Blue Anchor Café in Sutton Street the day before, it wasn't the same. After all, they couldn't really canoodle surrounded by dockers scoffing their dinners down.

'I shouldn't wonder if he doesn't pop the question soon,' said Beattie.

Connie winked. 'If he hasn't already.'

Millie felt a blush rising in her cheeks. 'Don't be silly, we've only been seeing each other for a few weeks.'

'How's your mum?' Beattie asked.

'As busy as ever. When I got around there yesterday she'd just finished making jam tarts for the Sunday School's Christmas party this week,' Millie frowned. 'I'm a bit worried she's doing too much though as she still seems below par. But every time I mention the subject she says it keeps

241

her out of trouble. I thought I might take a week's holiday and take her away somewhere in the summer to give her a rest. Perhaps to East-bourne or Brighton, or maybe even Torquay.'

'I might join you,' said Connie. 'I could do with a bit of a break myself, if your mum doesn't mind.'

'I'm sure she won't,' Millie replied.

'I'd come, too,' said Beattie. 'But I've got a feeling Alex isn't the only man around here thinking about popping the question. So me and Colin might have plans of our own in June.'

Connie's face lit up. 'Oh, Beattie,' she squealed. 'How do you know?'

Beattie laughed. 'Because he's insisted on coming home with me next Saturday and he wanted to make sure my dad wasn't playing in a golf tournament all day.'

A little jab of unhappiness caught Millie in her chest as she remembered her father joking that he'd send packing any young man who wanted to run 'his little girl' up the aisle.

The refectory door burst open and Annie dashed in, followed by the other three student Queen's Nurses.

'They've just arrived,' she shouted, waving a buff envelope above her head.

All the nurses in the room looked expectantly at them.

Millie beckoned Annie over and she wove her way towards them through the tables and chairs.

The other students did the same to join their nurse tutors, and then they tore open their enve-lopes.

Annie sat down opposite Millie, held the envelope out in front of her with both hands, and stared at it.

A loud cheer went up on the other side of the room as Eva and Sally hugged their student, Joan.

'What are you waiting for?' asked Connie.

Annie looked forlornly around. 'What if I've let you down?'

'For the love of all mercies,' said Millie, 'open the ruddy thing.'

Annie stared at the envelope for a second longer, then shoved her finger under the flap and tore along the fold. She drew out the one-page letter and unfolded it with trembling hands. Millie and her two friends held their breath as Annie's blue eyes scanned down the page twice and then looked up.

'Well? Have you passed?' asked Millie.

Annie offered her the letter. Millie took it and quickly read it.

'Well, put us out of our misery. What's it say?' asked Connie.

Millie grinned. 'Not only has our Annie passed, but she got a merit on her first paper and a distinction on her second.' She turned the sheet around so the other two could see.

'Oh, Annie!' shouted Connie as she threw her arms around her.

Beattie did the same, creating a nurse sandwich with a sobbing Annie as the filling.

After a moment they let go of her and went over to congratulate the other students, all of whom had also passed their exams.

Millie stood up and went around the table to Annie.

'Thank you,' said Annie, laughing and crying all at the same time.

'You did it, not me,' said Millie, hugging her.

'But I couldn't have done it without your help,' said Annie, wiping her wet cheeks with the back of her hand. 'And it's the best Christmas present.'

Millie hugged her again. 'Congratulations, Sister Fletcher, and how do you fancy taking on the Turner Street patch in the New Year?'

Arm in arm, Millie and Alex turned into Anthony Street just a few moments after five-thirty. The fog from the river that swirled around them seemed to reach right into Millie's bones and she was glad they would be snug inside her mother's front room very soon. Mr Gilbert and his wife, dressed in their Sunday best, waved to Millie as they hurried off to evensong.

Alex glanced along the street. 'Which house does your mum live at?'

'Number seventy-one. With the green door,' Millie replied.

'I'm looking forward to meeting her,' Alex said. 'Do you think she'll have some baby photographs of you that I can see?'

Millie rolled her eyes. 'Unfortunately, she will.'

They stopped in front of her mother's door and Millie noticed a couple of curtains at the windows opposite flickering.

'Will I pass muster, Miss Sullivan?' he asked, double-stepping to attention.

Millie's gaze ran over his well-fitted suit, regimental tie and polished shoes, and then moved on to regard his abundant black hair, square chin and the strong jaw. He most certainly would, in any woman's book.

The corner of her mouth lifted in a crooked smile. 'You might just about scrape through.'

He grinned and Millie knocked on the door.

Alex's eyes held hers for a moment, and then the lock clicked and Millie looked away. The door opened and her mum stood there smiling at them.

Doris was wearing one of her best dresses, a russet-coloured one that highlighted the streaks of auburn remaining in her hair. Tied around her waist was the totally impractical but very pretty frilly apron Ruby had bought her for her last birthday.

Millie stepped in. Alex ducked his head and followed.

Millie gave her mother a peck on the cheek. 'Hello, Mum. This is Alex Nolan.'

He offered her mother his hand. 'Good afternoon, Mrs Sullivan. I'm so pleased to meet you.'

'And I'm pleased to meet you, too, Alex.' Doris slowly looked up at him. 'Millie's told me all about you.'

He winked. 'I 'ope not.'

Doris laughed. 'You didn't tell me how cheeky your young man was, Millie.' She ushered them in. 'I'll make us all a nice cup of tea.'

She started towards the kitchen, but Millie stepped in front of her. 'I'll make it, Mum.'

'All right dear, if you don't mind,' her mother replied, settling herself into the armchair by the fire.

245

Alex took the seat opposite and Millie left the room.

She returned ten minutes later carrying the tray of tea just in time to hear her mother tell Alex how amazed she was that so many people had turned up to her husband's funeral.

'From what Millie has told me about her father, Mrs Sullivan, I'm sure he's fondly remembered by all who knew him.'

'That's very kind of you to say so,' Doris said. 'What about your family? Are they local?'

Millie poured them all a cup of tea and then handed them around as Alex told Doris briefly about his mum and gran, and brother and sisters.

'What was the service like today, Mum?' Millie asked.

'Splendid, and I told the vicar so when I left,' her mother replied cheerfully. 'I've been asked to be on the committee of the Mother's Union and help organise next summer's fete.'

'But you're already doing the flower rota and church cleaning,' Millie said, unable to hide her concern. 'Not to mention being on your feet for eight hours a day in the shop.'

'Well, it keeps me out of trouble,' Doris replied. She picked up the cake slice. 'A piece of sponge, Alex?'

'That would go down a treat,' he replied, picking up a tea plate. Doris gave him a slice of cake and cut herself and Millie one too.

'Did Millie tell you, Mrs Sullivan, that she thought I was a crook?' Alex said, as Millie sat next to him on the sofa.

'Alex!'

Her mother laughed. 'No, she didn't, but I'm not surprised. She always was one to let her imagination run away with her.'

'And that she only found out what I really did for a living because some idiot on A Relief arrested a pregnant woman who went into labour in the cells,' he added, shifting position and moving a little nearer to Millie.

'She told me about the poor girl in the cell, but not about meeting you there,' Doris replied.

Millie glanced shyly at Alex. 'Well, we hadn't really got to know each other then.'

He smiled at her and Millie's heart did a double step. 'And it's a bit of a miracle we have at all, what with my and Millie's shifts being at odds most of the time.'

'But she did tell me you were a gunner in the Eighth Army. Arthur sat up every night listening to the BBC commentary about the battles in El Alamein. Do you remember, Millie?'

'Yes I do,' replied Millie, thinking of those nights behind the blackout curtains with bombs dropping all around.

Alex popped the last square of his cake in his mouth and washed it down with his tea. 'It weren't no picnic, Mrs Sullivan, and I've seen some things I won't forget in a hurry, but it weren't all death and destruction. We had some laughs, too.' A smile spread across his face. 'There was this one time when me and the boys had been stuck in the same fox-hole for almost three weeks and we had to do something about the blooming lice.'

Doris looked puzzled. 'Lice?'

'Yer, great big fat ones,' he held up his little finger, 'the size of your nail, that lived in your underwear by day and feasted on you all night.'

'Oh dear,' said Millie's mother.

'Well, one day me and the boys had had enough, so we found an empty petrol drum, which we filled with water and lit a fire under. Then we stripped off and dumped our vests and pants in to boil off the parasites like you do with bed bugs.'

'What a good idea,' said Doris.

Alex laughed. 'I'm afraid it wasn't, Mrs Sullivan, because Army-issue underwear is made of wool and the whole lot shrank and,' he slapped his knee, 'we all had to march in our birthday suits through camp to the quartermaster to get new sets issued.'

Doris put her hand up to cover her mouth. 'Oh no.'

'Oh, yes,' replied Alex holding his side. 'Can you imagine what a right bunch of Charlies we looked like?'

Millie's gaze flickered over Alex's broad shoulders and long legs, and tried not to.

She picked up the teapot. 'More tea?'

'Yes, please,' said Alex. 'And if there's a bit of spare cake to go with it that would be grand.'

'There you go,' Doris said, cutting him another thick slice and plonking it on his plate. 'Is there anything else you'd like?'

Alex's eyes twinkled. 'Well, now you ask, Mrs Sullivan, I don't suppose you have any photos of Millie as a baby?'

248

Chapter Twelve

Millie and her mother took their places at the back of the queue at the cooked-meat counter, in Watney Street Sainsbury's. The shop was, in fact, two shops on the west side of Watney Street, with a connecting passage between them. Both parts of the shop were decorated exactly the same, with dark green tiles to waist height on all the walls, and cream above.

On one side of the shop there were two long, marble-covered counters behind which the white-coated assistants stood ready to help customers. This was where dry groceries such as tea, sugar and dried fruit were sold. Each purchase would be shovelled from a large sack behind the counter and on to a sheet of grey sugar-paper on the scales, the assistant swiftly moving brass weights off and on until the needle hovered in the middle. Then, with a deft twist of the wrist they would scoop it off and fold it into a packet before sealing it with a tight tuck.

The other side of the shop, where Millie and her mother stood now, had four wooden-fronted counters, each with a particular speciality: cold meats, cheeses, butter and eggs. The shopper had to purchase what they required from one counter before joining the queue at the next. It was long-winded and time-consuming, but woe betide anyone who sent in a child to hold a place in a queue.

Doris tutted. 'You'd think we'd seen the back of all this now it is all over but, if anything, it's worse.'

The stout woman in front, with a snotty-nosed infant clinging to her skirts, turned. 'And have you heard the latest? They're going to ration bread.'

'No!' said the woman behind Millie who'd just joined the line. 'I don't know why they don't just ration the air you breathe and have done with it, Dot.' She folded her arms across her ample bosom. 'My youngest boy's just come back from France and is nothing but skin and bone. 'Ow am I supposed to feed him up on a forkful of gristle each week, I ask you?'

'Mine was just the same, Rita,' Dot replied, pulling her child out of the path of a woman hobbling with the aid of a wooden stick towards the cheese counter. 'I don't know what that Army was feeding them all this time.'

The queue shuffled forward and Dot looked Millie over. 'Weren't you at Maurice Lamb's funeral?'

Millie nodded. 'I was his district nurse.'

Dot clicked her fingers. 'That's right. You were standing at the back. I didn't see you at the Rose after though.'

'I had to get on with my visits.'

'Pity, as it were a lovely spread,' said Dot.

'This is my mother, Doris,' said Millie. 'She's just moved into Anthony Street.'

'Number seventy-one?' asked Dot knowingly.

'Yes,' said Doris.

'That were old Eli Pinnock's place. He lived

250

there for more years than I care to remember.' Dot's work-worn face lifted in a nostalgic smile. 'I don't know. I still can't get used to walking past the 'ouse and not seeing him sitting outside in that scruffy old jacket of his. Out there in all weathers he was, waving an empty bottle of brown ale at people as they went to work.' She chuckled. 'And Gawd alone knows how they got those old trousers of his off when they took him away.'

'When did he die?' ask Doris.

Dot looked surprised. 'He's not dead. They just took him away.'

The woman in front of them took her items and Dot turned to the assistant. 'Ain't you got nothing but Spam?'

Doris looked at her watch. 'Are you still all right for time?'

'Yes, Mum. It's Annie's turn to do the tea-time insulins,' Millie replied.

'Well, well, well, Sister Sullivan,' a woman's voice said behind them. 'Fancy meeting you here.'

Millie turned to find herself face to face with Mrs Callaghan. She was in the line for the cheese counter on the other side of the shop just ten feet away. Beside her stood a pretty, dark-haired young woman in her early twenties.

'Good afternoon, Mrs Callaghan,' replied Millie, forcing a smile.

'I didn't realise you girls from Munroe House had to get your own shopping now,' she said.

'We don't,' replied Millie. 'I'm here with my mother. She's moved in around the corner.'

'So I heard. In old Eli's house,' Mrs Callaghan

251

said, looking Doris over.

Doris smiled at her. 'Yes, the woman in front was telling us. So you know my daughter?'

Amusement lifted the corners of Mrs Callaghan's mouth. 'We run into each other from time to time, don't we, Sister?'

'Now and again,' Millie replied. 'And is this your daughter?'

'No, this is my daughter-in-law, Bernadine,' Mrs Callaghan replied. 'She's married to my youngest, Joe.'

'I'm pleased to meet you,' said Bernadine, giving Millie a shy smile. Her coat was unbuttoned and Millie cast her eyes over the slight swell pushing the front of her frock out.

'I see you're expecting,' Millie said. 'When's the baby due?'

'In about four months, I think,' Bernadine replied.

'And is this your first?' asked Millie, casting her experienced gaze over the dark smudges under the young woman's eyes.

'Yes,' Bernadine replied. 'And I can't wait.'

Millie gave her a professional smile. 'And have you been keeping all right?'

Bernadine nodded. 'I can't keep anything down but–'

'She's grand,' Mrs Callaghan cut in.

Millie ignored her and focused on the mother-to-be. 'If you're past three months the morning sickness should have settled by now. Perhaps you ought to come to the antenatal clinic so we can monitor you.'

'She doesn't need to,' Mrs Callaghan said, be-

252

fore her daughter-in-law could reply. 'I'm keeping an eye on her.'

'But it wouldn't do any harm,' said Millie, noting the young woman's small hands and feet, which might indicate a narrow pelvic space.

'And it wouldn't do no good either, and,' Mrs Callaghan glanced slowly around at the dozen or so women listening to the conversation, 'at least with me looking after her she knows I'll arrive before the baby does.'

A low chuckle went around the shop and Millie's cheeks felt warm.

'I'll have you know, Mrs Callaghan, my daughter was top of her class at the London, and she's a qualified midwife,' said Doris, in support.

Mrs Callaghan laughed. 'That she might be. But I've delivered more babies than Sister Sullivan has had hot dinners, and so I don't think my son's wife needs to waste her time being poked and prodded in some clinic, thank you very much. Now, if you'd excuse me, I've got my old man's tea to get on the table.'

She tucked her basket in the crook of her arm and marched out of the shop. 'Bernadine!' she called behind her.

Bernadine gave Millie an apologetic smile and followed her mother-in-law out of the shop.

'What a horrible woman,' said Doris quietly, staring after Mrs Callaghan. 'And how dare she say such things about you?'

'Don't take any notice,' Millie said, acutely aware of at least two-dozen pairs of eyes looking at her. 'She's just an old busybody.' She forced a laugh. 'And I'm glad she's not my mother-in-law.'

Dot had moved on to the cheese counter and so Doris stepped forward. As her mother bought her four ounces of bacon, Millie looked through the front window at Mrs Callaghan and her daughter-in-law who were now by the greengrocer's stall in the market. No, Millie thought, she wouldn't want Mrs Callaghan as a mother-in-law, but even less would she want her to deliver her first baby.

Millie gave Connie one end of the fabric and took the other herself. They shook it out and laid the rich chocolate-brown cloth on the table. Outside the storm that had raged since dinner-time still lashed the windows behind the heavy drapes, although thankfully Trudy was the nurse on call this evening. It was only nine o'clock but already some of the nurses had taken their cocoa up to bed, and Millie had decided that as no one was using the long table in the nurses' recreation room she would cut out the new dress she'd been promising for over a month to make for herself. She was seeing Alex on Saturday and she wanted to look a bit special.

Connie smoothed out a couple of wrinkles. 'This will look beautiful on you, and I know someone else who will think so too.'

'I can't think who you mean,' Millie replied, trying to keep her expression noncommittal.

Connie grinned. 'Liar. So where is he taking you this time?'

'He managed to get some tickets for *Appointment with Death* at the Piccadilly Theatre for Saturday night,' Millie replied.

'I would have thought, after dealing with

murders all day, he'd want to watch something more cheerful,' Connie said.

'You wouldn't say that if you'd seen him fidgeting all the way through *Oklahoma!* last month,' Millie laughed. She pulled out the tissue-paper pattern from the envelope and unfolded it. 'Now, let's get the pieces pinned on and cut before lights out or it'll be next Christmas before it's finished.'

Millie had just twisted and turned the sleeves into place when the telephone rang.

'I'll get it,' said Gladys, putting down her *Picturegoer* magazine and standing up.

Millie picked up the shears and turned back to her task but within a few minutes Gladys walked back in.

'It's for you. Says he's your uncle Tony,' she said, eyeing Millie suspiciously.

Millie hurried out and, tucking herself under the stairs, put the receiver to her ear.

'Hello, Tony.'

'Millie?'

Her heart skipped a beat. 'Alex? For goodness sake, you frightened the life out of me. I thought something had happened to my mother or Ruby.'

'I'm sorry, Millie. I didn't mean to frighten you, but whoever answered the phone started giving me the third degree so I just said I was your uncle and she shut up,' he said. 'Look, I'm ringing from the front office of the nick so I've only got a few moments but I need to see you.'

'Well, I'm on duty early.'

'Tonight. Can I come round when I've finished at ten-thirty?'

'We're not supposed to have visitors after nine

255

o'clock,' Millie said.

'Please, Millie, I have to talk to you. It can't wait until Saturday.'

'All right, come around the back and wait under the lamp-post on the other side of the road. I'll come and fetch you,' Millie said, as anticipation fizzed through her.

'Thanks,' he said. 'I'll see you later and sorry again for giving you a scare.'

He hung up and Millie put down the receiver and walked slowly back into the recreation room.

'Everything all right?' asked Gladys as Millie walked back in. Millie smiled.

'Yes, thanks.'

Turning her back on Gladys, Millie hurried over to Connie. Picking up the scissors, she slid the blade under the fabric.

'That was Alex,' she said, in a low voice and then recounted to her friend the conversation. 'He needs to see me,' Millie finished.

'You're not going to sneak him in, are you?' Connie asked.

Millie glanced at Gladys, who was pretending to read. 'He said it was urgent,' she whispered.

Connie sliced the scissor blades decisively through the almost forgotten material. 'Well, don't let Miss Dutton catch you, or you'll be urgently looking for another job.'

Millie's heart thumped expectantly in her chest as she stood by her window in the dark room looking across the street. Somehow she'd managed to stay calm and get through the rest of the evening but now, pressing her forehead against

256

the cold windowpane, she wondered what on earth was so important that it couldn't wait until Saturday.

Millie strained her eyes and looked up the street towards Commercial Road. The fog from the river had barely shifted all day but was now swirling so thick Millie could hardly see more than twenty feet beyond the back gate. Then, suddenly, out of the mist Alex appeared.

He was still dressed in full uniform, as he was required to wear it even when off duty, but the absence of the red-and-white-striped band on his right arm indicated he'd finished his shift.

Before he'd stopped under the lamp-post Millie snatched up her coat from the back of the chair. She unlocked the catch on the landing window and lifted it slightly, then headed downstairs to the back door.

She could barely see the back entrance through the smog, but that also meant anyone looking out from any of the windows above couldn't see it either. The cold air chilled her cheeks as she dashed to the gate and slid back the bolt. As she opened the gate, Alex slipped inside and Millie closed it behind him.

She beckoned Alex to follow and then led him up the iron fire escape to the first-floor landing window. Trying to be as quiet as possible, she raised the window frame so she could climb in and then turned to Alex. 'I'll make sure the coast is clear and then I'll call you,' she mouthed.

Millie climbed in and stood stock still for a moment, listening to the sounds of the sleeping house, then she tiptoed to her room and opened the door. She crept back to the window.

'Alex,' she hissed. His head appeared through the lace curtains. 'My room's on the left – step over the squeaky board as you climb in.'

Alex nodded and climbed in. He dashed down the hall on tiptoes and through her bedroom door. Millie shut the window and went back to her room.

'What's so important?'

But before she could say more Alex caught her around the waist and covered her mouth with his. Millie held out against his kiss for a moment and then surrendered. She slipped her arms around his neck and kissed him back. After a long moment he released her.

Millie rested her hands on his chest and tried to look annoyed. 'I shouldn't have let you in, you know,' she said, enjoying the feeling of his arms around her.

Instead of the expected cheeky grin and a quip, Alex gave her an apologetic smile.

'I know, and I wouldn't have asked, but I had to talk to you,' he said, still holding her close.

'It sounds serious,' said Millie, her heart thumping uncomfortably in her chest.

He released her. 'It is. Perhaps we could sit down.'

They both glanced at her bed and then back at each other. Alex pulled out her dressing-table chair and took off his greatcoat, hanging it over the back. Putting the chair a respectable distance from Millie, Alex sat down.

He pulled out a page from the *Daily Mirror* from his pocket. 'They are advertising for experienced police officers to serve in the Mobile Police Force in Palestine and I'm going to apply.'

Millie took the sheet and looked blindly at it. 'Are you?' she said, as a choking weight settled on her chest.

'I am. I have to.' He stood up and paced to the window. 'Now that all the grammar-school boys are flooding back into the job market there's rumours that those promoted for the duration of the war might have to take a step down in rank to allow those who've served to take up their old posts. That means I'll lose any chance of promotion for years, and I just can't do that,' he said in an unyielding tone. He turned from the window. 'The war gave me the chance to crawl out from under the bottom of the pile, Millie, and I'll be dammed if I'm going to allow myself to be shoved back under. Can you understand what I'm saying?'

As his intense gaze captured her, Millie wondered how long it would take her to get over him.

'Of course I can, and I'm sure I'd feel the same. And it's not as if you haven't got the ability to go further.' She forced a smile. 'I'd say, given the right opportunities, you could make it right to the top and be a chief superintendent or even a commander.'

He strode towards her. 'Do you really think so?'

'I do.'

His shoulders relaxed and he let out a long breath. 'Then you understand why I have to apply right away.'

She nodded as a lump lodged itself in her throat.

Alex took her hands. 'I intended to do things

right, not rush you or come on too strong because I know you're not that sort of girl but...' he dropped down on to one knee in front of her, 'Millie Sullivan, will you marry me?'

Millie looked at him in astonishment. 'Alex, I ... I...' she stammered, as joy jostled with apprehension, 'you're going to leave England?'

'For a few years,' he replied. 'Just until I've climbed the ranks high enough to return to the Met as an inspector; six or seven at the most, and I want you to come with me to Palestine.'

Millie stared at him. 'Where would we live?' she asked, trying to imagine living anywhere other than London.

'In married quarters,' Alex said, 'with the other police families. It'll be a bit like being on an Army base, and we'd have flights back twice a year.'

Millie laughed. 'Fly! Goodness, I've never even been abroad and now you're asking me to live in another country.'

Alex looked unsure. 'I know I'm asking a lot, and of course there's no certainty I'll actually be given an interview.'

'Yes!' Millie shouted, pushing her doubts and fears aside, and flinging her arms around him.

Alex didn't move for a long second, and then his arms tightened around her and he lowered his mouth on to hers. His right hand slid up her back and anchored her head as he kissed her deeper. Lowering her to the bed he moved his leg across her, pinning her under him. Millie gripped his hair and pulled his head towards her, capturing his lips. He arched his body over hers and a thrill ran through Millie as she felt his erection against her hip. He pressed his mouth on to hers for a long moment, then drew back. He rolled off her and propped himself up on his elbow.

'We should wait,' he said, looking down at her.

'I know,' Millie said, reaching up and kissing him along his strong jawline.

'Not that I don't want to but because I want it to be right.' He ran his finger lightly down her cheek, 'And when you've got my ring on your finger.'

Alex closed his mouth over hers again as Millie's fingers clawed at his back through his police shirt. His hand slid up and cupped her breast, then he broke away from kissing her.

'I ought to go,' he said, breathing hard.

Millie ran her fingers through his hair and smiled up at him. 'Not just yet.'

He rose up to his knees and, with his eyes locked on hers, ripped off his jacket and tie.

Millie lay with her head in the dip between Alex's shoulder and neck, and ran her finger idly through the dark hair on his chest.

Not wanting to break the peace surrounding them just yet, she raised her eyes so she could study his profile without moving. His eyes were closed and there was a relaxed smile lifting the corners of his lips.

Although Alex still wore his shirt, the rest of his clothes were mingled with hers on the floor in the corner in the same abandoned and shameful way their owners had been behaving for the last half an hour. Well, not shameful really, just recklessly abandoned. But Millie didn't care. She loved Alex, and that was an end to it.

Her eyes strayed down to the corner of the top sheet, currently barely covering his hips. Although they had made love in the dark, there had still been enough light for her to make out details. Her gaze returned to Alex's face, deciding she wanted to kiss it again, Millie pulled the sheet over her breasts and got up on to her elbow. His eyes opened.

'Hello,' Millie said.

'Hello yourself,' he replied, his arm tightening about her. 'Are you all right? I mean, I tried to be as gentle as—'

Millie kissed him. 'I hardly felt a thing, and I only finished my monthlies two days ago and so I'm pretty sure we'll be safe.'

'I don't care if we're not, although you might need a bigger bouquet.' Alex regarded her with a happy twinkle in his eye. 'I thought perhaps three or four children – what do you say?'

Millie laughed.

'You know, when I visited that gypsy girl after she had the baby, her old grandmother told me my son would have his father's green eyes,' Millie said, smoothing a stray lock from his forehead.

'Did she now?' he replied, as his hand slid down her arm.

Millie nodded.

Alex smiled. 'Well then, it seems I've got a lot to look forward to. The prettiest wife in the world, a green-eyed son and a new career in the Middle East.'

Millie bit her lip. 'Do you think they will call

you for an interview?'

'Hopefully,' Alex replied, running his fingers idly over the skin of her shoulder. 'But I suppose that depends on who else applies.' His gaze hovered on the edge of the sheet she held over her breasts and his eyes darkened. 'But no matter. You're mine now, Millie Sullivan, and I'm not letting you get away.'

Millie ran her fingers through Alex's chest hair and then up around his neck. 'What makes you think I'd try to escape, Alex Nolan?'

A slow smile spread across Alex's strong angular face. He rolled her over, pulling away the sheet covering her in one swift movement and then lowered his mouth on hers again.

Chapter Thirteen

Alex pushed his plate away and patted his belly. 'Thank you, Mrs Sullivan, that was a feast and a half.'

'Yes, Mum, it was lovely,' Millie said, putting her knife and fork together on her empty plate.

She glanced at Alex on her left and they exchanged a private look.

They were sitting around the small square table that Alex had carried through from the kitchen. It was covered with Doris's best tablecloth on which lay two tureens, one with the remnants of the sprouts and carrots and the other with a couple of crusty bits of roast potato. The gravy boat with prints of dairymaids and cows on it had been drained dry and the little spoon used to scoop out the redcurrant jelly had slipped into the pot.

The culinary festivities were complemented by the paper chains pinned in each corner and hanging diagonally across the room, the brightly coloured Chinese lanterns attached to the ceiling with tacks and the three-foot-high artificial Christmas tree complete with glass baubles and tinsel in the window.

'I thought it was a bit stringy,' Millie's mother said, looking dubiously at the pigeon-sized carcass sitting in the middle of a huge oval plate.

'No!' Millie and Alex cried in unison.

Doris wasn't satisfied and looked at Alex. 'And

264

was it enough? I mean, you're a working man.'

He raised his hand. 'Honestly, Mrs Sullivan, it was delicious and more than enough. And I can put my hand on my heart and say it's the best Christmas dinner I've had since war broke out.'

Doris looked relieved. 'Well, if you're sure. Although you ought to thank Millie, too. She was the one who queued for two hours outside the butcher's to buy the chicken.'

Alex smiled at Millie. 'She told me.'

'Although how the butcher sleeps at night, charging ordinary people twelve shillings for one, I don't know.' Doris tutted then stood up and started to collect up their plates. 'Well, I hope you've both left room for pudding and custard?'

Alex rubbed his knee against Millie's under the table and caught her eye.

'Mum,' Millie said. 'Could we leave afters for a moment?'

'Because there's something we want to tell you, Mrs Sullivan,' Alex concluded, in a firm voice.

Doris looked from one to another, then put the crockery down.

'It sounds important,' she said, resuming her seat.

Millie smiled nervously at her mother. 'Mum, Alex and I are going to get married.'

'This is all very sudden,' said Doris. 'I mean, you've only known each other a few months.'

'I know, but we have to get married,' Millie said.

The colour drained from her mother's face. 'Millie Sullivan! You haven't–'

'No!' cut in Millie, blushing to the roots of her hair. 'Not like that.'

Alex laughed, and then he told Doris about applying for the Palestine Police Force.

'Alex is still waiting to hear if he has an interview, but either way we thought we'd get married at Whitsun in St George's,' Millie added.

Doris looked from one to another. 'But isn't there a lot of trouble with the Jews out there at the moment?'

Alex shook his head. 'There's a few hot-heads trying to form their own state, but the British have a mandate from the League of Nations to govern the area. I stayed for a bit in Haifa before Monty's big push. The Arabs are an excitable bunch, but I'm sure once the British have taken up the reins again properly things will settle down.'

'And when will you go?' asked Doris in a quiet voice.

'Not until the autumn,' replied Alex. 'September at the earliest. I'll find us some temporary lodging in the area so Millie can stay working at Munroe House until we ship out to Cyprus.'

Millie smiled encouragingly at her mother. 'It's only for a few years until Alex can make regional inspector and then he'll be able to come back to the Met. We'll be home twice a year.'

'And once we've got ourselves set up, you can come to visit as often as you like,' Alex said. He took Millie's hand. 'I want you to know that I love Millie very much, Mrs Sullivan, and I promise to look after her and make her happy.'

Doris looked at them for a moment, and then smiled. 'Well, if you make Millie half as happy as Arthur made me then you won't go far wrong.' A flicker of pain passed over her mother's face. 'I

266

only wish he'd lived to see Millie so happy.'

'So do I, Mrs Sullivan, as I would have liked to have asked him for his permission to marry Millie,' Alex replied.

Millie let go of Alex's hand and hugged her mother. She felt Doris tremble slightly.

'Are you all right, Mum?' she asked, noting a small muscle twitching in her mother's cheek.

'Of course. I was just thinking of your dad,' Doris replied, wiping her eyes quickly. 'And I'm allowed to shed a tear at Christmas when I remember how happy we used to be, aren't I?'

'Yes, you are, Mrs Sullivan,' replied Alex. He stood up and his arm slipped around her daughter's waist. 'I'm sorry I might have to take Millie away from you for a little while, but,' he captured Millie's gaze in his own dark green eyes, 'I just have to have her as my wife,' he said in the vibrant tone that always sent a shiver through her.

Doris smiled fondly at them. 'That's just what Millie's dad said to me. Has Millie told you how I met her dad, Alex?'

'She said you met him when he nearly knocked you over with his delivery bike,' Alex replied.

Doris picked up the plates again. 'I'll fetch in the pudding and when I come back I'll tell you all about it.'

Millie took them from her. 'I'll fetch the sweet so that you can tell Alex how, after waiting an hour for dad to cycle by, you jumped out in front of him because it was the only thing you could think of to do to catch his eye.'

Standing in the shelter of the doorway, Millie

267

wriggled the all-encompassing waterproof over her head. After a moment of darkness surrounded by the smell of galvanised rubber, her head popped out of the top. She flipped up the hood so it acted as a peak, and left the shelter of the shop awning to face the storm. Rain splashed on to her face and up her legs as she walked through the icy water streaming down the pavement and into the bubbling drain.

Millie lifted her bike away from the railing and grasped the handlebars. She was just about to roll it into the road and hop on when she spotted Bernadine Callaghan coming out of the butcher's. She was carrying a shopping bag in either hand and was wearing a hooded mackintosh, out of which her rounded stomach protruded. An uneasy feeling crept over Millie as she watched Mrs Callaghan's daughter-in-law waddle towards her.

Bernadine stopped and looked at the display of fruit and vegetables in the window with its handwritten notice stating 'Yes, we have no bananas' hanging above.

Millie rolled her bike under the awning out of the rain. 'Hello, Mrs Callaghan.'

Bernadine looked around. 'Oh, you mean me.'

Millie smiled. 'Yes, who else?'

'I thought perhaps my mother-in-law'd suddenly arrived.' The young girl glanced nervously up and down the road. 'You haven't seen her, have you?'

Millie shook her head. 'Not in my travels today.'

Bernadine relaxed. 'I'm very fond of Joe's ma, but she can be a bit...'

'Overprotective?' Millie helped her out, although bossy and domineering were the words that had

268

first sprung to mind.

'Yes, but she's got a heart of gold,' added Bernadine quickly. 'And busy? She's forever popping in on someone who's having a bit of bother or is under the weather. She only has to hear there's trouble and she's straight around there.'

'That's kind of her,' Millie said, meanwhile adding nosy and interfering to her list. 'And how far gone are you now?'

'Just over five months,' Bernadine replied.

Millie looked surprised. 'You look further on than that to me. Are you sure of your dates?'

'I ain't had a monthly visit since the Election Day in July and it's seventh of January now.' She looked down and ran a hand lovingly over her stomach. 'Joe was ten pounds born so this one must take after his dad.'

'But how are you?' she asked, noting the dark circles around the young woman's eyes. 'Any aches and pains? Trouble with your waterworks?'

Bernadine shook her head. 'I have terrible heartburn and...' she put her hand on her forehead.

'And what?' asked Millie, noting how Bernadine's wedding ring was cutting into her finger.

Bernadine forced a laugh. 'I seem to be getting more headaches than usual. I told Bridget and she said it's just the baby upsetting my liver.'

Millie cast an experienced eye over her again. Something was definitely not right. Perhaps her dates were wrong and she was nearer to delivery that she thought. That could account for the top of Bernadine's womb being only a few inches from her breastbone and her puffy ankles; or, more worryingly, if her dates were right, then the

269

headaches and water retention might mean she was developing toxaemia, which could be very serious. However, unless she examined her properly there was no way Millie could be sure.

'I know it's awkward, but you should come to the clinic so I can take a proper look.'

'I would, Sister,' Bernadine bit her lip and shook her head, 'but Joe's mum's bound to hear about it and you know how she'd be then.' She gave an apologetic shrug.

'Then will you take my advice and rest with your feet up every afternoon, make sure you eat all your rations and get Joe to give you half his cheese and fat allowance?'

Bernadine nodded and then caught sight of the clock over the watchmaker's shop. 'Oh, is that the time? Joe will be home in an hour and I ain't even started his tea yet. If it's not on the table when he walks in, his mum will create.'

She turned to go but Millie caught her arm. 'Remember, if you need me, Mrs Callaghan, you only have to ring Munroe House and I'll come straight round.'

She smiled at Millie. 'That's kind of you, Sister.'

Bernadine pulled her plastic rain-cap over her head, stepped out from under the awning and hurried off down the street. As Millie watched the young woman lumber through the market stalls, her sense of foreboding increased.

Millie tucked the bag of gauze into her bag and handed Annie the large brown bottle of proflavine.

They were standing in Letterman's chemist's shop on the Highway with the nose-tingling smells of surgical spirit, carbolic soap and castor oil enveloping them.

Wooden display cabinets that decades of polishing had honed to smooth darkness surrounded them. The one to their right displayed potions, medicinal plasters and patent medicines behind which, stacked neatly on shelves, were glass bottles with names such as *Aqua Phenocola*, *Chloral et Bromide* and *Titu Boric Salts* on scrolled labels, as well as more sinister-looking green bottles containing poisons. On the opposite side of the chemist's were displayed the more personal wares, such as shaving sticks, bottles of brilliantine and safety razors alongside face cream, home perm kits and lipsticks.

There was a beam-balance weighing machine with weights at one end and a worn rubber footplate, as well as a bench-top variety with an enamel scoop for weighing babies.

'Will that be enough to see you through to the delivery tomorrow?' Mr Letterman asked, peering over the rims of his spectacles.

The pharmacist wore country tweeds under his white coat. His sandy-coloured hair was always precisely combed and his fingernails clipped. With his well-worn wooden pipe and polished brogues he looked more like a gentleman farmer than a chemist in an East End street market.

'I could do with a pack of Gamgee if you've got one,' Millie replied. 'I've got a new patient with weeping leg ulcers and I'm going through a roll every other day.'

'I've a box out the back, Sister, I'll be but a moment.' He disappeared behind the opaque glass screen for a moment then reappeared with a cylinder wrapped up in dark blue paper and handed it to her.

Mr Letterman rested the order book between a display of tweezers and a cardboard advertisement for Cow & Gate baby milk on the counter and Millie signed the chit. Annie picked up their dressings and they left the shop.

'Shall I take these back to the clinic on my way through to Mrs Ingles?' asked Annie, her warm breath making little clouds in the cold air as she spoke.

'If you could, as I–'

'Sister Sullivan!' a woman's voice boomed out. 'I want a word with you.'

Millie turned to see Mrs Callaghan charging towards her, scattering bystanders and with an expression like a bulldog with toothache on her face.

Millie forced a nonchalant expression. 'Oh, Mrs Callaghan, how nice to–'

'Wot you been saying to my Joe's wife?' she bellowed as the late-afternoon shoppers froze mid-motion and stared at them.

'I just asked how she was,' replied Millie as Annie cowered behind her.

'Sticking your oar in where it's not wanted, more like,' snorted Mrs Callaghan. A crowd started to gather around them.

Millie straightened her shoulders. 'I happened to see her outside the greengrocer's and said I thought she looked further on in her pregnancy than five months.'

'Don't give me that! You just wanted to scare the girl so you can prod and poke her about at your ruddy clinic,' Mrs Callaghan sneered.

'I did no such thing,' replied Millie hotly. 'I was concerned, that's all.'

Mrs Callaghan jabbed her finger at Millie. 'Well, keep your bloody concerns for someone who needs them. I suppose that's why you told her to lie down every afternoon like Lady Muck.'

Millie's knuckles cracked as her grip tightened on her case. 'She mentioned she was having headaches.'

'She's strained her eyes reading.' Mrs Callaghan tutted loudly and cast her gaze around at the audience. 'I don't know what they teach 'em at that bloody 'ospital.'

There were a couple of sniggers and, despite the chilly air, Millie felt her face grow warm.

'It could be toxaemia,' she said, annoyed at the slight squeak in her voice.

Mrs Callaghan waved away her words impatiently. 'She ain't got no toxaemia or any other kind of aemia, for that matter.'

'But if she has,' countered Millie, 'she should rest with her feet up.'

Mrs Callaghan rolled her eyes. 'I tell you, there's nothing wrong with her. And while we're on the matter of unwanted advice, why did you tell her to ask my son for half his rations?'

'Because I think she needs extra protein and calcium,' Millie replied.

'Well, my son's a working man and he needs all his grub if he's going to hump sacks in Albert Dock all day.'

'But–'

'Now you listen to me, girl,' Mrs Callaghan said

273

taking a step closer and looming over Millie. 'My daughter-in-law's head is already full of rubbish. I don't want you or any of the other bleeding nurses from the clinic stuffing it with any more. Women have been having babies since Noah was a boy without the help of so-called qualified midwives and my son's wife will do the same 'cos she's got better. Me. And I've delivered more nippers than you've had hot dinners.' She leant forward until her nose was almost touching Millie's. 'So, Sister Sullivan, don't let me hear about you sticking your twopenneth-worth into my business again.'

She glared at Millie for a moment, then turned around. The crowd parted like the Red Sea to let Mrs Callaghan clump past. All eyes remained fixed on the old woman's rear for a moment and then they turned to stare at Millie.

Annie stepped out from behind her. 'Are you all right, Sister?' she asked, looking apprehensively up at her.

'Of course I am,' Millie replied in a quivery voice.

Annie let out a long breath. 'Well, thank goodness for that. For one moment I thought she was going to sock you one. And, after all, you were only trying to help.'

'One thing you have to learn if you want to work on the district, Annie, is that you can offer help and advice until you are blue in the face, but some people always think they know best,' Millie said as she continued to watch Mrs Callaghan stomp her way between the market stalls. 'I only hope that it doesn't take the loss of her grandchild to make Mrs Callaghan think otherwise.'

Chapter Fourteen

The gate squeaked as Alex closed it behind them. Millie hooked her arm in his and hurried him along the path towards her aunt's front door.

'I still can't believe it,' she said, looking at her watch for the fourth time since they'd got off the 663 trolley-bus in Ilford Broadway fifteen minutes before. 'Why is it the blooming bus we get on has to be the one that breaks down at the Rabbits?'

'Just our good luck, I guess,' Alex said,

'Aunt Ruby's a stickler for time-keeping,' Millie said, already seeing her aunt's disapproving look in her mind's eye.

He slipped his arm around her and squeezed her playfully.

'Stop it,' Millie giggled. She tried to wriggle away, but Alex caught her.

'And watch out. If you knock Aunt Ruby's gnome over she'll never forgive you,' she said as his brogue skimmed dangerously close to the china garden ornament. 'And try not to kick the gravel too much, as she hates having to clear it out of the flower borders.'

'Perhaps your Aunt Ruby should think about having a paved pathway put in,' Alex replied as they crunched up the path.

'I'm sorry, it's just...' Millie said with a sigh.

Alex drew her to him. 'It will be fine.'

'And you mustn't mind if Tony, Aunt Ruby's gentleman friend, nods off after dinner.'

'After seven days of earlies I might join him,' Alex replied.

Millie looked alarmed.

'I'm only joking.' He squeezed her arm. 'For goodness sake, Millie. Your family can't be that bad.'

'No, of course they aren't.' Millie pressed the doorbell. 'It's just that although she's got a heart of gold, my Aunt Ruby has views on things. And she insists on calling me Amelia.'

He laughed. 'Don't you worry, Amelia, once we get acquainted, me and your folks will be getting on like a house on fire.' He gave her a peck on the cheek just as the door opened.

Aunt Ruby stood in the doorway wearing a frilly floral apron over her tailored french-navy dress and with high heels instead of her pink slippers.

'Oh, good afternoon, Aunt Ruby,' Millie said, feeling the colour rise on her cheeks.

Ruby's eyes flickered to the house across the street then, satisfied none of the neighbours had seen the debauchery on her doorstep, returned to Millie. 'Good afternoon, Amelia. We've been back from church almost two hours.'

'I'm sorry, Aunt Ruby,' replied Millie. 'The trolley-bus broke down and made us late. Aunt Ruby, this is Alex Nolan. Alex, this is my mum's elder sister.'

Ruby gave him her hostess smile. 'Good afternoon, Mr Nolan.'

Alex thrust out his hand. 'Millie's told me so much about you that I feel I already know you.

And call me Alex, please.'

Ruby gingerly gave him the tips of her fingers. 'Perhaps when we are better acquainted. Do come in.'

They stepped into the hall and Ruby closed the door behind them. Millie hung their coats on the hall stand.

Alex looked around. 'You've got a lovely home, Mrs Dixon,' he said, smiling charmingly.

Ruby inclined her head. 'Thank you. I strive to create an elegant yet inviting home,' she said, indicating the green-gold flock wallpaper, Art Deco coat stand and mock-Tiffany chandelier with a sweep of her arm. 'Now, if you'd like to follow me into the lounge you can meet everyone. Oh! And could you make sure you've wiped your feet? I've just had the carpet shampooed,' she called over her shoulder, as Alex finished doing just that on the coconut mat.

Millie gave him an apologetic smile and he blew her a kiss. Millie followed Ruby into the front room with Alex close behind.

Ruby had taken her decorating philosophy of elegant homeliness through to the parlour or, as Ruby insisted on calling it, the lounge. The walls were covered with oriental-style wallpaper that had swallows darting between spindly willow branches and long-gowned Chinese fishermen casting their nets. She had a Utility round-armed sofa and two chairs like everyone, but instead of the dour beige and brown of most wartime furniture, hers had been reupholstered in brick red, which matched the heavy chenille curtains at the window. Even the three ducks pinned in mid-flight to the wall weren't common or garden mallards, but colourful mandarins. To finish off the sophisticated look, there were two aluminium statues of scantily clad nymphs holding grapes and flowers while pivoting on Bakelite plinths on the top of the grey-tiled fire surround.

As she looked around her aunt's front room, Millie's heart sank as she realised that when Ruby had said everyone, she really had meant everyone.

'Uncle Bill,' Millie said looking at her mother's younger brother, 'I didn't know you or Aunt Martha were coming for Sunday dinner.' She looked at her mother's little sister. 'And Aunt Edie, too.'

'Ruby told us we had to,' Bill answered, smoothing back his thinning hair and blinking rapidly. 'Didn't she, Martha?'

Martha, wearing a limp grey gown a tone darker than her hair, nodded. 'She did.'

Edie looked excitedly at Millie. 'She told us to be here as she was going to give your young man the once ov–'

'I asked Wilfred and May,' Ruby cut in. 'But their Scout troop is having some sort of Jamboree and, as he's Akela, they have to be there.'

Millie gave a silent prayer of thanks for Baden-Powell.

'Your young man's very tall, Amelia,' her Aunt Martha said, fiddling with the buttons on her cardigan and looking up at Alex like a bashful schoolgirl.

'And such a lot of hair,' added Edie, as if they were admiring a new baby.

Millie squirmed but Alex maintained his

pleasant smile.

'It's nice to meet you all.' He shook their hands in turn, setting off the twitch in Bill's right eye.

'And this is my friend, Anthony Harris,' Ruby said, ushering him away from the two spinsters.

'Afternoon, Mr Harris,' Alex said, shaking Tony's hand firmly.

'And to you. It's Tony, by the way.'

Alex spotted Doris in the corner. 'Good afternoon, Mrs Sullivan,' he said, smiling warmly at her. 'Nice to see you again.'

Doris smiled back. 'And you, Alex.'

Ruby clapped her hands lightly. 'Now that Amelia and Mr Nolan have arrived, perhaps we could come through to the dining room.'

Bill struggled to his feet and headed for the door with Martha and Edie hot on his heels.

'Can I help you up, Mrs Sullivan?' Alex asked, offering Millie's mother his hand.

'That's very kind.' She grasped it and stood up.

'Now,' Alex said hooking her mother's arm in his. 'Why don't you show me where the grub is?'

Millie put her spoon and fork together and glanced around. They were now squashed around Ruby's dining table in the back room of the house that overlooked the small rear garden. The family had talked politely enough about the weather and petrol rationing and what should be done to the Nazis at Nuremburg over the roast shoulder of lamb, boiled potatoes and carrots, before turning to the wedding.

'Couldn't you have the reception somewhere a little more refined?' said Ruby when Millie finished telling them the arrangements.

'There's nothing wrong with the Hoop and Grapes in Aldgate, Aunt Ruby,' said Millie.

'So, Alex,' Tony cut in before Ruby could speak again. 'After you and Millie are wed, you might be off to give those blooming Zionists a taste of Eighth Army steel, I hear.'

'I've got to get through the interview in three weeks first.'

As Alex explained what he hoped to be doing in the Middle East, Millie studied his strong profile. When he'd finished, and sensing Millie's eyes on him, he looked around. He pressed his leg against hers, then let his spoon rest against the side of his bowl.

'Well, that was a treat, and no mistake,' Alex said, wiping his mouth.

Ruby was sitting opposite them and her eyes flickered on to Alex's unused dessert fork. 'I can see that by the way you polished it off.'

'My dad was just the same,' Millie said, giving Alex a reassuring smile. 'He would be scraping his plate while me and mum were only halfway through our dinner.'

Alex laughed. 'My mum used to say that I ate so much I must 'ave hollow legs.'

Ruby wiped the corner of her mouth delicately with the edge of her napkin. 'And speaking of family, are your mother and father still alive?'

'I'm afraid not.' Alex told her then about his brother and sisters.

Ruby looked politely sad. 'What did your father do when he was alive?'

'As little as possible.'

Millie nudged his knee with hers under the table.

'He was a docker,' Alex said.

Ruby tried hard to look happy about the fact.

Alex regarded her levelly. 'So was I, but when I was in the desert having nine colours of you-know-what bombed out of me, I swore if I survived I'd never stand on line for some cow-son of a guvnor to throw me a work-ticket ever again.'

Edie looked down and pushed a couple of peas around her plate while Billy started to blink rapidly again. Ruby's neck flushed.

'Did I tell you that Alex is going to take a degree in modern history?' said Millie brightly.

'Are you?'

'As a correspondence course,' Alex replied. 'I started thinking about it in Malta before I was discharged from the Army and I'll be enrolling to do it soon.'

'Well done,' said Ruby as if congratulating a schoolboy for tying his shoelaces properly. 'It's a pity it won't be from a real university.'

Millie glared at her but Alex contented himself with a sardonic smile.

Ruby just stood up and smiled at everyone. 'Now, if everyone has finished perhaps we should clear away and have a cup of tea.'

'I'll help you,' Millie said through tight lips.

Leaving Alex in her mother's care, Millie collected the dirty crockery and followed her aunt into the kitchen.

Ruby was lighting the gas under the kettle on her New World cooker.

'What do you think you're playing at?' Millie

asked, shoving the dishes on the table.

'I don't know what you–'

'You insist I bring Alex here and then spend the entire meal trying to belittle him,' Millie said. 'And don't think I didn't see you watching to see which fork he picked up.'

'Well, he didn't know, did he?' Ruby replied, a look of triumph on her face. 'Really, Millie, I'm no snob, but you have to admit your young man is a bit, a bit, unsophisticated?'

'You mean common.'

'You said that, not me, Amelia.' Ruby looked contrite. 'Look, dear, I'm sure Alex is a very nice chap, but I do think you could do a little better. Like that nice Dr Yates you were friendly with.'

Millie rolled her eyes. 'And how many times do I have to tell you, I went to the flicks three,' she held up the required number of fingers, 'yes, three times with William Yates, and considering it was like sitting in the dark with an octopus I'd say it was two times too many.'

'Well, perhaps not him then.' Ruby took a breath. 'I never told you this, Amelia, but me and Bernard had tried for years to start a family and I think, although neither of us said it, that by the time you were born we both knew we weren't going to be blessed with our own children.' Ruby reached up and tucked a stray lock back behind Millie's ear. 'I remember the day I first saw you, all red and wrinkled when your dad brought you and your mum home from hospital. You were so little.'

Despite her crossness, Millie felt her eyes prickle.

'You had all the opportunities in life that we never had, going to grammar school and then to train in something you wanted to do, and you were never going to have to get just any old job because the family needed your money,' Ruby said. 'I've watched you grow from a pretty girl to a beautiful and intelligent woman, hoping that one day you'd meet some nice young man, with letters after his name, who can give you the nice things like a house of your own, a car and even a week on the beach at Eastbourne in the summer each year.'

'I understand all that, Aunt Ruby, and I do appreciate your feelings. But the truth of it is that I love Alex,' Millie said firmly. 'And he may not speak with a plum in his mouth, I know, but he's got more brains than half the doctors I know put together. And he will make me very happy.'

Ruby sighed a resigned sigh. 'I do hope so, dear.' She lifted out her blue and cream Poole pottery coffee set, regarded it for a moment, before putting it back in favour of the everyday one from Woolworths.

'If a piece of my best set gets broken, I'll never get a replacement,' she explained as she put it on the tray. She added the small tongs into the bowl of sugar cubes and set the milk jug alongside. 'I'll take these through if you put the plates in to soak.'

Holding the tray in front of her, Ruby swept past Millie.

'And Alex's degree will be a real one,' Millie said emphatically into the empty kitchen.

With a weary sigh Millie pushed the front door of number fifty-four Dorothy Street open, the home of Ada and Eddie White and their grown-up daughter, Flora. Like so many in the area, they lived in the two downstairs rooms of a dilapidated terraced house, with a minute scullery at the back. Eddie White was one of Millie's daily visits, and he had been on her books off and on for years for one thing and another.

In his younger days Eddie had worked as a docker, but after tumbling into the hold of a ship a few years back, he'd taken a job as a night watchman in one of the riverside warehouses.

Millie closed the door behind her and made her way down the hall. Putting her bag down, she took off her coat, folded it up and then slipped it into the large brown-paper bag she carried for the purpose. She set it next to the door and untucked her apron. It was standard practice for nurses to fold and pin it up to avoid contaminating the lining of their coats.

Ada White was working on her sewing machine, with a pile of completed trousers on one side of her and a stack of cut fabric on the other. She was nudging fifty but looked older, as the war years had stripped every last bit of fat from her bones. Like most women in the area, she was wearing a wraparound overall of an indeterminate colour, with a matching scarf over her hair that was knotted at the front of her head. She raised her head and smiled.

'Oh, come in, love,' she said, stopping the flying wheel of the treadle with a bony hand.

The Whites' main living room was smaller than

Millie's room in Munroe House, and jam-packed. A sideboard dominated the space under the window, next to which stood a corner cabinet full of glass and china ornaments so tightly crammed in that you couldn't see the ones at the back. There was a pile of old newspapers on one side of the tiled hearth and a battered coal bucket on the other. Above the mantelshelf a large murky-faced clock stood along with a sand-filled lighthouse from the Isle of Wight and two chalk-painted pixies from Devon.

'I'm sorry I'm late,' Millie said, squeezing around the back of the sofa and into the room.

Mrs White's eyes waved her apology away. 'We don't mind, do we, Father?'

Eddie White sat, or rather sprawled in the deep, upholstered armchair by the window. He was dressed in a yellowing short-sleeved vest with the top button undone to reveal grizzly chest hair. An empty cup and saucer balanced on one arm of the chair while a dangerously full ashtray teetered on the other. Ada had cleared their small tea table and set it next to him for Millie to work on.

'I'll go and get your fings, Sister,' Ada said.

'Thank you,' Millie said turning back to her patient.

'Can I fetch you another, Father?' Ada asked.

'A fill-up would be grand.' He handed her his cup. 'And a bit more sugar if you can spare it.'

A simpering expression spread across her face. 'And perhaps a couple of bits of bread and dripping?'

'Not just now, pet.' He patted his stomach,

which was hanging over the top of his stretched belt. 'I'm still stuffed from breakfast.'

Ada looked concerned. 'Are you sure? You only had a spot of porridge and toast and that was three hours ago. You have to keep up your strength. Doesn't he, Sister?'

Millie didn't answer.

'Perhaps later,' Eddie conceded.

Ada wrinkled her nose up in an oddly girlish way. 'That's better, and don't forget our Flora's going to bring in a nice bit of fish for your supper if she can,' she added as she left the room.

'And how are you today, Mr White?' Millie asked, setting her bag on a clean sheet of newspaper on the floor.

Eddie smiled at her, revealing a row of uneven black teeth. 'All the better for seeing you.'

'And the foot?'

Eddie raised the offending article swathed in bandages. 'Bugger kept me awake all bloody night.'

'Well, let's have a look, shall we?'

Millie spread another sheet of newspaper on the floor for the dirty swabs and set out her bottle of surgical spirit, safety pins and bottle containing half-and-half Dettol solution. With a couple of twists and folds she made a bag out of a sheet of paper and set that on the floor, then took her soap and nailbrush out of the side pocket of her bag. The door opened and Ada reappeared with a towel over her shoulder and carrying a tray with a bowl, a square tin and a small china bowl on it. She set it on the sideboard and brought over the larger bowl.

'There you go, Sister,' she said, then went back for the rest of the stuff.

Millie picked up the brush and soap and started washing her hands.

'I've baked them for five minutes, as you said,' Ada said as she placed the tin and small bowl on the sheet of paper.

'Thank you.'

Ada offered her the towel and Millie dried her hands. She prized the lid of the tin open and inspected the squares of gauze she'd left with Ada the day before. The frayed edges were golden brown from their roasting in the Whites' oven, so Millie knew they were sterile.

'Could you?'

Ada spread a sheet of newspaper on the ash-sprinkled rug in front of her husband and making sure she stayed within its perimeters, Millie knelt down. She made quick work of the bandages and, using forceps, peeled off yesterday's dressing to expose Eddie's foot.

She inspected his black toes. When Eddie's GP had instructed her to change Eddie's dressing each day, only his big toe and the two next to it were black, but now all of them had the distinct shiny skin that indicated gangrene caused by lack of circulation.

Ada peered over her shoulder. 'Are they ready to come off yet, Sister?'

Millie shook her head.

Eddie rolled his eyes. 'For Gawd's sake, can't you just chop 'em?' He winked. 'Go on, I won't tell if you don't.'

Millie laughed. 'As I told you last time and the

time before, nature has to take its course and I'm just here to give it a little help.'

Eddie muttered something about 'bloody nature' and reached for his tin of tobacco. Ada glared at him and he withdrew his hand. Millie leaned forward, thankful that at least this time she wouldn't leave the house with her hair reeking of cigarettes. She made quick work of the dressing and within a minute or two she was securing the bandage around the top of Eddie's stout calf.

She stood up, put her hands in the small of her back and stretched, then pulled the collection register and a small zipped purse out of the side pocket of her bag.

'Thank you Mrs White, and I'll see you to-morrow,' she said, slipping the two half-crowns into the purse and making a note of the payment.

'I hear that you're getting hitched in a couple of months.'

Millie gave her a questioning look.

'Eddie's cousin is the verger at St George's and told me you'd booked to have your banns read,' Ada explained. A sentimental expression spread across her face. 'You'll make a beautiful bride.'

Millie blushed. 'Thank you.' She snapped her case shut. 'I'll see myself out and come again tomorrow.'

Chapter Fifteen

Millie watched with barely concealed amusement as Alex hopped about her room trying to get his foot in the other trouser leg.

'Stop laughing,' he said in a loud whisper as he bumped into her chair.

Millie swung her legs off the bed.

'Stop making so much noise,' she replied, scooping up his shirt from the floor.

She offered it to him, but he grabbed her hand and pulled her towards him. 'I'll teach you to laugh at an officer of the law.'

He crushed her to him and pressed his mouth on to hers. Millie slipped her arms around his back, enjoying the feel of his skin under her fingertips.

'Do you have to go just yet?' Millie asked, kissing his shoulder.

'I do, before Georgie nods off and I can't get in the back door,' Alex replied. 'I've already had to sign in the late book once this week; twice, and the superintendent will want to know why.'

'Well, tell him you're preparing for your wedding,' Millie said, tugging on his trouser belt.

Alex removed her hands. 'You are a wanton woman, Millie Sullivan.'

Millie laughed and let him go. She sat back on her bed and watched him button his shirt.

'I'm sure you'll hear back from the Foreign Office any day now,' she said, as excitement at becoming Alex's wife fought with the anxiety of leaving London.

'I'm not,' Alex replied, looping his tie around his neck. 'It's been over six weeks since the interview. The top brass were probably knee-deep in applications from Redcaps and Navy provosts, and didn't have to bother with us ordinary blokes.'

Millie studied his disappointed expression for a moment, then got off the bed and padded across the room in her bare feet.

'I'm sure they'll advertise again next year,' she said, sliding her arms around him.

Alex kissed her forehead. 'Course they will,' he replied in a tone that said otherwise. He forced a smile. 'But it's Good Friday next week, which means,' he took her hands, 'it's just over eight weeks until we get married.' He kissed her, then broke free of her embrace and knotted his tie.

'Eight weeks, three days, actually,' Millie said.

Alex grinned. 'And then I won't need Georgie to sneak me in the back of the section house.'

'So I won't see you until next Tuesday?' she said, gliding into his arms again.

'I'm afraid not, sweetheart,' replied Alex, hugging her to him. 'And I suppose I ought to chase the estate office about allocating us a flat in Warren House.'

He took his comb out of his breast pocket and, half-crouching to see his reflection in her dressing table mirror, combed his hair. 'Ought to go.' He picked up his police jacket.

Millie unhooked her dressing gown from behind her door and put it on over the under-slip she'd hastily donned. She switched off the bedside lamp

290

and they went to the bedroom door. Opening it just enough for her to slip through, Millie crept out on to the landing, checked all was quiet, and then swiftly opened the window at the far end. Millie scooted back to her door and half-twisted the handle. The door opened and Alex slipped out, holding his boots in one hand and his helmet in the other. As fast as they could, Millie and Alex tiptoed noiselessly back to the window and he climbed out. Millie followed and stood beside him on the metal fire escape while he put on his boots.

He straightened his jacket and pulled her to him. 'Sleep tight,' he whispered, kissing her briefly on the lips before heading towards the ladder at the far end.

'You too,' she whispered back. 'Not long now.'

Alex blew her a kiss. 'Just eight weeks, three days.'

Millie flicked a few pages of the latest copy of *Woman and Home* over to the knitting section.

'I'm thinking of making this for Alex for his birthday next month,' she said, turning the magazine so Connie could see the Fair Isle jumper pattern. 'I think it will look good on him.'

Connie raised an eyebrow. 'You think he'd look good in a sack.' They were sitting at a table tucked into the corner of Kate's Café surrounded by dock workers finishing off their midday meal before the local factories and docks sounded their back-to-work hooters. Above them a wooden radio played the final few bars of *Workers Playtime*'s signature tune.

Kate's was one of the oldest shops along the

Highway and judging by the accumulation of grease splattered behind its ancient range, it had been a working-man's eating house for a very long time. To be honest, it was a bit rundown, but it had a lot of things going for it. Despite having its windows blown out almost weekly, Kate's had kept open all through the Blitz. There was always a fresh pot of tea brewing and a cheery welcome. But its overriding attraction had to be that Miss Dutton would only have set foot in the place if someone held a gun to her head.

'Any news on the results of Alex's interview yet?' Connie asked.

Millie shook her head. 'He's trying to keep chirpy and he mentioned last week about putting in his application to take the Inspector exam, and so I think he's come to terms with the fact that he hasn't got the job.'

'Poor Alex,' said Connie. She grabbed Millie's hand across the table and squeezed it. 'Still, at least it means I won't be losing you to foreign parts. Now, what about the vicar?'

Millie shook her head. 'We've tried four times to sort out an appointment but what with Alex's shifts and mine, it's been impossible. But I've swapped next Tuesday with Eva so we can have the same rest-day, and so we're booked to see him then.'

'Well, it's March already, and if you leave it any longer all the Saturdays in June will be taken,' Connie said. 'What about your dress? Have you thought about that?'

'I have, but after getting a new uniform last year I'm very low on coupons. As much as I'd like to have a proper wedding dress, there's a waiting list for bridal fabric and so I don't think I'll be able to manage it in time. I thought instead that I might just treat myself to a new suit and hat, and get married in that.'

'Why don't you wear mine?' Connie said in a nonchalant tone.

An image of herself walking towards Alex in Connie's beautiful ivory dress floated into Millie's mind. 'Oh, Connie. Could I? I mean, I'll give you my coupons and pay you for it.'

'I wouldn't say no to a fiver and half-a-dozen coupons, but I'd be happier to see you wearing it than leaving it creased up at the bottom of my wardrobe.' Connie shrugged. 'And it's not as if I'm going to be needing it.' She gave a brittle smile. 'Did you hear that Charlie's wife is pregnant again?'

Millie shook her head.

'Annie booked her into the maternity clinic last week. She's three months gone. They didn't waste much time. The first one was only born in November.'

Millie reached across and squeezed her friend's hand. 'One day, when you meet the right man, you'll go around and personally thank Charlie's Italian wife for taking him off your hands.'

Connie's expression remained glum for a second or two longer, then she wrinkled her nose. 'Let's have another look at your ring.'

Millie scooped her finger into the thin ribbon tied around her neck and pulled it out. She slipped it on the third finger of her left hand and held it out.

Connie sighed admiringly. 'It's so pretty.'

'I think so too,' replied Millie, moving it back and forth so that the two entwined diamonds caught the light from the bulb overhead.

The doorbell jingled, and Millie and Connie looked up as Annie, Sally and Joan stamped in, bringing the biting cold and fog with them.

They spotted Millie and wove their way between the tables to join her. 'I've seen some pea-soupers in my time,' said Sally, unwinding her scarf and taking off her gloves. 'But with this one you can hardly see your hand in front of your face.'

'It's more like two o'clock in the morning than two o'clock in the afternoon,' added Annie, glancing towards the steamy shop window. 'And everyone's coughing as the fog is holding the smoke from everyone's chimneys.'

'Cuppa tea, girls?' Pearl Watson, the owner of Kate's Café, called over to the new arrivals.

'Yes, please. And a top-up for us,' Connie said back, holding up her empty mug.

Sally pulled up another chair and Annie and Joan squeezed themselves around the other side of the table.

Pearl, dressed in her usual faded overall and with her obligatory roll-up dangling from her lips, shuffled over to them carrying a tray of mugs that she slid on to the table between them, sloshing tea everywhere. 'There you go, girls,' she said, the metal curlers in her orange fringe clinking together as she spoke. 'And there's a cake each to 'elp keep your strength up.'

The nurses muttered their thanks and Pearl went back to the counter, her down-trodden slippers making little slapping noises against her heels as she walked.

Millie and Connie distributed the cakes. Annie and Joan shook their heads and cradled their mugs glumly.

'What's the matter with you two?' Connie asked.

'The same as ever,' replied Joan.

'What's she done now?' asked Millie.

'Added three patients to Joan's afternoon list and another five to mine,' Annie said, her blue eyes hot with indignation.

'And she's swapped my day off from Tuesday to Friday without asking me,' Joan added.

Annie stirred her tea noisily. 'It's not fair. She's picking on us because we're new.'

Millie, Connie and Sally exchanged a look. They'd said as much over cocoa in Sally's room only two evenings ago.

Annie looked nervously around the table. 'I don't know if I should tell you this, but Doreen has had enough and has applied for a job with the Bethnal Green and Hackney Association.'

'And I can't say I blame her,' chipped in Joan. 'In fact, I'm considering doing the same myself.'

Annie put her cup down. 'Will you speak to her, Millie?'

Millie bit her lower lip. 'I would if I thought it would do any good. But you know me and her get on like oil and water, and so I don't think she'll take any notice.'

'Oh, Millie, please,' said Joan, clasping her hands together in supplication.

Millie sighed. 'All right. I've got to speak to her anyway about getting married, and so if I get a chance I'll have a word, although I'm not promising.'

Millie stepped out from the darkness of the Crosses' house into the bright morning light. Heaving her bag into the basket on the front of the bicycle she unfastened the chain and pulled the bike away from the railings. She stood on the pedal to roll the bike forwards and then jumped on the saddle. Tilting her face so that the sun could warm her cheeks, she pedalled at a leisurely pace along Sutton Street to her next visit, Mrs Frazer in Swedenborg Gardens. As she shot past the coal lorries and delivery vans parked up along the street, Millie's mind wandered over the list of things she had yet to do for her wedding.

There was a trip to the local Food Office for extra coupons for the wedding breakfast and then she needed to find dried fruit for Mrs Pierce to make the cake. Added to which there were the flowers to order and the seating plan to agree.

Acknowledging the milkman setting milk bottles on doorsteps while his horse ploddcd dolefully along its morning route without breaking stride, Millie stuck her right arm out and swung into Cable Street. As she straightened after taking the corner there was a screech of brakes and then the frantic clanging of a police Black Maria bell echoed around the street.

Millie grabbed the brakes and jolted to a halt just in time to see the police van tearing towards her, sending a small flock of grey pigeons scratching in the gutter into panic. The van bumped into the curb and stopped. The driver of the greengrocer's lorry behind pulled on the wheel to swerve around it, shouting out a series of colourful oaths as he did. The window cleaner on the ladder opposite halted mid-wipe and the handful of people at the bus stop turned and stared.

The police wagon passenger door opened and Alex scrambled out. He flipped his helmet on his head and ran across the road. 'Millie!'

Millie stepped off her bike. 'Alex, what on earth are you doing?'

'Thank goodness I caught up with you,' he cried, skidding to a halt in front of her. 'The nurse who answered the phone said you had visits along Cable Street, and me and Georgie have already been up and down three times trying to find you.'

Millie glanced past him at Georgie, who was leaning nonchalantly on the side of the police van, having a quick smoke.

'What's happened?' Millie asked, as her gaze returned to her fiancé.

'This, my darling wife-to-be, this.' He tore a sheet of paper from his breast pocket, dislodging his whistle at the same time. Alex laughed. 'It was waiting for me in the post box this morning. It's from the Foreign and Commonwealth. The Palestine Police force has accepted me.'

His eyes sparkled with triumph as he looked down at her.

Millie stared at him for a second before her attention shifted to the letter in his hand.

Alex flicked the letter open with the tip of his finger. 'They can't confirm my start date but, as we thought, it's sometime in the autumn. We're off to Cyprus first for training and language lessons, and then deployment to one of the main bases. They'll send me the full details a month or so beforehand, which gives us plenty of time to give notice and pack up. And we'd better get your passport sorted as soon as we're married.' He took off his helmet and ran his fingers through his hair. 'Oh, Millie. Isn't it brilliant?'

'Yes, brilliant,' she said, flatly.

Alex laughed again. 'You might sound a bit more enthusiastic, sweetheart.'

Millie blinked and summoned up her warmest smile. 'I'm sorry, Alex. It's just a bit of a surprise, that's all. I'd sort of got used to the idea that we weren't going, and from what you've been saying about trying to buy a house in a year or two I thought you had, too.'

Alex grinned wildly at her. 'To tell the truth, Millie, although I've been trying to put a brave face on it all, I've been bitterly disappointed to think I'd been overlooked and missed out on such a golden opportunity.' Noticing her grave expression, he gave her a puzzled look. 'What's wrong?'

'Nothing,' she said, renewing her smile. 'Nothing at all. It's just a lot to take in.'

Alex's shoulders relaxed. 'I know. I had to read the blooming thing twice myself before the penny fully dropped. Whoo!'

He punched the air with excitement then, heedless of the onlookers, Alex caught her around the waist and pulled her close.

'This is it, Millie,' he said, as his lively green eyes captured hers. 'It's you and me and our new life.'

He kissed her and his police helmet slipped off and clattered on to the pavement. Someone wolf-whistled but Alex ignored them and kissed her deeper. Millie raised her free hand and rested it on his chest for a second before he released her.

'I've got to go,' he said, snatching up his helmet and jamming it on his head again. He kissed her on the cheek. 'See you later.'

He turned, putting his hand up to stop the traffic, and strolled back to the van. Georgie stamped his cigarette butt under his size eleven boot and climbed in behind the wheel as Alex swung into the passenger seat. The van revved and, giving her a quick blast on the bell, it shot away down the street.

Millie stared after it for a second or two and then kicked her pedal to the up position ready to pedal off, but as she stepped forward her knees started to wobble. She rested her bike against a nearby lamp-post then took her notebook from her pocket and fanned herself.

'Oi, Sister!'

Millie looked across the road at an old woman pushing an old battered pram with a scruffy-looking dog sitting on top.

The old woman grinned, showing her one remaining upper tooth. 'I'd feel a bit beside meself too, if some 'andsome copper gave me a smacker like that.'

The people at the bus stop laughed and Millie gave a good-natured smile. She pulled her bike upright and walked it on a little way. Although Alex's kisses usually left her a little breathless, it was the stark reality that she would soon be waving goodbye to everything and everyone she knew that had truly sent her head reeling.

Chapter Sixteen

Standing under the awning outside the pie and eel shop to keep dry, Millie waited until the half-a-dozen people alighted from the trolley-bus and then looked at her watch. Where on earth was her mother? They'd arranged to meet at two and it was half-past now.

Millie strained her eyes westwards to where another red bus trundled along the road towards Stratford Broadway, sparks from the cable above flashing as the runners tripped over a point. After a couple of moments it stopped and Doris stepped down. She spotted Millie and waved cheerily at her and, putting up her umbrella, trotted over.

'Hello, dear. I'm sorry I'm a bit late. The bank rang Mr Pugh at dinnertime about the wages, and so he went to see them and I said I'd stay until he got back. And then I had to pick up the scones from the baker's and take them to the church for Saturday's Mother's Union tea.'

Millie stifled her irritation. 'Well, I suppose you're here now.' She gave her mother a peck on the cheek. 'Now, let's get to Boardman's before the heavens open again.'

An hour later, after much deliberation, Millie had settled on a sage-green square-shouldered suit with velvet lapels and a single box-pleated skirt as her going-away outfit. Ruby had already promised her one of her many hats and so, after parting with eighteen coupons and one pound seventeen shillings and sixpence, Millie and her mother made their way to the department store's tearoom upstairs.

They settled into one of the booths and Millie gave their order to the waitress.

'I'm hoping to finalise the guest list once Alex has heard back from his sister, and then I can give the final number to the Hoop and Grapes,' Millie said.

'You know, Ruby still isn't happy about you having the reception in a pub,' her mother said.

'She made it plain enough last time I saw her,' Millie replied. 'But there's nowhere else to have it. Everywhere is fully booked or too dear. It'll only be a small do as we're saving all we can to set up house. I'll have to make do with a plaster-of-Paris cover over a fruit cake, but the landlady said she'd do us a nice spread of sandwiches for everyone.'

'I'm sure it will be a lovely day, dear.' Her mother opened her handbag and shakily pulled out her handkerchief. 'I just wish it was your dad and not Uncle Bill walking you down the aisle.'

'So do I, Mum. And there's something else.' Millie took a deep breath. 'Alex has been accepted in to the Palestine Police.'

Doris's face drained of colour. 'You told me he hadn't.'

'I know,' replied Millie. 'And as it's been over two months since the interview, we'd both assumed he hadn't got through, but he had a letter yesterday.'

They sat in silence for a moment then Doris picked up her spoon and stirred her tea noisily. 'I would have thought, after five years away from home comforts, men would be glad to put their feet up instead of dashing off to the four corners of the globe again.'

'The world's changed, Mum,' Millie said patiently. 'Men like Alex want something more from life than living in a damp couple of rooms and a dead-end job.'

'But Alex hasn't got a dead-end job,' Doris replied. 'He's a police sergeant. And you would have police accommodation when you got married.'

'He's only a temporary sergeant,' Millie said, 'and unlikely to go any further for a very long time. And as for somewhere to live – there's only those awful police flats in Jamaica Street and they're worse than some of the houses I visit. As it is, we'll have to find somewhere that the divisional commander will permit us to rent for a few months and that won't be easy or cheap.'

'When will you go?' her mother asked, stirring the sugar into her tea with slow deliberation.

'Not until September, at least,' Millie replied. 'We'll stay in Cyprus on the Army base at Akrotiri until Alex is posted, then we'll transfer to the family quarters.'

'It sounds as if you've got it all sorted out,' replied Doris, trying to look enthusiastic.

Millie put her hand over her mother's. 'It's only for a few years, Mum, until Alex has moved up the ranks a bit. Then we'll be back. And we'll be home twice a year on leave.'

Doris gave her a bright smile. 'Well, that's all right then. And I've got plenty to keep me occupied.'

Millie regarded her mother thoughtfully for a moment then put her cup down carefully in the middle of the saucer. 'Mum, you know I'm so pleased you're getting on well at your job and have made so many new friends since you moved, but I've been wondering...'

'Wondering what, dear?' Doris asked innocently.

'If perhaps you're doing a bit too much,' Millie said. 'I worry that you're going to wear yourself out. I mean, what with working at the shop, you're on the church's welfare committee, packing boxes for the Red Cross, and helping out at the Army resettlement office, and Aunt Ruby told me you've just volunteered to help out in the WVS canteen at King George's Dock.'

'Well, what do you want me to do, Millie? Sit at home all by myself?' her mother asked a trifle crossly.

'No, of course not. But—'

'But nothing,' her mother said briskly. 'I'm up bright and early each morning, sometimes before the sun's up, and I'm on the go all day, raring to go. And what's wrong with me spending my time helping people? Isn't that what you do?'

'Yes, but I also have at least four hours a day to myself plus a day off each week.' Millie's shoulders sagged. 'I'm sorry, Mum,' she said wearily, 'I'm just worried that you'll make yourself poorly, that's all.'

Doris smiled. 'Well, stop it, because I'm perfectly all right. Now, let's have another cuppa.' Millie slid her saucer over and her mother picked up the teapot. 'After all,' continued Doris, as she set the strainer on Millie's cup, 'keeping busy

303

stops me dwelling on things.'

Millie waved goodbye to the Buntons' three young children, who had their noses pressed against the cold window pane of number twenty James Street, and rolled her bike along to old Mrs Ashley at number four at the far end of the street. She knocked, but thankfully there was no answer. It was only a routine call to see if the old lady needed her ears syringing, and it could wait until next week.

Millie leaned her bike against the streetlamp and then pulled off her gloves. She shoved them in her pocket, took her visits diary from the side pocket of her case and flipped it open.

Although it was only three-thirty in the afternoon, a combination of a low cloud and river fog meant, even with the light from the lamp above, she had to hold her record book close to read the names.

She scanned down the remaining names: just two, and they could wait until the evening round. Thank goodness!

At least now she'd have time to pop in on her mother on the way back to the clinic. She'd meant to visit earlier in the week, but Sally had been in bed for the past four days with a temperature of 102, and so she, Annie, Beattie and Connie, whose patches all butted on to Sally's, had had to visit her patients in addition to their own. And this was crammed in alongside the school visits, antenatal clinic and doing two nights maternity on-call to cover Eva's holiday. It meant that since Monday Millie had only just finished the morning visits before she had to turn her attention toward the evening ones.

She put her diary back in the bag and, pulling her bike upright again, she rolled it forward and jumped on.

Ten minutes later, after weaving through a pack of dogs sniffing around in the gutter for scraps, Millie swung into Anthony Street and pulled up outside her mother's house. Lifting her bag out to take in with her, Millie slipped her hand in her pocket for the key, but it wasn't there. Thinking she must have left it on her dressing-room table, Millie knocked on the door. After waiting for a couple of minutes she knocked again, this time a lot harder. The sound echoed through the house but there was no other sound.

Millie went to the window and peered through the net curtain. The front room was neat and tidy as it always was, with her mother's sewing box sitting on the table next to a cup and saucer.

Was it Mothers' Union this afternoon or was she at the packing station for the Jewish refugees or was she minding a child for one of the neighbours? Millie couldn't remember.

'Are you looking for your mum, Sister?' a woman's voice shouted.

Millie turned around to see a woman dressed in a faded wraparound overall with curlers in her hair and a half-smoked roll-up hanging from her bottom lip. Balancing a baby on her hip, she shuffled across the road towards Millie.

'Yes,' replied Millie. 'Do you know where she is?'

The woman shook her head. 'I ain't seen her all day.'

Millie cupped her hands around her face and looked through the window again. 'She wasn't expecting me, so she's probably just out at the church or somewhere.'

'Come to think about it, I ain't seen her yesterday neiver.'

Doors were opening along the street and soon a crowd formed on the other side of the street with people craning their necks to see what was going on.

Millie turned back to the window and banged on it with the flat of her hand. 'Mum!' she shouted.

Still nothing.

Mrs Gilbert, who lived next door, came out.

'Wot's 'appened?' she asked, tucking a stray curler back under her grubby headscarf.

'Doris ain't answering the door,' the first woman replied.

'Can I climb over your fence, Mrs Gilbert?' Millie asked, hurrying towards her.

'Course.' Mrs Gilbert stood back as Millie rushed past.

Millie bolted through the Gilberts' living room and into the back scullery then out of the door. Ducking her head to avoid the limp, grey washing hanging on the clothesline, she threw her bag over the fence then, with her heart pounding in her throat, Millie stepped on an upturned zinc bucket and scrambled into her mother's backyard.

Without breaking her stride, Millie crossed the yard and opened her mother's unlocked back door.

The sickening smell of gas caught in her throat. Millie fumbled in her pocket for her handkerchief and clasped it over her nose and mouth. Throwing the door wide to let in air, she stumbled into the kitchen.

Her mother was lying on the scullery floor with her head in the open oven and all the gas taps turned fully on.

Millie turned the gas off and then, grabbing her mother's legs, pulled her back. Her head thumped on the slate floor but Doris didn't murmur. Millie ran to the front door and tore it open.

'Call an ambulance,' she screamed to the astonished crowd and then ran back in.

Her mother was where she'd left her, motionless and grey. Millie bent down and, hooking her arms under her mother's, she heaved her up and dragged her towards the front door. Others had followed her in and one of the men lifted Doris's lower half while another took some of the weight from Millie.

With her heart pounding Millie stumbled backwards into the street and they laid Doris down. Millie collapsed on her knees beside her mother and lifted her in her arms.

She put her hand on her mother's chest and felt it rise ever so slightly and a faint beating deep within. *Thank God!*

'Mum!' she screamed, shaking her and slapping her face. Doris's head rolled back and her mouth dropped open. Millie shook her again and someone handed her a newspaper.

Millie waved it frantically over her mother's face. 'Mum! It's me. Millie! Wake up!'

Doris's eyes rolled under her closed lids. Finally she coughed, gagged, and then rolled her head and vomited.

Her eyes flickered open a little. 'I just want to be with Arthur.'

Pain cut through Millie like a knife.

'It's all right, Mum,' she whispered, cradling her mother and pressing her lips to Doris's clammy forehead.

The clanging bells of the ambulance from the local station grew louder as it turned into the street. It screeched to a halt and two ambulance men jumped out from the back. They pulled a stretcher out and lay it down beside Doris while the driver brought over a cylinder of oxygen. They lifted Doris on to the stretcher and then one of them placed the rubber mask over her mouth and nose, and secured it behind her head.

Someone said they would take care of her mother's house and Millie thanked them and then dumbly followed the ambulance men as they loaded her mother into the back of the wagon. She climbed in and sat beside her mother. Doris had lost consciousness again but now she was being given oxygen her breathing was visible and regular.

'You her nurse then, darling?' asked one of the ambulance men as he climbed in.

'No, she's my mother,' Millie replied, holding her mother's unresponsive hand.

The engine roared into life and they juddered off with the emergency bell ringing above them.

The ambulance man turned his head and studied Doris. 'She's lucky you came by. What happened to her?'

'She fell asleep in the kitchen and the cooker

light must have blown out,' Millie said, not looking him in the eye.

Millie sat with her eyes closed and her head resting back on the dull green Victorian tiles that lined the London Hospital's second-floor corridor. She thought she must have been waiting outside Paulin Ward for almost half an hour but it could have been longer. Time seemed to have become oddly distorted since she'd burst into her mother's kitchen, but it must be close to midnight now, as the night-shift nurses had finished their rounds. She could hear them cleaning the metal trolley in the sluice just on the other side of the ward's double doors.

The sound of someone hastening up the stairs echoed along the empty passage. Millie rolled her head and opened her eyes to see Alex striding towards her in full uniform. As she rose to her feet he enveloped her in his arms. Millie put her head on his shoulder and sobbed.

He kissed her hair. 'It's all right, sweetheart,' he murmured.

'Oh, Alex, it was so scary.'

He held her while she cried out the tension of the past hours, then he sat her back on the bench.

'Now,' Alex said, taking off his coat and helmet and sitting beside her. 'Tell me what happened.'

Somehow, between sobs, Millie ran through the events of the afternoon. 'Although Mum had oxygen in the ambulance she remained unconscious all the way to the hospital and even when they examined her she barely responded and then just with incoherent murmurs. Her blood pressure and heart rate were through the roof, so we had to stay in casualty for hours until they came down from their dangerous level. The doctor is with her now.'

Alex raked his fingers through his hair. 'Well, thank God you arrived in time.'

'But, Alex, I should have realised she wasn't well. All the clues were there,' Millie blurted out. 'The straightforward way she accepted Dad's death and the move, her jolly attitude to everything, the frantic business to stop herself dwelling on things. I should have known she was unwell.'

He looked confused. 'They said in casualty there'd been a fault with the gas cooker and your mum was overcome.'

Millie bit her lower lip. 'I found her lying with her head in the oven and the taps turned on.'

Alex looked shocked. 'Bloody hell.'

'I know. And telling her that we were leaving in a few months the day before yesterday must have been the final straw. She just couldn't face life any more.' Millie covered her face with her hands. 'It's all my fault.'

Alex gathered her to him. 'It's not,' he said, pressing his lips on her hair. 'You couldn't have seen this coming.'

'But I should have because I'm a nurse and she's my mum,' Millie replied, burying her face in the rough barathea of his police greatcoat.

The ward door swung open and Millie and Alex stood up.

A young, dark-haired nurse dressed in the hospital's lilac-striped dress, white apron with matching puffy sleeves and frilly hat came out.

'How is my mother?' Millie asked.

'As well as can be expected,' the nurse replied. She looked at Alex.

'This is my fiancé,' Millie explained.

The nurse gave them a sympathetic look. 'If you'd like to follow me, Dr Roberts will see you now.'

Millie and Alex followed her into the ward and were ushered into the doctors' office to one side of the short passageway. Dr Roberts, a man in his early thirties with the tanned skin and clean-cut look of a recently demobbed officer, looked up from his notes as they walked in.

'This is Mrs Sullivan's daughter and fiancé, Doctor,' the nurse explained as Alex pulled out a chair for Millie.

Dr Roberts gave them a professional smile.

'How is my mother?' Millie asked, edging forward on the chair.

'Very lucky to be alive,' Dr Roberts replied. 'Although, we're not out of the woods by any means, your mother's chances of recovery are better than even. Unfortunately, until she wakes up, we have no real way of gauging the extent of her injuries and, depending how much carbon monoxide she breathed in, there may be some long-term effects to her cognitive function.'

'Meaning?' asked Alex,

'She might have brain damage,' replied Millie flatly.

Dr Roberts gave her a questioning look.

'I'm a district nurse at Munroe House,' she explained.

'Are you?' Dr Roberts' thick eyebrows rose. 'Well then, Miss Sullivan, you also know, and I'm

311

sure your fiancé will confirm, that the law no longer prosecutes attempted suicides.'

Millie's shoulders slumped. 'I know, I–'

'Then why did you tell the ambulance men that your mother's asphyxiation was an accident?'

Millie shook her head and looked helplessly across at her mother's doctor. 'I don't know, I just–'

'She was in shock,' Alex cut in. 'I'm sure, like me, you've seen enough of it in recent years to understand.'

Doctor Roberts' unyielding expression softened a little. 'Indeed.' He glanced at his notes again then looked up at Millie. 'I'm afraid it will be a few days before we know how she's been affected.' He closed his file. 'Perhaps you would like to sit with your mother for a few moments before lights out.'

Millie nodded and Alex helped her up. The nurse who had fetched them earlier beckoned them and they walked silently down the dimly lit ward to a bed opposite the nurse's desk. The nurse moved one of the screens aside and Alex guided Millie through the gap.

Her mother lay peacefully in the middle of the bed with an oxygen mask over her face. The pale blue hospital counterpane draped over the bed was similar to the one that had covered her father almost a year before.

Millie sank on to the chair beside her mother's bed and took her hand then lowered her head to rest her cheek on it. She felt her mother's wedding ring against her skin and tears welled up in her eyes again.

'Please get better, Mum,' she whispered, kissing

her mother's limp fingers. 'It would be too much to bear if I lost you, too.'

Millie lay staring dry-eyed up at the ceiling listening to the first trolley-bus trundle along Commercial Road towards the City and guessed it must be almost six o'clock. She could hear the nurses on the floor above getting ready and she would have to get up soon but just now she didn't have the energy, either physical or mental, to rise from her bed. She rolled her head and then turned to study the pale morning light seeping out from behind the curtains. It was going to be another lovely spring day.

There was a faint knock on her door and then it opened. Connie's head appeared around the corner. She had been on call last night and by the look of her crumpled uniform and bleary look she'd been called out to a delivery in the early hours of the morning.

'I just thought I'd pop in and see how things were,' she said in a half-whisper, coming in and closing the door quietly behind her.

'More or less the same.' Millie threw off the blankets and sat up.

'Is she awake yet?' Connie said, coming over and sitting beside her on the bed.

Millie shook her head wearily. 'Although the doctors said yesterday her reflexes responded when they tested them.'

Connie put her arm around her shoulders and squeezed. 'There you go. I bet by the time you get in today your mum will be sitting up and drinking a cup of tea.'

Millie gave her a feeble smile.

'Well, I hope you get some decent explanation out of the cooker company for the safety mechanisms on their appliance not working properly,' Connie said.

'I really should get up,' Millie said, without making an effort to do so.

'What time are you going to the hospital?' Connie asked.

'When visiting starts at three.'

'Is Alex going with you?'

Millie shook her head. 'He's on a late shift but he's going to ring this evening when I get back. He's been marvellous and I don't know what I would have done without him these past four days. Aunt Ruby will be there this afternoon.'

'I would have thought, under the circumstances, the old bat would have given you a couple of days off,' Connie said.

'There's no point at the moment, although I've asked to take three days' holiday when Mum comes out,' Millie replied, forcing aside the thought that she might not.

Connie gave her an encouraging smile. 'Well at least you've got four weeks until the wedding and she's bound to be fit and well by then.'

Millie looked past her friend at her wedding dress hanging on the end of the wardrobe and forced herself to stand. 'Well, Mrs Pierce will be ringing the breakfast gong any moment, so I'd better get dressed.'

Connie yawned. 'I'll see you at supper.'

She left. With her arms feeling like lead and her head stuffed with cotton wool, Millie dragged on

314

her uniform, then opened her bedroom door and made her way downstairs. As she passed the treatment room, the bell rang and Millie heard someone unbolt the outer door. She smiled. Some anxious father no doubt, Millie thought as she rested her hand on the knob at the bottom of the banister. The treatment-room door opened and Sally looked out.

'Oh, Millie, there's a–'

'Joan's doing the early on-call,' Millie said, holding her hand up. 'I'll see if she's having breakfast.'

'No, it's not a delivery. It's a, er, young lady asking for you in particular,' said Sally, looking nervously towards Miss Dutton's office.

'What about?' asked Millie.

'She didn't say,' Sally replied, signalling urgently for her to come.

Pushing aside the wave of weariness washing over her, Millie followed Sally into the treatment room. As she entered, the faint smell of cheap perfume tickled Millie's nose and she looked up. Standing awkwardly beside the pile of freshly cleaned bedpans on the cabinet was Olive from the Shangri-La Café. She wore a tight skirt, box-shouldered three-quarter-length jacket and last night's make-up. She shifted from one high wedge-heeled shoe to the other and gazed around at the shelves of lotions and potions. 'I ain't never seen so many bottles and jars in one place. Do you know what's in every one, Miss?'

'Yes,' said Millie, noting a fading bruise on Olive's right cheek.

'Well, you must be powerful brainy, that's all I

can say.' She smiled nervously and tugged her skirt down to cover her knees. 'I hope you'll not mind me dropping in on you like this.'

'Not at all,' replied Millie, forcing a cheerful smile. 'It's good to see you again, Olive. How is Gina?'

'Grand, so she is,' Olive said. 'Margie's been letting her take it easy.'

'Good, I'm glad she's feeling better,' Millie said. Her eyes flickered on to Sally. 'Now, I hope as how you won't be offended Sister, but me and the girls clubbed our coupons together and got you this.' Olive delved into the shopping bag and pulled out a box of Quality Street chocolates.

Millie reached out and took the quarter-pound box. As she gazed down at the soldier in his bright red uniform and woman in a pink dress holding a parasol beside him, Millie felt the corners of her eyes pinch.

'It ain't much,' continued Olive. 'But me and the girls just wanted to say thanks for what you did for Gina.'

'That's very kind of you,' Millie could hardly speak as tears gathered in her eyes.

Olive looked embarrassed. 'It's just a box of chocolates.'

'Sister Sullivan's mother's not very well,' Sally said to Olive, putting her arm around Millie.

Olive's painted face became a picture of sympathy. 'You poor ducks,' she said, reaching out and patting Millie's hand.

Millie took out her handkerchief and wiped her eyes. 'Please tell the girls it was very kind of them and it's really cheered me up.'

The treatment door opened and Gladys strolled in.

Her eyes flickered over Millie and then she looked at Olive.

Olive lowered her head. 'I ought to be going,' she said, stepping aside as Gladys pushed past to get to the dressing cupboard.

Millie took a deep breath and blinked. 'Thank you again for the chocolates. And I'll come by soon to see how Gina is for myself.'

Olive gave her a shy smile and shot out of the door.

Gladys spun around. 'I don't know what Miss Dutton will say when she finds out you've got women like *that* calling in on you.'

'She won't know unless you tell her, will she?' said Sally. 'And lay off Millie, will you?'

'Oh, yer, I'm sorry about your mother,' Gladys said, although her belligerent expression remained unaltered. 'And if you want my advice – straight in the bin,' she nodded at the chocolates. 'God only know where they've been.'

'And if you want mine,' retorted Sally, still holding on to Millie, 'I'd say you'd better get on your rounds before Mrs Atchison complains about not having her insulin in time again.'

Gladys glared at them both for a moment then snatched up her bag and stormed out of the room, banging the door behind her.

Millie ran her hand over the silky smoothness of the box then smiled up at her friend. 'Mum's favourite is the one with the nut in the middle,' she said, 'so I'll take them into her this afternoon and we can enjoy them together.'

Chapter Seventeen

Ruby straightened the starched sheet across Doris's chest for the umpteenth time since she'd arrived half an hour ago.

'I spoke to Edie and Bet, and told them you're being well looked after, Doris, and they said they will be in over the weekend,' Ruby said, looking through red-rimmed eyes at her sister. 'I'm sure you'll be back to your old self by then.'

The mild expression on Doris's face didn't flicker as her eyes remained fixed to the ceiling.

Ruby looked up at Millie. 'Are you sure she can hear me?'

'Yes, Aunt Ruby.'

'Then why doesn't she answer me?'

'She will. We all just have to be patient.' Millie forced a sunny smile. 'The flowers are nice. Are they from the garden?'

'But for how long?' Ruby replied, looking anxiously at her sister. 'It's been three days already since the doctors gave her the all-clear.'

'Maybe tomorrow,' replied Millie, wishing it so.

They lapsed into silence. Millie rested back and her gaze ran down the sunlight-flooded ward to where the elderly orderly was pushing the tea trolley along the ends of the beds. Ruby fiddled with the covers again. 'I still can't believe it,' she said.

'Mum couldn't help it, Aunt Ruby,' replied Millie. 'She just couldn't cope without Dad any more, that's all.'

'Well, I've been widowed and I didn't stick my head in the oven.' She looked down at her sister and frowned. 'Haven't I told you time and again not to wallow, Doris?' Ruby dabbed her eyes with her handkerchief and blew her nose. 'And what about poor Amelia? Four weeks from her wedding day and now this dumped on her shoulders. And what do you think her young man makes of it?'

'Didn't you say Tony was picking you up at four o'clock, Aunt Ruby?' Millie asked, feeling a headache threatening.

'Yes.'

'Well it's almost five to now,' she said, indicating the ward clock above the door.

Ruby looked at her wrist then held it to her ear. 'My watch says twenty to, but perhaps it's losing time again. I'll have to have it cleaned.' She stood up. 'I'll be back in tomorrow, Doris.' She patted her sister's hand again. 'You just do what the nurses say and get better, do you hear? Or you'll have your big sister to answer to.'

Ruby stood and came around the bed. She hugged Millie and kissed her on the cheek. 'I wish I could do something more.'

'You're here and that's enough,' Millie said, giving her a kiss back.

Her aunt enveloped her in another shaky embrace, then stood back and adjusted her hat.

Her chin wobbled ever so slightly as she took a last look at Doris and hurried down the ward.

Millie sat down again.

A fat bluebottle buzzed in through the open window above Doris's bed and, after doing a lazy circuit around them, flew out again. Millie stifled a yawn as her eyelids suddenly became heavy.

'I'm sorry.'

Millie sat bolt upright and her gaze fixed on her mother. 'Mum!' she said, grasping Doris's hand.

Her mother rolled her head and a tear escaped from the corner of her left eye. 'Ruby's right, it's not fair on...' She started to sob in little gasping croaks. 'But I miss him so much.'

The grief-stricken tone of her mother's voice cut into Millie's heart, but she squeezed her hand again.

'I know you do, Mum, I know,' Millie smiled encouragingly. 'You'll soon be better and what about if we go on a little holiday before me and Alex ... to Devon or somewhere. What do you say?'

Doris shook herself free of Millie's grasp. 'You should have left me.'

She rolled away from Millie and buried her face in the pillow. Anguish rose in Millie's chest and for a moment threatened to overwhelm her, but then she held it in check. She stared helplessly at her mother's shaking back for a moment and then went around to the other side of the bed.

'Come on, Mum,' she said, in a jolly tone. 'What do you think Dad would say if he heard you talking like that?'

Doris responded by pulling the covers over her head. Millie's hand fell limply to her side.

The ward bell sounded out, signifying the end of visiting times and the patients' friends and families started to leave. Millie leaned forward and awkwardly hugged her mother's shape under the covers.

'I'll be in tomorrow,' she said.

Again there was no response. Millie turned and walked up along the row of beds towards the double doors at the end.

'I thought it was you,' a cultured voice said as Millie passed the sluice room.

She turned and found Nurse Villiers standing behind her.

'How nice to see you again, Sister Sullivan.'

'Hello,' Millie said in a dull tone. 'I wondered if you were still working on the ward.'

'Yes, I've been home for a few days,' Nurse Villiers replied. 'Are you visiting another patient?'

'My mother, in bed seven,' Millie replied.

Nurse Villiers was contrite. 'I'm sorry. Mrs Sullivan, of course. Please accept my apologies for not realising.'

'It's quite all right. There are a lot of us Sullivans in this neck of the woods.' Millie forced a smile. 'Mum's still not quite feeling herself this afternoon.'

'She's been through a lot.'

'Yes. I know.' Millie's gaze returned to her mother's hunched form. 'I've tried to take some of the burden since Dad died but...' From nowhere tears welled up in her eyes and ran down her face. She brushed them away. 'I'm sorry ... I...'

Nurse Villiers gently put her arm around her shoulders and led her into the sluice room. She handed Millie a gauze washcloth and Millie dried her eyes.

'Thank you.' She looked around at sparkling clean urine bottles and bedpans stacked on wire shelves. 'It makes a change. When I was on the wards I used to flee to the linen cupboard to have a good sob.'

Nurse Villiers smiled. 'I always head for the lavatory myself.' She put her hand on Millie's arm. 'You mustn't blame yourself.'

The sluice door opened and the matron, a stout woman with frizzy grey hair and more than a hint of a moustache, poked her head around the corner.

Her eyes flickered over Nurse Villiers. 'The appendix in bed four is ringing her bell,' she snapped.

'Yes, Matron,' Nurse Villiers replied. 'It was so nice to see you again, Miss Sullivan,' she said to Millie as she gave her a warm smile.

The matron's lashless eyes bulged as the regal nurse glided past her and then she turned to Millie.

'Miss Sullivan,' she said, forcing her lips into a semblance of a smile. 'May I have a word with you about your mother before you go?'

'Of course,' Millie replied.

The matron, with her white cap flying behind, led her out of the sluice and into the ward office opposite. The junior doctor sitting in the corner with a full ashtray at his elbow and a pile of notes on his lap looked up as they walked in, then returned to his scribbling.

Millie took the chair by the small rickety-looking desk while the Matron settled her rear on the one on the other side. She opened the file in front of her and scanned down it briefly, then looked up at Millie.

'I'm pleased to tell you, Miss Sullivan, that des-

322

pite the amount of gas your mother inhaled, the doctors feel it will not have had any permanent physical effects on her.'

Millie slumped in the chair. 'Thank God.'

'However,' continued the matron. 'The same cannot be said of her state of mind.'

The matron clasped her hands together and rested them on Doris's notes. 'Dr Roberts, in conjunction with his psychiatric colleagues, reviewed your mother's case this morning and decided that she should be transferred to St Colombo's.'

A cold hand clutched at Millie's heart as the image of the old workhouse in Mile End Road flashed into her mind.

'But you must believe me, this is completely out of character,' Millie said. 'She just had a moment of weakness. After all, she lost my father, moved house and now I'm going to Palestine. It's just all got on top of her, that's all.'

The matron's thick eyebrows rose. 'You're going abroad?'

Millie explained briefly.

A pompous expression settled on the matron's face. 'Well, I'm sure you flitting off with your new husband has nothing whatsoever to do with your mother putting her head in the oven, but as I'm sure you'll appreciate, it's the hospital protocol to refer cases like your mother's to a lunatic asylum.'

Millie stared at her in horror. 'But surely, Matron, if I could talk to Dr Roberts?'

'I'm afraid that won't be possible. Your mother is being transferred on Friday.' The matron closed the book and her patronising smile returned. 'And don't worry, Miss Sullivan. All the staff at St

323

Colombo's have a great deal of experience dealing with mental cases.'

Lying in the dark on her bed, Millie repositioned the cold flannel over her eyes and prayed the two aspirins she'd taken just after supper an hour ago would soon start to work. With jumbled thoughts about Alex, her wedding day and St Colombo's barred windows still crashing around in her mind, she wasn't convinced they would.

There was a tap on the door and then it creaked open. 'Millie?' Connie's voice asked in a loud whisper.

Millie removed the flannel and opened her eyes.

'It's Alex.'

'I didn't hear the telephone,' Millie said struggling on to one elbow.

Connie shook her head. 'He's here downstairs in the small lounge.'

Relief flooded through Millie.

'Could you tell him I'll be straight down?' she said, switching on the bedside light and swinging her legs off the bed.

'Course.' Connie left.

Millie put her slippers on, put a comb through her hair then went into the hall. The glare of the landing lights made her blink but, thankfully, didn't exacerbate her headache. Swinging around the upright banister at the bottom, Millie dashed towards the small visitors' parlour beside the main recreation lounge and burst through the door.

Alex was standing in full uniform with his back to her and his hand gripping the marble fireplace, staring into the empty grate. He turned as

324

she rushed in.

'Alex, I'm so pleased you came instead of phoning,' she said, almost hysterical at the sight of him.

He crossed the space between them and took her in his arms. 'I had time owing so took the last four hours off. And I needed to see you.' He kissed her deeply and Millie clung to him.

'And I needed to see you, too,' Millie said, feeling her headache slowly recede.

He released her and they sat on the sofa.

'How's your mother?' he asked, twisting her engagement ring on her finger.

'A little better,' Millie replied. 'She's still not saying much but the nurses gave her a bath today and washed her hair so she's looking more like her old self. And the doctors don't think the gas did any permanent damage—'

'Thank God!' Alex raked his fingers through his hair as his old relaxed smile spread across his face. 'So when's she coming home?'

'Not just yet,' replied Millie. 'The matron caught me before I left.'

She told him about St Colombo's.

Alex looked horrified. 'For how long?'

Millie felt her eyes sting. 'I don't know. Perhaps a week or so.'

'But we're getting married in less than four!' He stood up and walked to the window and back.

'I don't want her in St Colombo's hospital any more than you do, Alex, but the doctors think it's best,' Millie snapped, watching him pace back and forth. 'And my mother can't help being ill.'

Alex came back and sat beside her. 'I'm sorry, sweetheart,' he said taking her hands. 'I know she can't, but it couldn't have happened at a worse time.'

Millie's annoyance evaporated. 'I know.' She traced her thumb up the back of his index finger. 'But I couldn't get married without her, so if Mum's not better in a week or two we'll have to postpone the wedding.'

'I understand how you feel, sweetheart.' He reached inside his jacket and pulled out an envelope. 'But I got this in the post today. It's from the Palestine Police Force's central offices in London. I have to report for duty on the seventeenth of June, so we can't postpone the wedding.'

A chill ran through Millie. 'But that's a week after we get married.'

'I know.'

'Surely if you tell them there's illness in the family or something, you'll be able to defer,' Millie said, hearing the panic in her voice.

'All right, Millie. I'll phone them and see.' He drew her to him and slipped his arm around her waist. 'And even if they can't, we're only shipping out a few months earlier than we thought. I do understand what I'm asking of you, but I love you and, selfish though it may be, I can't see a future without you, Millie.'

Millie shoved aside her anxieties and gave him a dazzling smile. 'I'm sure once the doctors at St Colombo's get her on the right treatment, Mum will be her old self and on her way home. I can almost see her now, throwing rice at us outside St George's at Whitsun and waving us off on the quayside.'

'I'm sure you're right,' said Alex, looking

mightily relieved. His dark eyes captured hers for a moment or two, but as he lowered his mouth on to hers Millie's head started to thump again.

Millie had just snuggled down under the covers when the telephone in the hall downstairs rang. With a heavy sigh she threw back the eiderdown and swung her legs out of bed. She'd cycled all the way to Jamaica Street to find that Mrs Gunn's stomach cramps were due to too many jellied eels rather than her ninth child arriving.

Still, she thought, as she shoved her arms into her dressing gown, at least it's my last night on call for three weeks.

Stifling a yawn, Millie made her way downstairs. She picked up the telephone and put the receiver to her ear. The pips went, the caller pressed button A, and they were connected.

'Good evening, Munroe House. Sister Sullivan speaking, how can I help?' Millie said, trying to sound as if she wasn't still half asleep.

'It's Joe Callaghan,' said a man's voice down the phone. 'My wife's having a baby and you need to come quick as you can.'

'Of course. Has your wife had a show?'

'Yesterday evening – at least, that's what she said.'

Millie smiled. 'That's fine,' she said reassuringly. 'It can happen a day or two before proper labour. Has your wife had any pains?' Millie asked.

'They started just before dinnertime and they've been getting stronger ever since.'

Millie glanced at the clock opposite. 'That was over twelve hours ago.'

'I know and her waters went as the factory hooter went off at six. Me ma said there's nothing to worry about but I think there's something right amiss. You really need to come and sort it out.'

'Why didn't you call me ... Callaghan?' asked Millie, as something akin to ice water washed over her. 'Are you Bridget Callag–'

'Yes I'm Ma Callaghan's son, but it's my wife Bernie that needs you. You must come now,' he said, the anxiety in his voice palpable down the line.

'I'll be there straight away,' said Millie. 'You live in Richard Street, don't you?'

'Yes, number four. But hurry.'

The phone clicked down. Millie replaced the receiver.

Trying to put the nasty thought of coming face to face with Bridget Callaghan in her own lair out of her mind, Millie sped back to her room and slipped into her uniform. Picking up her maternity bag as she dashed through the treatment room, Millie was cycling through the back gate within five minutes and turning into Richard Street some ten minutes after that.

A young man hovering on the pavement halfway down dashed towards her, causing Millie to put on the brake sharply.

'Sister Sullivan?' he asked, as she came to a screeching halt.

Millie dismounted. 'Yes.'

He grabbed her arm. 'This way, quick.'

Millie grabbed her bag as he hurried her towards the open front door of a two-up, two-down cottage.

Joe ushered Millie along the dark corridor and up the stairs to the small half-landing. Without stopping, he shoved open the door and they went in.

Bernadine Callaghan lay in the middle of a double bed with her hair plastered across her forehead, her sweat-drenched nightdress clinging to her and with blind terror in her eyes. Bridget Callaghan, dressed in her usual shapeless dress and wraparound, was bent over, massaging her daughter-in-law's distended stomach.

'Joe, help me!' screamed Bernadine as she saw her husband.

He dashed to her side. 'It's all right, ducks. I've got help. You'll be fine and dandy now.'

The old woman looked around sharply and her eyes narrowed to slits. She dragged herself to her feet and turned around.

'What's the matter with you, boy?' she spat at her son. 'I thought I told you I had everything in hand.'

Beads of perspiration sprang out on Joe's forehead. 'I know, Ma, but Bernie's in pain–'

Mrs Callaghan waved her hand dismissively. 'Dry births are always more painful, but she'll forget all about it once it's over.'

Millie went around to where Joe stood and put her bag on the bedside table, then took off her coat and unpinned her apron. She opened her bag and started to set out her equipment. As she put on her mask, Bernadine's hand shot out and gripped her wrist.

'Don't let my baby die, Sister,' she pleaded.

'Now, now, don't you worry, everything will be

329

just fine,' Millie replied, patting her shoulder gently. 'Can I examine you, Mrs Callaghan?'

Bernadine nodded. 'But call me Bernie. So I know who you're talking to.'

Millie placed her palm on the young woman's abdomen. Something, a knee or a bottom perhaps, was low in the young woman's pelvis but before Millie could distinguish what it was, it shifted away from her touch.

Please, God, don't let the baby present shoulder first, she thought.

'What's the matter?' Joe asked, looking anxiously at her face.

'Nothing's the matter, I tell you,' cut in his mother. 'I delivered more babies that you've had hot–'

'Will you shut up about fucking hot dinners, Ma,' Joe yelled. 'And either let the midwife do her job, or clear out.'

Mrs Callaghan's face mottled an unhealthy purple and she glared at her son. 'Shouldn't you be going down the pub instead of getting underfoot?'

Bernadine's eyes flew open and her knuckles cracked as she held on to her husband's hand. 'Don't leave me, Joe.'

Joe smiled. 'It's all right, chick, I'm not going anywhere.'

Millie continued to search for the baby's position. Her finger found the firmness again and she closed her hand around the distinctive roundness of the head. Thank goodness!

The next contraction gripped Bernadine and she gasped.

'Try to stay above it,' Millie said, placing a hand on the young woman's distended stomach and glancing down at her upside-down watch.

One, two ... Millie got to forty-five, and then the contraction subsided.

'Oh Joe,' Bernadine whimpered.

'It's all right, it's all right,' he said, gently stroking his wife's forehead.

Millie smiled encouragingly. 'It won't be long now.'

Bernadine gave a cry, then curled up and strained.

'Look up and pant, Bernie, but don't push just yet.' Millie snapped on her rubber gloves and gently slipped two fingers into the birth canal. She almost wept with relief as she felt the baby's head through the neck of the womb. The contraction subsided and Bernadine flopped back on the pillows. 'Is everything all right, Sister?'

Millie nodded. 'And it's got a full head of hair.'

Bernadine laughed and gripped her husband's hand. 'Did you hear that?'

'See, I said she was fine,' Mrs Callaghan said, giving Millie a derisory sneer.

Millie ignored her and patted her hip. 'Brace yourself on me, Bernadine, and push with the next contraction.'

'I can feel it coming,' she gasped, doing as she was told. Millie placed a gloved hand under her, ready to guide the infant into the world, but couldn't feel movement.

'Can you see my baby?' Bernadine gasped.

'Not yet,' Millie replied as her anxiety returned. Millie slipped her fingers in again and sweat

331

broke out between her shoulder blades. Somehow, the baby's head had retracted. It was too late to send Joe to call the doctor or for an ambulance, and if she didn't do something the baby would become wedged and die.

She snatched the pillows behind Bernadine's head.

'What's wrong?' asked Joe.

'The baby's misaligned and I'll have to get it back in position,' Millie replied. 'Now lay your wife flat and lift her hips.'

'How?'

'I don't care,' shouted Millie. 'Just get them as high as you can so I can get the pillows under.'

Joe jumped on the bed and, bending forward, heaved his wife's hips in the air. Millie shoved the pillows under and tilted her pelvis. Millie knelt on the bed and massaged Bernadine's stomach firmly. Another contraction started.

'For the love of God, don't push!' Millie yelled as the momentum started to build.

Mrs Callaghan stepped forward. 'In my experience, the pains will sort the position out if it's not quite right, so if you want my advice, let her–'

'Be quiet and let me concentrate,' Millie snapped back. Suddenly she felt a powerful movement under her hands as the baby shifted position.

Millie pulled out the pillows. 'Sit up and hang your legs over the end of the bed!'

Joe pulled his wife upright and she swung her legs on to the edge of the bed. Millie knelt down and ran her hand under the stretched skin.

Thank God, she thought, as the baby's head

pressed through the widening aperture into her hand.

'Breathe slowly with the contraction,' Millie said, as she checked for a tangled cord.

She cupped her hand and eased the baby's head clear, then manoeuvred the shoulders out. Gripping it firmly, she lifted it up and on to Bernadine's stomach.

The baby did indeed have a lot of hair, but its lips were blue and it lay unmoving. Swiftly Millie placed the mucus-smeared infant on a towel on the table and hooked her finger into its mouth to clear any muck, then rubbed it vigorously. The baby jolted and then it cried. Millie let out her breath and smiled down at the newborn child.

Bernadine and Joe laughed. 'What is it?'

Millie lifted the infant up and smiled. 'You have a healthy baby boy,' she said, clamping the cord, wrapping the infant in a towel and placing him in his mother's arms.

'Thank you, Sister,' said Bernadine, breathlessly. Her hand went to her stomach and she grimaced.

'It's just the afterbirth,' said Mrs Callaghan, hobbling up to the bed. 'I'll take care of it.'

Millie gave her a sweet smile. 'I'm afraid I can't allow that, Mrs Callaghan. Bernadine is my patient.' She turned back to Bernadine. 'If you shift on to your back and lift your knees, please.'

Millie picked up the enamel kidney bowl and put it in position to catch the placenta, but then, instead of the afterbirth, a head, covered with the same mop of dark hair as the first, popped out, followed by a shoulder and arm. In a swift move-

333

ment Millie lifted the baby. It hiccupped and then let out a wail.

Millie threw her head back and laughed.

'Two?' said Joe, looking shocked.

'Congratulations, Mr Callaghan, you are the father of twin boys,' Millie said cutting the cord and wrapping the second infant in another towel.

Joe looked down at his two sons with a stunned expression on his round face.

Millie washed and weighed the two babies, then dressed them and gave them back to their proud parents. Then, while the new family got to know each other, Millie tided away her equipment and, after making sure the babies had taken their first feed, she top-and-tailed them into the cupboard drawer that would serve as their cot for their first few weeks.

'Good night, I'll be around in the morning,' Millie called pleasantly to Bernadine and Joe as she picked up her case.

On her way to the door she stopped and glanced down at her night's work lying curled peacefully together asleep. Mrs Callaghan heaved herself out of the chair and lumbered over.

Her beady eyes flickered over Millie. 'As anyone around here will tell you, I speak as I find, and you did a good job with these two.' She smiled fondly down at her grandchildren. 'I'd say my Joe's a lucky chap having two for the price of one.'

'Would you, Mrs Callaghan? Would you indeed?' replied Millie, sharply. 'If you ask me, I'd say your daughter-in-law is the lucky one. Lucky that, despite having small hands and feet, there was just enough room for a baby to squeeze through her pelvis, lucky that her pre-eclampsia, which could have been treated weeks ago if you'd let her come to the clinic, hadn't developed to the full-blown version, lucky that her husband had the presence of mind to call for help in time, and lucky that your years of so-called midwifery experience didn't result in her delivering two stillborn children.'

Millie gave the old woman a withering look and then pushed past her to the door.

Chapter Eighteen

As the ambulance drew to a halt, Doris sat bolt upright on the stretcher and grabbed Millie's arm. 'Where are they taking me?'

'Just to another hospital so you can get better,' Millie said, over the thick lump forming in her throat.

Doris nodded and lay down again although she still clung to Millie's hand. Millie peered apprehensively through the small side window at St Columbo's Hospital.

The local asylum sat like a fat toad on the old road from London. Built when Queen Victoria had been on the throne, it had the classic layout of a mid-nineteenth-century workhouse. It was constructed of yellow bricks with white masonry around the windows and doors. The two-storey wings jutted out either side of the imposing central block and dull grey roof tiles. In front of it was a low wall with iron railings shaped like up-ended spears.

The ambulance jolted forward and her mother's grip tightened. 'It's all right, Mum.'

Doris looked trustingly at her as guilt stabbed at Millie.

They rolled forward a few more yards and then stopped again and the engine was turned off. Millie helped her mother sit up and swing her feet on to the floor, then she pulled down her skirt and made sure her shoelaces were still fastened.

Thankfully, as Friday was her morning off and as Nurse Villiers had been in charge, she'd allowed Millie to get her mother ready. So now, dressed in her light blue frock with her hair washed and combed, Doris looked much better. Perhaps Alex was right, and Doris would be back to her old self in good time for the wedding.

The back doors of the ambulance opened. 'Ding, ding. End of the line. Everybody out!' called the ambulance driver.

Millie held her mother's hand and walked her to the ambulance door. Doris looked around.

'Where are we?' she asked, a confused expression on her face.

'At the Barmy Farm, missus,' the driver said, taking her hand to help her down the step.

Doris's eyes grew wild with terror. 'Where?'

Millie put her arm around her mother's shoulders reassuringly. 'It's all right, Mum,' she said, giving the driver a furious look.

The ambulance man, a red-faced individual with a receding hairline, shrugged, took a half-smoked cigarette from his top pocket and re-lit it.

A large woman wearing an orderly's uniform came over. 'Wotcha, Len,' she said, puffing to a halt in front of them. 'What you doing 'ere?'

'Just delivering you another customer, Mo,' the ambulance man replied. He flicked the cigarette butt in a high arch and then closed the ambulance doors. 'And now I'm off for me grub.'

'This is my mother, Mrs Sullivan,' Millie said as the ambulance drove off. 'Dr Roberts has referred her.'

The ward orderly looked them up and down without introducing herself. 'Well, you'd better come this way.'

Millie followed her through the institution's half-glazed double doors and into the sparse entrance hall. The listless-looking woman sitting behind the reception desk looked up as they approached.

'Sullivan from the London,' Mo snapped.

The woman behind the desk picked up a clip-board and glanced at it. 'Rose,' she said, without moving her lips.

Mo led them past a patient rocking back and forth in the middle of the hallway towards the sweeping central stairs. Hooking her mother's arm in hers, Millie followed the orderly to the first floor and along to the far end of the corridor and into Rose Ward.

As Millie stepped inside, the throat-clogging stench of stale urine, disinfectant and floor polish filled her nose. Her stomach heaved. Although it was a warm day outside, the temperature in the ward was decidedly chilly and the lack of warmth was intensified by the stark black and white tiles on the floors and dank grey-emulsioned walls.

There were probably thirty beds in the ward, arranged in the traditional Nightingale fashion down each side of the room, but that's where the resemblance to an ordinary hospital ended.

At the far end of the ward two orderlies were securing an old woman wearing a faded dress in a tilt-back chair, while a third orderly was shoving the spout of an invalid feeder into another woman's tightly clamped mouth.

A nurse in an ill-fitting blue uniform shambled

towards them.

'This is my mother, Mrs Sullivan,' Millie said, before Mo could do the introductions. 'She's been referred by Dr Roberts at the London Hospital.'

The nurse turned her attention to Doris.

'Hello, my pet, I'm Nurse Dunn,' she said, in a squeaky little voice as she reached out for Doris's hand. 'You come with me and I'll show you where your nice little bed is.'

Doris looked anxiously at Millie.

'It's all right, Mum. I'm coming too.'

She started forward but Nurse Dunn blocked her way. 'We don't allow family in for the first day or two after a patient is admitted. It unsettles them.'

Doris grabbed Millie's hand. 'But my Millie's a nurse and a midwife, and so she can come in.'

The nurse's piggy eyes flickered over Millie. 'Where do you work then?'

'She's a Sister on the district,' Doris piped up. 'Top of her class she was at the London.'

Nurse Dunn's pugnacious attitude ebbed a little. 'Well, all right, but you'll find things on the mental side a bit different from the general.'

'I'm sure,' replied Millie, glancing around at the patients wandering aimlessly up and down the ward.

Nurse Dunn gave Millie the once-over again and then led them down to the empty bed at the end of the ward. A woman with wild hair sitting cross-legged on her bed screamed out as they passed. Doris shrank back.

'Take no notice of old Peggy,' Nurse Dunn said in the squeaky voice that was already grating on

Millie. 'She's only after some attention. There we go. This is your little place.' She indicated the bare iron bedstead with a threadbare throw over it. 'I'll leave you to unpack.'

Millie glanced at the clock on the wall above the door. 'I have to be on duty at five. Do you think the doctor will be long?' Millie asked, as she put her mother's suitcase on the bed.

A puzzled expression spread across Nurse Dunn's flat face 'The doctor?'

'Who's in charge of my mother's care?' Millie replied. 'I'd like to explain to him what my mother's been through recently and discuss her treatment.'

'Oh, he won't be here until Monday,' Nurse Dunn replied. 'But don't worry, he'll talk to you then.' She glanced down the ward. 'If you don't mind, I have to...'

'Of course,' replied Millie.

Nurse Dunn smiled fleetingly at Millie and then looked past her. 'Florence! Put your clothes back on!'

She marched off.

Millie turned to her mother. 'Right then, Mum, shall we unpack?'

There wasn't much, just two nightdresses, some underwear and a change of clothes.

'That should keep you going until I come on Monday,' Millie said as she closed the locker door beside her mother's bed. 'I'm afraid I have to be going, Mum.'

Fear flashed into her mother's eyes and she grabbed her hand. 'Don't leave me, Millie. I don't like it here.'

Millie's throat tightened but she forced a jolly

smile. 'I have to, Mum, so you can get the right treatment. It's only for a few days until you're well, and then I'll be taking you home.'

'I can go home in a few days?' echoed Doris.

Millie smiled reassuringly at her. 'I promise you can, but first you must rest and get well because I need you there beside me on my big day.'

Doris rested back in the chair and patted Millie's hand and smiled at her. 'You're a good girl.'

Millie bent forward and kissed her mother on the cheek. 'You just have a quiet weekend and I'll be in Monday to see how you're getting on.'

Doris gave her a brave little smile and nodded.

Millie kissed her again and then, before she changed her mind, she walked briskly back down the ward. As she got to the door she turned.

In the bed on one side of her mother a young woman with unkempt blonde hair nursed a china doll while on the other a stick-thin woman with bruises on her face tapped out a soundless tune on her knees.

Doris waved, and guilt pressed down on Millie like a physical weight. Somehow she managed to smile and wave back before, blinded by tears, she stumbled out of the ward.

Millie sat in the corner of the nurses' lounge with her feet up on the leather footrest and her eyes closed as the strains of the BBC Symphony Orchestra drifted out of the radio behind. As it was Friday night everyone except Sally, who was the nurse on call, was out enjoying themselves. They'd invited Millie, but thankfully Alex had left a message that he would pop by later, so they didn't press her to come, which was just as well, because after her trip to St Colombo's she wouldn't be good company.

She must have drifted off to sleep because she jolted awake as the telephone rang and someone thumped down the stairs to answer it.

Millie settled down again and rested her head back.

The door opened and Sally came in. 'Oh Millie, you are here. It's Alex.'

Millie got up, walked out of the room and down the corridor to the desk at the front entrance.

She picked up the receiver. 'Hello.'

'Hello, Millie,' Alex said in a warm tone. 'Look, love, there's been a knife fight in the Ship and Compass and so we've been kept on.'

'Oh,' said Millie.

'I'm sorry, darling. I really am. How was it today?'

Millie turned towards the wall and cupped her hand over the mouthpiece. 'Oh, Alex, it was so awful.' In a low voice she told him about her mother's admission.

'It was only the first day,' he said when she'd finished. 'I'm certain things will look a bit more on the up and up when you see her on Monday after they've started the treatment.'

'Maybe,' the ache in Millie's chest deepened. 'I wish you were here.'

'So do I.'

'Can we meet tomorrow in Kate's Café?' Millie asked. 'I could slip in there about midday for dinner.'

'I don't know,' Alex replied. 'This thing at the

Ship is pretty big and I've got a feeling our leave will be cancelled tomorrow.'

'Oh.'

'But if it's not, I'll give you a tinkle.'

'Did you manage to get through to the Palestine Police office today?' she asked.

'I did.' There was a pause. 'Look, I didn't want to tell you over the phone, but the upshot is that the chap at the other end wasn't very helpful.'

Millie couldn't speak.

'I know you've got a lot on your plate at the moment without all this, honey, but don't worry. I'm off on time next Friday so I'm going up to the Foreign and Commonwealth office to sort it all out face to face.'

'Oh, Alex,' Millie said as relief flooded over her. 'If we could just postpone going for six months then I'm sure Mum–'

A klaxon and a clangour of bells sounded.

'I'm sorry, Millie, I've got to go,' Alex shouted down the phone. 'I'll call you tomorrow.'

'All right. I love yo–'

The phone went dead.

Millie replaced the receiver. Although she ached to see him, perhaps it was as well Alex couldn't come around tonight. Once he had postponed his commission then she'd tell him her monthlies were a week late.

Millie had intended to catch Miss Dutton after her morning round to discuss Doreen and Joan, but perhaps, as the superintendent was working late, it might be better if she spoke to her now. Turning from the kitchen, Millie walked back down the hall to the room at the far end.

As she raised her hand to knock she heard a man's voice say something on the other side of the door. Thinking it must be one of the tradesmen, Millie tapped lightly. A chair scraped and then Miss Dutton called, 'Come in.'

'I'm sorry to disturb you,' started Millie. She stopped when she spotted who was in Miss Dutton's office.

Mr Shottington was sitting in the easy chair by the filing cabinets with a fat cigar clamped between his teeth and a blasé expression on his face. He was wearing a three-piece dinner suit with a white silk scarf draped around his neck, and patent evening shoes.

Although not as splendidly attired as the surgeon, Miss Dutton was nonetheless smartly dressed in a snugly fitting maroon sateen dress and had applied a touch of blush to her cheeks and colour to her lips. In contrast to the chairman's relaxed appearance, the superintendent looked tense as she hovered in front of her desk.

Mr Shottington's piggy eyes ran slowly over Millie. 'Ah, Sister Sullivan, How nice to see you, again.'

'Good evening, Mr Shottington,' Millie replied. She looked at Miss Dutton. 'I'm sorry. I'll come back tomorrow.'

Mr Shottington heaved himself to his feet. 'No, no. I must be on my way.'

Miss Dutton put her hand up as if to stop him. 'I'm sure whatever Sister Sullivan wants can wait until tomorrow.'

'Please don't leave on my account,' Millie said,

wishing she'd stuck to her original plan.

Mr Shottington stubbed out his cigar and smiled congenially at her. 'I'm not. Gielgud's playing Hamlet at the Aldwych and I don't want to miss curtain-up. Good night, Miss Dutton, Sister Sullivan.'

He strode out of the room and closed the door behind him.

Miss Dutton stared after him for a moment then turned her attention to Millie. 'He happened to be passing, so popped in to tell me a couple of things.'

'That was kind,' Millie replied, for want of anything else to say.

Miss Dutton returned to her side of the desk and sat down. 'Well, now you're here, what is it you want to see me about?'

Millie told her about her wedding plans but omitted to mention the Palestine Police. Although Connie, Annie and Beattie knew about it, Millie decided not to make it generally known until after the wedding.

'I'm surprised your husband is allowing you to work after you're married,' said Miss Dutton when she'd finished.

Millie looked puzzled. 'Why?'

'Well, most men don't want people to think they can't provide for their family,' she said, with just a trace of a smirk.

'My fiancé isn't most men,' Millie replied coolly. 'And he's happy for me to continue at Munroe House.'

'You'll still have to do your on-call rota, you know,' Miss Dutton said with an expression like

345

she'd been sucking lemons.

'I know,' replied Millie. 'And we'll apply for a telephone as soon as we have somewhere to live.'

'Then I suppose I ought to wish you well, Sister Sullivan,' Miss Dutton said sourly.

Millie smiled sweetly. 'Thank you, although I would have thought you'd be relieved I was staying, not implying I should leave.'

'Of course, it would be a great loss to us all if you left, Sister Sullivan, but...' She sighed wearily. 'I'm worried that married nurses will put their husbands first and neglect our poor patients.'

'So you're worried about our patients,' Millie said.

Miss Dutton put on her Florence Nightingale-with-constipation expression. 'Of course. They are my overriding concern, as they should be for all nurses.'

'Well then, it's a pity your constant swapping around nurses' rest days, half-days and on-call rotas means that some patients have to wait until lunchtime before they are washed and dressed, that others can't have their breakfast until almost ten because the nurse has too many insulins to do, while patients with wounds have to get their families to do the dressing because the nurse is so late in coming.'

A flush spread up Miss Dutton's neck. 'There have been some minor hiccups since I reorganised the nursing areas, but that's to be expected of course. And don't forget we're not fully staffed. After all, there is a shortage of nurses in London.'

'I grant you there's a shortage, but why have three of ours left in the past month? And to my

346

certain knowledge there are two others planning to follow them. I'll tell you, shall I?' Millie said, before Miss Dutton could answer. 'Our general and maternity cases have almost doubled since VJ day, we're already working on our days off, and you're rota-ing us for additional work without even asking. And if that wasn't bad enough, before the girls set out on a long day's work they have to spend half an hour tidying their rooms so you don't dock money from their wages for leaving their stockings on the bedroom floors.'

Miss Dutton's face turned purple. 'I suppose you think you could do a better job.'

Millie didn't answer.

The superintendent's mouth pulled into an ugly line. 'Well, it doesn't matter what you think, Sister Sullivan. Because the Association's board appointed me to run Munroe House to ensure that patients are cared for properly. And as to being short-staffed – I can't stop nurses leaving, and nor can I conjure them out of the air.'

'If you're genuinely worried about neglecting patients, why don't you actually recruit some more nurses?' Millie asked.

'I don't expect you to understand, but I can't just put an advert in the *Nursing Mirror*,' Miss Dutton explained, as if speaking to a child. 'I have to get the board's agreement before I can employ more nurses.'

'Well, why don't you just ask your friend Mr Shottington?' asked Millie.

'I told you he only popped in because he was passing,' replied Miss Dutton sharply. 'He's never been here before.'

Millie looked her square in the eye. 'I know about your association with the board's president, Miss Dutton.'

The blood drained from Miss Dutton's face. 'You do?'

'Mrs Archer told me you worked under him at the Brompton,' Millie continued.

Some of the colour returned to the superintendent's face.

'Look, I really don't care how you know Mr Shottington. All I ask is that you use your influence with him to get us some more nurses,' Millie said.

'Well, I suppose I could ask him.' Miss Dutton cleared her throat. 'Was there anything else you wanted me to do?'

'Well, you could stop harrying the newly qualified QNs from pillar to post,' Millie replied. 'They are all good nurses and I wouldn't want them to look for pastures new.'

'I'll review their caseload at the end of the month,' Miss Dutton said stiffly.

'Thank you,' Millie said, more than a little shocked now at her own boldness. 'Then I'll wish you a good night.'

Miss Dutton gave a sharp nod and opened the daily ledger.

Millie walked across the room but looked back as she reached the door. 'And, Miss Dutton, when you next see Mr Shottington, please could you ask him to raise the issue of the St George's and St Dunstan's District Nursing Association's pay scale, as both the West Ham and Hackney Associations are paying ten shillings a week more.'

348

Chapter Nineteen

Stepping carefully between the puddles left by the spring shower, Millie hurried along Jubilee Street. On the bomb-site to her left a gang of boys, still in their school uniforms, fought a pretend battle and fired imaginary guns at each other as they jumped in and out of the blackened beams and tumbled-down walls. Opposite, outside the houses that had survived the incendiary bombs, women dressed in their drab overalls and carpet slippers paused in their conversations to acknowledge Millie as she dashed by with a cheery wave.

Holding her breath as she passed the pickled onion and smoked salmon factories in Assembly Passage, Millie emerged on to Mile End Road just in time to see a number twenty-five shoot past.

Suppressing the urge to scream, Millie dodged behind a fully loaded brewers' wagon pulled by two dray horses resplendent with their harness brass shining merrily, and a Sainsbury's delivery lorry, and crossed the road.

Making sure she was out of the spray range of the passing traffic, Millie leaned against the bus stop sign and yawned. Her eyelids felt heavy and she had to force them open.

'Yoo-hoo, Sister Sullivan.'

Pushing the foggy feeling in her mind away, Millie looked around, and inwardly groaned.

Not because of Bernadine Callaghan, who was

pushing a deep-bodied pram with one hand and waving happily at her with the other, but because of the old woman hobbling along beside her. Although Millie had seen Mrs Callaghan a couple of times in the street since the night the twins were born, it had been in passing and so they hadn't had to speak. Nevertheless Millie forced a pleasant smile.

'Hello, Bernadine,' she said as the young mother stopped in front of her. Millie's eyes flickered on to her mother-in-law. 'Good afternoon, Mrs Callaghan.'

A chilly expression fixed on the older woman's face. 'And to you, Sister Sullivan,' she said from taut lips.

Millie looked into the pram at the two babies curled asleep. 'How are the boys?'

'They're grand.' Bernadine smiled fondly into the pram. 'James, he's the one with his hand against his ear, is a few ounces heavier, but John is catching up with him.'

'Are you feeding them yourself?' Millie asked, conscious of Mrs Callaghan's beady eyes fixed on her.

Bernadine shook her head. 'Joe's Ma said I didn't have enough, so I had to top them up with a bit of connie-onnie. That's all right for them, isn't it?'

'As long as you dilute the condensed milk as it says on the tin.' Millie smiled down at the sleeping infants. 'And are they good babies?'

Bernadine laughed. 'They would be if they didn't wake me up two or three times in the night.'

'I've told you to thicken the last feed with a bit

350

of Farley's rusk,' Mrs Callaghan cut in.

Bernadine's head snapped around. 'The nurse at the clinic said they were too young for that.'

Mrs Callaghan rolled her eyes. 'I gave it to mine and it didn't do them any harm.'

'That was in the old days,' Bernadine replied tartly. 'I prefer to take notice of people who are trained properly in how to look after babies.'

The two women exchanged a couple of sharp looks before Mrs Callaghan turned her attention back to Millie.

'You look a bit peaky, if you don't mind me saying so.'

'I was called out for a delivery last night,' Millie replied.

In fact she'd been back in bed by 1 a.m., but had just lain there until dawn staring at the ceiling, restless as worries about Alex, her mother and her wedding were running around in her head. It had been much the same for the previous three nights, too.

'I hear your mother had an accident with her gas cooker,' Mrs Callaghan said. 'Is she all right?'

Somehow Millie managed an unconcerned smile. 'Yes. I expect the doctors will send her home soon.' She spotted a bus trundling towards her. 'In fact, I'm just off to visit her now.' Millie put her hand out to stop the bus. 'Well, it's nice to see you and I'm glad the twins are doing well.'

The bus stopped and Millie jumped on the backboard.

Mrs Callaghan's penetrating stare flickered over Millie's face. 'So your mother's in the London, is she?'

351

Millie smiled brightly. 'Yes.'

The conductor rang the bell and the bus rolled away.

'Well, then,' called Mrs Callaghan, 'the London Hospital's behind me, so you're going the wrong way.'

Millie jolted awake just in time to realise she was about to miss her stop. Thankfully she was sitting on one of the long seats at the back of the bus, so managed to jump off just before it pulled away.

Millie looked across at St Columbo's on the other side of Mile End Road and then, shoving the cloud of despondency aside, she crossed the road toward it.

The main gates were secured with a rusty lock, so Millie entered through the less imposing side entrance. Walking swiftly past the inmates tending the garden, she pushed open the half-glazed front doors and entered the main corridor. Her heels echoed around the vast space of the foyer and up the stairs to the first floor.

A porter pushing an old man slumped in a wheelchair passed her as she hurried towards Rose Ward. Pausing for a second, Millie took a long breath and then shoved the door open.

Inside the ward it was much the same as it had been when she'd left her mother there on the Friday except, as it was visiting time, there were one or two visitors sitting at some of the beds. Smiling briefly at the orderly mopping the floor, Millie made her way to her mother's bed at the far end.

Doris was lying with her eyes open and an

empty expression on her face. She was wearing the same dress she'd been admitted in except now there was what looked to be a gravy stain down the front of it. Her stockings had been left off and her hair uncombed. A hollow feeling flickered in Millie's chest but she managed to find a cheery smile.

'Hello, Mum,' she said, pulling up the chair and sitting beside her mother's bed.

Doris rolled her head and puzzlement flickered in her eyes. 'Is that you, Millie?' she muttered.

'Yes, Mum. I've come to see you,' Millie said. 'How are you?'

Doris looked muddled. 'I don't know. Where am I?'

Millie took her mother's hand, and stroked it gently. It was cold, and Millie noticed discoloration on her forearm that could have been a hand mark.

'You're on Rose Ward in St Colombo's,' Millie replied, as her misgivings suddenly multiplied. 'Don't you remember?'

Doris shook her head. 'My mind is a bit of a jumble at the moment, dear. Why am I here?'

'So you can get better,' Millie replied. She reached around the back of her mother's locker and felt the dry towel and flannel. 'Have you had a wash today, Mum?'

'I suppose so,' Doris replied.

'And what did you have for dinner?'

Doris looked blank.

Millie spotted a nurse coming out of the office carrying the files containing the nursing notes. She sat down behind the desk and opened the

353

first set of notes.

'I won't be a moment, Mum,' Millie said.

She stood up and hurried back down the ward to the nurses' station.

'Excuse me.'

The nurse, a thin individual with mousy hair and a uniform at least two sizes too big, looked up. 'Yes?'

'My mother, Mrs Sullivan in bed six, doesn't seem to have had a wash today,' Millie said.

'She must have if she's dressed,' the nurse replied.

'But she's not wearing her stockings and her hair isn't brushed,' Millie said firmly. 'And there's a bruise on her arm. And I'm a bit concerned that she seems confused.'

'A lot of our patients are confused,' replied the nurse, drily. 'That's why they're here in the first place.'

Millie gave the nurse behind the desk a steely look. 'Is the doctor around?'

'I'm not sure.'

'Perhaps you could find out?'

A disgruntled expression settled on the nurse's lean features but she picked up the telephone receiver. 'Could you put me through to Dr Benfield, please?'

There was a pause.

'Hello, Dr Benfield, it's Nurse Williams on Rose Ward. I'm sorry to interrupt you but Mrs Sullivan's daughter is here and would like to ask some questions about her mother.' Her eyes flickered over Millie again. 'Yes, she's the district nurse. Thank you, Doctor.' She replaced the receiver and

354

smiled at Millie. 'He'll be with you in a few moments.'

'Thank you. I'll wait with my mother.'

Millie left the nurse to her clerical duties and returned to her mother. Doris lay curled up like a child and had gone to sleep, so Millie sat down quietly beside her.

Thankfully, she didn't have long to ponder on whether she should have agreed to her mother being sent to St Colombo's, because within a few moments the doors to the ward swung open and a young man, with his white coat flapping behind him, marched into the room. He said something to the nurse, she handed him a set of notes and he walked down the ward towards Millie. She stood up as he approached.

Dr Benfield was probably a year or two older than Millie and was wearing baggy-kneed corduroys, a country-weave shirt and a tweed jacket and tie. He had straw-coloured hair, pale eyes and a painful-looking shaving rash.

He stopped at the bottom of her mother's bed. 'Good afternoon, Miss,' he consulted his notes, 'Sullivan. I'm glad the nurse called me because I wanted to have a little chat with you about your mother's treatment. If you'd like to come with me?'

Millie followed him to the ward office. He offered her a seat and then took up his position behind the desk. He pressed his hands together as if in prayer, and then rested his chin on his fingertips.

'Well, Miss Sullivan. What would you like to know?'

Millie took a deep breath and gave him a friendly smile. 'My mother seems a little listless.'

'It's probably the sedative.'

'Sedative?'

He extracted a curved wooden pipe from the pocket of his white coat. 'We thought it best,' he said, drawing out a tobacco wallet and packing his pipe. 'She was very agitated after she was admitted.' He smiled condescendingly. 'Just a little something to jolly her along until the main treatment kicks in.'

'And what is the main treatment?'

'ECT,' he replied in a matter-of-fact tone.

Millie gasped. 'Electro-convulsive therapy! Didn't Mengele use that in the concentration camps?'

'It was never proven. And in any case the type of therapy we use is quite different.' Dr Benfield stuck his pipe in his mouth and lit it. 'Your mother, Miss Sullivan, is suffering from what we in psychiatry call depression.'

'I know. It's because of the strain she's been under. You see, doctor, my father–'

'A century ago your mother would have been labelled insane and chained to a wall in an asylum, never to be seen again,' he interrupted, puffing energetically on his pipe. 'But this is the modern age and we can treat mental weakness.'

'But isn't ECT dangerous?' Millie asked, feeling more than a little uneasy questioning a doctor's treatment.

Dr Benfield shook his head. 'Not at all. We secure the patient so they can't fall off the bench when they convulse and a wooden block is placed

356

between the teeth to protect the tongue, so they are perfectly safe.'

'The poor patient must be terrified,' said Millie.

'We're not savages, Miss Sullivan. We anaesthetise them first.' He rested his arms on the table and leaned across. 'Rest assured a couple of bursts of the old ECT and your mother will be on her way home as good as new.'

'She will?'

'I promise you.' He pulled a sheet of paper from her mother's notes and laid it in front of Millie. 'Now if you could sign to say you'll allow us to go ahead, we can start your mother's treatment this week.' He pulled a tortoiseshell fountain pen from his pocket, unscrewed the top and handed it to her.

Millie took the pen. 'And it's perfectly safe?'

Doctor Benfield smiled superciliously. 'Perfectly.'

Millie gripped the pen and reluctantly scratched her signature along the dotted line at the bottom.

As Miss Dutton read out the last few items from the clinic diary, Millie slipped her hand into her pocket and ran her fingertips over the resignation letter. The familiar flutter of uncertainty ran through her, but Millie pushed it aside.

She would definitely give it to the superintendent this morning. After all, her mother had had her second treatment two days ago and seemed to have improved. Well, perhaps improved wasn't quite the word, as she'd gone from being listless and uncommunicative to slightly nervy and overly talkative, but at least now she was reacting to her surroundings. As the doctor had said, it was a step

357

in the right direction, and so Millie had no excuse for holding on to her resignation letter any longer. If she didn't put it in tomorrow she would have to work to the eighth of July and then only have a day to say goodbye to everyone before catching the train to Southampton.

Miss Dutton's shrill voice cut across Millie's thoughts. 'And finally, nurses, remember to leave your cases in the treatment room by six o'clock this evening for my inspection.' She closed the diary with a thump. 'That will be all.'

The nurses stood up and started to make their way out. Millie picked up her nurse's bag from under her chair and went over to the superintendent.

'Excuse me, Miss Dutton. May I have a quick word with you?' Millie said with her heart thumping in her chest.

Miss Dutton's ice-blue eyes flickered over her. 'Could it wait until later?'

'It is quite pressing,' Millie insisted.

'Very well,' Miss Dutton replied grudgingly.

Millie followed her out of the treatment room and along the hall towards her office.

Miss Dutton sat down behind her desk. 'So, what is it you wanted to see me about?'

Millie put her hand in her pocket and fingered the letter again. 'As you know, I'm getting married next Saturday and well, Alex, my fiancé, na–'

'For goodness sake, spit it out, Sullivan, I haven't got all day,' Miss Dutton barked.

The door behind them burst open and Mr Shottington, dressed in a charcoal frock coat, tartan waistcoat and pinstriped trousers, strode in.

'Good morning, Superintendent,' he boomed, throwing his hat on to the papers on Miss Dutton's desk.

She jumped up and bumped her hip on the side of her desk in her eagerness to greet him.

'Good morning, Mr Shottington,' she twittered, her ill-temper evaporating in an instant. 'What an unexpected but very pleasant surprise.'

'I thought that as it was such a fine morning I'd stroll down and discuss a couple of Association matters in person.' He beamed at her. 'Any chance of a coffee?'

'Most certainly.' Miss Dutton turned to Millie. 'Tell Mrs Pierce to make Mr Shottington a coffee straight away.'

'But–'

'Straight away.' The superintendent glared at her. 'And tell her to make it strong and sweet–'

'Just like myself,' chipped in Mr Shottington ebulliently.

'And be quick about it,' Miss Dutton added.

Millie shoved her resignation letter back in her pocket. 'Yes, Superintendent.'

Chapter Twenty

'Yes, we need two plates of both meat paste and egg and cress sandwiches, along with the pork pies and pickles,' Millie said, feeding the telephone box another couple of coins.

The two women waiting outside rolled their eyes and shifted impatiently on the spot. Millie gave them an apologetic smile. She was in the telephone box in front of the Black Boy public house next to Stepney train station.

'That's very kind of you, but I'll bring the cake when I pop by on Friday night. Yes, the wedding's at eleven-thirty, so we should be back from the church by one.' Millie glanced at her watch. 'And you will make sure there's lemonade and cream soda as well as beer for people? Lovely.'

One of the women outside, a chubby woman with her hair in curlers and a roll-up hanging out of her mouth, tapped on the glass. Millie smiled and nodded.

'Yes, it's just over a week,' she said. 'Of course I'm excited. And thank you for your help, Mrs Kemp. Bye.'

Millie put the telephone down on the landlady of the Hoop and Grapes, pressed button B and collected her unused pennies.

She pushed open the door and the woman outside caught it.

'About blooming time, too,' she said, pushing

past Millie into the kiosk. 'Wot you doing? Sorting out Buckingham Palace?'

'My wedding, actually.'

The woman's rounded face lost some of its annoyance. 'Well, good luck to you.'

Millie smiled. 'Thank you. That's very kind.'

The woman pinched out her cigarette and stored it behind her ear. 'You'll need it, gal, if your old man is anything like my lazy bugger.'

Millie ran to the bus stop and jumped on the backboard of the bus just as it rolled away on the twenty-minute journey to Mile End.

Millie walked into Rose Ward just as the minute hand of the ward clock juddered on to the Roman numeral for twelve, indicating the time as four o'clock. Without pausing, she headed for her mother's bed, running through the guest list in her mind as she strolled down the centre of the ward. Oddly, there were a couple of screens around her mother's bed, but as they weren't closed, Millie walked in. As she looked down at her mother unconscious on the bed, something akin to a sledgehammer hit her in the chest.

Doris was dressed in the same dress she'd been wearing the day before, and she was lying with her arms and legs thrown out. Her eyes were closed and there was vomit around her mouth, matted into her hair and on the pillow under her head. There was also a wet patch seeping out from under her and the distinctive smell of fresh urine hovered.

Millie leaned over her mother and gently shook her. 'Mum!' Doris's eyelids flickered and her lips twitched.

361

'Wake up, Mum,' Millie urged.

She rubbed her mother's hand vigorously and felt her pulse. It was regular but slow, probably due to sedation of some sort.

A dribble of saliva trickled out of the corner of her mother's mouth, and then she turned her head and moaned. The screens were pulled back and Nurse Dunn appeared.

'Oh, Miss Sullivan,' she said, her eyes flickered from Millie to Doris and back again nervously. 'We weren't expecting you so soon.'

'What's happened to my mother, and why has she been left like this?' Millie demanded.

'There was a bit of an accident this morning during her treatment. It's nothing to worry about, I'm sure,' Nurse Dunn added hastily.

'Nothing to worry about?' Millie repeated in astonishment. 'I come in and find my mother unconscious and lying in her own vomit, and you tell me there's nothing to worry about! Where is Dr Benfield?'

'I'll fetch him.' Nurse Dunn scooted away.

'And fetch me a bowl of water, a flannel and a change of bed linen too,' Millie shouted after her.

By the time Doris's doctor bustled on to the ward, Millie had washed and dressed her mother in her nightgown and changed the soiled sheets.

'Good afternoon, Miss Sullivan,' he said, smiling ingratiatingly.

'Not really,' replied Millie sharply, putting the bowl of dirty water on the bedside locker. 'Can you explain what's wrong with my mother?'

He glanced at Doris. 'Perhaps it would be better to discuss this in the office?'

'Here will be fine, Doctor,' Millie replied. 'It's not as if she can hear, is it?'

The doctor's professional demeanour wavered for a moment. 'Very well. Electro-convulsive therapy works by stimulating the brain into minor convulsions – fits, in layman's terms.'

'I know what a convulsion is,' Millie told him tersely.

'Well, in extremely rare cases the treatment can trigger a *grand mal*. Unfortunately that's what happened to your mother this morning. But be assured that one *grand mal* fit won't have done any permanent damage or made her epileptic, although we will have to monitor her more closely next time. Once the sedation has worn off she will be as right as rain,' he continued, in a deliberately unconcerned tone. 'You can stay with her until she fully recovers, if you so wish.'

'Thank you, I will.' Millie decided to say nothing more for the moment. She took her mother's hand and sat on the chair beside the bed.

Millie yawned as the late-duty nurses said their goodnights to the night nurses and left for home. Nurse Dunn'd brought her three cups of tea over the course of the afternoon and two slices of thinly buttered toast from the supper trolley at five. Millie had forced one slice down but couldn't work up the appetite for the second and it remained untouched on the plate on the over-bed table.

Other than phoning Connie to tell her where she was, Millie hadn't strayed from her mother's bedside for the past five hours. She hadn't phoned Alex because, firstly, he was on a late shift and,

363

secondly, she wasn't certain what she was going to say.

The orderly and the nurse in charge went into the ward kitchen and Millie heard the chink of cups as they prepared the night drinks. She shifted and tried to relieve her numb behind.

'Is that you, Millie?' Doris croaked.

Millie sat up and looked at her mother. Although her complexion was still deathly white, Doris had her eyes open, although unfocused, and there was a little more colour in her lips.

Millie took her mother's hand. 'Yes, Mum. I'm here.'

Doris put a shaky hand on her temple. 'I feel so strange.'

'It's just the medicine,' Millie reassured her, stroking her hair back from her forehead and feeling her temperature at the same time.

'Where am I?' Doris gripped Millie's hand as her eyes grew wide with fear. 'Get me out of here.'

'It's all right, Mum,' Millie said.

'You don't understand what they did.' Doris looked fearfully down the ward. 'They made me lie down and they buckled straps across me to hold me there,' she said in a broken whisper. 'I begged them to stop but they wouldn't. Then they shoved this horrible thing in my mouth so I couldn't breathe and I couldn't move my head. And someone stuck a needle in me.' She sat bolt upright and grabbed Millie's arms in panic. 'Then I started falling and falling.'

'It's all right, Mum,' Millie said soothingly, as she tried to loosen her mother's painful grip.

'I tried to stop them, Millie, but they were too

strong.' Doris pulled Millie towards her and into the over-table so the cup and plate on it crashed to the ground. The nurse and the orderly came out of the kitchen and ran down the ward towards them.

Doris caught sight of them and screamed. 'Don't let them kill me!'

'No one's trying to kill you,' Millie said, trying to ignore her mother's nails biting into her upper arms.

'We'll have to sedate her,' the nurse said, casting her gaze over Doris.

Doris let go of Millie and an expression of terror transfixed her face. 'No!' she shrieked as she crawled backwards up the bed.

Millie caught her mother and cradled her in her arms. Doris tucked her head into Millie's chest as she clung on to her.

Millie held her mother tightly. 'Don't worry, Mum. I'm not going to let anyone do anything,' she said, looking pointedly over her mother's head at the nurse.

The nurse hesitated for a moment then, nudging the orderly, they headed back to kitchen.

Millie stroked her mother's hair soothingly. 'Look, they've gone.'

Doris peeked out and then relaxed a little when she saw that she and Millie were alone.

'That's better,' said Millie, helping her mother back under the bed covers. 'Now, what you need is a good night's sleep.'

Doris rolled towards her and curled up, slipping her hand under the pillow, and allowed Millie to tuck her in. She lay there quietly with her eyes closed for a moment, then opened them again.

'You won't leave me here, will you, Millie?'

Millie's throat constricted, but she smiled reassuringly and pulled her chair closer. 'I'll have to go back to Munroe House tonight. But don't worry, Mum,' she took her mother's hand and pressed it to her lips, 'I'll be back tomorrow to sort everything out, I promise.'

With her heart hammering in her chest, Millie stared at the brass knob of the small sitting-room door, then gripped it firmly and went in. Alex, who was standing looking out of the window, turned immediately.

He studied her anxiously for a moment, then crossed the space between them and took her hand. 'You look awful, sweetheart, are you un-well?'

Millie shook her head. 'I'm just tired, that's all.' She reclaimed her hand. 'Mother had a really bad reaction to the treatment yesterday, so I was at St Colombo's with her and didn't get in until almost five o'clock this morning. How did you get on?'

Alex's face fell. And so did Millie's heart.

'I'm so sorry, sweetheart,' he said. 'I tried every-thing I could but the commander in charge of recruitment wouldn't budge. Unless I take up my commission on the appointed day, it will be with-drawn.' Alex reached into his breast pocket and pulled out a large manila envelope. 'And this arrived this morning. It's the final arrangements. I'm to report to the HMS *Celeste* at Southampton, and the families are to follow on three weeks later aboard the *Northern Princess* on the tenth of July.'

He handed the thick letter to Millie.

366

'I explained about your mother being unwell and asked if she could come with us. But the rules state that only wives and children can accompany officers,' Alex concluded in a gloomy tone. 'I'm sorry.'

Millie stared down at the list of neatly typed instructions and the words seemed to shake on the page. 'Then I can't go,' she said in a low voice.

He looked bemused. 'Look, Millie, I tried my best but they won't budge.'

'I know, but I can't leave her,' said Millie, each word slicing deep into her heart.

'All right,' Alex cut in, raking his fingers through his hair.

'I won't leave,' Millie said firmly. 'While Mum's the way she is, I'll never be able to go to Palestine – or anywhere else, for that matter – and right now there's no guarantee she'll ever recover.'

Alex looked bewildered. 'Let's not be hasty, sweetheart. You're just upset, that's all. Let's talk it through properly. What about if I tell them you'll be joining me later?'

Millie shook her head. 'I've had all night sitting by my mother's bedside to think it through. And I wish there was another way. But as much as I love you, Alex, I can't turn my back on her.'

'Don't tell me you love me in one breath and then tell me you can't marry me in the next,' he spat out angrily. 'We've planned it! Our wedding, starting a family and everything. And now, just two weeks before we're to be married, you're backing out.' Alex covered his face with his hands.

His palpable anguish cut through Millie like a knife. 'Don't you think I want all those things, too?' she said softly. 'A home and children of my own?'

Alex looked up. 'What about if your mum went to stay with your Aunt Ruby and she looked after her until we could work out a way out of this mess?'

'Mum's my responsibility, not Aunt Ruby's, and what sort of daughter would I be if I just abandoned her in a mental hospital?' Millie forced herself to hold his gaze. 'I'm sorry, Alex, but I can't marry you.'

Alex balled his fists and then turned and stalked to the window. He slammed the window frame then put his hand up on it and, with his shoulders tense and his head bowed, stared out of the window. After a long pause, he turned back to face her.

'You're right, of course,' he said with a resigned sigh. 'I'll speak to the divisional commander tomorrow and withdraw my resignation. I'll tell Estates we'll have that flat in Warren House, and your mum can move in with us so you can look after her.' A bitter expression twisted his lips. 'I've got a better than even chance of being put forward for the inspectors' exam next year, and who knows, maybe then one of the other colonial police forces like Singapore or Rhodesia might start recruiting.'

Millie shook her head. 'It's no good, Alex. I can't marry you.'

Alex grabbed her hand. 'Please, Millie.'

The sensation of his fingertips sent Millie's senses spinning, but she forced herself to take back her hand. 'I'm sorry, but if you turned down this one chance to make something of yourself, you'd end up resenting me,' Millie said.

'Don't be bloody ridiculous,' he said angrily.

'If, instead of being an area superintendent, you were still plodding the beat in ten years' time because all the grammar school boys and the Freemasons had been promoted over your head, can you honestly say you wouldn't look at me across the kitchen table every morning and think to yourself how marrying me had held you back?'

Alex stared back at her for several heartbeats. For a second or two Millie's hopes soared. But then his gaze flickered.

Millie looked at him, taking in his long legs, athletic frame, thick black hair and angular face in one glance, and then she twisted off her engagement ring. She offered it to him.

Time stood still as they stared at each other before Alex stepped forward and gently took it from her.

'What about your "son with his father's green eyes"?' he asked, looking deeply into her sad eyes.

'I'm sorry, Alex,' she whispered, as tears blurred her vision.

Alex looked at the ring they had lovingly picked out together only four months before – it felt like a lifetime ago – and then he slipped it into his pocket.

'I'm sorry, too, Millie,' he said in a cracked voice, and then marched across the sparsely furnished lounge and banged out of the room without a backward glance.

Millie stared at the door, praying Alex would come back. And yet she knew he wouldn't.

Chapter Twenty-One

With her mother holding on tightly to her arm, Millie turned into Anthony Street and her heart sank. The sunny afternoon had brought the women of the street outside for a natter. They nudged each other as they spotted Millie and Doris, and before they'd walked more than a few yards mother and daughter were the centre of attention. Doris gripped her arm and drew in closer.

'It's all right, Mum,' Millie said, patting her mother's arm. 'There's nothing to be afraid of.'

Her mother looked up with the same mild expression she'd worn since Millie arrived on Rose Ward an hour ago to collect her.

Millie chewed her lip anxiously. There was probably enough gossip about her mother's accident, so Millie prayed she could get Doris into her house without fuelling speculation further.

''ow you doing, ducks?' shouted a woman on the opposite side of the road with two children playing at her feet.

'Glad to see you're looking better, Mrs Sullivan,' called a stout old woman sitting on a stool that had a mangy-looking dog asleep beneath.

'My mother's pleased to be home,' Millie called back.

The women returned to their nattering and Millie breathed a sigh of relief.

'There you go, Mum,' Millie said, opening her

mother's front door and helping her inside.

Doris stepped in and looked questioningly at Millie. 'What shall I do?'

Millie closed the door. 'Take your coat off, Mum.'

Doris unbuttoned her coat, slipped it off and stood holding it.

'Now hang it up in the usual place, Mum,' Millie said gently. 'By the door.'

Doris gazed around the room then spotted the pegs beside the front door. She padded over, hooked up her coat and then turned back to Millie.

Millie forced a smile. 'Why don't you sit down and I'll make us some tea?'

Doris looked blankly at her, so Millie took her mother's hand and led her to the chair by the fire.

'Do you like the flowers, Mum?' she asked, as she sat her mother down.

'They're lovely,' replied Doris, staring at the little vase of lily of the valley on the side table. 'Did Alex buy them for you?'

A pain cut through Millie. 'No, Mum. I got them on my rounds this morning in the market.'

Her mother smiled innocently. 'Is Alex coming around later?'

Fighting to keep hold of her emotions, Millie forced a cheery smile. 'No. Alex won't be coming today. Now you put your feet up and I'll get us that cuppa.'

Millie fled to the kitchen.

She leaned on the scrubbed table and, staring at the kitchen dresser that she'd restocked before catching the bus to St Colombo's at three-thirty, took a couple of deep breaths. When she'd regained her composure, Millie filled the kettle, set it on the stove and lit the gas beneath it.

Just as the kettle started whistling, there was a knock on the door. Turning the heat off, Millie walked through the lounge and pulled the net curtain back half an inch. Her heart sank further when she saw who was standing on the doorstep. She let the curtain fall and opened the door.

'Aunt Ruby. I was going to ring you,' Millie said nervously.

Ruby gave Millie a withering look, then swept past in a cloud of cigarette smoke and Coty *Muguet de bois*. She deposited her handbag on the table and hurried over to her sister.

'How are you, Doris?' Ruby asked, looking at her anxiously.

Doris looked bemused for a moment, then smiled. 'Ruby, what are you doing here?'

Ruby forced a jolly smile. 'I've just popped by to make sure you're all right, that's all.'

Doris laughed. 'Don't be silly, I'm fine; and I've got Millie looking after me.'

'I know.' Ruby's lips drew together.

Millie matched her aunt's cool look. 'I'm just making Mum a cup of tea. Would you like one?'

'That would be lovely,' replied Ruby. 'I'll help you.'

Millie walked into her mother's small scullery and her aunt followed.

'What on earth do you think you're doing, Amelia?' Ruby asked in a whisper, as soon as they were out of earshot.

'Looking after my mother,' Millie replied, striking a match to relight the gas ring.

'That's not what the doctor at the asylum called it,' retorted Ruby. 'He said stopping your mother's treatment could seriously damage her chances of a full recovery.'

'It's called a mental hospital, not an asylum,' replied Millie, setting the cups out on the tray. 'And I don't happen to agree with Dr Benfield.'

Ruby looked incredulous. 'But he's a doctor. He's passed exams, been to university and everything.'

'You didn't see the dreadful state she was in after treatment began. She was left to lie in filth, and was terrified. And she's my mother and I want what's best for her. I am not convinced that shooting electricity through her brain will help her get better. Not to mention the fact no one washed her or changed her clothes the whole time she was in St Colombo's.' Millie took the milk bottle out of the stone keep on the draining board. 'Mum needs rest so she can recover, and she won't get that on Rose Ward with people yelling at the top of their voices day and night. She'll be better off at home where I can pop in a couple of times a day to make sure she's all right, and I'll spend the evenings with her after my late visits. I'm sure that if I can ease her back gently into her daily routine, then she'll start to improve. I might not have Dr Benfield's qualifications, but I've cared for enough grieving people in the past five years to understand a little bit how to help them back to health.'

'Well, that's all very well and good, Amelia,'

said Ruby, as Millie spooned the tea into the pot. 'But what's going to happen when you go to Palestine in a few weeks?'

'I'm not going,' Millie replied in a resigned voice as she placed the teapot alongside the cups and saucers on the tray. 'And I've called off the wedding.'

'You've done what?' Ruby asked in disbelief.

The familiar choking lump in Millie's throat reappeared. 'I told Alex yesterday that I couldn't go to Palestine with him because I had to look after Mum and so it was best we called the wedding off.'

Ruby's mouth dropped open. 'But surely he could postpone his posting or something.'

Millie shook her head. 'He's tried to, but the Ministry of Defence won't budge. Alex wanted to give up his commission and stay in London so that we could marry. But I told him I couldn't let him throw everything he'd worked so hard for away. I know you never liked Alex, but I love him and it's because I love him that I've let him go.'

Ruby exhaled. 'I know you probably can't see it now, but perhaps it's for the best. You're still young and pretty, and there's lots of time yet.'

'Please, Aunt Ruby,' Millie begged, balling her hands into two tight fists. 'I've just had to tell the man I love that I can't marry him, knowing that I'll never see him again. Added to which I haven't slept for three nights, I've got a blinding headache, and I can barely keep a glass of water down, so please no "there's more fish in the sea" or "you'll find someone else someday" at the moment, because I just couldn't take it.'

Ruby nodded understandingly. 'I know you might not feel like it now. But I promise you, Amelia, you will get over it.'

'I'm sure I will,' Millie replied, knowing she would not.

Ruby smoothed a damp strand of hair from Millie's forehead, then picked up the tray. 'Why don't you bring the cake through and then we can all have a nice cup of tea.'

Millie took out the large brown bottle with 'Methane Hair Oil' written on the label and stood it on the trolley.

'Let's hope we don't need too much of that today,' she said to Connie, who was still putting her hair up under a tight cap by the mirror over the sink.

They were in the white-tiled medical room of Glamis Street School just about to start the bi-weekly nit inspection. This week it was the turn of one of the infants' classes to be checked. Although it didn't need two of them, Millie had offered to help Connie to attack the headlice lurking in Miss Palgrave's class because Connie was helping her with the evening round so that Millie could put Doris to bed.

Connie tucked the last few strands of hair out of harm's way and joined Millie. 'I can't hear them yet.'

'No, we're a bit early. The afternoon registers are still being taken,' Millie replied, putting her metal comb in the beaker of turquoise antiseptic fluid.

She unfolded the rubber gloves from the paper covers and set a pack of gauze next to them.

'How's your mum?' asked Connie.

'Fretful and restless.' Millie sighed.

Connie looked sympathetic. 'With you skipping meals, dashing in and out of Munroe House at all hours of the day and night, I guessed as much.'

'She can't help it, of course,' said Millie, with a twinge of guilt, 'but she won't eat unless I prompt her, and so I've had to drop in each dinnertime, too.'

'As well as cook, shop and clean,' sympathised Connie.

'I know. But she's only been home a week and she's already a bit cheerier.'

Connie still looked perturbed. 'Well, you be careful, because you'll be in ten types of trouble if Miss Dutton hears about you visiting your mum while on duty.'

'Don't worry, I always park my bike in the back yard,' Millie replied. 'It won't be for long, as I'm going to start taking her out for a little walk each day from next week. I thought I might start with a trip to...' tears welled in her eyes, and her words were choked off.

Connie reached across and squeezed her hand. 'Oh, Millie.'

'Alex ships out today,' Millie whispered, as a yawning chasm opened in her chest.

Connie left what she was doing and put an arm around Millie's shoulder. 'Have you heard from him?'

Millie shook her head. A tear escaped and rolled down her cheek. 'Also, I came on today.'

'You mean...?'

'I thought I might be.' Millie pulled her handkerchief out from her sleeve and blew her nose. 'Alex always used something and we were careful, but sometimes...' she gave her friend an apologetic shrug.

Connie looked relieved. 'Well, I bet you're bloody glad your monthlies have arrived.'

'Of course,' replied Millie, unsure if knowing absolutely that she wasn't having Alex's baby was worse than fearing she was.

She quickly dabbed her face dry. 'I think I can hear the children outside.'

The voices of the chattering children rang as they came down the corridor and then lined up outside the medical room. Millie placed a chair in front of her, and pulled on her rubber gloves.

The door opened and Miss Palgrave, an elderly lady wearing wrinkled surgical stockings, marched in the first five children.

'Stand there quietly until nurse calls you.' Miss Palgrave jabbed her finger toward the wall. 'And Terence Casey!' A little boy with hair sticking out at all angles looked up. 'Stop picking your nose.'

He extracted his finger from his nostril and stood up straight next to his classmates.

The teacher turned to Millie. 'Just send them back to class when you're done, Sister.'

'Thank you, Miss Palgrave. We should only be an hour.' Millie took the metal comb from the beaker and tapped off the excess antiseptic mixture. She looked at the five children.

'Who's first?'

The little girl at the end of the line with long ginger hair walked over and climbed on to the chair.

'Now, let's see what we can see,' she said, gently

running the teeth of her comb down the length of the little girl's scalp, looking for lice.

One hour, and twenty-eight children later Millie dropped the comb back into the cleaning solution for the last time.

'Off you go, mister, you've no new friends today,' Millie said in a jolly tone as she helped a boy down.

He trotted off back to his class, making the glass rattle in the door as he slammed it behind him.

'Well, that's not too bad,' Connie said, indicating the seven children sitting on the row of half-sized chairs by the sink. 'We should be done in no time and might even get back to the clinic in time for tea.'

'No, not bad at all. Let's make a start. I'll wash if you dry,' Millie said, picking up the brown bottle of diluted insecticide.

'Right, young lady, what's your name?' she said, to a little girl on the first chair fiddling with the hem of her skirt.

'Violet,' she replied, looking nervously up.

'Well, Violet, I'm afraid I've found some nasty little monsters in your hair, but don't worry,' Millie said, giving her a happy smile. 'I'm going to rub in some of my special magic lotion and they will all disappear. Your mummy can't wash it out for two weeks, but I'll send a note home with you to explain. Now, come with me and we'll make a start.'

She led the child to the chair in front of the sink and lifted her on to it. She unbound her tight braids and then tucked a towel around her neck. Bending the girl's head over the sink, Millie uncorked the bottle and half-filled the small galley pot on the side of the basin.

'Close your eyes very tight, Violet,' Millie said.

The child nodded. Millie poured the glutinous brown liquid slowly through the child's hair and rubbed it in.

'There you, go,' Millie said, when she'd used up all the solution. 'Now pop over to my friend Nurse Byrne over there and she will comb your hair through.'

Millie lifted Violet down from the chair and she trotted over to Connie waiting on the other side of the room.

'Come on, lad. You're next,' Millie said beckoning to the lad sitting on the next chair.

He slid off and ambled towards her with his eyes fixed to the floor and dragging his feet.

'And what's your name, little chap?'

He didn't answer.

Millie hunkered down so her face was level with his. 'Don't be afraid,' she said softly. 'You're not in trouble.'

His gaze flickered up briefly.

'Mickey. Mickey Walters,' he mumbled before continuing to study his toes.

Although most six-year-old boys were an inch or two shorter than the girls, the little boy standing submissively in front of Millie looked more like a four-year-old. And whereas most mothers washed and darned the hand-me-downs they dressed their children in, the frayed collar on Mickey's jacket had never seen needle or, judging by the stains down the front, a wash tub. He also had a barely healed scar across his chin and the last yellowy hue of bruising around his right eye.

'Where did you get that shiner?' Millie asked, turning his head to see the deeply ingrained tide-mark around his neck a little better.

'I bashed into the table,' he replied, not looking up.

'And this?' she asked, running her fingers over a bump on the back of his head.

He shrugged.

Millie took his hands and turned them over and back, noting the bitten black fingernails and what could well have been burn marks. 'How many brothers and sisters have you got, Mickey?'

'Two and the baby in our house.' A twinkle lit up his bright blue eyes. 'She's called Susie and she laughs at me when I pull faces at her.'

'How old is she?' Millie asked.

Mickey shrugged. 'A year, I think, and I has three other brothers, big ones, who live around the corner with Dad and *Her*. But Mum gives me a belt if I say about them,' he added.

Millie ran her finger lightly across his dirty cheek. 'And where do you live, Mickey?'

'Stebbins 'ouse. Number fifteen,' he said.

Millie lifted him on to the chair and placed a towel gently around his slender shoulders. 'Well, Mickey, I'm going to get rid of your unwelcome chums now, and then I might pop around and see your mum tomorrow for a chat.'

Millie stepped niftily over the whirl of dog dirt in the middle of the pavement. As any bike – even a district nurse's – would be pinched within minutes of being chained to the railing at Stebbins

House, Millie had decided to walk the half-mile there to the west end of Cable Street.

The tenement had been built in 1884 and had the fact emblazoned on the oval plaque above the main entrance. In those days the three blocks that made up the complex would have been counted as a revolutionary design of dwelling for the respectable working man and his family. Unfortunately the respectable man had long since departed, taking his family with him, and now the flats were let to anyone who had the rent. No questions asked.

Gripping her bag firmly in her hand, Millie left the warmth of the daylight and walked past the wrought-iron staircase winding up to the floors above and passed into the triangular courtyard between Stebbins, Fallow and Garrett Houses, which formed St Katherine's Building.

Curious eyes from the balconies above watched Millie duck between the grey washing hanging limply on the communal washing lines. Somewhere above an infant wailed and jazz music drifted down. Millie looked up and saw Mickey Walters hanging over the second-floor balcony. He waved and she waved back. Picking her way through the cigarette ends, bacon rinds and ash that had spilled over the top of B block's large rubbish bin, Millie made her way to the stairs.

Holding her breath to keep the stench of urine at bay, Millie made her way up to the second floor.

Mickey was waiting for her at the top of the stairs. ''ello, Miss. I told Mum you were coming to see her. Come and see Susie.' Millie followed the lad along the landing.

'This is my Susie,' he said, indicating a beaten

pram by the last door. He stuck his thumbs in his ears and waggled his fingers. The baby giggled.

Millie picked her up from the pram, wrapped in a grubby shawl. 'Shall we go and see your mum?'

'Mum's popped down to the shop and I'm in charge until she gets back,' Mickey said, puffing out his chest.

Millie stepped through the door and walked along the narrow corridor into the main living room at the end. There she found two toddlers, a girl in a crumpled dress and no knickers and a boy wearing only a grubby jumper, playing on the bare lino in front of an open fire. There was a small table shoved up against one side of the room with the remnants of the family breakfast, complete with an uncovered jam pot with a couple of flies hovering around, a baby's bottle laying on its side and a full ashtray.

Balancing the baby on her hip, Millie bent down and gently pulled the two children away from the fire.

The front door banged and Millie turned.

A woman wearing an old green dress with a missing button and a dark stain down the front stood in the doorway. Her short brown hair sat in tangled clumps on her head and her pendulous breasts and unsupported midriff strained against the fabric of her clothes. She held a canvas shopping bag in her hand.

'I suppose you're the bleeding nurse,' she said, lumbering into the room. 'And why couldn't you leave her be? I've only just settled her.'

'Hello, Mrs Walters,' Millie said, with a pleasant smile. 'I'm Sister Sullivan and when I saw this

382

little poppet,' she jigged the child in her arms, 'I thought I'd bring her in with me while I have a chat. I saw your son Mickey at school yesterday. Do you mind if I sit down?'

'Suit yourself.'

She dumped the groceries on the table. A potato rolled out and fell on to the floor. Mrs Walters ignored it and flopped into the chair by the fire.

Millie perched on the wooden chair by the table, put her bag down and set the baby on her knee. Mickey came and stood beside her.

'I thought I'd just pop by and explain that you have to leave the lotion on for two weeks,' Millie said

Mrs Walters shrugged. 'That's all right. I often skip their bath on Friday. It's a lot of trouble lugging all the water up from the pump below and they're dirty again an hour later.'

'And what about the baby?'

'I give her a dunk in the sink once or twice a week,' replied Mrs Walters. She looked suspiciously at Millie. 'I thought this was about our Mickey's nits.'

'It is,' replied Millie.

Mrs Walters took the cigarette out of her mouth and flicked it into the fire. 'It had better be, 'cos I ain't having no one poking their nose into my business, let me tell you. Nurse or no nurse.'

'I've come to see you because if Mickey has headlice then the chances are you all have them too.'

'Little bugger.' She glared at her son and raised her hand. Mickey flinched. 'I bet he picked them up from that half-caste nigger kid in number

383

seven. I told you not to play with 'im.'

'He could have got them from anywhere, but the Council's Medical Board says I have to treat all of you,' Millie said firmly. 'In fact, you should go to the Thursday afternoon clinic in Cartwright Street, but Mickey said you had three other young children and so I thought it might help if I came to you.'

'It won't cost me, will it? Me man hasn't had much work this week,' Mrs Walters asked.

Millie shook her head. 'I'll start with this little one, then I'll settle her again and do the others.'

Half an hour later, with Mickey trailing behind her all the way, Millie had deloused the family, cleaned the table, washed up, emptied the rubbish bin into the hopper at the foot of the stairs, fed the baby – after boiling the bottle for five minutes – and plastered her bottom with zinc and castor oil, cleaned urine off the little boy's legs and fetched the potty from the kitchen to save further accidents. She'd glanced into the kitchen and bedroom and decided to leave tackling them to her next visit.

As Millie busied herself around the flat, Mrs Walters made a couple of token gestures to help, but in the end just rolled herself another cigarette and remained in her chair.

Finally, after Millie had wiped the pots, recorked the bottles and screwed the lids back on the tubs, she packed them all back in her bag.

'There, Mrs Walters, all done and dusted. Just don't wash the lotion out for two weeks, and you should all be fine.'

'I bloody hope so,' Mrs Walters said, shooting

another irritated look at Mickey as she struggled out of her chair.

'Your husband will have to go to the clinic at Backhouse Lane after work, I'm afraid,' Millie said.

'I'll tell him,' Mrs Walters replied, not meeting her eye.

Millie snapped her case shut. 'I'll come back next week to make sure the treatment's worked.'

'If you have to.' Mrs Walters turned her back on Millie and lolloped over to the dirty cooker to make a cup of tea.

'You know, with such young children you really should have a fire guard,' Millie said.

'Can't afford one,' Mrs Walters replied. 'And they only have to touch it once to learn not to do it again.'

'I think I have a spare one at the clinic. Would you like it?' Millie asked, stepping to the side to block the little boy's path to the smouldering embers.

Mrs Walters flicked the ash off the end of her cigarette by way of an answer.

Millie picked up her case. 'I'll bring it with me next time, then.'

She left, and Mickey followed her out.

'I'm glad you come, Miss,' he said chirpily, as they walked back to the top of the stairs. 'And I shall look out for you every day.'

Millie ruffled his hair and, squeezing between two young men drinking in the stairwell, made her way down the stairs.

As she crossed the yard towards the entrance, she looked back. Mickey was leaning on the balcony watching her. He waved and a strange tightness caught in her chest. Millie waved back and resolved to drop the fireguard in to Mrs Walters after her morning round tomorrow.

'Are you sure you don't want a nice cuppa while you do that, Sister Sullivan?' Mrs White asked for the third time since she arrived.

Millie yawned as she stood beside the small table in the Whites' front room while Grace Jackson, a curvy redhead with large limpid eyes who was the Association's new trainee Queen's Nurse, got the equipment ready to dress Eddie's toes. Millie was supposed to be supervising Grace, but her eyes were so heavy she could barely keep them open. Before she could stop herself, Millie yawned again.

'Mother! Get our nurse a cuppa,' Eddie said. 'She's almost asleep on her feet.'

'That's very kind, but I can't dawdle,' Millie said, handing her improvised newspaper bag to Mrs White.

'I don't expect you can,' Mrs White replied. 'What with dashing from pillar to post all day, and then running around to see to your mum.' Her thin face pulled into a sympathetic expression. 'How is the poor love?'

'Recovering slowly,' replied Millie, making a play of tidying her equipment. 'How did you know?'

'I met Sadie Ryman – you know, her with one leg shorter than the other who got a room above the baker's – a couple of days ago when I was getting Father some new underpants in Sheldon's. She said her sister, who lives in Tarling Street, ran

386

into Flo Baxter, the shop assistant in Caters, who heard it from Iris Clark, who lives opposite your mum at number twenty-four.' Mrs White shook her head and tutted. She turned to Grace. 'What about you, dearie?'

'Thank you, Mrs White, but I've just had one, too,' she said, smiling at the older woman.

One of the many things understood but not written in district nursing textbooks was when you were asked if you'd like a cuppa in a house with flies lazily circling unwashed plates in the sink, you had always just finished one in the last house.

Mrs White looked disappointed. 'Well, I'll just fetch Father one, then.'

She sidestepped around the bundles of unmade clothing that had been delivered just before they arrived, and headed for the door.

Millie turned back to her patient, who was waiting good-naturedly in his usual chair for his dressing to be changed. He sat with his trouser buttons undone to relieve the pressure on his bloated stomach, and ash flecked his moth-eaten jumper.

'We won't be long,' Millie told him, giving him a reassuring smile.

Eddie White shrugged. 'Don't worry. I ain't going nowhere.'

Millie turned to the student nurse. 'Have you got everything ready?'

Grace surveyed the table with the assembled equipment spread out on the open pages of yesterday's *Daily Sketch*.

'I've fifty-fifty water, and Dettol in the cup, the tin of dressing is nicely toasted and the forceps are in soak. All I have to do is pour the surgical spirits and make sure the safety pin for the bandages is where I can see it and of course, the paper bag for the dirty dressings.' Grace indicated the improvised bag folded out of another sheet of newspaper on the floor under the table.

'Very good. Now get yourself prepared,' Millie said.

Grace turned to the washbowl set up alongside the dressing equipment and lathered her hands.

The door opened and Mrs White returned carrying two china mugs with a donkey in a hat and the word 'Southend' painted on the side. She put one on the mantelshelf and the other beside her husband.

'Are you sure you don't want a bit of bread and jam to keep you going until suppertime?' she asked.

Before Eddie could reply the front door banged.

The Whites' daughter, Flora, stuck her head around. 'Coo-ee, only me,' she yodelled.

With her father's round face and trunk and her mother's petite hands and feet, Flora White was a perfect blend of her parents, and from the bulges of fat spilling over her waistband and creasing around her ankles and wrists, she'd inherited their hearty appetites, too. The fact she worked in the Meredith and Drew biscuit factory on the Highway didn't help either.

'I was expecting you home half an hour gone, Flora,' Mrs White said.

'I would have been if the blooming conveyer belt hadn't snapped and we had to make up the time lost later,' Flora replied.

388

'Well, never mind, you're home now, so come and give your old dad a smacker,' her father said, screwing up one side of his face.

Flora's chubby features formed themselves into a fond smile and she trotted, with little baby steps, over to him. 'And how is the best daddy in the world?' she asked, kissing Eddie noisily on his bald head.

'All the better for seeing my little princess,' Eddie replied, basking in his offspring's adoration.

'I've brought you these, Dad,' she said, opening the bag and offering it to her father.

'My favourite,' said Eddie, pulling out a handful of broken biscuits coated with different coloured icing and stencilled pictures.

Flora spotted Millie. 'Hello, ducks,' she said, depositing a shopping basket on the sofa with a huff.

'Afternoon, Flora,' Millie replied, spreading two sheets of newspaper on the floor in front of Eddie. She and Grace knelt down. Grace unpinned the safety pin and started unwinding the bandage. There was a rustle of paper as someone behind them helped themselves to more biscuits.

Flora peered over Millie's shoulder. 'How's me dad's foot doing, Sister?' she asked, munching noisily behind her.

'I'll let you know as soon as we have the dressing off,' Millie replied.

'There's a lot of muck seeped through,' said Flora, as Grace discarded the outer layer, stained yellow with leaking fluids.

'That's quite natural,' replied Millie. She removed the wadding with the forceps. The gagging

389

smell of decaying flesh rose up.

Flora plonked herself on the sofa and the springs twanged in protest. 'It's funny you being here, Sister, 'cos I've just passed your mum in Cable Street.'

'My mum?'

Flora nodded. 'She must have popped out to the corner shop because she was still in her slippers.'

A cold hand clutched at Millie's heart.

'If you apply pressure to the dressing, I'll dribble the water over to loosen the gauze,' Millie instructed, trying to concentrate on Eddie's gangrenous foot.

'Yes, Sister.' Grace gripped the crusty bandage with her forceps and pulled it gently away.

Millie picked up the pot of cooled water and held it over Eddie's foot. Her hands started to shake, splashing water over Eddie, Grace and herself.

Millie put the bowl down before it slipped from her grasp. 'I'm sorry, I–'

Grace took it from her. 'I can finish off here,' she said softly.

'Thank you,' replied Millie, feeling both guilty and grateful. She stood up and ripped off her gloves. 'I'll meet you at Mrs Frogmore's in half an hour.'

Millie dashed down the street towards Cable Street, praying that her mother would still be there. Turning sharply at the Crown and Dolphin, Millie put her hand on her hat to keep it from flying off and ran westwards towards St George's

Town Hall.

Someone wolf-whistled as her skirts flew high, and a couple of scruffy-looking navvies loitering on the pavement made a play of catching her as she tore past them, but for the most part, when they saw her uniform, people stepped aside.

Millie paused outside St George's Town Hall and then climbed a couple of the steps to scan the crowds of dock workers milling around outside the betting shops and cafés.

Relief flooded over Millie as she spotted her mother by the bus stop at the corner of Denmark Street. There were a couple of rough-looking lads, who were clearly playing the hop from school, milling around her, but otherwise she looked all right.

Millie jumped down from the steps and ran the final thirty yards to reach her mother. As she grew closer, Millie noticed that although, thankfully, Doris had put her coat on before leaving the house, one stocking was gathered loosely around her left ankle. More worryingly, she had her handbag hooked over her arm and it was wide open.

Gathering up her last ounce of breath, Millie sprinted the last few yards and stopped just in front of Doris.

One of the boys had her mother's purse in his hand and was rifling through it.

'Give me that,' Millie said, wresting it from his hand.

'Bugger off,' he shouted, trying to snatch it back.

Doris stared bemusedly at them as Millie fought to get her mother's purse back.

'Police!' screamed Millie, now getting the attention of passers-by. Suddenly the young man lurched to one side and knocked into Doris with his shoulder, as his friend made himself scarce. Doris tumbled off the pavement. Millie let go of the purse.

'Mum!' she screamed, jumping in the path of a rag and bone man's cart that was trotting towards them.

The thief turned and, shoving people aside, fled.

Heedless of the dirt and refuse in the gutter Millie knelt beside her mother and lifted her up, casting her gaze quickly over her. Other than a nasty red mark on her cheek and dirt in her hair, Doris seemed unharmed.

'Are you all right, Mum?' Millie asked, as people came and helped Doris to her feet.

'My elbow hurts,' Doris replied, cradling her right arm.

'I'll look at it when we get back,' replied Millie, dusting down her mother's clothes.

The crowd around them parted, and Georgie Tugman, who would have been Alex's best man, strode through dressed in his police uniform. His gaze hardened as he recognised her.

'All right, you lot,' he said to the people gathered around. 'Be about your business.'

The crowd lowered their heads and hurried away. Georgie turned back to Millie and her mother.

'What's all this then?' he asked coolly.

'My mother's been robbed,' Millie replied, forcing herself to look him in the eye.

He raised an eyebrow. 'Has she now?' He turned to Doris. 'So what happened, Mrs Sullivan?' he

392

asked, not bothering to take his notebook from his breast pocket.

Millie's mother smiled blandly up at Georgie, 'This nice boy asked me if I had any money. I said yes and then he asked if he could have some so I gave it to him.'

Georgie smiled. 'Well, that's all right then. If your mother gave it to him then there's no robbery.' He looked at Doris again. 'That's what you said didn't you, love?'

Doris nodded. 'Yes.'

Georgie sneered at Millie. 'See?'

Millie looked up at him in amazement. 'But surely you're going to do something to try and find him? My mother isn't well. And, after all, he did knock her into the road. And he's run off with her purse.'

'Did he?'

Millie glared at Georgie. 'Of course he did. You saw for yourself.'

'She probably slipped off the pavement, that's all. And she gave him the money,' Georgie replied. 'Now, if there's nothing else?'

Millie's head started throbbing. 'But aren't you even going to make a report of the robbery?'

'My daughter is marrying a policeman,' Doris chipped in.

Georgie's mouth pulled into a harsh line. 'That's nice,' he said, bitterly. 'I had a mate who was getting married. He had it all planned, he did. Happy as Larry, too, until she changed her mind and called the whole thing off.'

'Oh, poor man,' said Doris. 'Is your friend all right?'

393

Georgie's unforgiving stare rested on Millie. 'He will be when he realises what a lucky escape he's had. But I ain't worried about him because I know he'll soon find someone better.'

Millie's head spun as she felt the blood drain to her feet.

Grim satisfaction spread across Georgie's face. He touched the brim of his helmet and then, whistling 'Here Comes the Bride', sauntered down the street at the regulation three miles an hour. Millie stared after him as images of Alex smiling, holding and kissing another woman tortured her mind.

Doris's voice cut through her thoughts. 'He was a nice policeman. Do you think Alex knows him?'

Chapter Twenty-Two

Walking swiftly back to the main road, Millie unchained her bicycle from the town hall railings and started off towards the Compass public house at the far end of Wapping High Street, where landlord Tubby Watts had tumbled down the loading hole and gashed his arm.

Pushing hard on the pedals, Millie scooted through the puddles left by a summer shower. It had brought a breeze with it that played with the escaped curls around Millie's face and cleared some of the cobwebs caused by weeks of broken sleep.

Tilting her face to the warm mid-summer sun, Millie freewheeled down Wapping Lane towards the river. Weaving through the file of lorries parked along the kerb being loaded, she was just about to swing left at the bottom when Joe Kemp, the landlord of the Saracen's Head, rushed out and waved at her. Millie applied the brakes and squealed to a halt.

'Thank goodness I caught you,' he said, bending forward and putting his hand on his thighs to catch his breath. 'Sister Byrne's been trying to get hold of you. She knew you had a visit to one of the pubs along the High Street but forgot which one, so she rung the lot of us. It's your ma. She's at Munroe House.'

Millie jumped off her bicycle in Munroe House's backyard. Throwing it vaguely in the direction of the bike rack, she ran in the back door and down the hall to the nurses' refectory.

Although it was now only three, Annie and Sally were already sitting in the far corner having their afternoon tea and cake.

Millie hurried over to them. 'I've just got the message that my mother is—'

'It's all right, Millie,' Annie said, meeting her halfway. 'Your mum's upstairs with Connie.'

Panic filled Millie's mind. 'Upstairs! If Miss Dutton finds her there'll be hell to pay.'

Annie caught her arms. 'Miss Dutton's out and won't be back until after supper. Now tell me what visits you've got left, and me and Sally will do them while you sort your mum out.'

'Just Mr Watts at the Compass,' Millie said, feeling light-headed with relief. 'Are you sure you don't mind?'

'Course not,' replied Sally. 'You'd do the same for us.'

The door opened and Gladys and her friend Trudy strolled in.

'What's brought you back so early?' Gladys said, looking suspiciously at Millie.

'Nothing,' replied Millie, as casually as her thundering heart would allow. 'I just fancied a quick cuppa before cycling down to Limehouse, that's all.'

She went to the long table and poured herself a cup from the large cream enamel teapot then turned and looked at Annie and Sally. 'I'll see you girls at suppertime as I've got to rinse my stockings through.'

Feeling Gladys's eyes burning into her back, Millie strolled out of the refectory and then rushed upstairs.

When she got to Connie's room she found Doris perched on the edge of the upholstered easy chair wringing her hands and with an anxious expression on her face.

Millie had been in early that morning to help her wash and dress and had left her in a turquoise gown. Sometime during the course of the day Doris had discarded them and was now wearing her pale blue dress inside out, with the frill of her nightdress hanging beneath, and without her stockings.

'There we are, Mrs Sullivan,' said Connie as Millie closed the door swiftly. 'I told you Millie would be back soon.'

Millie gave her friend an appreciative look.

Doris stood up and scurried over to Millie.

'Where have you been, Millie?' she asked gripping her hands. 'I haven't seen you for weeks.'

'I saw you this morning, Mum,' she replied, walking her back to the chair. 'And I told you that I'd be back to put you to bed.'

Doris looked puzzled. 'Did you?'

'Yes, I did.'

Doris's face crumpled. 'I'm sorry Millie,' she said, twisting her fingers together. 'I thought you'd gone away and left me. Have I got you in trouble being here?'

'No Mum, it's fine.' She handed her mother the cup of tea. 'Here you go. I brought this for you.'

Her mother took it and smiled up at Millie.

'You're a good girl, so you are.'

'We'll go home when you're done, but don't rush,' Millie replied, wanly.

Doris nodded but only drank a couple of mouthfuls of tea before her eyelids fluttered down. Millie took the cup from her hands. The tight band around Millie's forehead eased a little.

'Thank goodness,' she said, slumping down on to the corner of Connie's bed. 'She hasn't slept more than a couple of hours in a row for the past three days, so she could do with forty winks.'

'What about you?' asked Connie. 'You've hardly had a full night's sleep yourself since your mum came out of St Colombo's.'

'I'm all right,' replied Millie, trying unsuccessfully to stifle a yawn.

'You don't look it,' replied Connie with a worried frown. 'How long do you think you can go on like this?'

'I'm fine, I tell you,' replied Millie. 'She's only been out of hospital just over four weeks and it's bound to take a bit of time for her to settle.'

'I know you want to do the best for your mum, but you can't go on staying up with her until the early hours every night and then dragging yourself out of bed at six in the morning to do a full day's work as well,' Connie replied.

Doris's eyes blinked open and she looked puzzled for a moment until she spotted Millie.

'Are we going home now?' she asked.

Millie stood up. 'Yes, Mum.'

'It's nice to see you, Mrs Sullivan,' Connie said, helping Doris to her feet. 'Is it all right if I pop around to see you next week?'

'That will be nice,' said Doris, smiling cheerfully.

Millie opened the door and checked that the corridor was empty, and then took her mother's hand.

'Oh,' said Connie as Millie led her mother out. 'I picked up your post.'

She ducked in and came back to the door with a handful of letters. Millie took them and thrust them in her pocket.

She gave her friend a peck on the cheek. 'I'll see you later – and thanks.'

Connie nodded and gave her a meaningful look. 'Just remember what I said.'

It had gone eight p.m. by the time Millie pulled the bed covers over her mother and then crept down the stairs to the living room. Thankfully, by the time she'd left Munroe House the nurses in the refectory had already gone off on their rounds, so she managed to smuggle Doris out of the nurses' home without anyone being any the wiser.

Stretching to relieve the tightness in her shoulders, Millie switched on the radio just in time to hear a professor from Cambridge tell Roy Plomley his fifth choice in music if he were ever to be cast away on a desert island.

Millie closed the curtains and turned on the standard lamp behind Doris's chair, setting the fringing around the bottom of the shade swaying as her arm brushed against it. She went into the kitchen and made herself a cup of tea. Making sure the back door was locked, Millie went back into the lounge, snuggled into her mother's chair and put her feet up on the leather pouffe.

Millie took a sip of her tea and then pulled the letters Connie had given her out of her pocket. Resting them on her lap, she picked up the first one and opened it. It was a letter from Aunt Edie asking how she and her mother were. Millie picked up the next. She opened it and read the note from the landlady of the Hoop and Grapes confirming the cancellation of the wedding reception. Putting it and the hollow feeling in her chest aside, Millie picked up the last letter and, as her gaze rested on her boldly written name on the envelope, her heart thumped painfully in her chest.

With trembling hands she ripped open the envelope and something fluttered to the floor. Millie picked it up, only to stare at the photograph of herself and Alex taken that cold afternoon in Oxford Street. She looked for a moment at the happy couple caught on camera, then pulled out the sheet of paper still inside the envelope.

As she traced the well-formed swirls and curves of the words, an image of Alex flashed into Millie's mind, taking her breath and quickening her pulse in the same moment.

Dear Millie,

I had promised myself that for both our sakes I wouldn't write, but I can't sail tomorrow without telling you what I should have told you before we parted in Munroe House. To be honest, I can't write everything I'm feeling because most of it I can't put into thoughts let alone words, but I have to try. Let me say straight off that I don't blame you one bit for deciding you couldn't leave your mother. She needs you and you wouldn't be my Millie if you hadn't

400

fetched her out of that hospital. You were right and no one could say otherwise.

But when I offered to give up the Palestine Police so we could be married and you still gave me back my ring, I couldn't believe it. I left Munroe House that day convinced that you had called off the wedding not because of your mum but because you didn't really want to be my wife. I stuck with that belief, hurt, furious and hateful right up until the morning my papers, ticket and warrant arrived from the Palestine Police central office. And then I knew you were right about me, too.

As much as I love you – and I do love you, Millie – if I'd turned my back on this chance to make something of myself I know eventually I'd hate myself for it. A part of me wishes I'd never smashed my leg up in Sicily because then I wouldn't have had my eyes opened to what the world can offer, but you can't turn back time and now I've seen the opportunities out there, I know that I would never be satisfied just plodding on in the same old rut.

So there we have it. When it comes down to it, we have to put love and dreams aside and do what we have to so we can look at ourselves in the mirror each morning.

You'll always have a special place in my heart and I've sent you a photo so that perhaps when you look at it you'll think of me fondly, too.

All my love
Alex

Tears misted her vision. Millie closed her eyes and rested her head on the back of the chair. The closing strains of Desert Island Discs played out and the plummy tones of a BBC presenter announced the next programme although Millie had long ceased listening.

When the news began there was a long piece about the plight of the German people, followed by a story about the government's on-going negotiation with America for further assistance.

'And now Palestine,' the newsreader said.

Millie opened her eyes and sprung to attention.

'A spokesman from the Foreign and Colonial Office has told the BBC that although the Commissioner has had no further contact with the Zionist rebels who kidnapped the three British soldiers in Jerusalem two days ago, they are still confident that they will be able to secure their release in a matter of days. And now for the weather forecast.'

Millie picked up the photo and lightly ran her fingertips over Alex's grinning face poking out above the sailor's painted body.

She smiled sadly, then pressed Alex's image to her lips. 'Please, God. Keep him safe,' she whispered.

Chapter Twenty-Three

'Sullivan, are you paying attention?' Miss Dutton asked.

Millie sat up immediately. 'Yes, Superintendent,' she said, stretching her eyes wide as she looked at Miss Dutton.

Her thin face took on an expectant look. 'Well?'

Millie stared blankly at the superintendent, and Gladys, who was sitting opposite Millie, started to smirk.

Annie spoke. 'Sister Sullivan is—'

'Please don't interrupt,' Miss Dutton cut in, her voice cracking down the table like a whip. 'I was asking Sullivan, whose mind seems to have another appointment this morning.'

The superintendent's icy blue eyes fixed on Millie again.

'I apologise, Superintendent, but could you repeat the question?' said Millie.

Miss Dutton's lips pulled so tight together they almost disappeared. 'I asked when are you going to organise the next round of teaching sessions for our Queen's Nurse students?'

'Er, um.'

'It's a perfectly simple question, Sullivan,' said Miss Dutton.

Millie gathered her wits. 'I'm waiting for a reply from the sewage works and the Co-operative Dairy, but I will telephone them again and make sure the list of visits is on the notice board by Friday.'

Miss Dutton smiled sweetly. 'Now, that wasn't so difficult, was it, Sullivan?'

'No, Superintendent.'

Millie and Miss Dutton stared at each other for a long moment, and then the superintendent turned her attention back to the report book in front of her.

As Miss Dutton's voice droned on, Millie concentrated on staying awake. Thankfully, after a couple of other small notices the morning report was concluded, and the nurses picked up their bags from under their chairs and started to leave. Millie prepared to do the same.

'Sullivan,' Miss Dutton said. Millie looked up. 'If you would wait, please.'

Giving Millie sympathetic glances as they passed, the other nurses trooped out. Millie rested her case on her chair and waited. When the door closed behind the last one, Miss Dutton closed the report book and folded her hands across it.

'I have to tell you, Sullivan, I'm beginning to have serious doubts if you are committed and dedicated enough to be a district nurse in the St George's and St Dunstan's District Nursing Association.'

Millie's mouth dropped open. 'But I didn't hear what you said.'

'I'm not talking about this morning, although that is the sort of thing that proves that you have become very blasé and slapdash in the last few months. And it cannot continue.'

'I'm never slapdash!' Millie retorted.

Miss Dutton's eyes narrowed. 'What about leaving half your equipment at Mrs Unwin's last week?'

Millie spread her hands. 'I got distracted for a moment.'

'What about sending Barrett to the wrong address?'

'That was a mix-up between Rope Street and Rope Walk.'

'*Your* mix-up, Sullivan,' Miss Dutton shot back. 'And what about asking Dr Hayhurst to call on Mrs Tyler when she's not even his patient.'

'I made a mistake, that's all,' replied Millie, as her temples started to throb.

Miss Dutton's sharp features pulled into a disapproving expression. 'Well, it was a mistake he complained about, and in no uncertain terms, to the Association president, Mr Shottington, who, I can tell you, Sullivan, was very displeased indeed.'

'I'm sorry.'

'Well, I'm afraid it's not good enough,' continued Miss Dutton, her voice rising in pitch as she spoke. 'Added to which, your lack of respect and insubordination is becoming a problem.'

'I beg your pardon, Miss Dutton but I have done everything I can to–'

'From the first day I took up my appointment I knew you were trouble.' Miss Dutton's razor-sharp gaze flicked over Millie. 'I know you thought you should have got the post, but that's no excuse for the way you've constantly undermined my authority ever since I arrived. Don't try and deny it.' The superintendent's face took on an ugly expression. 'I've seen the way the nurses go to you for advice and how they look to you to direct them. And I'm tired of the way every doctor who phones here asks for you first before telling me what the problem is. It's as if everyone thinks you're in charge, and not me.'

'I'm sorry,' said Millie. 'I can only say that I'll be more careful in future.'

The corners of Miss Dutton's lips lifted slightly. 'Nurse Potter told me about your fiancé breaking off your engagement, but that's no excuse. And you know that a nurse cannot let her private life prevent her from doing her duty to her patients. They must come first in all things.'

Millie's shoulders slumped. 'I know, and I am sorry,' she sighed. 'It won't happen again.'

Miss Dutton regarded her unfavourably for a second or two, and then spoke. 'I'm afraid "sorry" won't do this time, Sullivan. I am placing an official reprimand on your file, which means if it ever comes to light that you have acted in such a manner again, you will be brought before the board and most likely dismissed without a reference. Now, you'd better get on your rounds before someone else complains.'

She waved a dismissive hand at Millie and looked down at the report book.

Her hands hanging loosely at her sides, Millie stared dumbly at the top of Miss Dutton's blonde head.

The superintendent jabbed her pen towards the door. 'I said you can go.'

Grasping the handle of her bag, Millie lifted it from the chair. With Miss Dutton's words ringing in her ears and her head pounding, she staggered out of the treatment room.

Millie held out her arms. 'That's a clever girl,' Millie said to Susie Walters as she held on to Millie's fingers and pulled herself up. Susie's mother was sitting in the chair opposite with a rolled-up cigarette hanging out of her mouth. The two other children were playing quietly in the corner with a couple of dolls and an old wooden train that Millie had brought over on her last visit. As it was the middle of the morning, Mickey was at school.

'She's coming on really well,' Millie said, feeling how cold her hands were.

'Yer.'

'What are you feeding her on now?' Millie asked, feeling a slight dampness as she sat the child back on her lap.

'Bit of bread and milk in the morning and whatever the rest of us have at dinnertime,' Mrs Walter replied.

Millie set Susie on the lino and stood up. 'And what would that be?'

'Pie and chips and a bit of fish on Friday,' Mrs Walters replied, watching Millie search for a clean nappy in the cardboard box of clothing under the table.

'And what about vegetables?' Millie asked, pulling out a grey towelling square frayed around the edges.

Mrs Walters looked puzzled. 'Chips are made of taters, aren't they?'

'I meant greens, carrots and peas.'

Mrs Walters shrugged. 'It's a long trek to the market and when you do there's always a queue.

Bloody veg costs money, and he always keeps me short.'

'But if you just boiled a couple of carrots or a spoonful or two of cabbage for the children each day it would help them grow big and strong.'

'You saying my kids are stunted or summink?' Mrs Walters threw her cigarette into the fire, then struggled forward to pick up her tobacco tin.

'No, I'm not. But a portion of greens on their plate will help them fend off runny noses and colds, especially as they're saying it's going to be a harsh winter.'

Mrs Walters continued to roll her cigarette and didn't answer.

'Won't be a moment,' Millie said, heading towards the small kitchenette off the main room.

As she walked in, Millie recoiled at the stench of rotting food and clogged drains. The room, which was no more than nine or ten feet wide by the same across, had a twenty-year-old iron-framed cooker black with burnt-on grease in one corner, and a dilapidated kitchen dresser against the far wall. There was one window, which had what could only be described as a rag hanging from a couple of nails above and a stained enamel sink beneath filled with unwashed crockery.

Picking up a tea-towel to turn the tap, she filled a handleless cup and took it back into the main room.

Millie rubbed her hands together. 'In fact, it's a bit chilly in here now. Why don't you light the fire before the baby gets too cold?'

'It's 'im – he don't leave me enough,' Mrs Walters replied in a plaintive little voice.

408

Setting the cup of water on the table, Millie picked up the baby and laid her on the table. Millie pulled out a jar of zinc and castor oil from her bag and then unpinned Susie's nappy.

'I don't know if you know, but St George's Church has an emergency fund for people who–'

The front door banged open and Millie looked around.

A man with dark, Mediterranean features dressed in an expensive three-piece suit, a flamboyantly knotted tie and a trilby set at a jaunty angle strolled in. The two children immediately stopped what they were doing and pressed themselves against the wall.

His dark eyes darted around the room and settled on Millie. They slid slowly over her as Millie suppressed a shudder.

Mrs Walters heaved herself up and hurried over to him. 'Oh. Marco,' she said, looking adoringly up at his callous face. 'I've been hoping you'd come today.'

'Who this?' he asked without looking at the woman beside him.

'I'm Sister Sullivan from–'

'A nun?' he said, the matchstick between his lips moving as he spoke. 'I've never seen a nun dressed like zat.'

His eyes slid down and lingered on her legs. Resisting the urge to tug her hem down, Millie put Susie's nappy back on and then set her on her hip.

'No, Marco,' Mrs Walter said, putting her hand on his arm tentatively. 'She's a nurse and–'

His mouth pulled into a thin hard line. 'What, you tink I a stupid Dago just off the boat?' he said, poking her head with his forefinger.

'I'm sorry, Marco,' she replied, shying away. 'I didn't mean anything by it.'

'I met your son Mickey at school and now I come to help your wife with the children a couple of times a week,' Millie said, mustering a pleasant tone.

Marco's gaze ran over her again and then he turned back to his common-law wife and threw a couple of crumpled pound notes and a couple of coins on the table.

Mrs Walters stared at it, then grabbed his arm. 'Can you spare a few bob more, please?'

He shook her off. 'Money, money, money – that's all you want.' He kicked the table leg and the cup of water toppled over. 'And look what I get for it – a place that in my country we would not keep a pig in.'

He turned to leave but Millie stepped in front of him. 'I was just saying that it was too cold in here for the baby, and your wife said she couldn't afford any coal.'

Marco's expression hardened. 'She can now.'

He went to push past her but Millie blocked his way. 'But not if she wants to pay the rent and buy your children food as well.'

He glared down at her hatefully. Millie forced herself to hold his glower.

She adjusted the child in her arms. 'I could always telephone the council and ask them to come and assess your wife for welfare tokens,' she said innocently.

His face darkened and he clenched his fist. 'Get out of my way.'

410

Millie stood her ground. 'Of course, they will want to know all about you.'

She heard his teeth scrape together and for one moment she feared he would knock her aside. But instead he shoved his hand in his pocket and slammed another ten-shilling note on the table.

Millie stood aside. Marco stormed past her and out of the door.

There was silence for a moment and then Mrs Walters snatched up the money and grabbed her coat.

'Where are you going?' Millie asked.

'Out. I won't be long. You can leave them with 'er next door when you go,' she shouted as she disappeared into the hall.

The little girl in the corner burst into tears. Millie put Susie down and went to comfort her and noticed the boy clutching on to her had a dark patch at the front of his trousers.

'It's all right,' Millie said, hugging them both.

'I'm hungry and so is Keith,' said the girl.

Keith stuck his thumb in his mouth and pressed his face into his sister's shoulder.

'Well, then,' Millie said, straightening up. 'I'd better make you dinner.'

Millie stood beside Annie in the middle of Nelly Wiseman's living room and studied the damp patch of serous fluid seeping on to the carpet under the old woman's feet.

'So how many days is it since the nurses called, Mrs Wiseman?' Millie asked.

Nelly's wrinkled face took on a puzzled expression. 'Yesterday, I think. Or was it the day before?'

Nelly Wiseman, like her mother before her and no doubt her mother's mother too, had been in the shellfish trade. With an oversized basket containing prawns, cockles, whelks and other salty delicacies over one arm, and a zinc bucket full of oysters in brine hooked over the other, she had been a familiar sight selling seafood brought up through the Thames estuary from Leigh and Southend in the dozens of pubs around the docks until her ulcerated right leg made it impossible. She now lived with her daughter Noreen, who had taken over her mother's trade and expanded the business by opening a pie and mash shop around the corner as well. Sad to say, over the last year Nelly's mind had also started to let her down, so now some days she didn't know her whelks from her cockles.

'Can you remember who?' Millie asked.

Nelly looked at Annie. 'Wasn't it you?'

'No, Mrs Wiseman. Could it have been Nurse Potter?' Annie asked.

'Who's she?'

'About my height with brown, curly hair,' Millie said encouragingly.

Nelly looked blank.

'She should have dressed your legs yesterday, and the day before,' replied Annie. 'Are you sure you can't remember her coming?'

Mrs Wiseman shook her head. 'I remember the jolly one with glasses and the blonde with big eyes and you,' she pointed at Annie, 'the little one, but I can't say as how I remember no one with curly hair. But then my memory isn't what it used to be.'

Millie smiled reassuringly. 'Don't worry, Mrs Wiseman, we're here now and I'm just going to unwrap your bandage so I can have a little look.'

'All right, Sister, if you must,' replied Nelly, taking a sip from her afternoon glass of stout. 'But it seems a bit of a waste of time to have both you and ... what did you say her name was?' she asked, looking apologetically at Annie.

'Sister Fletcher,' said Millie.

She lifted Nelly's leg on to the footstool and then knelt down on the front page of last week's *Sunday People*. Annie did the same on the sports page.

Millie unfastened the safety pin and put it in the pot of Dettol sitting alongside the forceps, gauze and iodine on the table beside them. She put on her boiled rubber gloves and unwound the bandage then dropped it in the newspaper bag. Taking the forceps, Millie lifted one corner of the gauze square and the sickly sweet smell of leg ulcers wafted up.

Annie coughed as Millie peeled off the dressing to reveal the doughy green and yellow pus beneath.

Nelly looked at her leg. 'Is it any better?'

Millie and Annie exchanged a quick look.

'A little,' replied Millie, dropping the sodden gauze in the rubbish bag. 'Now just rest back and let us make you more comfortable.'

Millie and Annie washed and redressed the old woman's leg in iodine-soaked gauze, while Nelly hummed along with the factory workers on *Workers' Playtime* drifting out of the old Bush radio on the windowsill.

'There you go, Mrs Wiseman,' Millie said at

last, standing up and stretching out the ache in the small of her back.

'Ta, ducks,' Nelly said, gazing admiringly at the neat bandaging.

'Nurse Fletcher will come and dress your leg again tomorrow,' said Millie.

Nelly smiled. 'Is that the dark-haired one?'

'No, that's me, Mrs Wiseman,' replied Annie, wedging the cork stopper on to the top of the iodine bottle.

Millie parcelled up the rubbish and placed it in the empty grate for Nelly's daughter to dispose of.

'I'll leave this for Noreen to put in the oven for tomorrow,' Millie said, holding up the dressing tin repacked with fresh gauze before putting it alongside the radio. 'Good day.'

Millie stepped out of Mrs Wiseman's house and Annie closed the door behind them.

'So what do you think?' asked Annie, securing her bag in the basket between her handlebars.

'You're right,' replied Millie. 'No one's touched that dressing for at least three days.'

'Do you think I should tell Miss Dutton?' asked Annie, clearly not relishing the prospect.

Millie shook her head. 'I'm pretty sure Gladys was allocated Nelly for the last two days, but I'll have to check the book. If she was, then I'll speak to her and warn her that if it happens again, I'll be informing Miss Dutton.'

Annie brightened instantly. 'Thank you, Millie. I knew you'd know what to do. You always do.'

After the last of the pregnant women waddled

414

out of the antenatal clinic that afternoon, Millie set to tidying the treatment room to make sure she caught Gladys as soon as she returned. It was almost five o'clock and after all the other nurses had already stowed their cases in the storage cupboard Gladys finally rolled in at the end of her afternoon visits.

Millie smiled professionally at her. 'Can I ask you about Mrs Wiseman?'

Gladys slung her bag into the bottom cupboard. 'What about her?'

'Did you do her legs yesterday, and the day before?' Millie asked.

Gladys's gaze flickered. 'Course.'

'I went to see her today and found the bandages wet, loose and reeking of infection,' Millie replied.

'She must have fiddled with them,' Gladys replied.

'She couldn't remember you calling, either,' Millie said, holding Gladys's gaze.

Gladys snorted. 'I'm not surprised. The batty old bird don't remember her own name most days. But if you don't believe me, you can check her notes.' She nodded towards the wooden filing cabinet containing the patients' notes. 'It's all there.'

She started towards it but Millie stepped in her path. 'I bet it is. But if you changed those dressings yesterday, then I'm a Chinaman.'

A belligerent expression twisted Gladys's features. 'What do you mean?'

'I mean that because you skipped a visit, Mrs Wiseman hasn't had her legs dressed for at least two days,' Millie replied.

Although Gladys's face flushed, she forced a casual laugh. 'You've got no proof.'

Millie gave her a cool look. 'I'm not going to take it any further this time,' she said. 'But if I find you've falsified patient records or neglected a patient ever again I'm going to–'

'What?' snarled Gladys, thrusting her face close to Millie's. 'Tell Miss Dutton? I wouldn't if I were you or I'll have to tell her how you've sneaked your policeman boyfriend in at night to have a bit of how's-yer-father. And that you've been popping in to wash and dress your daft old mother while you're on duty.'

An icy finger seemed to run up Millie's spine.

'I'll also tell the superintendent how your mother's been making a nuisance by turning up here half-dressed and babbling on about a lot of nonsense.'

'That was once when she was upset,' countered Millie.

'Upset!' Gladys circled her finger next to her temple. 'Trudy saw her and told me she was away with the fairies.'

'My mother's not been well,' said Millie.

'Bonkers, you mean.' Gladys jabbed her finger at Millie. 'Then you should have left her in St Colombo's nut hutch where she belongs instead of getting the other nurses in Munroe House to do your work so you can slip off whenever you feel like it.'

Millie's hands balled into fists. 'Don't you dare speak about my mother like that!'

'I also think Miss Dutton will be interested to know you've been staying out all night and then sneaking in at dawn, but all the while pretending you've been tucked up in bed. And I surely don't need to remind you of the Association rules that all unmarried nurses are to live in.' Gladys's lips twisted into a mockery of a smile. 'And you're certainly not married, are you?'

An image of Alex flashed into Millie's mind, sending a dart of pain through her chest. It must have showed on her face because Gladys's smug grin spread wider.

'But don't worry, Millie dear, as soon you'll be able to spend as much time as you like with your mad mother. Because if you start telling tales, I'll let Miss Dutton in on all your little secrets and she'll certainly give you your marching orders.'

Chapter Twenty-Four

Shifting her cumbersome bag into the other hand, Millie yawned as she plodded down the stone stairs of Tate House. The brick-built three-storey building in Shadwell Gardens was one of the first attempts at improving the living conditions of the poor. Although the triangular structure retained much of its ponderous Victorian character, its ornate wrought-iron banisters had been stripped out as part of the war effort to salvage metal, and had been replaced by a rope handrail. It was therefore advisable for those going up and down the stairs to keep as close to the wall as possible.

Millie had five patients to see in Tate House. As her list included an insulin injection, dressing deep bedsores, tending a festering breast abscess and two bed baths, she'd been there most of the morning.

Over the last few days her mother seemed to be improving slightly and Millie had had Doris settled in bed by ten o'clock, which meant she had been tucked up under the covers herself on the right side of midnight. Not that Millie felt it had done her much good, because she was still arguing with Gladys in her head until St Martha's and St Mungo's church clock struck one.

Of course, Gladys was right: she shouldn't be popping in to see her mother while she was on duty. But what choice did she have? She was

418

between a rock and a hard place, as Doris needed to be cared for. After all, that was why Millie had called off her wedding.

The women pegging up their washing on the communal clothesline in the courtyard of Tate House greeted her as she passed, and Millie waved to them and the handful of children playing alongside them as she made her way to the main entrance.

Outside the gloom of the enclosed blocks of flats, the midsummer sunshine dazzled her eyes for a second. Turning left, Millie headed towards Watney Street just as the twelve o'clock factory hoots sounded. Intent on cutting through the market to her last morning visit, Millie didn't take much heed of the person stepping out of Shelstone's, the local haberdasher's shop, until she heard a too-familiar caustic voice call her name.

'Sister Sullivan, 'ow's your mother?'

Millie turned. 'Good afternoon, Mrs Callaghan.'

The old woman lurched towards her, setting the loaded shopping bags she was carrying swinging around her.

'So, how is she?' Mrs Callaghan asked, puffing to a halt a few feet from Millie.

'She's fine, thank you,' replied Millie, forcing herself not to shift under Mrs Callaghan's intense stare.

'I only ask because I saw her in the ironmonger's yesterday and she seemed a bit emotional, poor love. Kept going on about she weren't going back to that place again, although I couldn't rightly make out what place she was talking about,' Mrs Callaghan continued. 'Perhaps you know?'

'She didn't like being in hospital much,' Millie replied. 'Mum's had a rough couple of months and she's still not properly back on her feet.'

'Is that why you've been staying over each night, then?' asked Mrs Callaghan.

'Who told you that?'

'Don't be daft,' Mrs Callaghan said scornfully. 'Everyone knows you're in and out of your mother's all the time. I hear your aunt ain't been near or by for the past two weeks. Have you and her fallen out?'

'No, we haven't fallen out, Mrs Callaghan.' In her head Millie counted backwards from ten slowly. 'My aunt has been sick, that's all, and she lives a long way away.'

'Ilford, isn't it?'

'Yes.'

'Owns her own house, does she?'

'Yes.'

Mrs Callahan crossed her arms and adjusted her bosom. 'Very nice, I'm sure.'

'Now, I really must–'

'And I thought you were getting married to that Alex Nolan,' Mrs Callaghan interrupted, fixing Millie with her steely gaze again.

A surge of desolation welled up inside Millie. 'I'd rather not talk about it, if you don't mind,' she said, as her lip wobbled.

Mrs Callaghan continued regardless. 'Course, people round here don't have no truck with the rozzers unless they can help it like, but I knew his old gran and she was a tru'un so, although some I could name wouldn't, I'll give him the benefit of the doubt. He was a bright kid, too, although a bit

420

on the cheeky side for my liking.' Her sharp eyes flickered over Millie's face. 'I suppose you sent him packing because of the way your mum is.'

Millie gasped as if she'd been punched in the stomach. She opened her mouth to say 'no' but found she couldn't speak.

Mrs Callaghan gave her a knowing look. 'I can see 'ow it is.' Her hard features softened a little. 'It's as it should be. Honour thy father and mother, that's what the good book says, don't it?'

A roaring started in Millie's head. 'I'm sorry, Mrs Callaghan I've got patients still to see and I really must get on. Good day.'

She stumbled forward, then regained her balance.

'Well, I'll not stop you,' replied Mrs Callaghan as Millie passed her. 'But to my mind you're looking right off-colour yourself, so if you don't want your poor mum ending up back in that "place" she's so afraid of, you want to start looking after yourself proper.'

Millie checked the cork was firmly in place and then slid the refilled bottle of surgical spirit into the side of her bag ready for the next day's work. She opened the cupboard and stared at the shelves of dressings and bandages. The thick fog of tiredness clogging her mind threatened to overwhelm her thinking, but she forced it away and selected a couple of packs of gauze, then closed the glazed door. The treatment-room door opened and Connie came in.

'There you are,' she said, visibly relieved as she spotted Millie standing by the enamel sink. 'I tried to catch you after tea but by the time I finished talking to Eva, you were gone.'

'Sorry, if I'd known I'd have waited, but I had a full afternoon list and wanted to get on,' Millie explained. 'What were you after me for?'

Connie ambled over and lolled against the work-top. 'Do you know that as part of this nationwide health service the government's talking about bringing in, the Association is opening a clinic in Spitalfields?'

'You mean the clinic that's been talked about in the old mission house?'

'That's it,' replied Connie. 'Well, they need experienced district nurses, and so I'm considering asking for a transfer. But I want to know what you think of the idea before I do.'

'Is it because Charlie's wife has had the second baby?' Millie asked.

'You heard then?'

Millie nodded. 'Sally told me.'

'Another boy. Just eleven months after the last.' Anger flitted across Connie's face briefly but then she sighed. 'It's not just about Charlie's blooming wife, although I am sick to death of bumping into her all the time, but it's more because I feel like I'm stuck in a rut here, and if I have to end up an old maid I'd rather not be so close to Charlie.'

'Oh, Connie,' Millie laughed. 'You, an old maid? Never.'

Connie smiled. 'Well, even so, while I'm waiting for this Mr Right you seem so sure is waiting just around the corner, I might as well do something useful with myself.'

Ignoring the oddly bereft feeling that suddenly

422

loomed up, Millie mustered a smile. 'Well, I suppose we can't remain the terrible twins of St George's and St Dunstan's for ever, and I think Munroe House's loss will be Spitalfield's gain. I'm sure you'll be the superintendent within the year.'

Connie scoffed. 'I doubt it, but I am pleased you think it's a good idea. And I'm only half an hour away, so we'll still see each other at least once a week.'

'We'd better,' replied Millie, struggling to maintain her light tone. 'It won't be easy though,' she warned. 'If you think it's rough in Wapping and Shadwell, the streets around Brick Lane and at the back of St Leonard's are like something out of *Oliver Twist*. And where will you live?'

'There's an old house in Dorset Street they're doing up as a nurses' home,' replied Connie.

'Isn't that where one of Jack the Ripper's victims lived?' Millie asked, looking innocuously at her friend.

'Just around the corner. But I'm not worried,' said Connie in a blasé tone. 'Because old Jack wouldn't stand a hope in hell's chance if he tackled a district nurse in a hurry.'

Millie laughed but Connie's expression became serious. 'Have you been crying?'

Millie had. For a full hour on her bed after her run-in with Mrs Callaghan earlier. But now she shook her head and blinked her eyes open wide. 'I'm fine. I just had a rough night, that's all.'

'Wouldn't your mum settle again?'

'She wasn't too bad,' replied Millie. 'No, it was Gladys.'

She told Connie about Mrs Wiseman.

'Why didn't Annie just go straight to Miss Dutton?' Connie asked when she'd finished.

'I think she wanted to make sure she wasn't imagining things,' Millie replied.

'I suppose that's fair enough, but she should have gone to the superintendent and not you,' replied Connie crossly. 'And it's not as if you haven't got enough on your plate without adding more.' She gave Millie an exasperated look. 'You take too much on to yourself.'

Millie's shoulders slumped. 'You're probably right, but I was so furious with Gladys that I just steamed in. And it's just as well I did or she would have told Miss Dutton about Mum. And if that wasn't bad enough, I've just had Mrs Callaghan giving me the third degree about mum outside Shelstone's.'

Millie's head started to throb again and she put her hand to her temple. The floor seemed to sway and she grabbed the edge of the cupboard to steady herself.

'Millie, are you sure you're all right?' Connie asked from what seemed to be a long way away.

Millie took a couple of deep breaths and the dizziness faded. 'Honestly, I'm fine,' she replied, smiling reassuringly at her friend. 'It's just Mrs Callaghan. She always riles me.'

Connie didn't seem convinced. 'If you say so, but you're looking very pale to me. Come to the sitting room, and I'll make you a cuppa.'

Millie glanced at the clock above the door. 'I'd love to, but I've got to get around to Mum's.'

'Well then, give me a knock when you get back

and we'll have a nightcap together,' Connie said, still scrutinising her closely.

'I might stay with Mum until she's properly settled, so don't wait up.' Millie closed her bag and put it away in the store cupboard. She locked the door and turned back to her friend. The dizziness threatened to return but she forced it away.

She smiled at Connie. 'If I don't see you later, we'll catch up at breakfast.'

A blinding light set Millie's heart pounding in her chest and panic racing through her as she sat bolt upright and looked around. For a moment she wasn't sure where she was, then she realised she was on the sofa in her mother's front room. She'd taken off her dress and stockings as she usually did when she had to sleep on her mother's couch, but was still in her underwear.

'Would you like a cup of tea, dear?' her mother said pleasantly as she shuffled across the lounge towards the kitchen. She was still in her night-clothes with her hair in curlers.

Millie rubbed her eyes. 'What's the time?'

Doris rolled back her dressing-gown sleeve and looked at her watch, then back at Millie. 'I haven't got my glasses on.'

She carried on to the kitchen. Millie forced her eyes open and peered at the clock on the mantelshelf. The numbers on it seemed to dance about on the face, so Millie threw off the blanket and stood up. Half asleep and her head thick with tiredness, she staggered over to the fireplace and picked up the clock.

Four-thirty! Her mother hadn't gone to sleep until almost twelve o'clock. That was five nights in the past week that she'd been unsettled.

With her head pounding fit to burst Millie stumbled backwards to the couch just as Doris came back in carrying a tray of tea. She set it on the small coffee table and sat down on her chair.

She smiled at Millie. 'Shall I be mother?'

Millie raked her fingers through her hair. 'It's four-thirty in the morning, Mum. It's too early to be up yet.'

Doris looked surprised. 'Is it?' she sighed. 'Oh, well. Never mind.'

'But don't you understand I have to go to work at six?' Millie said, as an invisible band seemed to tighten around her forehead.

'Well, then, you've got plenty of time to enjoy a nice cuppa before you get ready,' Doris said brightly, as she poured them both a cup of tea. A sentimental expression settled on her face. 'Not long now.'

A heavy weight settled on Millie's chest. 'No, Mum.'

Doris reached across and squeezed her hand. 'You're going to be the most beautiful bride that, ever walked down the aisle. I only wish Dad was here to see it.'

'So do I,' Millie replied, feeling tears sting the corners of her eyes.

Doris let go of her hand and handed Millie her tea. 'Is Alex coming around today?'

'Not today.'

Doris smiled sadly at her. 'Never mind, I'm sure he'll come around tomorrow.' She stood up and went to the window. She drew back the curtains.

'Another nice morning,' she said, as the first few pink rays of the August dawn streaked across the sky.

The hammering in Millie's head suddenly intensified and she jumped up. She rushed at her mother and grabbed the drapes from her hands. 'It is not a nice morning! It's the middle of the bloody night!' she shouted, and wrenched them closed.

Doris looked shocked. 'Millie!'

'And Alex isn't coming around tomorrow, or the next day, or ever again, because he's gone.' Millie began to sob, falling against the back of the chair.

'Gone? What do you mean?'

'For goodness sake, what do you think it means, Mother? He's gone, left, departed, not here anymore,' screamed Millie, as tears streamed down her face. 'He sailed for Palestine over a month ago.'

Her mother stared at her daughter in bewilderment. 'But you're getting married.'

Millie shook her head. 'Not anymore.'

'Why?'

Millie wiped her cheeks with the heel of her hand. 'We're just not. That's all.' She ran her hands over her face. 'Drink your tea,' she said more calmly.

She tried to walk past her mother, but Doris threw her arms around her and hugged her. 'My poor sweetheart,' she said, stroking Millie's hair gently, as she had done for as long as Millie could remember.

For a couple of seconds Millie remained rigid in her mother's embrace, and then she lowered her head on to her mother's shoulder and cried heartily. After what seemed like hours, and with her chest aching and her eyes stinging, Millie took a deep breath as she regained control.

Feeling empty and drained, Millie untangled herself from her mother. Doris gave her a sad smile and moved away a damp lock from Millie's cheek.

'Tell me what happened,' Doris said.

Millie wiped her face with her hands. 'There's nothing to tell, really,' she said, feeling the raw sense of loss claw at her chest again. 'Now, come on, drink your tea before it gets cold.'

Doris's gaze ran over her face. For a couple of seconds there was a look of understanding and deep sorrow in her mother's expression, then she nodded and allowed Millie to guide her back to her chair.

Millie returned to the sofa, tucked herself into the corner and rested back. She pulled the covers up, closed her eyes and although her mother started singing quietly to herself, Millie drifted back to sleep.

Chapter Twenty-Five

Millie packed the last piece of her equipment back in her bag and then pinned up her apron.

'I'll see you on Friday, Mrs Wallace,' she said, taking her lightweight summer mac from the brown paper bag and putting it on. 'And don't fiddle with the bandages.'

The old woman sitting in the chair pulled a face. 'I'll try, nurse, but it do itch like buggery.'

'That's because it's healing,' Millie said, giving her a pretend scowl.

Mrs Wallace chuckled, showing off her one remaining tooth. 'All right, ducks, I'll try. Now you look after yourself, do you 'ear?'

Millie smiled and took the thruppeny bit for the visit out of the chipped cup on the mantelshelf. Gerty Wallace had been on and off the Association's books for years, but because she only had her old-age pension, she was charged only a token rate for a nurse's visit.

Leaving the old woman's small flat in the Greenbody Building in Settle Street, Millie yawned as she turned around the top of the stairs.

She'd managed to get another hour on her mother's sofa before sneaking back to Munroe House at a quarter to six, but felt less than rested. Still, she only had two more visits before dinner. But as she reached the last couple of steps her head swam and she stumbled. She grabbed at the stone banister to save her from falling, dropping her case in the process. Millie found her footing again and dusted herself down. She picked up her bag and checked it. Mercifully, nothing had broken, so she closed it and continued down the stairs. Her eyes felt heavy but she hoped the fresh air as she pedalled her way to Greenbank would wake her up soon enough.

After stowing her bag in the usual place, Millie unchained her bike from the lamp-post and, putting her foot on the pedal, scooted forward a couple of feet then hopped on. Passing the old school on her right, Millie picked up speed as she bounced over the cobbles heading towards Commercial Road.

Swinging left into the main road, she waited until one of Maguire's coal lorries had passed before moving to the right to turn at the traffic lights into Cannon Street Road.

The red light showed as Millie approached, so she eased up. Despite the wind in her face, Millie's eyes started to silt up, so she took a couple of deep breaths to clear her head. As she coasted towards the stop line, the amber light joined the red. Shaking herself into action, Millie stood up on the pedals and, sticking her right arm out and seeing there was no oncoming traffic, sailed across the junction.

Something blasted out and there was a screech of brakes. Millie's heart thumped uncomfortably in her chest and her pulse set off at a gallop. She turned to find herself staring into a set of headlights and a metal grille. Someone yelled as Millie's cycle was knocked from under her and she flew through the air. She landed on her back and stared upwards at the blue sky, lamp-posts and faces swirling around in her vision. She tried to move but couldn't. She was hurt, badly, she knew, although she couldn't work out where the pain was. A man's face loomed over her, asking her something, but Millie couldn't understand what he was saying. She tried to answer but no words came out.

Somehow, as the commotion raged above her, Millie raised her hand and flexed her black and bloody fingers. Thank goodness they moved, but the effort exhausted her, and so she let her hand fall again. Someone covered her with a coat and then she heard bells. People were talking to her and to each other. Soon hands were gently lifting her from the tarmac. Millie's head swam again as the black fog that had hovered at the edge of her consciousness surged forward. An image of Alex and then her mother flashed through Millie's mind as darkness engulfed her.

The sound of metal scraping on metal brought Millie back to consciousness. Although her head pounded as if her brain was trying to punch its way out, her thoughts were clear. She lay still listening to the familiar sounds of a hospital ward for a few moments, then wiggled her toes and gently flexed her fingers under the covers. Despite a tingling in her forearms, her fingers seemed to be working properly now, and she could even feel the texture of the smooth sheet beneath her. Relief swept over Millie but, oh, the pain!

Millie drew in a deep breath and felt a couple

of ribs protest. She opened her eyes. The first surprise was that although she was certain she raised both lids, she could only see out of her right eye; the second was that Connie was sitting by her bedside.

'Where am I?' Millie mumbled.

'Hanbury Ward,' her friend replied, with a slight crack in her voice. 'And thank goodness you're awake at last.'

'How long have I been here?' Millie asked, struggling to sit up.

With an experienced hand Connie helped Millie to sit forward. 'Since yesterday,' she replied, as she buckled the backrest in place and repositioned the pillows.

Millie started to sink back but then sat up again. 'My mum?'

'Don't worry. Your mum's fine, Millie,' Connie said, smiling reassuringly and patting the pillows. 'She's being well looked after.'

Despite the pain in her wrist, Millie grabbed Connie's hand. 'She's not been taken back to St Colombo's, has she?'

'Of course not.'

'Where is she, then?' Millie said, as panic started to rise in her chest. 'Is she with my Aunt Ruby?'

'No, she didn't want to go to her sister's. But everything is in hand,' Connie replied.

The throbbing in Millie's head started to build, and she let herself sink into the pillow and closed her eyes.

'That's better,' said Connie in her sister-knows-best voice. 'Aunt Ruby came yesterday to see you for a couple of hours, and she will be down tomorrow again. Now don't worry.'

Millie nodded and wished she hadn't. 'I don't think there's one inch of me that doesn't hurt.'

'I'm not surprised – you've taken half the skin off your arms and legs, not to mention knocking your head on the kerb,' said Connie, looking at her sympathetically. 'Thank God you weren't killed. Can you remember what happened?'

'Not really,' replied Millie. 'One moment I was cycling down Commercial Street and the next I was lying on the ground with people around me.'

'The policeman who came to see us said the lorry jumped the lights, so he'll be prosecuted,' Connie said. 'The doctor in accident and emergency thought you'd done more damage, but when the x-rays came back clear a couple of hours ago they stopped the morphine.'

Millie shifted position to ease the numbness in her bottom and a pain shot down her leg. 'I can tell.'

'Here.' Connie picked up a small china pot. 'The nurses left this for when you woke up.'

Millie stretched out her hand and her friend tipped out two white tablets.

'It's codeine. It'll take the edge off the pain,' Connie concluded, putting the pot back.

Millie popped them in her mouth and Connie held a glass of water to her lips and helped her drink.

Millie swallowed the tablets and let her head fall back. Connie took her hand gently. 'Oh, Millie, you gave us all such a fright. When the police rang and said you'd been knocked off your bike by a lorry, well,' Connie's chin trembled, 'I can't tell

433

you how relieved I was when I arrived and they told me you were alive and not too seriously injured.'

Although she knew it would hurt, Millie squeezed her friend's hand. They smiled at each other.

'The girls say they'll pop in when you're feeling a bit better. And we all clubbed together and bought you these.'

She delved into her bag and pulled out something Millie hadn't seen for almost six years: a bunch of bananas.

Millie's mouth fell open. 'Where on earth did you get those?'

'Don't ask,' replied Connie with an amused expression. 'Let's just say Annie has a patient who can "acquire" things, and leave it at that. Do you want one now?'

'Yes, please,' replied Millie, realising suddenly she was hungry. Connie peeled it and handed it to her. Millie bit the top off and closed her eyes.

'Oh my goodness,' she said, rolling the perfectly ripe fruit around in her mouth. 'I'd forgotten how sweet they are.'

She broke the rest of the banana in half.

'Here, you have some,' she said, offering her friend the bottom half.

Connie hesitated for a split second, then took the fruit and bit into it. 'Mmm, so tasty,' she said through a mouthful of banana. 'Perhaps I should tumble off my bike, too.'

'I wouldn't recommend it,' Millie replied. She smiled lopsidedly. 'I owe you and the girls for taking care of Mum, Connie.'

Connie's gaze flickered nervously over Millie. 'Look, I was going to tell you when you'd recovered a bit more, but perhaps you ought to know now.'

Cold dread washed over Millie. 'Tell me what?'

Connie shifted uncomfortably from one foot to the other. 'Well, Millie, me and the girls are popping in once a day but – and promise you won't get annoyed – Mrs Callaghan is the one who's taken charge, and she's got a rota of neighbours caring for your mum.'

For a moment Millie thought she was hearing things, but Connie's sheepish expression told her she had not.

'Mrs Callaghan!' Millie screeched, setting the pain in her head banging again.

'When we heard you'd had an accident, Annie, who was on her day off, went straight round to sit with your mum, but just as she was about to make tea, Mrs Callaghan and a couple of your mum's neighbours turned up and, well, they took over. Before you could say Jack Robinson, they were doing your mum's cooking and cleaning. The woman from across the road sat with your mum all evening and then got her to bed and when I arrived the next morning your mum was already up and dressed and having breakfast with another neighbour. And this is the plan until you are out of hospital. Someone gets your mum breakfast and sits with her all morning, and then someone else comes to give her dinner and keeps her company all afternoon until the late shift arrives to do supper and bedtime.'

Millie was dumbstruck.

'I know,' said Connie, seeing the look of be-wilderment on Millie's face. 'I couldn't believe it either.'

'I didn't think Mrs Callaghan even liked me,' said Millie, still unable to believe what she was hearing. 'So why would she look after my mother?'

'I have no idea, but if you want to know why Mrs Callaghan has galvanised the whole neigh-bourhood into action, you'd better do as the doctors say and get out of here, and then you can ask her yourself.'

Feeling slightly dazed after three days in a hos-pital, Millie waited outside her mother's house while her aunt concluded negotiations with the cab driver who'd brought them home.

'Glad to see you're better,' a woman who was scrubbing her step on the other side of the street called to Millie.

'I bet you're right glad to be home,' shouted another, hanging out of an upstairs window and polishing the glass with a screwed-up sheet of newspaper.

Millie smiled wanly at them and the dozen or so women on the other side of the street. Just like the woman in a cuckoo clock who nips out to tell you the weather is fine, Doris's neighbours had all popped out of their front doors as soon as the taxi drew up.

The cab pulled away. 'I don't know: people these days!' Ruby said as she joined Millie. 'He had the cheek to try to charge me five shillings for a half-mile journey. I told him if he'd come straight here instead of taking the long way around it would have been half that and I'd give him not a penny more than three.'

'What did he say?'

'It doesn't bear repeating,' replied Ruby, patting her pillbox hat into place. 'I blame this Labour government for all this racketeering.' She glanced up at the heavy, grey sky. 'You'd better get indoors before it buckets down.'

Millie lifted the latch and walked in. Her mother was sitting by the fire knitting, and a young woman, who looked vaguely familiar, sat alongside her with a little boy playing with three metal soldiers on the floor at her feet.

Doris stood up as soon as Millie walked in. 'Oh, my dear,' she said, hurrying over to her. 'I was so worried.'

Millie had asked Ruby not to bring her mother to visit her because she was concerned about the effect both seeing her and being in a hospital might have on Doris.

Doris put her arms around Millie and hugged her for a moment, and then ran her hand gently over Millie's forehead. 'Your poor face.'

The deep purple on Millie cheeks and around her eyes now had yellow tinges, and she could now see out of both eyes. But she still looked a mess.

She smiled down at her mother. 'I know, but there's no bones broken, and in another week I'll be as good as new.'

'Come and sit down,' Doris said, leading Millie to the sofa.

Feeling quite exhausted from the journey home, and a little light-headed from standing up,

Millie sank gratefully on to the sofa.

'Now put your feet up and I'll make us a cuppa,' her mother said, manoeuvring the pouffe in front of her. 'You may be on the mend, but you need to rest.'

The young woman put aside her magazine and stood up. 'It's all right, Doris, I'll make it.'

With her little boy trotting behind her, she went out into the kitchen.

Doris covered Millie's legs with a knitted blanket and then sat beside her. Ruby came downstairs and plonked herself in Doris's chair. 'I've unpacked your suitcase and your friend Connie will be dropping by later with some more clothes. Anthony has set up a camp bed next to your mother's. It's a bit of a squeeze but I'm sure you'll manage. I went to Munroe House yesterday and spoke to Miss Dutton. I told her you won't be back to work for two weeks and that your mother was looking after you.'

'What did she say?' asked Millie.

'What could she say?' Ruby replied, with more than a hint of smugness. 'She went on about you needing a doctor's certificate before the Association paid you for your time off, but I'm sure Dr Golding? Godwin? Or whatever her name is will give you one.'

'You mean Doctor Gingold?' asked Millie.

'Yes,' Doris said. 'She came around to see me as soon as Bridget told her what had happened to you. I made her tea and told her all about Dad.'

'Bridget?'

Doris looked surprised. 'Bridget Callaghan.'

The young woman came back with the tray of

438

tea. 'I'll make a move now, Doris,' she said, putting it down on the table and gathering the toys from the floor. 'Peggy from number four will be in later with your supper.'

'Thank you, Jill,' Millie's mother said. 'And I'll see you soon.' Jill nodded, then scooped up her son, settled him on her hip and left.

'I'd better head off, too, Doris,' said Ruby, rising to her feet and hooking her handbag over her arm. 'Anthony and I are going to a reception at the Ilford Chamber of Commerce tonight.' She leant over and gave Millie a gentle kiss on the forehead. 'You gave us all a real fright, Amelia, so make sure you don't start doing too much until you're properly better. Understand?'

'Yes, Aunt Ruby.'

Ruby gave her a severe look. 'Promise?'

'I promise,' Millie replied.

'Good.' She kissed her again. 'I'll be down next Tuesday.'

She left, closing the front door firmly behind her.

Doris put Millie's tea in front of her on the coffee table. 'Do you mind if I put the wireless on quietly, Millie?'

Millie shook her head. It took a few moments for the valves to warm up, but then they heard the Greenwich time pips and the presenter announced *Much-Binding-in-the-Marsh*, and ran through the list of players while the lively signature tune played.

The nasal tones of Richard Murdoch launched the first exchange and Millie drank her tea and settled further down into the sofa. Doris returned to her own chair and picked up her knitting.

As the audience in the Broadcasting House Concert Hall laughed at the goings-on at the fictitious airfield base and as Doris's knitting needles clicked together, Millie's eyes slowly closed and she started to drift off to sleep. Suddenly, her eyes blinked open.

Doris looked concerned. 'What's the matter, dear?' she asked, looping the wool between the needles and then slipping one through.

'You're knitting,' said Millie, staring in astonishment at her mother.

Doris held up her needles to show Millie the small sleeve she was working on. 'It's the wool from that pink and blue jumper Aunt Edie knitted you for Christmas a couple of years ago that you never really wore,' her mother said, making another stitch. 'It's a jumper for Lilly Farmer's little girl. It's her birthday next week. Do you like it?'

Millie nodded. 'It's beautiful,' she said, staring at the intricate pattern of the small garment.

Doris smiled. 'Good. Now you shut your eyes again and have a rest.'

Millie did as she was told. For as long as she could remember, Doris had always had a garment on her needles and one of her enduring childhood memories was of her father reading the paper in a chair on one side of the fireplace while her mother sat opposite knitting. She'd always had the knack of transforming a couple of skeins of wool into finely worked matinée jackets and bootees.

In comparison to some of the pretty cardigans, socks and gloves Doris had knitted over the years, the little pullover for her neighbour's daughter wasn't anything out of the ordinary to look at.

But to Millie's mind it was the most precious garment her mother had ever knitted. It was the first knitting Doris had had on her needles since her husband died.

Narrowly avoiding being knocked down by a pack of dogs who had been turned out for the day while their owners were at work, Millie made her way along Richard Street. Two young women on the other side of the road turned and stared at her for a moment before they recognised her out of uniform and waved. She acknowledged them and continued on until she reached number four.

Although she could have just pulled the string dangling through the letter box or, as most people did, walked down the side alley and entered the house via the back door, Millie felt her visit warranted a more formal approach. So, straightening her Peter Pan collar and being careful not to scuff her feet on the immaculately white step, Millie reached out and raised the wooden knocker. She waited a couple of minutes and Mrs Callaghan, wearing her faded wraparound apron and with a potato peeler in one hand, opened the door.

'I thought you were the tally man,' she said.

Millie gave her a friendly smile. 'Good afternoon, Mrs Callaghan. If I'm not disturbing you, could I come in for a moment?'

Mrs Callaghan's gaze flickered over Millie and she stood aside. 'Go through to the back.'

Millie had of course been in the house before, but then Joe had whisked her so swiftly up the

441

stairs to his wife's bedroom that she hadn't had time to see the kind of house Mrs Callaghan kept.

Now, walking down the hallway with its dust-free picture frames and polished banisters, Millie suspected that the old woman was one of the daily top-to-bottom brigade, and when she reached the scullery the evidence was overwhelming. Although the deep butler sink was supported by Victorian ironwork and had only one tap, it was spotless. The ancient dresser on which the family's crockery was stacked had seen better days, but its bleached wood bore witness to years of scouring.

'I thought you only came home yesterday,' Mrs Callaghan said, lumbering into the room behind her.

'I did,' replied Millie.

A sour expression pulled Mrs Callaghan's lips together. 'Well, in my day invalids were supposed to be resting up, not gadding about the street.'

'I hardly think walking from my mother's house two streets away is gadding about, Mrs Callaghan,' Millie replied, feeling her familiar antagonism towards the cantankerous old woman begin to rise.

Mrs Callaghan didn't look convinced. 'You look a bit pale to be out and about, so perhaps you'd better sit down before you fall down.'

'Thank you,' said Millie, sliding on to the hard-backed chair in the corner.

'I'll make you a cuppa.' The old woman set the kettle on the back ring of the ancient cooker. 'You look as if you could do with it. Did Lil Rackham turn up this morning?'

'Yes, she'd already made breakfast by the time I got downstairs,' Millie replied.

Mrs Callaghan gave a satisfied nod. 'Her old man's been a bit off-colour so I wasn't too sure she'd be able. How's your ma today?'

'Much better. In fact, that's why I've come to see you.' Millie took a deep breath. 'I want to say thank you for organising people to look after her while I was in hospital. I am most grateful.'

'You don't have to thank me,' Mrs Callaghan replied. 'We take care of our own around here.'

'That's very—'

'We always have and always will. And where would we have been when the Luftwaffe came calling, if neighbours hadn't pitched in?' Mrs Callaghan cut in.

'Perhaps so, but I still want to thank you,' insisted Millie. 'And for asking Dr Gingold to visit.'

Mrs Callaghan crossed her arms and adjusted her bosom. 'I don't hold with doctors and their ways, as you know.' She put a mug of tea on the shelf beside Millie. 'But after seeing Dr Gingold dodging bombs to treat people, I'll make an exception in her case. It's action that shows what's really in people's 'arts. Help yourself to sugar,' she added, indicating the bowl on the dresser.

'Thank you, but I couldn't use up your ration,' Millie replied.

'You're not. My Joe's a docker and gets plenty as spillage,' Mrs Callaghan replied. 'It'll give you a bit of energy.'

Millie smiled and spooned in two heaped measures. Mrs Callaghan did the same and then perched on an old stool, which creaked ominously

443

under her weight.

'Perhaps you and I haven't always seen eye to eye on things,' Millie said, blowing across the top of her tea. 'But if you hadn't stepped into the breach like that, I don't know what would have happened to Mum.'

'She'd probably been carted away to that bloody mental hospital again, and much good that would have done her,' Mrs Callaghan replied.

Millie looked astonished. 'You knew!'

The old woman nodded. 'My cousin's girl is a cleaner in St Colombo's. It was 'er who told me your mother had been taken in, and,' an expression of approval spread across Mrs Callaghan's deeply lined face, 'how you fetched her out. I never met your dad, God rest 'im, but I'm sure he'd have been right proud of what you did.'

A lump formed in Millie's throat.

'And,' continued Mrs Callaghan, 'even though you had to turn your back on your own happiness with that copper, you put your family first, and that's what counts. You're a good daughter, Sister Sullivan, and there ain't none around here would say different.'

A wave of gratitude suddenly welled up in Millie and tears clouded her vision. They stared at each other for a few seconds, then a loud cry cut between them.

Mrs Callaghan eased her ample rear off the stool.

'Nanny's coming, sweetheart,' she called, hobbling through the back door.

Millie blinked, then stood up and followed her into the tiny back yard.

444

Mrs Callaghan had already reached the old-fashioned deep-bodied pram standing by the side wall. Millie walked over to her and looked down at the two babies she'd delivered only a few months before, lying side by side. They were well wrapped up in matinée jackets, hats and mittens to allow them to get the full benefit of the hours spent in the fresh air without becoming chilled. One of them was still fast asleep but the other was awake and niggling.

'You've got another hour before your bottle, John, my boy,' Mrs Callaghan said, reaching in and picking up his dummy. She stuck it in her own mouth for a second or two to clean it, then popped it back into the child's mouth.

John's little chin started bobbing up and down and his eyelids started to flutter. An expression of pure love settled on Mrs Callaghan's face. 'As I say, Millie Sullivan, it's family that comes first.'

Chapter Twenty-Six

'Well, congratulations on your new post,' said Millie, raising her cup of tea to Connie. 'Although, I'm not sure the Spitalfields and Shoreditch Nursing Association knows what it's in for.'

Connie pretended to be offended. 'Well, if they ask, I'll tell them I learned all the tricks of the trade from you.'

They laughed and chinked teacups.

Millie sighed. 'Although I'm sad to lose you, I really wish you all the best with your new job, Connie. It will be strange not having you around. After all, we've been together since our first day of training, except when I did my midders at Woolmers Park.'

'Yes,' agreed Connie. 'We've been through the lot together, haven't we? Training under Miss Alexandra, and the Blitz, courtesy of Goering.'

Millie grinned. 'And I'm not sure which was worse.' She shifted in her chair and winced.

'Are you sure you're well enough to come back to work next week?' Connie asked.

'Of course,' Millie replied. 'I'm all but healed, and the last few bruises will be gone by then. And besides, it's been almost three weeks and although it seems odd to say it, I'm missing my patients,' Millie confessed. 'It was all well and good resting up, but now I'm better it's getting a bit boring.'

'I can't say we don't need you back, what with

Beattie being away on a course and one of the trainee QNs leaving because she was homesick. But what about your mum?'

'She's a great deal better,' Millie replied. 'And the neighbours are going to keep on popping in while I'm at work. Mum's even talking about going along next week to the Mother's Union at St George's with Mrs Rogers from across the street. I think seeing someone every day is what she needs to help her recover, not having electric shocks passed through her brain. Dr Gingold's been very kind, too. She's been down to see Mum every week to talk to her about Dad.'

The latch on the front door opened, and Doris and a young woman walked in.

'Hello, Connie,' Doris said as she untied her rain hat and shook it out. 'We nearly missed it, didn't we, Hannah?' she said to the young woman who was taking off her coat.

Hannah nodded. 'If we hadn't had to queue for so long at the greengrocer's, we would have been back half an hour ago.'

'And after all that they only had potatoes, cabbage and woody carrots,' Doris replied. 'And you'll never guess – you know those old houses in Cannon Street Road up by the old school?'

'Yes,' said Millie and Connie in unison.

'They've all been taken over by squatters,' said Doris, as she plonked her shopping bag on the table.

'What, all of them?' asked Millie.

'Every blooming one of them,' replied Hannah. 'And good luck to them, that's what I say. Do you know, there was some spiv asking fifteen bob a week for one poky room? It's disgusting. We're fortunate enough to be bunking in with me mum in Richard Street until we can find somewhere, but others aren't so lucky.'

'I knew I knew you from somewhere,' Millie said. 'You're Hannah Green, aren't you?'

Hannah nodded. 'I didn't know if you recognised me.'

A wry smile lifted the corner of Millie's lips. 'How could I forget delivering your baby on the east-bound platform of Stepney Green Station in the middle of a bombing raid?'

The letterbox rattled and a handful of letters fluttered on to the floor. Millie stood up and fetched them.

'Who are they from?' asked Doris, looking anxiously at an electricity bill.

'Nothing for you to worry about, Mum,' Millie replied reassuringly.

She handed her mother a small letter. 'This one's for you and by the look of the handwriting it's from Edie, and this one's for me,' she said, turning over the large official-looking manila envelope.

Millie ran her finger under the flap and opened it. Taking out the two-page letter she read down the first page.

For one moment the floor seemed to go off kilter and a sensation like icy water trickling over her gripped Millie.

'Shall I make us all a nice cuppa?' Connie asked, in a strangely distorted, faraway voice.

Millie slipped the first page behind the second and read to the end.

'Not for me,' replied Hannah, 'I've got to get back.' She looked at Doris. 'Mum says she'll be around at eight so you can... Sister Sullivan, are you all right?'

The words danced on the page as Millie reread the letter, setting her heart pounding in her chest.

'Millie!' The fear in her mother's voice brought Millie back to the present.

Millie looked up. 'It's from Mrs. Harper, the chairwoman of the Association.'

'Is she writing to ask how you are, dear?' her mother asked.

Millie shook her head. 'She's writing to tell me I'm to be investigated for disregarding the Association's rules, flouting the superintendent's authority, and negligence, and that I have to appear in front of the Association's board when they meet on the third of October.'

'That's ridiculous,' said Connie indignantly. 'It's Miss Dutton trying to make trouble for you.'

Millie held the letter aloft. 'Well, she's succeeded, because this letter informs me that if the board finds that the allegations are true, I'll be dismissed with immediate effect.'

Having secured the bandage around Mrs Fallow's foot, Millie rose from her kneeling position and started to clear away her equipment.

Mrs Fallow had gone down to the bar in the middle of the night a week ago in her slippers and had stepped on a broken glass. Millie had been in every day since to dress it.

'There you go, Mrs Fallow,' she said, wrapping the dirty dressing tightly in newspaper. 'And try and keep off it if you can.'

Vi Fallow's crimson lips turned down at the corners. 'Fat chance,' she said lifting her leg off the footstool. 'Have you ever tried to run a pub hobbling about on a set of crutches?'

Millie laughed. 'I can't say I have, but if you don't, it will take twice as long to heal. Isn't Bert running the Boatman while you're out of action?'

Vi tutted and rolled her eyes. 'That's what he's telling people, but since he got elected on to the East London Labour Party's executive committee, he's been out more than he's been in. I tell you, every blooming day there's someone from this ministry or that coming to get a "feel" for the area. Thank goodness I've got Gert to help out or I don't know what I'd have done.'

She reached for the crutch resting on the side of the armchair and thumped on the floor. 'Would you like some tea, nurse?'

Millie closed her bag. 'Thanks, Mrs Fallow but I should be going.'

'You poor love,' Vi reached over and her manicured hand patted Millie's. 'I was only saying to a couple of the regulars at the bar yesterday, it's a right liberty the way that bloody nursing lot are treating you. Not after all you've been through, what with your muvver being Tom and Dick and all,' she said with a surprisingly maternal expression on her face.

Millie gave her a wan smile. There was no point asking Vi how she knew about the Association's board, because every patient she'd visited since she returned to work three weeks before had said the same. Her precarious situation was clearly the talk of every shop, pub and street corner in the area.

The door at the bottom of the stairs leading into the public house below opened again and feet tramped up the stairs. Millie turned, expecting to see the barmaid, but instead her eyes found a well-dressed man in his late twenties.

Although not as tall as Alex, he still hovered just under the six-foot mark. His tweed jacket had leather-patched elbows, but was clearly of quality, as were the buff-coloured trousers. With high cheekbones, pronounced jaw and a mop of tousled blond hair, he caught Millie's attention, epecially his striking blue eyes, which were scrutinising her with interest.

There was a thump-thump up the stairs and Bert appeared. Ignoring her husband, Vi smiled lavishly at the young man who had just come in.

'Oh, Mr Smith, you're back,' Vi said in her best telephone voice. 'H'I was beginning to wonder if you and my h'husband had fallen in the drink, don't you know.'

'Give over, Vi,' Bert said, scowling at his wife.

'I'm sorry Mrs Fallow,' Mr Smith said in a deep, well-modulated voice. 'We were a great deal longer than I expected. But I just find the history of the dockers' struggle against the vested interests of the wharf owners so fascinating.' He turned and smiled charmingly at Millie. 'I don't think we've met.'

'This is our nurse, Sister Sullivan,' Bert said, hobbling over to her. He grinned. 'And there's many a time she's—'

'Jim Smith,' the young man said, stretching out

451

his hand.

Millie took it. 'Millie, Millie Sullivan.'

He smiled winsomely. 'Is that Millicent or Amelia?'

'Amelia,' Millie replied, enjoying the sensation of his fingers enclosing hers.

'Mr Smith's father is a baron.' Vi beamed adoringly up at him.

'Jim, please,' he said to Millie, while contriving to give the landlady an embarrassed look. His gaze returned to Millie. 'Vi has flushed me out of the long grass. I have to admit to being the Honourable James Percival Woodville Smith, actually.' His smile went from charming to captivating. 'But I never mention it. Not now we are all equals in our fight to throw off capitalist oppression. You should join the party, Millie, and be part of the struggle.'

Millie smiled sadly. 'You sound just like my dad. And I suppose I should. But just at the moment I'm weighed down by shackles of my own.'

She tried to retract her hand but Jim held it firmly. 'Are you?'

'I should say,' cut in Bert. 'It's those bloody—'

'Language, Albert, please,' Vi said, batting her eyelashes at Jim. 'We have a guest.'

Bert glared at his wife but corrected himself. 'The *blooming* stuck-up bunch on the Association's committee have it in for Sister Sullivan. Victimisation is what I call it.'

'What's happened?' asked Jim, finally releasing her hand.

'It's nothing,' Millie replied.

'Nothing!' bellowed Bert. 'If it happened to a

comrade in the docks the shop steward would have 'em down tools and out in the wink of an eye.'

'All h'our Sister Sullivan was trying to do was look after her mother like a good daughter should,' explained Vi. 'But someone went running to that hoity-toity Miss Dutton and she went straight to the Nursing Association's board.'

'It's just a mix-up, really,' Millie said, feeling her cheeks grow increasingly warm under Jim's unwavering stare.

'It was a right mix-up when that Miss Dutton got the job of superintendent instead of you, dearie,' Vi said. 'I don't know what Mrs Archer was thinking. I told her as much when I met her at the Masons' ladies' night. Of course, she tried to blame Mr Shottington but–'

'Shottington,' Jim interjected. 'Is he one of the Hertfordshire Shottingtons?'

Vi looked puzzled. 'I wouldn't know, but it were him who took my sister's boy's appendix out two years back in the London. The lad's got a scar from here to here.' She ran her painted fingernail from her right hip to her navel.

Millie picked up her case. 'I really ought to be off. I still have four visits before dinner. Now keep off that foot, Mrs Fallow, and I'll be back tomorrow.'

As she walked towards the stairs leading into the pub, Jim stepped in front of her. 'Let me carry that for you,' he said, taking hold of the handle of her bag.

'That's quite all right.'

He smiled. 'I insist.'

453

Millie couldn't help but release her case.

Jim followed her down the narrow stairs to the bar and then out into the street. He put the case in the basket of her bike. Millie unlocked the chain and Jim pulled it away from the fence for her.

'Which Nursing Association is it you work for?' he asked.

'St George's and St Dunstan's.' Millie put her foot on the pedal and rolled forward. 'It's been very nice to meet you, Mr Smith.'

'The pleasure's all mine,' he replied, slipping his hands in his pockets and stepping back as he watched Millie get ready to ride away. 'And please. Call me Jim.'

Trying not to look again at the clock above the boardroom door, Millie pressed her knees together and smoothed her skirt down again. She was sitting on the same long bench in St George's Hospital that she'd sat on just over a year ago, waiting to be interviewed for the superintendent's post.

The solid oak door creaked as it opened. Millie stood up. Mrs Overton, the board's secretary, came out and walked across the parquet floor towards her.

'The board is ready for you now, Sister Sullivan,' she said, giving Millie a sympathetic look.

With her heart thumping uncomfortably in her chest, Millie followed the secretary into the boardroom.

In the same way as when she'd last faced the board at her interview, the members of the committee were ranged along the polished table. Mrs Archer, sporting a hat with a delicate veil, sat in the central chairwoman's seat, with Algernon Shottington, suitably attired in a brightly coloured bow tie and fob chain, to her right. Mrs Fletcher sat, with Mrs Overton to her left. There was, however, an addition to last year's panel. There was a man in his late twenties or early thirties dressed in a grey suit with a club tie, sitting next to Mr Shottington.

On a chair to one side sat Miss Dutton, dressed in her navy superintendent's uniform with a newly starched frilly matron's hat balanced on her blonde curls. She shot a quick glance at Millie as she entered, and then looked straight ahead again.

'Good afternoon, Sister,' Mr Shottington said, looking over his half-moon glasses.

'Good afternoon, Mr Shottington,' Millie replied, her voice wobbling just a little.

The surgeon jabbed towards the solitary chair in front of the table with his pen. 'If you would take a seat.'

Millie scooted her skirt under her and sat down.

Mr Shottington's gaze ran over the panel. 'I think you know everyone here except Mr Braithwaite.'

Millie inclined her head toward the newcomer. What looked like a hint of amusement flickered across Mr Braithwaite's finely chiselled features.

'Good afternoon, Sister Sullivan,' he said, in the impeccably English tones of a radio announcer. 'It's a pleasure to meet you.'

'Mr Braithwaite is the acting regional officer for the Ministry of Health, and he joins us today as

455

part of his fact-finding tour of the London District Nursing Associations,' explained Mr Shottington smoothly.

A genial smile lifted the corners of Mr Braithwaite's mouth. 'I work very closely with Sir Clifford, the under-secretary who has the ear of the Minister, Mr Bevan. He is, as you are probably aware, grappling with the details of the nationwide health service the Labour movement has promised the nation, but he still likes to be fully informed of grass-roots issues.' His gaze flickered briefly over Mr Shottington.

'Thank you, Mr Braithwaite, your presence is most welcome.' A sycophantic expression slid across the consultant's face. 'And please assure Sir Clifford that we at the St George's and Dunstan's District Nursing Association are most eager to help his efforts in any small way we can.'

Mr Braithwaite inclined his head. 'Be assured I will be appraising the under-secretary fully on today's proceedings.'

The consultant turned back to Millie. 'Now, Sister Sullivan, although you had a letter explaining why you are here, I will read out for the benefit of the rest of the panel the allegations Miss Dutton has brought against you.' He lifted a piece of paper on the table in front of him. 'Miss Dutton states that on numerous occasions over the last few months you have neglected your patients in order to spend time socialising with your mother. That instead of being resident in Munroe House, as stipulated in the rules of the Association, you have stayed overnight at your mother's house on countless occasions. Added to which you have

456

been inattentive, which has led you to be derelict in your duty towards the poor souls in your care. She goes on to say that she has already given you a formal warning about your conduct, but that there has been no improvement. In fact, if anything, your behaviour is worse.' He put down the letter and looked at Millie. 'I am disappointed to hear of such goings-on. I therefore—'

'Excuse me, Mr Shottington,' interrupted Mr Braithwaite. 'I know I'm only an observer, but perhaps we should hear what Sister Sullivan has to say before you make any pronouncements.'

Mr Shottington's heavy eyebrows rose in surprise. 'It seems a little unnecessary, don't you think? After all, Miss Dutton has investigated the matter thoroughly and has several statements—'

'How many?' asked Mr Braithwaite, conversationally.

'Just three,' replied Mrs Fletcher before the consultant could answer.

Mr Braithwaite looked puzzled. 'Just three nurses out of thirty?' he mused.

'Yes, and two of them have instances of misconduct recorded on their files,' said Mrs Archer, the veil on her hat shaking a little as she spoke.

An unhealthy flush darkened Mr Shottington's face. 'Very well,' he replied, grudgingly. 'What have you got to say for yourself, Sister?'

Millie looked unwaveringly at the committee. 'Firstly, I swear that I have never in eight years of nursing ever neglected a patient. And if anyone says otherwise, they are lying.'

Miss Dutton bristled, but Millie maintained her unflinching composure.

457

Mr Shottington held her gaze for a moment, then shifted his attention to the letter on the table. 'What about visiting your mother when you were on duty and staying over at her house.'

Millie's shoulders slumped. 'That's true. But I wasn't socialising with her, I was caring for her. As you know, my mother has been very ill, and the only way I could be sure she was washed and dressed and eating properly was to call in. But it was never for more than five or ten minutes, and I have always made the time up later. I did everything else, like the cleaning and laundry, on my day off. And I admit that I've stayed over at my mother's house when she wouldn't settle, but never when I was on call. What else could I do? She's my mother!'

The three women sitting behind the table nodded in agreement, and Millie's spirits lifted just a little.

'We quite understand,' said Mrs Archer.

'I did the same for mine,' added Mrs Fletcher.

Mr Shottington gave them an exasperated look. 'I'm sure you did, Mrs Fletcher, but you weren't employed as an Association nurse at the time, were you?'

Mrs Fletcher shrunk back under the consultant's fierce gaze. Mr Shottington turned his attention back to Millie.

'So you admit your guilt then, do you, Sister Sullivan?' he said with more than a glint of triumph in his eye.

Mr Braithwaite looked disdainfully at him. 'Really, Mr Shottington, we're not in the Old Bailey.'

458

The consultant's eyes bulged as he grappled with his temper.

Millie's head started to buzz so she put her hand on her forehead to ease the tension. 'Yes, I have broken two of the Association's rules and I suppose a combination of long days and lack of sleep meant I haven't quite been myself. But still I can assure you that not one of my patients has suffered because of my family responsibilities.'

A syrupy smile spread across Mr Shottington's face. 'While we all commend you for being a dutiful daughter, you have, by your own admission, broken the Association's regulations, so I'm left with no other option but to dismiss you–'

'Surely, with a quarter of the nursing posts in London unfilled, you don't really intend to sack one of your best nurses?' Mr Braithwaite said with an innocent glance at the consultant.

Mr Shottington smiled. 'I'm afraid I can't see any alternative. If the other nurses see that Sister Sullivan gets away with flouting the Association's rules, then everyone will follow her example and, as much as I value your insightful input into our deliberations, Mr Braithwaite, might I remind you of your own words about being only an observer?'

Mr Braithwaite matched the consultant's stare. 'In the interest of fair play I feel there should be someone to speak on Sister Sullivan's behalf.'

'There is, Mr Braithwaite,' said Mrs Archer excitedly, pulling out a thick handful of papers from the file in front of her and holding them up. 'I have over two dozen letters from Sister Sullivan's patients, and at least that number of letters again from the other nurses resident in Munroe

House, as well as in addition three ringing endorsements from local general practitioners.'

Millie stared at the thick wad of letters in the chairwoman's hand.

'Patients have written letters in my support to the board?' she said incredulously.

Mrs Archer's eyes sparkled with a hint of amusement. 'Well, some are little more than pencilled notes but, without exception, every last word details Sister Sullivan's devotion to duty and her hard work. I have at least half-a-dozen from women who, after long and complicated labours, have been delivered with healthy babies absolutely because of Sister Sullivan's midwifery skills; and many more from patients who talk of how her care helped them cope with the passing of a loved one. The nurses talk about your tremendous kindness towards them, and your cheery and approachable manner; while the doctors state unanimously they trust your judgement so much that if you tell them a patient is unwell, they know they jolly well have to visit them.'

An urbane expression spread across Mr Braithwaite's refined features. 'It seems to me – purely as an observer, of course, Mr Shottington – that you should think carefully before making any rash judgements. The Minister will be looking for doctors and consultants who share his belief in taking patients' views seriously, as doctors who should be part of the new health system that will be introduced soon.'

Mr Shottington's belligerence vanished in an instant. 'Two dozen you say, Mrs Fletcher?' he pondered. 'And three doctors? Well, that puts a completely different complexion on the matter.'

'What about her insubordination?' Miss Dutton's shrill voice rang out. 'From the moment I arrived, Sullivan has done everything she can to usurp my authority. She's mollycoddled the younger nurses so much that they look to her for guidance instead of me. And while she's been slipping off on her own business, they've all covered for her. I wouldn't have known about her deranged mother's visit to Munroe House if it hadn't been for Nurse Potter informing me about the incident.' She gave Millie a look that would have cut glass. 'Anyone would have thought she was the superintendent, and not me.'

'Well, as Sister Sullivan seems to command the total loyalty of ninety per cent of the nurses, perhaps she should be,' replied Mr Braithwaite, looking coolly at her.

The colour drained from Miss Dutton's face. For one moment Millie thought she might collapse in a heap, but Miss Dutton pulled herself together with a thunderous expression.

Mr Shottington cleared his throat. 'I think perhaps we are straying from the point, Miss Dutton,' he said, looking at the table in order to avoid the superintendent's furious face. 'Although Sister Sullivan has broken some of the Association's minor rules, she is clearly an exceptional nurse.' He beamed benevolently at Millie. 'And in view of the strain she's been under, and as no patients were neglected, I think we must view Sister Sullivan's actions as exceptional. I'm sure the superintendent would not wish to lose such a valuable member of her team.' Mr Shottington

461

risked looking at Miss Dutton over his glasses. 'We are most grateful for your contribution this afternoon, Miss Dutton, but I'm sure you're eager to return to your duties.'

Miss Dutton stared at the committee members at the table for a second or two. Then she stood up and marched out of the boardroom, the door banging behind her.

Mr Shottington spread his hands out in front of him. 'In view of the all the evidence, I accept that Sister Sullivan acted as she did because of her duty to her mother, and therefore she should not be dismissed from her post. All those in favour?'

Mrs Fletcher, Mrs Archer and Mrs Overton's hands shot up.

Mr Shottington nodded approvingly. 'Please record in the minutes, my dear Mrs Overton, that the motion is carried unanimously.'

Millie laughed in relief. 'Thank you, Mr Shottington. I promise I won't let things get on top of me again.'

'I'm sure you won't,' he replied, with an oddly affectionate look on his face.

Mr Braithwaite coughed.

Mr Shottington was immediately attentive. 'You have some other observation that might assist us, Mr Braithwaite?'

'Perhaps, in order to ensure that Sister Sullivan doesn't find herself torn between her mother and her patients in future, the committee would consider granting her permission to reside with her mother permanently?'

The three women looked at each other and then questioningly at the Association's president.

462

Millie held her breath.

One of Mr Braithwaite's arched eyebrows rose slightly. 'It would be in keeping with some of the ideas the Minister is considering.'

Mr Shottington beamed at him. 'What a splendid suggestion!' He turned to Millie. 'You have the Association's approval to live away from Munroe House, so long as it is within easy travelling distance and provided you agree to sleep in the nurses' home when you are on night cover. Do you agree?'

Millie nodded. 'Oh yes. And thank you. All of you.'

Mr Shottington straightened his papers. 'Well then, I think that concludes business.' He stood up. 'If you'd excuse me, ladies, I have a hospital to run.'

'Of course,' Mrs Overton twittered.

'Such devotion,' Mrs Fletcher remarked, giving him a very girlish smile for one on the wrong side of sixty.

'Thank you for your valuable time,' added Mrs Archer.

Mr Shottington offered Mr Braithwaite his hand. 'It was good to meet you, sir, and please tell Sir Clifford of my eagerness to be involved in this new national health scheme.'

'Be assured your name will be on the top of my list when I next meet with the undersecretary.'

Mr Shottington's eyes lit up and then he bestowed another avuncular smile on everyone before strolling out.

Millie stood up and hurried towards the door. 'Sister Sullivan.'

Mr Braithwaite slid out from behind the table and came towards her. 'Congratulations, Sister Sullivan,' he said, stopping just in front of her.

'Thank you,' replied Millie. 'And for your suggestion that I might live at home. That will help a great deal.'

'I was pleased to help and I'm very pleased to meet you.' His gaze flickered over her, and then one corner of his mouth lifted.

Millie felt her cheeks start to glow. 'Thank you once again.' She walked through into the corridor.

'And, Sister Sullivan.'

Millie turned.

'Jim Smith sends his regards.'

Chapter Twenty-Seven

The door banged open and Aunt Ruby staggered into the room carrying a turkey that probably weighed only a pound or two less than she did.

'There we go,' she said, heaving it into the middle of the table. 'Merry Christmas everyone.'

Everyone actually meant *everyone* this year because six weeks of Ruby's nagging, cajoling and threats had produced more than the usual quorum of members of the family for the festive dinner.

Cousin Gwen and her husband Len, whom Millie hadn't seen since their wedding eight years before, had battled the freezing temperatures from their home in Wickford on a motorbike and with their two children snuggled in the sidecar. There was the perpetually single Cousin Bob, who'd arrived in a smart new Rover, and Wilfred and May had made the effort too. As Millie and her mother were staying with Ruby until the day after Boxing Day, her mother's cousins were being put up around the corner with Wilfred's trainspotting cousin Edgar, or Igor, as Ruby always called him.

'Shove around, so Anthony can sit down,' Ruby instructed.

As most of the roasting birds Millie had seen hanging in butchers' windows weren't even half the size of the one now sitting in the middle of the table, she guessed they had her Aunt's gentle-man friend to thank for their dinner.

Tony jokingly squeezed himself into the space next to Millie's Uncle Bill and sat with his back to the French doors. Ruby, bending herself into a half-crouched position, slid into the seat beside him.

Her eyes flickered over the table to check that there were no unfolded napkins or misaligned cut-lery and then, satisfied that no one had wrecked her master plan for the perfect Christmas dinner, Ruby's 'hostess' smile spread across her flawlessly made-up face. 'I'm so pleased you could all make it today,' she said benevolently.

'Not that we had much choice,' muttered Wilf-red.

May nudged him sharply in the ribs. 'He's only joking,' she said with an apologetic shrug.

Ruby let a glacial gaze linger on Wilfred for a second or two, then she smiled at them all again. 'And I hope the bird's not tough.'

Everyone assured her it would be delicious.

'And that the lights don't go out again,' said Aunt Martha. 'I sat in the dark for three hours on Sunday because the electricity went off. I didn't even have the wireless to keep me company.'

'The same happened to us last week,' said Gwen. 'I was just getting the kids' tea when – pop! – it all went dark.' She ran her hand lightly over the five-year-old sitting next to her. 'We had to eat our tea by candlelight didn't we, poppets?'

The two poppets, Rex and Basil, presumably after Harrison and Rathbone, sitting on cushions between their parents, nodded.

466

'It's a disgrace,' agreed May. 'And in this weather too.'

'Well, I blame Atlee,' said Ruby. 'Him and that blooming Shinwell. It would never have happened if dear Winston was still in charge.' She turned to Tony. 'Would you do the honours, darling?'

'I certainly will,' Tony replied, picking up the carving knife and two-pronged fork.

A lump lodged in Millie's throat as an image of Alex carving the chicken at her mother's house the year before flashed into her mind. She pushed it aside. After all, Alex was a thousand miles away at this moment, and what was the point of dwelling on what might have been?

As everyone tucked their napkins into their collars and necklines, Ruby and Tony worked as a well-oiled machine: one plonked slices of meat on the plates while the other loaded them with Brussels sprouts, carrots and, due to the fat rationing, dry-roasted potatoes. The family, knowing the drill of old, passed them down the table until everyone had a dinner in front of them.

Tony sat down and, pulling his fully laden plate towards him, said, 'Right, round the teeth and round the gums, look out belly, here it comes, Amen. Now get stuck in!'

As the family worked their way through the mountain of food they complained about the coal shortage, grumbled about the rationing, criticised the council and moaned about the weather. It had rarely been above freezing for the past three weeks, causing two of the nurses from Munroe House to skid off their bikes on the ice.

'It's delicious, isn't it, Millie?' Doris said, casting a loving look at her daughter.

Doris had been seeing Dr Gingold on a weekly basis since August. For the first couple of months the hour-long visit didn't seem to have much effect, but Dr Gingold insisted that for Doris to recover fully she needed to face the things troubling her. And gradually, as the weeks wore on, Doris became less agitated and started to sleep better. At first Millie dare not hope for too much, but when she took her mother Christmas shopping in Stratford two weeks ago and Doris brought out the list of presents she was going to buy for the family, Millie finally allowed herself to believe that her mother would eventually be her old self again.

Millie smiled. 'Yes, it is. Do you want some gravy?'

'Please.'

'There you go, Doris,' said Bob, handing her a jug with meaty rivulets running down the side.

He gave her a schoolboy grin, which sat oddly on a man who was forty-three next birthday and who sported a hairline somewhere north of his crown.

'I hear you and Millie have just moved,' he said, through a mouthful of sprouts.

'Yes, but only around the corner to Jane Street,' Doris replied. 'The new house isn't much bigger downstairs, but there are two bedrooms and so poor Millie doesn't have to sleep on the put-up bed anymore.'

'And I've got somewhere to hang my clothes,' Millie added, dipping a potato in her gravy.

'I was surprised to hear you'd moved in with your mother, Millie,' said Gwen, wiping a spot of potato from her son's cheek.

'I had special permission from the president of the Association,' said Millie.

'No, I mean because I hadn't realised you didn't get married. What happened?' May asked.

The hurt that had dulled over the past few months surged up in Millie. She forced a smile. 'Oh, you know...' She tried to change the subject, 'But the house in Anthony Street was cramped with both of us living there, and we were lucky to find the one in Jane Street empty.'

'Your gran, Millie, brought up all of us,' Uncle Bill swept his knife in an arc to include his sisters. 'And May and Bob's dad Arthur, our Frank and little Bette, God rest 'em, in a house half that size. Do you remember, Doris? You, Edie, Martha and Ruby all squashed into that old bed in Mum and Dad's room?'

Doris laughed. 'I do, and you boys in the other, but all the responsibility Millie has with her job, she needs to have a bit of space of her own.'

'I was only thinking of Bette, the poor little mite, last week,' said Martha, sadly. 'I can remember her quite clearly sitting on Ma's knee just a few days before she was taken.'

'They were lucky to lose just one still in the cradle,' added Edie. 'I can think of a dozen families down our street who lost at least three or four children who never made it out of nappies.'

'I remember my poor mum being out of her mind after the funeral,' Ruby said. 'She just sat staring at the wall for weeks. Barely eating and

469

hardly sleeping.' A tear shimmered on her lower eyelids but she dabbed it away before her mascara ran. 'I don't know why people call it the good old days. Things are much better now.'

'For some,' said May, with an envious glance around the comfortable room. 'We still live in two rooms above a hardware shop.'

Tony tapped his knife on his beer glass. The talking stopped and all eyes turned towards the head of the table.

He removed his napkin and stood up. 'As most of us are done, there's a little announcement I'd like to make.' He cleared his throat. 'I'm a man of actions, not words, so I'll say it straight. Two weeks back I asked Ruby to marry me.' He gazed down at her with an odd mix of tenderness and accomplishment. 'And she said "yes".'

The men hammered their fists on the table while the women squealed with excitement.

'Where's the ring?' demanded May.

Ruby beamed like a young girl as she fished out a ring on a chain around her neck, and then slipped it on her finger. 'And the wedding's on the twelfth of July next year.'

'Right, Ruby. It's your turn,' said Bill, getting himself comfortable on the piano stool. 'What will it be?'

The women had washed up the dishes in the kitchen while the men slept off their dinners and the couple of pints beforehand, and now the whole family were together again in Ruby's seldom-used front room for the traditional family singsong before the women went back into the

470

kitchen to prepare tea.

As there were more people than chairs, Gwen's two boys were sitting cross-legged on the rug in the bay window playing with their new Meccano, Gwen was perched on the side table and Millie was sitting on the arm of her mother's chair.

'Let Edie sing something,' Ruby said, feigning reluctance, as always, to sing herself.

Tony hooked his arm around Ruby's waist and led her to the piano. 'Sing us the Jolson one, sweetheart.'

'All right. If you insist.' Ruby took her place beside the piano.

Bill's fingers ran over the notes of the introduction and then Ruby launched into a sentimental song about dying. It was Ruby's party piece that she always sang. Everyone swayed back and forth until the chorus, when all joined in until the song finished with a full-throated last note, and then everyone clapped vigorously and Bob wolf-whistled while Ruby gave a modest little bow.

'Sing "Irish Eyes", Ruby,' shouted Gwen above the din. 'I've got to put the kettle on for tea,' Ruby replied.

'Just sing it, Ruby. We can make tea after,' Doris said.

Bill struck up the opening bars but this time no one waited for the chorus and so the whole room came in together with the refrain. Millie joined in with the singing as heartily as the rest of the family, until she got to the second chorus. As she sang an image of Alex's green eyes, inherited from his Irish forbears, flashed into her mind, and tears sprang up too swiftly for Millie to stop

471

them while the lump in her throat silenced her voice. She got up and hurried out of the room.

With tears threatening to stream down her face, she stumbled into the kitchen. She went to the sink, rested her hands on the edge, and wept.

'Millie, are you all right?' her mother's voice called from the hall.

Millie took a deep breath and quickly wiped her eyes. 'Yes, I'm fine,' she called back.

Doris came into the kitchen. 'Are you sure, dear?'

Keeping her back to her mother, Millie picked up the kettle. 'Of course, I just thought I'd start the tea, that's all. You go back in.' Millie put the kettle under the cold tap and turned it on. 'So, Aunt Ruby's getting married again.'

'Millie, I–'

'Who'd have thought it?' said Millie in a wobbly voice. 'And after all these ye–'

'I'm sorry,' her mother said softly.

'For what?'

'For everything I've put you through in the last six months.'

Millie tried to give a light laugh. 'I've told you before, Mum, you don't have to apologise, and you never will. You couldn't help it.'

'But mostly I'm sorry about Alex,' Doris continued. 'I would have said something before but I've been waiting for a chance. I know it's my fault you called off the wedding.'

'It's not. You were ill and I looked after you in the same way you've looked after me all these years.' Tears bubbled up again but Millie held them back and turned to face her mother. 'It's history and it doesn't matter now. It's just Ruby's sentimental old song that set me off, that's all. I'm fine, honestly.'

The sound of the family crooning 'You Made Me Love You' drifted into the kitchen.

Millie smiled brightly. 'I only came out to start tea for Aunt Ruby.'

'I'll give you a hand.'

'It'll be a while yet,' Millie replied. 'You go and join them and I'll give you a shout when the kettle boils.'

'If you're sure?'

Millie nodded.

Doris gave her a little smile then left the kitchen. Millie watched her until she disappeared into the front room and then, leaning against the yellow and black tiled wall, she sobbed silently until her chest ached.

Millie stood with her gloved hands tucked under her arms in a vain attempt to bring some circulation back into them. Despite the extra vest and two jumpers, after just an hour of her morning visits she was already frozen to the bone. Although she was inside, it was only a couple of degrees warmer than outside, which made the temperature in the room where she was standing just a little over freezing.

It had been overcast and very cold all January, but as February approached people had started to look forward to the longer days and a rise in temperature. But that was almost four weeks ago, and instead the first snowflakes of the year had fallen, bringing the country, quite literally, to a grinding halt. The radio commentators and people in the streets alike were already talking about the winter of 1946-47 as being the worst in living memory.

Millie was waiting for Doctor Gingold to finish her examination of old Dolly Travers, as was the policeman, also kitted out as if he was about to cross the Antarctic, on the other side of the bed.

Dolly lived with three other families in one of the old houses in Cable Street, just a few doors up from Doctor Gingold's surgery. The small, sparsely furnished room Dolly occupied at the top of the house had once been the servants' quarters and was grimy even by local standards. Millie glanced out of the window overlooking the small yard below. Everything outside was white.

As she watched a couple of thin wisps of smoke curling up through the murky atmosphere, Millie prayed that the hundredweight of coal she and her mother had ordered over a week ago would arrive today. Dr Gingold lifted her stethoscope from Dolly's bony chest and stuffed it back in her case and rose to her feet.

'There's nothing for you to do here, officer,' she said. 'I'll record hypothermia as the cause of death and, judging by the fact that rigor mortis isn't yet complete, I'd estimate the time between three and four hours ago.'

The officer made a note in his pocket book. 'Thank you, Doctor. I'll not detain you further.'

Dr Gingold rebuttoned her coat, wound a scarf around her neck and put on her gloves. 'Will you pop in to the surgery when you've finished here, Sister?' she asked Millie. 'I've some more customers for you.'

'Yes, Doctor,' replied Millie.

'If I could ask you a couple of questions, Miss,' the officer asked after Dr Gingold left, his breath escaping in little puffs of steam as he spoke.

'Of course,' replied Millie, stamping her feet to return the circulation.

'What time did you find Mrs Travers?'

'Just after eight-thirty.' Millie gazed at the old woman lying cold and stiff but with a peaceful expression on her face, covered by a thin faded pink eiderdown. 'I came up as I usually do, to wash her and make her comfortable for the day, and I found her like this, poor love. She's been on our books for years, and the girls will be upset when I tell them. We come in morning and evening to sort her out, give her breakfast and supper, and Belle Freeman from downstairs cooks her a dinner.'

The officer glanced at the handful of burnt coal and cinders in the grate. 'And who set her fire?'

'We do,' replied Millie. 'The nurse last night would have banked it to last all night but like the rest of us, Mrs Travers had only half her delivery of coal this week and so we've been trying to eke it out.'

The officer scribbled down her answer and then closed his pocket book.

'Well thank you, Miss. I think that will do, but I'll contact Munroe House if there's anything else.' He tucked his scarf tightly around his neck. 'Good day, Miss, and mind how you go.'

He clomped down the stairs, leaving Millie alone with the body. Although she'd only given the old lady a full bed bath the day before, Millie would have given the body a full wash as part of the last offices, but as the water was frozen in the pipes that wasn't possible. Millie picked up the brush from Mrs Travers' rickety dressing table and smoothed it through the dead woman's hair, then she stripped off the covers. Carefully she arranged the body with the legs straight and the arms across the chest then, using the bottom sheet and rolling the old lady back and forth, Millie wound it around until the body was completely swathed.

As she finished, Tom Wells, the youngest son of Albert Wells of Wells & Co undertakers and embalmers, who had been burying and cremating East Enders for almost a hundred years, strolled in.

Tom, like most undertakers, was a jolly individual. He was wearing a long coat with an elbow-length cape that made him look like someone from a Dickens novel.

'Morning, Sister,' he said, stomping into the middle of the room and depositing a flurry of snow on the bare floorboards. He glanced at the old woman lying stiff on the bed. 'Poor old girl. She's the third one we've had freeze to death this week. Any family?'

'Not as far as I know,' replied Millie.

'All right, I'll contact the council when we get back,' he said, as one of Tom's assistants appeared carrying a stretcher.

Millie stepped back. The assistant plonked it on the floor beside the bed, then in one swift movement he and Tom lifted the old woman on to the canvas and covered her with a black drape they had brought with them.

As they carried Dolly out, Millie put on her gloves, picked up her bag and after locking the door, followed them down to the street. There was a small crowd, with suitably solemn faces, standing around in the snow by the undertaker's van.

Tom jumped out of the back and closed the door. 'See you around, Sister,' he said cheerily, climbing in behind the steering wheel.

The van drove away, leaving a cloud of diesel fumes behind it. Millie watched it slip and skid along the deep, ice-packed ruts in the road for a moment. And then, as it was impossible to cycle in such weather, she set off on foot towards her next patient, her Wellington boots making neat imprints in the crisp blanket of snow.

The sun had already set by the time Millie reached home. She slipped off her boots and put them on the tiled hearth to dry. Unlike the fireplace in Anthony Street, this one was the old Victorian original with a wrought-iron grille across the top of it and Millie noticed that her mother had put a pot containing water on the grille. Because of the shortage of coal the gas supply had to be shut off from time to time, and so they had taken to heating water over the fire just in case. The lack of coal had affected the electricity too, as was evident from the weak glow given by the central light.

'Is that you?' Doris called from the kitchen.

'I hope so,' Millie shouted back as she flopped in the armchair.

'There you are, sweet,' her mother said, handing her a steaming cup of tea. 'That'll soon bring the colour back to your cheeks.' She turned on the radio on the sideboard and once the valves warmed up it crackled into life. Millie inwardly groaned as Mrs Mopp asked yet again, 'Can I do you now, sir?'

Ignoring Tommy Handley's quick-fire chat with the fictitious cleaning lady, Millie cradled her tea in her hands, enjoying the warmth.

'Thank you, I feel like a block of ice.' She took a sip. By the time rationing did finally end she would be quite used to tea without sugar. 'Did the coalman arrive today?' she asked.

'Yes, but he only delivered half our order,' her mother answered.

'I suppose it's better than nothing,' Millie replied. 'What's for tea?'

'Lambs' hearts with leek and potato followed by bread pudding,' Doris replied. 'It'll be about five minutes.'

'Good, because Sally's sick and I'll have to cover,' Millie said, wishing she could just curl up in her own bed instead of the rickety one in the on-call room.

'Not again,' said Doris crossly. 'Can't that sour-faced superintendent find someone else for once?'

Actually Miss Dutton had been reluctant to ask Millie because it meant she had to speak to her, which these days she avoided doing at all costs.

Millie shook her head. 'There isn't anyone else, and I'm only doing tonight. Connie and Annie are doing tomorrow and the next day.'

'Well, you put your feet up while you can,' Doris said.

She went back into the kitchen. Millie cradled her cup and took a sip.

Millie put her drink down and closed her eyes. Her head fell back as a wave of exhaustion swept over her. She must have dropped off because she woke with a start when her mother came back into the room. Reluctantly, Millie woke up. Her mother put their plates on the table and Millie dragged herself across the room and sat down.

'So, how was your day?' she asked, sitting down opposite Millie. 'I heard it was you who found Dolly dead.'

'Yes,' she said with a sigh. 'And if that wasn't enough, I had to send another old lady to hospital with a broken hip after she fell on the ice.'

'Was that Fanny Wright?' Doris asked.

'You know I'm not supposed to talk about my patients, Mum. It's confidential.'

Doris nodded sagely. 'I understand. But I saw her daughter in the newsagent's and she said her mother had had a fall and been taken in. I said I'd pop around and see if she needed anything in the morning.'

Since the locals had taken her into their homes and hearts, Doris had embraced her role as one of the neighbourhood mothers. So much so that she and Mrs Callaghan were almost partners in crime for searching out snippets of news and neighbours who might need some help.

'This is the five o'clock news,' the announcer on the radio said.

479

Millie and her mother listened to the daily catalogue of disasters, from herds of sheep being lost in snowdrifts, spring vegetables too frozen to be dug out of the ground and ice floating in the North Sea. There was a reiteration of the Prime Minister's words from his broadcast the week before begging everyone to use less electricity.

'And now the shipping forecast. Humber, Dogger and Forties will experience—'

There was a pop. The lights went out and the wireless died.

'Not again,' sighed Doris. 'That's the third time this week.'

Leaving her dinner, she got up and fetched the matches from the mantelshelf. She lit the old oil lamp that they'd used in the Anderson shelter. It spluttered into life and illuminated the room with a buttery glow.

'At least we've finished our tea,' said Doris, placing it on the table to one side of them.

Millie glanced down at her watch hanging upside down on her chest. 'I'd better go,' she said, standing up.

Doris rose to her feet too. 'I'll cut you a wedge of bread pudding to take with you.'

'Thanks, Mum,' she said, stifling a yawn and praying that Munroe House's telephone remained silent until morning.

'And cheer up. After all, you and the girls have the Association's dance to look forward to on Saturday,' reminded Doris as Millie opened the door.

Millie gave a wan smile. 'Night, Mum.'

Outside the temperature had plummeted again

and as she walked towards the main road her feet crunched over freshly laid frozen snow.

Millie turned her face into the wind and headed for Munroe House as her thoughts turned to the Association's annual fundraising dance. Unless they were on duty, it was compulsory for the nurses to attend, although the thought of having her toes trodden on all night by council officials and bank clerks with roaming hands filled Millie with dread. As much as she didn't relish being called out in the dead of winter in the middle of the night, Millie seriously considered volunteering to cover Sally's Saturday night.

Chapter Twenty-Eight

Stanley Trotter, one of the junior accountants from the council's Highways Department, swirled Millie around in an awkward flourish as the last bars of 'In the Mood' faded. The dancers around them clapped the five-piece band enthusiastically while Millie breathed a sigh of relief as her partner's chubby hands released her from the too-close embrace of the dance.

Millie caught sight of Connie and Annie standing by the fire exit of St Martha's and Mungo's church hall. They pulled a face. Millie suppressed a giggle, knowing she'd won the prize for dancing with the most uncoordinated man in the room.

Although probably no older than thirty, Stanley had already made a respectable start on acquiring middle-age spread, and by the way he puffed and panted around the dancefloor, he'd have to watch his blood pressure before long.

'They're a cracking band,' Stanley said, taking a red handkerchief from his top pocket and mopping his sweating brow, cheeks and neck.

'Yes, they are,' Millie replied, clapping lightly.

'And I bet the committee are pleased to see that so many people have braved the snow,' Stanley said casting his eyes around the hall.

'I think people are just fed up of all the misery and are snatching at the chance of a bit of fun,' Millie replied.

The musicians struck up for a quickstep. Stanley returned his handkerchief to the pocket of his brown, chalk-striped suit. He smiled, revealing a pair of protruding front teeth.

'Why don't you let me buy you a drink?' he said, smoothing back his Brylcreemed hair.

'That's most kind but–'

'Maybe a port and lemon?' His eyes flickered to her breasts. 'While we get to know each other a bit better.'

He went to slip his arm around her waist but, pretending to adjust her stocking seam, nimbly Millie moved out of reach.

She gave him a dazzling smile. 'That's very kind but I ought to get back to my friend.' She indicated Connie with a nod. 'She's a bit down in the dumps today.'

Stanley looked across with puzzlement at Connie, who was tapping her feet merrily to her favourite 'Little Brown Jug' as she grinned around the room.

'She's putting a brave face on it,' explained Millie. She turned and headed off. 'Thanks for the dance.'

'Maybe I'll catch you for a waltz later,' Stanley called after her.

Millie just smiled, and scooted quickly around the end of the room to join her friends.

'You escaped then,' Annie said as Millie reached them.

'Not soon enough for my poor toes,' replied Millie, wriggling them inside her new wedge-heeled shoes. 'And now it's poor Eva's turn to suffer,' she added, watching Stanley doggedly make his way

483

over to her.

'The Wicked Witch of the East looks a bit dolled-up, doesn't she?' said Annie.

They glanced across at Miss Dutton, who was chatting to Mrs Harper. Dressed in a stylish red cocktail dress and with her fair hair bouffanted up, Betty-Grable-style, the superintendent would have looked quite attractive if not for the sour expression on her face.

'That dress must have cost a pretty penny,' said Connie.

'And do you think they're real diamond ear-rings?' asked Annie.

Connie laughed. 'Oh, Annie!'

'They could have been a present,' replied Annie, looking just a little bit crestfallen.

'What, from her lover?' asked Millie.

Connie and Annie laughed.

The church hall opened and Mr Shottington strolled in. Mrs Harper hurried over to greet him, leaving Miss Dutton to stare forlornly after her.

'Are you two ready for another drink?' asked Connie, draining hers.

Millie was about to answer when she sensed someone behind her.

'Hello again, Millie Sullivan,' a cultured voice intoned.

Millie turned and found herself staring up into Jim Smith's handsome face.

'Mr Smith, how nice to see you again,' she said.

'Jim, please,' he reminded Millie, as his gaze ran slowly over her. 'And I'm bound to say that colour suits you very well.'

484

'Thank you,' she replied, feeling ridiculously flustered. 'These are my friends Connie and Annie.'

Her two friends smiled girlishly up at him.

'And this is Jim Smith,' Millie said. 'We met at the Boatman last month when I visited Mrs Fallow.'

'Good evening, ladies. And thank you, Sister Sullivan, for not adding in all the rest,' he said with a good-hearted laugh. Connie and Annie looked enquiringly at Millie.

'Jim's full name is James Percival Woodville Smith,' Millie explained.

'Dreadful isn't it?' Jim said, looking utterly mortified. 'Even with "the Honourable" stuck in front of it doesn't make it sound any better. Of course, I never use it. So just call me Jim.'

Connie and Annie nodded dumbly.

The band played the opening bars of the next dance and Jim turned his attention back to Millie.

He reached out and took her hand. 'May I?'

Millie allowed him to lead her on to the dance-floor. He slipped his arm around her and a memory of dancing with Alex for the first time flashed into Millie's mind as they stepped off. She shoved it aside as they swirled into the middle of the dancers.

'So how are you, Millie?' he asked, as he guided her around another couple.

'Cold and overworked and in the dark mostly, but I'll survive,' she said.

'That's it, chin up.' He grinned. 'It's that sort of plucky East End spirit that put paid to Hitler.'

He guided her through a side-sweep just half a

485

step short, which meant Millie's foot brushed against his as they turned, something Alex would never have done.

'And what have you been up to?' she asked, forcing herself to concentrate on the man she was dancing with, and not the one she wished she was.

'Mainly advising the Dockers' and Stevedores' Union on the new Dock Labour Scheme we're introducing in the summer,' he replied as he glided her backwards. 'It's been one meeting after another; first the dock managers, then the shop stewards. I've been so tied up that as the Boatman is only a stone's throw from London, Royal and India Docks, I've taken up Bert Fallow's offer of lodgings, so I can be on hand.' He looked down at Millie. 'I also thought it might mean I might meet you again.'

Millie regarded him coolly. 'Mrs Fallow's off the books now,' Millie replied. 'So I've no reason to visit.'

'Pity.'

The music stopped and Jim released her.

'Let me buy you a drink,' he said, as people drifted from the dancefloor.

'Thank you.'

They strolled to the improvised bar in the corner. As Jim ordered their drinks, Millie looked around. Connie and Annie were chatting with two young men at one of the tables near the back of the hall, while Mrs Fletcher and Mrs Overton sold tickets for the raffle to people standing around the edge of the dance-floor. Jim handed Millie her drink and then smoothly guided her away from the

486

crush at the bar.

He sipped the froth off his beer. 'Marvellous! I tell you, you can keep all your Chateaux Mouton-Rothchilds and Courvoisier Cognac – just give me a pint of brown ale, and I'm happy.'

'I'm a G and T girl myself,' Millie replied, taking a sip of her drink.

Jim took a mouthful of beer and then regarded her thoughtfully. 'I wasn't looking forward to this evening at all,' he said. 'You know, rubbing shoulders with the local petty bourgeoisie.' His gaze ran lightly over the gathering of shopkeepers, tradesmen, merchants and their wives before returning to Millie's face. 'But when I saw you standing with your friends, I thought...'

'You thought what?'

'I thought I'm not going to let you go again until I've persuaded you to come out one evening with me,' he replied, giving an undeniably charming smile.

'I don't think so,' Millie said.

'Why not?'

'Well, for a start, I don't know you,' Millie replied.

He smiled at her confidently. 'All right, I'm twenty-eight, I boarded at Winchester, read History at Oxford and served in Fighter Command. I'm not married and have all my own teeth, and what else would you like to know before you say "yes"?'

A flash of red caught the corner of Millie's eye and she turned to see Mr Shottington twirling Miss Dutton around the dance-floor in a lively foxtrot.

A wry smile lifted the corner of Millie's lips. 'You can tell me why the observer from the Ministry of Health, Mr Braithwaite, gave me your regards after my disciplinary hearing.'

Jim looked surprised. 'Did he?'

'Don't try and come the innocent!'

'All right, you've found me out. Baggers Braithwaite and I were at Oriel together, and I happened to mention to him that you were having a bit of trouble, that's all.'

'Don't you mean you told him to step in and use his position to influence the board?' Millie said.

'I didn't tell him exactly that, I just asked him to make sure you got a fair hearing,' Jim replied, trying but failing to look repentant.

Millie regarded him dispassionately. 'I thought the Labour Party were against that way of doing things? You know: who you know, and not what you know?'

'We are. But I'm not against bringing the system down from within,' he replied with another winning smile. 'After all, in that hearing were you being rewarded for what you'd done for the Association, or was your very livelihood plus the welfare of your mother dependent on the whim of that old buffoon Shottington?'

'No. I mean, yes!'

'Well, there you have it,' said Jim. 'And now I've answered your question, what day shall I pick you up next week, Millie?'

'I haven't said "yes" yet.'

His cool, self-confident expression returned. 'But you will, won't you?'

'Don't be too sure about that.' Millie finished her drink and handed him the glass. 'Thanks for the dance and the drink. Perhaps I'll see you around sometime, Jim.'

She turned and headed across the dance floor.

'You certainly will, Millie,' he muttered in a low voice. 'You most certainly will.'

Millie knocked on the door of number fifteen Clementine Street, a small two-up, two-down terraced house in the middle of a dozen others, then pushed open the door and walked in.

'Hello, Mrs Mundey. It's the nurse!' Millie called, as she looked over the swept floor, dust-free pictures in the hallway and the polished handrails of the staircase.

'In here,' came a raspy reply from behind the front-room door.

Millie opened it and went in.

Mrs Mundey's front room was just as spotless as the hall. The walls were papered with an old-fashioned flowery design but without curled edges or any peeling at the top or bottom, and although the square rug that covered most of the floor had seen better days, it was without a speck of dirt. The heavy chenille curtains were arr-anged in even folds on either side of the window and the net hanging behind them looked fresh and newly washed.

Mrs Mundey, who had only slightly more flesh on her bones than the teaching skeleton in Munroe House's equipment cupboard, was sitting in an old armchair next to the fire with her feet up on a padded leather pouffe. She had a brightly coloured knitted blanket over her knees and there was a cup of tea and plate with a half-eaten piece of cake on the side table at her elbow. There was a packet of cigarettes and a half-full ashtray on her knees.

Revealing yellowing teeth set in receding gums, Mrs Mundey smiled and, stubbing out the cigarette held between her nicotine-stained fingers, said, 'Oh, Nurse. I'm so pleased you've come. Sit down.'

Millie perched on the chair on the other side of the fireplace. 'Good morning, Mrs Mundey, I'm Sister Sullivan. I'm from the St George's and St Dunstan's District Nursing Association. Dr Hayhurst asked me to call to see if I can make you more comfortable,' she said, retrieving a blank set of patients' notes from her case.

Mrs Mundey's wrinkled face took on an expression of heartfelt gratitude. 'That's very kind of you, Sister. You nurses at that there 'Ssociation are pure angels, so you are.'

'Thank you,' replied Millie, feeling a little uplifted by the old woman's appreciation.

Mrs Mundey pulled out another cigarette and stuck it between her colourless lips. 'I'd offer you a fag too, love, but I've only got a couple to last me until my daughter gets back,' she said breathlessly as she rummaged under the blanket for her lighter.

'That's all right,' replied Millie. 'I don't. Now, if I could ask you a couple of questions so I can decide what help we can give you?'

'Can I tell you, Sister, before you start,' Mrs Mundey put her hand to her throat, and took a

490

deep, chest-rattling breath, 'I'm just a poor old woman and have just enough to avoid a pauper's grave, so if it's going to be dear I can't have you.'

'Don't worry,' said Millie. 'Because of your condition–'

'You mean 'cause I'm dying and there ain't nuffink anyone can do,' Mrs Mundey said, looking at Millie with knowing eyes.

Millie felt a little awkward at the old woman's bluntness. Even if the doctor chose to tell the patient that they were dying, no one openly referred to it. If you were forced to say something, you said 'poorly' or 'ailing', but never 'dying' or 'terminal'.

'Yes, because you're incurable,' said Millie, not quite able to match Mrs Mundey's candour, 'the Association's services are free.'

Mrs Mundey put her hand on her chest and her sad eyes drifted upwards to the ornate glass lampshade. 'May the Blessed Mother herself shine her face on you,' she said, pulling a rosary from the neck of her blouse and kissing it.

Millie smiled. 'We do our best. Now, if you don't mind, could you tell me...'

She ran through the usual questions about medication, mobility, water supply and availability of clean linen, and then told Mrs Mundey that she would get a commode delivered so she didn't have to go on using the bucket tucked away at the back of the chair as a toilet, and that a nurse would come in each morning to check on her and give her a bed bath.

Millie crossed a couple of Ts and closed the file. 'That all seems fine, Mrs Mundey. And I believe your daughter Joy can give you your meals and do the housework.'

An odd expression swept over the old woman's face. 'Yes,' she said, stubbing out the cigarette butt forcefully.

Millie cast her eyes around the spotless room and the old woman's freshly laundered clothes, and smiled. 'Well, I have to say, Mrs Mundey, she's looking after you very well.'

Mrs Mundey grabbed a handkerchief from her sleeve, spat a green and brown globule of phlegm into it, then shoved it back into her clothing. 'It's no more than she ought.' She took out another cigarette and lit it.

'Well then,' said Millie, slipping her file into her bag and closing it. 'I'll be off. Nurse Byrne will call tomorrow between nine and nine-thirty.'

Through the closed lounge door she heard the front door open and close.

'I'm back, Mum,' a woman's voice called.

'I can hear that,' shouted Mrs Mundey. 'Have you got my fags?'

'Of course. Let me put the shopping away and then I'll bring them in.'

'Don't take too long,' gasped the old woman. 'I'm down to me last one.'

'All right, Mum.'

There was the sound of footsteps going through to the back of the house and then the parlour door creaked open.

Millie started in amazement as a little girl with coffee-cream skin, enormous dark eyes and a mass of dark curly hair trotted in. She fiddled nervously with the bows on her frilly pink dress for a moment and then smiled shyly at Millie.

Mrs Mundey gave a phlegmy growl and snatched up the walking stick leaning against the side table. 'Joy!' she yelled, coughing and spluttering as she struggled forward in her chair. 'Your fucking nigger bastard's in here again.' The old woman swung her stick at the child, who shrank back.

Millie jumped up, ready to step between the little girl and the flailing stick.

The door opened. A slender young woman with honey-coloured hair, soft sea-green eyes and a pretty, heart-shaped face came into the room. She scooped the toddler up in her arms and kissed her.

She gave Millie a warm, friendly smile. 'I'm Joy Mundey. You must be the nurse Dr Hayhurst sent.'

'Yes, er, yes. I'm Sister Sullivan,' replied Millie, in a shaky voice.

'Where are my ciggies?' croaked Mrs Mundey.

Joy fished a packet of Senior Service out of her jacket pocket. 'They only had tens,' she said, handing them to her mother.

'I suppose it will have to do,' replied Mrs Mundey, jabbing her second cigarette in twenty minutes into the ashtray and immediately lighting another.

Joy settled her daughter on to her hip and grinned at her. 'Shall we go and put the shopping away, Ginnie?'

The little girl nodded.

'Nice to meet you, Sister,' said Joy, smiling at Millie again.

'And you,' replied Millie, as the young woman

493

walked out of the room, the skirt of her blue flowered dress swinging around her shapely slim legs as she strode out.

Millie stared at the closed door in disbelief. If Mrs Mundey's stick had struck the little girl, it could easily have cracked her skull and knocked her unconscious or, if the knob had struck her on the temple, even killed her. Disturbed by what she'd just seen, Millie forced herself to turn back to her patient.

Mrs Mundey shook her head slowly and tutted. 'I can see from your face what you're thinking, Sister,' she said with a weary sigh. 'How can that poor dying woman hold her head up with the shame of it all? But it ain't nuffink of my doing and if I'd have had my way I'd have made her get rid of that GI coon's bastard before it even took a breath.'

Although she had seen four other patients after her visit to Mrs Mundey that afternoon, Millie was still shaken from the experience when she docked her bicycle under the rack. Taking off her hat and coat, she hooked them with the others on the hall stand and then started towards the treatment room. Before she reached it, the door opened and Annie's head popped out.

'Oh, it's you,' she said, hurrying down the corridor towards Millie. 'You've got a visitor. And you'll never guess who.'

Alex's image flashed into Millie's mind and for one dizzy moment she allowed herself to imagine that he'd returned. She pushed the painful thought aside.

'If it's Stanley from Highways, tell him I've emigrated to Australia,' Millie replied.

'No,' said Annie, almost beside herself with excitement. 'It's James Thingummy Whatsit Smith.'

'Jim's here?' Millie said, quelling a surprise sudden flicker of pleasure.

Annie nodded.

'He has been for almost an hour,' continued Annie. 'Miss Dutton tried to get rid of him by saying you wouldn't be back for hours, but he just smiled and said he was happy to wait. He said something else to her that I didn't catch, then she showed him into the small sitting room and ordered Mrs Pierce to make him a cup of tea.'

Millie looked amazed.

'I know,' said Annie. 'But I suppose underneath her starched knickers even Miss Dutton is a woman and, well, you know.' Annie held out her hand. 'I'll take your bag.'

Millie passed it to her and then made her way down the corridor to the guest sitting room, stopping briefly in front of the hall mirror to check her hair.

She took a deep breath and went in.

Jim was sitting with one long leg crossed over the other in the seat by the window. He rose immediately as she entered.

'Ah, my dear Millie has returned at last,' he said, giving her a dazzling smile.

Millie shut the door. 'I'm not your Millie.'

'Not yet,' he replied, taking two steps closer. 'But that's why I'm here.

'To be honest,' said Millie, trying to look in-

495

different, 'as it's been almost three weeks since the dance, I'll put your attentions down to just a bit of outrageous flirting.'

Jim raised an eyebrow. 'Yes, I'm sorry I've not called sooner, but the Ministry sent me to Liverpool for two weeks to advise the trade union officials up there.'

'What, are you trying to bring them out on strike like the local men?' Millie replied.

'The dock workers have legitimate grievances and have the right to withdraw their labour in pursuit of it,' Jim replied, with a serious frown. 'It's so we can make sure those who produce the wealth have fair shares.'

'Tell that to the women and children queuing in freezing weather for a pound of tripe or horse-meat,' replied Millie. 'It's all well and good for politicians, but the people I visit every day are just about surviving, and so I don't see how leaving food to rot in ships' holds while the country goes hungry is helping anyone.'

Jim stared at her for a moment, then smiled. 'It's a lot more complicated than that, but,' the expression in his eyes warmed as he looked deeply into hers, 'I make it a rule never to talk politics when I'm in the company of a pretty girl.'

'You sound as if it's an everyday occurrence,' Millie replied, trying to keep her tone even.

'I can only hope,' he replied smoothly. 'And you did agree to come out with me if I answered your question about John Braithwaite.' His smile widened. 'How about Saturday?'

Millie's heart gave a little double beat. It might be halfway around the world with Alex, but to her surprise she wasn't immune to Jim Smith's well-proportioned frame, tousled hair and self-assured charm.

'I'm visiting my aunt on Saturday,' she said, coolly.

Jim's confident gaze flickered.

And then Millie smiled. 'But I'm free the following week.'

Chapter Twenty-Nine

Millie sat staring at the magnolia-coloured walls of the council offices while she listened as the soft tap-tap-tap of the typing pool filtered through the half-glazed door at the far end of the corridor. She glanced down at her watch. Three-thirty. Although the town hall was only a stone's throw from the Watney Street surgery, she'd be late for Dr Gingold's child clinic if Mrs Grossman, the child welfare officer, didn't call her in soon.

The brass handle rattled and Millie looked up as the battleship-grey door opposite opened. A woman dressed in a baggy tweed suit, thick stockings and tan brogues with scuffed toes stepped out. She blinked through round-rimmed glasses perched on the tip of her nose.

'Sister Sullivan?' she asked, pushing her spectacles back to their rightful place.

Millie stood up. 'Yes. Mrs Grossman?'

Mrs Grossman nodded, setting wisps of grey hair fluttering. 'Do come in.'

Millie entered the ill-lit, dingy office and took the seat in front of the desk while Mrs Grossman closed the door and returned to her side. She sat down and her old chair creaked to accommodate her weight.

'I'm sorry to have kept you, but the resettlement committee overran this morning and I

498

haven't yet caught up,' she said, looking at Millie over the piles of manila files that littered the desk. 'Now is it about the Walters family again?'

'It is, and this is the fourth time I've come to you, so I hope this time you'll agree with me that one of the council welfare department should be involved. I'm still visiting once a week, but I'm making no progress with Mrs Walters, who still refuses to shoulder her maternal responsibilities,' Millie said.

Mrs Grossman shuffled her papers. 'I can't seem to see any reference to Mr Walters.'

'She isn't married,' Millie answered, holding the welfare officer's pale gaze.

Mrs Grossman's thin lips drew together. 'All those children and no wedding ring,' she said in a caustic tone.

'The children's father lives around the corner in Dock Street,' Millie drew in a steady breath, 'with his other family.'

Mrs Grossman's mouth grew smaller. 'I see.'

'But it's the children we should be concerned about, don't you think?' Millie said.

Mrs Grossman's expression softened a little. 'So you want me to send one of the welfare officers around to Mrs Walters?'

'I do, before one of the children has an accident or gets hurt in some way,' Millie replied.

Mrs Grossman shook her head. 'I'm afraid I can't do that. What you describe is no different to what I would expect to find behind any front door in Stebbins House.' She smoothed her grizzled grey hair back into place. 'I'm afraid, Sister Sullivan, that I really can't justify putting the Walters

499

family on the list.'

'But the children are living in abject squalor,' Millie replied. 'You should see the condition of the place. The little ones were playing amongst empty bottles and cigarette butts on the floor. There was no fireguard, and only bread and dripping in the larder. On three occasions I arrived to find the children alone in the house. The only wash the children have each week is the one I give them when I visit, and the tangles in little Vera's hair were so bad I had to cut them out last week.' A little knot lodged itself in Millie's chest. 'And they're such bright little buttons,' she added, with a slight waver in her voice. 'The baby's grasping at things and trying to pull herself up, the two-year-old can talk as clear as day. And although he's the youngest in the class, Mickey already knows his alphabet and is starting to sound out letters.'

Mrs Grossman's expression softened again. 'You have a good heart, Sister Sullivan, and I understand your concern. In normal circumstances I might be able to help, but with the strain of hundreds of illegitimate babies waiting for adoption, plus trying to find homes for Blitz orphans, my small team just can't take on ordinary domestic cases at the moment.' She clasped her chubby hands together and rested them on the blotting paper in front of her. 'I'll make a note of the family and keep it on file. But with you visiting the family each week I'd say the Walters children are a great deal safer than many I can think of.' Mrs Grossman smiled. 'But if anything changes feel free to pop back and tell me,

Sister, and I'll review the case.'

The first bars of the music started as the closing credits began to roll up. The small cinema just off Wardour Street erupted with spontaneous applause, which Millie joined in with enthusiastically. The lights went up and the people around her rose to their feet and started to sidestep along the seats to the ends of the rows.

'Did you enjoy that?' asked Jim as he stood up.

'Oh, yes,' replied Millie, hooking her handbag over her arm and standing. 'It was gripping. And when Sister Ruth stood on the edge of the cliff ringing the convent bell I couldn't bear to watch. But how on earth did you get tickets to the press showing?'

'A chum of mine works for the distributors and he owed me a favour.' Jim smiled. 'I'm glad you liked it.'

Their row shuffled forward and Jim took hold of Millie's elbow and guided her along the side aisle. They collected their coats from the cloak-room and then, shielding her from the press of the people behind them, Jim opened the cinema door and they stepped out into the bright afternoon sunlight of a perfect April day.

'Now,' he said, running his hand round the brim of his hat to straighten it, 'I know just the place for a coffee.'

Millie took his arm and Jim guided her through the crowds in Berwick Street Market and then into Beak Street. Keeping her eyes from straying to the billboards outside the strip clubs advertising the attractions within, Millie tucked herself in beside him as they walked along the narrow street. Within a few minutes they stopped outside a small café with an Italian flag crossed over a Union Jack in the window. Jim pushed the door open and a bell tinkled.

'After you,' he said, placing his hand lightly in the small of her back.

Millie stepped into the narrow shop and inhaled the inviting smell of fresh coffee and boiled milk. The café's walls were a rich cream, the woodwork picked out in chocolate brown while the chairs were painted pink, giving the place the look of a block of Neapolitan ice cream. It was no more than two arms-breadths wide and had a row of booths that could each seat four people running down one side, most of which were occupied. Opposite was a long counter with half-a-dozen customers sitting on tall stools.

The man serving behind the counter looked up as they walked in.

'Mister Woodville Smith!' he shouted, his face alight with joy.

'*Buonasera, Alfredo,*' Jim said, with perfect inflection. '*Due dei vostri speciali, per favore.*'

'Coming a-righta up,' Alfredo replied, unhooking two cups from the ornate rack above the counter.

'You speak Italian?' asked Millie.

'A smattering,' Jim replied.

He steered her towards a free booth near the front and they sat down.

'So, how am I doing for a first date?' Jim asked, as Millie set her handbag on the seat beside her.

'Quite well,' she replied. 'Although I have to

502

admit, you score double for the film.'

Jim laughed. 'Well, let me chalk up some more points by saying I always preferred blondes until I met you. But now,' he cast his eyes over her shiny auburn hair, and then back to her face, 'I'll never look at another. And your eyes are just extraordinary. One moment they're green, and then the light changes and they are brown.'

'Stop it,' said Millie, feeling her cheeks grow warm.

Alfredo arrived with two cups of frothy coffee that had little macaroon-looking biscuits balancing on the saucers.

'Specials for Mr Woodville Smith and his pretty lady,' the proprietor announced with a lavish roll of his eyes.

'Thank you, Alfredo,' Jim said, stirring in a heaped spoonful of sugar-substitute from the bowl on the table. '*Come sta la sua bella moglie?*'

'*Sta bene.*'

Jim and Alfredo exchanged pleasantries for a moment or two and then the owner's gaze flickered on to Millie. '*Si dovrebbe sposare questo,* Mr Woodville Smith.'

Jim looked at Millie and nodded slowly. '*Potresti avere ragione.*'

Alfredo chuckled and ambled back to the counter, collecting empty crockery on the way.

Jim studied Millie. 'Aren't you going to ask me what he said?'

'No.' She picked up her coffee.

'He said I ought to marry this one,' Jim said.

'Did he now?'

'He did,' replied Jim, raising an eyebrow.

Millie changed the subject. 'So, where were you stationed during the war?'

Jim stretched his arms along the back of the padded seat. 'At Hornchurch, in Essex, flying Spitfires with Seventy-Four Squadron. How was your war?'

'Babies and bombs,' Millie replied, taking a sip of creamy coffee. 'And very often at the same time.'

'My mother was a nurse in the Voluntary Aid Detachment during the Great War,' Jim said. 'She met my father there after the Battle of Ypres. He'd been shot in the leg and arrived on her ward. Of course, he wasn't the Baron of Tollshunt then, but just an ordinary solider.'

'As he's a baron, doesn't that mean that one day you'll inherit his title?' asked Millie.

An odd expression flitted across Jim's face. 'No. When the old man goes it will be dear Lionel, my older brother, who will get the lot,' he said, in a flat tone. 'Not that I'm bothered, of course.' Jim gave a hollow laugh. 'In fact, I'm quite relieved I won't be saddled with a title, a crumbling pile of medieval masonry and the estate because it will save me the trouble of renouncing the lot when I become a Labour MP.'

'You're standing for parliament?' said Millie.

Jim's good nature returned. 'At the next election,' he said with an assured grin.

'For where?'

Jim lowered his eyes and he stirred his coffee deliberately. 'I can't say just now, but there are a couple of local executive committees who are vying for me, and so I'm pretty confident that

504

one of them will adopt me as their prospective candidate before too long.'

'Is that why you're in Stepney and involved with the dockers' union?' asked Millie.

Jim nodded. 'Ever since I heard Ramsay Mac-Donald speak at the Oxford Socialite Club I've pledged myself to break the shackles of servitude and the subjugation of my fellow man.' He punched his right fist into his left palm. 'For too long the common man has had his back bowed and broken by oppression, and his work-cal-loused hands forced to produce wealth for the elite.' Jim's well-manicured fingers curled around Millie's, and a tingling sensation travelled up her arm. 'But what I'm even more pleased about is meeting you, Millie, a very uncommon woman. And I'd like to add that you look absolutely ravishing in that shade of green.'

Jim looked at her with undisguised admiration and Millie's heart couldn't help but be warmed and flattered by the attention.

She studied him over the rim of her cup. His chin wasn't as square as Alex's, nor were his eyes so compelling, and no man but Alex could set her pulse racing with a look. But all the same, Jim's clear blue eyes and eloquent phrases had an appeal of their very own.

Millie finished her coffee, and smiled. 'Thank you, Jim, and I'm glad we met, too.'

'Here you go, Sister,' said Joy Mundey, lifting a pile of soaking clothes out of the sink and plonk-ing them on the wooden draining board.

As it was Monday, Joy, like every other woman

505

in the area, had set up the wash tub early, and - dozen garments on the washing line in the small back yard. She was just starting on the second tubful of the day.

'Thanks.' Millie rested the enamel bowl on the edge of the sink and tipped the dirty water down the plughole.

'Your mum's all done and I've put her in the blue dress you left on the back of the chair. I'll give her a moment to catch her breath then I'll let her have her medicine.'

'How is she?' asked Joy, taking one of her mother's nightdresses and running it up and down the scrubbing board.

'Quite well, considering,' replied Millie. 'Where's Ginnie?'

'Playing upstairs.' Joy wiped her brow with her forearm.

'Ginnie is an unusual name,' Millie said, rinsing the bowl out under the solitary tap.

'It's Marvin's mother's name, Virginia,' Joy explained. 'He's from Detroit in Michigan. He was a sergeant in the Seventh Army and fought alongside our Eighth Army in Sicily.'

Millie forced a smile. 'I knew someone in the Eighth Army once,' she said as a pang of longing caught in her chest.

'I met Marvin at the American Red Cross Club just off Shaftesbury Avenue.' Joy hugged herself and looked into the distance. 'He was so tall and handsome, and the perfect gentleman. Although he worked in a car factory, Marvin's really a musician. When we used to dance he would sing and, oh my, it was just heavenly.' She looked at

Millie. 'Do you know what I mean?'

An image of Alex formed in Millie's mind, and she nodded.

'We saw each other whenever we could, but just a few weeks after we met, Marvin was shipped out to Germany,' Joy said, smearing Sunlight soap over one of her mother's nightdresses ready for a scrub.

'And Ginnie?'

Joy's cheeks flushed. 'Although my mother says otherwise, I was a good girl until I met him. And well, you know how these things happen.'

'Where is Marvin now?' asked Millie.

'Back home in Detroit, but he's coming back to marry me as soon as he gets out of the Army,' Joy said, her eyes wide with belief and hope.

Millie smiled politely, although she wondered just how many young girls left with GI babies had been told the very same story, only to be disappointed.

Joy picked up the bucketful of washing ready for the line. 'Can you see yourself out, Sister?'

'Of course,' Millie replied.

Joy left the kitchen. Millie took the tea towel from the bracket supporting the old butler sink and wiped the basin dry.

A piercing shriek of pain and fear ripped through the air. Millie dropped the bowl and dashed through the house as the screaming increased. Shoving the front-room door aside, she ran in and stared in disbelief at Mrs Mundey gripping Ginnie by the hair.

'Mrs Mundey, you're hurting the child!' Millie shouted.

'Hurt her!' Mrs Mundey shook the toddler viciously. 'I'll fucking kill her. Thieving little wog.'

The little girl turned her large tearful eyes on Millie and howled.

Mrs Mundey grabbed her stick. 'I'll teach you to touch what ain't yours.' She whacked the child around the head.

Ginnie stumbled and fell against the wooden arm of Mrs Mundey's chair.

'Let go of her,' Millie said firmly. She strode over and tried to prise the old woman's fingers loose.

Joy ran in. 'Ginnie!' she screamed, dashing to her daughter, enfolding the toddler in her arms.

She tried to pull Ginnie out of her mother's grasp, but Mrs Mundey held on with surprising strength.

'Mummy! Mummy!' Ginnie sobbed, clawing at her grandmother's gnarled knuckles.

Joy grabbed her mother's bony wrist, while Millie tried to help release Ginnie from the gnarly grip but without hurting the old woman. Mrs Mundey glared hatefully at her daughter for a moment and then released her hand, and suddenly they all broke apart.

Millie staggered back against the table, and Mrs Mundey rubbed her wrists and scowled at her daughter.

Joy scooped up Ginnie, holding her tightly. 'It's all right, Mummy's here,' she cooed in Ginnie's ear, rocking the toddler back and forth on the spot.

'Get that nigger kid out of my sight,' said Mrs Mundey.

Joy kissed Ginnie's forehead. 'Shall we see if there's a biscuit in the tin?'

Ginnie gave a little shuddering hiccup and nodded. Joy kissed her again and left the room with her daughter on her hip.

Mrs Mundey glowered after her until the door closed, and then she slumped back exhausted. Millie stared aghast at the frail, prostrate old woman for a moment, and then straightened the shawl over her legs and picked up her case.

'Goodbye, Mrs Mundey,' she said, in a clipped professional tone.

Mrs Mundey smiled sweetly up at her. 'Thank you, Nurse.'

Millie left and walked back to the kitchen. The room was empty, and through the window she could see Joy, with Ginnie still in her arms, at the far side of the yard looking at the clematis flowers on the wall.

She watched for a moment mother and child talking together in the warm afternoon sun, and then retraced her steps back through the house and out to the street. Millie put her bag in her cycle basket, scooted her bike forward and then hopped on.

As she turned out of the street she realised that in all the uproar she'd forgotten to give the opium for pain relief. But as the awful image of Mrs Mundey abusing her own small granddaughter played over in her mind, Millie decided her difficult patient could bloody well do without it just this one time.

Millie held her glass of sherry in readiness as

Keith Rosser, Tony's best man, turned to the newly-weds and raised his pint. 'I give you the new Mr and Mrs Harris.'

The hall of the Manor Park and District Working Men's Club was filled with Tony and Ruby's wedding guests, who pushed their chairs back and rose to their feet. Millie followed suit.

'Mr and Mrs Harris,' fifty voices shouted.

'Aunt Ruby and Tony,' she said, looking at her aunt and her husband of two hours happily sitting next to each other at the top table.

In her search for a wedding outfit, Ruby had visited at least a dozen of the Aldgate sweatshops who manufactured beautiful clothes for West End department stores like Derry & Toms, Bourne & Hollingsworth and Selfridges. She'd settled on a slim-fitting fern-green suit which complemented her trim figure. The jacket had an asymmetric front with large four-holed buttons fastening it in a diagonal line towards her left shoulder, and minimal flaps on the pockets. The streamlined cut was continued through in the straight skirt with a fishtail vent at the back. If the skirt was a little longer and the jacket sleeves a little fuller than clothes rationing might demand, it was because Ruby's suit was probably of the cabbage variety: that is, made from the fabric left over after the contracted order of outfits had been fulfilled.

Keith drained his glass and wiped his mouth with the back of his hand. 'Right now the formalities are over, lads,' he waggled his empty glass. 'Time for a top-up while our better and prettier halves clear away.'

Like a well-disciplined squadron of fighter

planes, the men peeled away from the trestle tables and headed for the bar at the other end of the hall. Aunt Martha lifted the wedding cake from its stand and transferred it to the small table in the corner, then popped the cardboard cover fashioned to resemble a three-tiered iced cake over it. The women in the hall immediately stacked the empty plates and glasses ready to be taken to the kitchen and washed.

Jim slipped his arm around Millie's waist and guided her towards the edge of the hall. 'Do you want another?' he asked.

Millie smiled at him. 'I'm fine. But are *you* all right? I mean, my family can be a bit overwhelming if you're not used to them.'

'Don't be silly,' Jim replied.

'And I'm sorry about the business at the church, but Edie always gets a bit emotional at weddings and if I hadn't sorted it out she might have started one of her sick headaches.'

'I was fine, and it gave me time to have a nice chat with your mum.' Jim winked. 'You didn't tell me you were the top student nurse in your class.'

Millie laughed. 'I always let her tell that story.'

'Your aunt looks happy,' said Jim, looking at the couple in the middle of a crowd of well-wishers.

Millie smiled. 'She is. It's almost fifteen years since Uncle Bertram died and none of us ever thought she'd marry again.'

'Well, I suppose when you find the right person you want to make them yours straight away,' Jim said, in a thoughtful tone.

Millie gazed at him as he looked deeply into her eyes.

The tension was broken as her mother's voice cut through the hubbub. 'Millie!'

They turned.

Doris was standing with Ruby on the other side of the room and waving for Millie to join them.

Millie slipped her arm in Jim's. 'Come and meet the bride.'

Dodging the men carrying the collapsed tables through to the storeroom, Millie and Jim walked across the hall.

'Congratulations,' Millie said, being enveloped in a cloud of Chanel No. 5 as she hugged her aunt. 'You look lovely.'

'Thank you, Amelia,' Ruby replied, kissing the air beside Millie's cheek. 'You look very pretty yourself.'

'This is Millie's young man, Jim Smith,' Doris said to her sister.

Ruby's eyes flickered over Jim and she held out her hand. 'I'm pleased to meet you, Mr Smith.'

Doris's eyes danced with excitement. 'He's a lord and his father's a duke.'

Ruby stared at Jim in wide-eyed wonder.

'My father's just a minor baron, actually, and I'm nothing more than an Honourable,' Jim said easily, taking Ruby's hand. 'But, as I told your sister earlier, I never mention it. It's a pleasure to meet you, and especially on such a happy occasion.'

Jim slipped his arm around Millie and squeezed. 'I ought to help the chaps set up the stage for the band, but I'll be back for the first dance.'

'Make sure you are,' said Millie, with a little laugh.

'If you'd excuse me, ladies,' he said to her mother and aunt. Ruby and Doris nodded mutely, and watched him goggle-eyed as he sauntered off to join the men.

Ruby grabbed her sister's arm. 'For goodness sake, Doris, why didn't you tell me our Amelia is walking out with a member of the aristocracy?'

'Because I didn't know myself until I talked to him outside the church, Ruby,' replied Doris, 'and I had to pry it out of him. But isn't it wonderful?'

Ruby nodded, setting the feather on her hat trembling. 'And he talks just like a BBC commentator.' Horror flashed across her face. 'Do you think we should have curtsied or something?'

Millie rolled her eyes. 'Of course not! And Jim's not interested in all the landed gentry business and he tries to keep his background quiet. He works for the Ministry of Labour and he hopes to become an MP at the next election.'

'An MP,' Ruby said, with a look of utter delight on her face. 'That's just what the Party needs: new blood.'

'He'll be standing as a Labour candidate, Aunt Ruby,' said Millie, suppressing a smile.

Ruby waved the notion away. 'He can always cross the floor. Like dear Winston.'

Doris smoothed a stray lock of hair from Millie's forehead. 'Dad would have been chuffed to bits to know his daughter's going to be a Labour MP's wife.'

'I think you're both jumping the gun a bit,' exclaimed Millie, feeling her cheeks grow warm. 'Apart from the fact that Jim and I have only

513

been going out a few months, he has to ask me.'

'But surely he must have hinted?' wheedled her mother.

Ruby clicked her fingers. 'Perhaps we should make enquiries about booking the town hall just in case.'

'Can we discuss my wedding *if* Jim proposes, and *if* I accept?' said Millie. 'And now, if you two *Shadchans* have finished matchmaking, I'm going to mingle.'

Millie turned and made her way across the hall. The band was now tuning up and the men were back at the bar, laughing and joking as they ordered their pints.

Millie spotted Jim tucked in the corner at the far end talking to the barmaid, a petite redhead wearing a tight blouse and lavish smile. Jim beckoned her forward and then whispered something into her ear. The girl giggled and coiled a strand of hair around her finger.

An unexpected twinge of disquiet caught Millie in the chest. But then Jim picked up the two drinks and turned his back on the girl. He spotted Millie and smiled as if she were the best thing he had ever seen. Millie's unease evaporated and she grinned back.

Jim strolled over and handed her a glass. 'Well, what's the verdict?'

'They think you'll do,' Millie replied.

Jim laughed and slipped his arm around Millie's waist. A thrill of excitement ran through her. The band struck up for the first dance and Tony led Ruby on to the floor.

As she watched her aunt and her new husband

glide around on their first dance as a married couple, a wave of sadness rose up in Millie. Try as she might, Millie couldn't help but picture herself in Alex's arms doing the same.

Jim's embrace tightened 'Are you all right, sweetheart?'

Millie smiled. 'Of course,' she said, blinking away the tightness in her eyes. 'Don't you know it's traditional to cry at weddings?'

Jim kissed her forehead. 'Shall we join the happy couple?'

Millie nodded and he led her on to the dance-floor.

'What about you?' Jim asked as he guided her on to a back step. 'Will I do for you?'

Millie held his gaze for a moment. 'I'm beginning to think you just might.'

Chapter Thirty

Bone-weary, Millie hopped off her bike and walked it the last few yards to the back gates of Munroe House. It was her second night on call and she'd just delivered a whopper of a baby in Turner Street. She couldn't wait to crawl into her camp bed.

After stowing her bike in the rack opposite Miss Dutton's accommodation, Millie made her way to the back door. Unsurprisingly, as it was well past midnight, the downstairs of Munroe House was dark and still.

Without turning on the hall light, Millie dragged herself into the treatment room and put her bag on the surface of the dressing cupboard. She snapped open her case, pulled out her dirty scissors, metal bowls and syringes, and then put them in the stainless steel tray full of Dettol solution to soak overnight. Yawning, Millie opened the glass-fronted cupboard and pulled out a fresh set of delivery instruments and popped them in her bag. She reached into her bag to pull out the set of kidney dishes and then remembered, because they were so bloody and mucus-stained from the delivery, she'd put them in her bike rack loose so they wouldn't contaminate the inside of her bag.

With a weary sigh Millie trudged out of the treatment room and back into the yard. She had just reached her cycle when Miss Dutton's front door opened.

The light from the hallway cut across the cobbles, illuminating Miss Dutton dressed in a pink lacy negligee with her hair cascading over her shoulders. Standing next to her was Algernon Shottington, complete with opera cape and top hat.

'Do you have to go just yet, my darling?' Miss Dutton said breathlessly.

'I'm afraid I do,' Mr Shottington replied in a tone heavy with regret.

Miss Dutton clung to him. 'I hate you going back to her, Algie.'

'Now, now, Lilly sweetheart, don't upset yourself. You know it's only until the children have grown.'

The lovers parted and Mr Shottington walked swiftly to the back gate. He stopped to blow Miss Dutton a silent kiss and then slipped out silently.

Miss Dutton stared after him for a moment then, sensing Millie's presence, turned and looked at her.

'Good evening, Miss Dutton,' said Millie in a crisp voice.

Miss Dutton jumped and clasped her hand to her chest. 'Sister Sullivan, it's not what—'

'I think?' asked Millie, not even trying to keep the sarcasm from her tone.

Millie tucked the three kidney bowls under her arm, turned and marched back into the nurses' home, finally understanding the real reason she was passed over for the superintendent's post.

Millie arrived at Munroe House at half-past one

517

the next afternoon and nearly collided with Annie as she opened the back door.

'Sorry, Millie,' Annie said, catching her hat before it slipped off her head. 'I'm in a bit of a rush.' She looked puzzled. 'I thought you had a day off today.'

'I have, but I'm interviewing prospective candidates for our Queen's Nurse training places and I thought it gave a better impression if I wore my new uniform,' Millie replied.

After almost twenty years the Institute had discarded the uniform designed in the roaring twenties and had approved a new design. Millie's had arrived two days ago and it seemed appropriate to wear it for selecting the next set of QNs.

'I can't wait to get enough coupons together so I can order mine,' replied Annie, looking a little enviously at Millie's new A-line uniform with its neat white collar and cuffs.

Millie smiled. 'Didn't you say you were in a hurry?'

'Oh, gosh, yes.' Annie stepped around her and dashed towards the bike rack. She threw her bag in the basket and yanked the front wheels out of the brackets. 'I promised Mr Tucker I'd be with him by two and you know what an old moaner he is if you're late.'

She pushed her bike forward, jumped on to the saddle and pedalled furiously out of the yard.

Millie turned back to the house and was just about to walk in when the door to Miss Dutton's accommodation opened and the superintendent stepped out. She, too, was in uniform but in her old hospital matron's one, with a starched, lacy collar and cuffs and nun-like white hat. As she spotted Millie, colour burst on to her cheeks and her gaze faltered.

'Good afternoon, Miss Dutton,' Millie said in a conversational tone.

The superintendent looked across at Millie. 'Good afternoon, Sister Sullivan,' she said, pulling herself together and walking purposefully across.

'After you,' Millie said, holding the door for her.

'Thank you,' Miss Dutton said, lowering her eyes as she stepped inside.

Millie followed her in and down the hall to her office.

Mrs Archer and Mrs Harper were already in the room. The chairwoman was sitting in the superintendent's chair behind the desk reading through a pile of notes, while the secretary was setting out the chairs ready for the first candidate. They both looked up as Millie and Miss Dutton walked in.

'Good afternoon, ladies,' Mrs Harper said regarding them over the rim of her glasses. 'I trust you are both well.'

'Thank you,' said Millie. 'I am, if a little tired from three nights on call.'

Miss Dutton yawned.

The chairwoman raised an eyebrow. 'You too, Miss Dutton?'

'Sorry, Mrs Harper,' the superintendent replied.

'I've set the papers out for both of you,' said Mrs Harper, indicating the sets of notes neatly stacked on either end of the table. 'I hope you don't mind, Miss Dutton, but I've put Madame Chair in your seat.'

'Not at all,' replied Miss Dutton, slumping down on the chair on the right-hand side of her desk.

Millie sat at the opposite end.

'There are seven candidates,' said Mrs Archer. 'And the first two are already here.' She looked at her watch and stood up. 'We've got a few moments yet, so if you'd excuse me, I've got to powder my nose before we start.'

'Good idea,' agreed Mrs Harper. 'I'll join you, then organise some tea for us all.'

The two women left.

Millie crossed her legs and, as the grandmother clock in the corner ticked off the seconds, she studied the opposite wall.

'Millie, I suppose you're just waiting for your moment before telling Mrs Harper about last night,' said Miss Dutton.

Millie turned. 'Don't judge me by your own standards.'

Miss Dutton stared at her incredulously. 'You mean you're not going to say anything?'

'What you do when you're off duty is none of my business,' replied Millie.

The superintendent let out a long-held breath and looked visibly relieved. 'Well, Millie, that's very generous of you.'

'But what you do when you're on duty is.' Millie's eyes narrowed as she looked down the table at the other woman. 'So from now on I want you to start running Munroe House like a modern district nursing service and not a bloody Victorian hospital ward as you have been.'

Miss Dutton's cheeks flushed. 'Whatever do

you mean?'

'For a start you could get out from behind that desk and visit the odd patient or two yourself when we're short-staffed, instead of always forcing the girls to do double shifts,' clarified Millie. 'Then you can get us some more equipment. And I'll let you know when I think of the rest.'

'This is blackmail,' said Miss Dutton, with a trace of her old venom.

Millie smiled. 'Then report me. I'm sure Mrs Harper would be pleased to hear what you have to say.'

Miss Dutton gave Millie a furious look, then her head snapped to the front.

The sound of Mrs Archer and Mrs Harper chatting as they walked down the corridor outside filtered through the office door.

'And one other thing,' Millie said without turning her head.

'What?'

'Don't ever call me Millie.'

Miss Dutton ticked the fourth question on her list and looked up. 'And lastly, Miss Norris, could you explain to us the correct way to store the rubber items?'

Miss Norris, a freckled, red-haired toothy young woman with bitten nails, mulled over the question.

'Er...' she started, blinking rapidly as she struggled for words.

Millie sighed inwardly. 'Let's say you've just brought a rubber ring back from a patient's house.' The young nurse nodded and shifted to the edge of her chair. 'Would you just put it on the shelf?' asked Millie.

'Oh, no, Sister,' the young nurse replied. 'I'd wash it.'

'And?' asked Millie, looking encouragingly at the young candidate.

'Then I'd put them away,' replied Miss Norris, looking puzzled by the question.

'Wet?' asked Miss Dutton.

Miss Norris looked affronted. 'Of course not, Matron. I'd dry them proper.'

'And then?' Miss Dutton asked.

Miss Norris's eyes drifted up to the ceiling and she chewed the inside of her mouth for a moment, then beamed at the panel. 'Then I'd stack it neatly on the shelf with the others.'

'You wouldn't consider inflating it to ensure it stays in shape or dusting it with powder to ensure there's no moisture left to rot the rubber?' asked Millie.

Miss Norris looked blankly at her.

Millie glanced at the chairwoman.

'Well, thank you Miss Norris,' Mrs Harper said, putting on her professional face and tidying her papers together. 'We won't take up any more of your time.' She smiled frostily. 'We'll let you know.'

Miss Norris stood up and, looking slightly bemused, walked to the door.

The four women remained still until the lock clicked and then they slumped in their chairs.

'I didn't think anyone could be worse than Nurse Gurney,' said Mrs Harper, holding her head in her hands.

'But that's because we hadn't had the pleasure of meeting Nurse Norris,' replied Miss Dutton.

For once Millie had to agree.

Mrs Harper scanned down her list. 'So after three hours and six candidates there's only two, Miss Crawford and Miss Kelly, who we'd consider offering a training position.'

Miss Dutton nodded. 'Miss Crawford definitely, but I'm not too sure about Nurse Kelly. She's very young.'

'Weren't we all at twenty-one?' commented Millie cheerily. 'But as a student she scored in the top five in all her state exams. She was promoted to junior sister after only two years and ran a surgical ward in Guy's all through the Blitz. I think she'll make an admirable Queen's Nurse.'

Millie gave Miss Dutton the friendliest of smiles.

'I'm sure you're right, Sister Sullivan,' the superintendent replied, now matching Millie's agreeable expression.

'What about the third candidate, Nurse Everett?' asked Mrs Archer. 'After all, she mentioned both inflating and powdering the rubber equipment.'

'She did,' replied Millie. 'And she was a very pleasant young woman. But as she'd visit a tuberculosis case before attending to a bed-bound elderly patient with a chesty cough, I don't think she would be suitable.'

Mrs Archer looked questioningly at Miss Dutton.

'I agree,' said the superintendent.

The chairwoman sighed. 'Perhaps, as we're still short of experienced nurses, it's better to have only half the trainee places filled this year.'

523

'There's still Nurse Williams to see,' said Mrs Harper.

'Very well,' said Mrs Archer, wearily. 'Show her in.'

Millie stifled a yawn and glanced at the clock, wondering if she'd have time to telephone Jim before he left the Boatman and tell him not to come around tonight as she was too tired to go out. The door opened as Mrs Harper returned.

'I'm embarrassed to say that I can't read my own writing,' she said, with a little laugh. 'It's Nurse Villiers, and not Nurse Williams.'

Millie's exhaustion vanished as the tall nurse she'd first met over a year ago on Truman Ward when she'd visited Gina walked in.

Daphne Villiers was dressed in an impeccably tailored mustard suit and a crisp white blouse fastened with a crystal blue brooch that matched her eyes. Her honey-blonde hair was gathered into a black snood under her Robin Hood felt hat and she wore low-heeled court shoes with a matching handbag.

'Good afternoon, Nurse Villiers. If you would take a seat,' Mrs Archer said, indicating the chair in front of the desk.

Nurse Villiers smiled and gracefully sat on the chair. She placed her handbag on the floor, pressed her knees and ankles together and rested her hands on her lap.

'I'm Mrs Harper, chairwoman of the St Georges and St Dunstan's District Nursing Association,' Mrs Harper said.

'Good afternoon.'

'You know Mrs Archer.' The chairwoman

nodded towards Miss Dutton. 'The superintendent of Munroe House, Miss Dutton.'

Nurse Villiers acknowledged the superintendent. 'Good afternoon.'

'And lastly,' continued Mrs Harper. 'Sister Sullivan, our senior nurse.'

Nurse Villiers turned to Millie and recognition flickered in her eyes. 'I'm pleased to meet you, Sister Sullivan.'

A broad smile spread across Millie's face. 'And I'm very pleased to meet you too, Nurse Villiers.'

'Another glass of wine, madam,' a waiter with hair so slick it looked as if it had been painted on his head, asked.

'No, thank you,' Millie replied, holding a hand over her half-full glass.

His pencil-thin moustache lifted at the corners and he slid back into the crowd.

She took a sip of her drink and glanced around the ancient hall and wondered if Jim would be much longer at the buffet table.

After finding Lenny Hayes on the floor when she'd called, by the time she'd got him back into bed and then finished her teatime insulins it was almost six-thirty. She'd barely had time to dress, put on her face and curl her hair before Jim arrived at seven and so she had missed both afternoon tea and supper.

'Sorry, sweetheart.'

Millie turned to see Jim weaving his way through the crowds, holding two plates.

'Oh, Jim I wondered where you'd got to.'

'Sorry, the undersecretary for Fuel and Power

collared me,' he said with an apologetic smile, offering her a plate.

Millie took it and looked down at the tiny morsel sitting in the middle.

'The little things on squares that look like little berries is caviar. You should try it,' Jim said. 'It's very good.'

Millie popped it in her mouth. It was tasty enough but it wouldn't be sufficient to stop her stomach rumbling later.

'Lovely,' she said, wishing there was a sausage roll or pork pie amongst the snacks.

'So what do you think of the place?' Jim asked, popping a little crunchy thing in his mouth.

'When you asked if I'd like to come to a small reception for the new US ambassador I thought we were going to a hotel with a couple of dozen people, not to the House of Commons itself.'

Jim glanced around. 'Yes, I suppose St Stephen's Hall is quite impressive.'

'And I wish I'd borrowed Sally's black cocktail dress,' Millie said.

She'd collected the coupons from three editions of *Woman and Home* to get the pattern, which it claimed was the latest style. But alongside women wearing the sleek satin gowns sweeping over the tiles nearby, Millie knew that her homemade pink taffeta dress didn't really pass muster.

'Don't be silly,' Jim said reassuringly. 'You look perfect.'

'And all the jewellery!' Millie replied, fingering the small cross at her throat.

'I'll tell you a secret, shall I?' Jim looked around conspiratorially. 'Most of it's paste.'

Millie laughed.

'That's better. Now bottoms up, and I'll get us another,' he said scanning the room over her head as he raised his hand.

A waiter appeared from nowhere and refilled their glasses.

'But who are all these people?' asked Millie.

'Members of the government mostly, you know. Under-secretaries of state, junior ministers, and senior civil servants and their wives.'

'But what about the rest? Like the man wearing a sash over there, or the soldier with all those medals across his chest next to the pot plant?' Millie asked.

'The Raj of Khommarn's ambassador Mr Juppa, and the exiled Prince Rudolf of Albania,' Jim replied.

Something red flashed in the corner of Millie's eyes and she turned. She wasn't the only one. Most of the men in the room had done the same.

In the doorway stood a slender woman wearing a figure-hugging flame-red full-length evening dress, long black satin gloves and a cool smile on her crimson lips. Her ash-blonde hair swept up into a high knot emphasised her long neck. And clearly none of the diamonds sparkling around her throat or hanging from her ears were paste. She stood for a moment to allow the room to appreciate her fully and then, taking a glass from one of the three waiters who had rushed to her side, glided impressively into the room.

'And that is the Countessa of Casiciano,' Jim said. 'Wife of the Argentinian Ambassador.'

'She looks more like a film star than a diplomat's wife,' Millie said, wondering how she was able to walk in such a tight skirt.

A wry smile lifted Jim's lips. 'That's probably because she was an actress when she caught the Count's eyes.'

The Countessa's gaze swept lazily around the room and alighted for the briefest of moments on Jim and Millie as she passed.

The buzz of conversation started up again.

'I want you to meet a few people,' Jim said, taking Millie's elbow and guiding her through the crowds.

From time to time as Millie chatted to ministers' wives, civil servants and cultural attaches, she caught sight of the Countessa holding court with various expensively dressed men who seemed to hang on her every word. She would stub out a cigarette held in her long ivory holder only to be offered another immediately, and no sooner had she finished one glass of wine than another appeared. She laughed elegantly and swayed like a reed in a summer breeze as her half-dozen admirers vied for her attention.

After half an hour of introductions and small-talk with a variety of people eager to speak with Jim, Millie and he reached the other end of the hall.

Something caught Jim's eye. 'Drat!'

'What's the matter?'

'I've just spotted Don Weatherfield,' Jim replied. 'He's a big cheese in the party and I need to keep in with him if I want to be adopted as the prospective candidate for Leytonstone and Wanstead.'

'Well, go and schmooze him then,' Millie replied. 'I don't mind.'

'Are you sure?'

'Of course,' Millie replied. 'I'm quite capable of being left alone for a few moments. I'll probably get myself some more snacks.'

'All right.' Jim grinned. 'As long as you promise not to be swept off your feet by some exiled duke or rich sheik while I'm gone.'

Millie giggled. 'Promise.'

'Meet me by Mr Pitt in fifteen minutes,' he said, indicating the marble statue of the statesman on the other side of the hall.

Jim winked and strode off.

Feeling a little self-conscious, Millie decided instead that as she didn't have the chance to wander around the Houses of Parliament every day she might as well make the most of it. Leaving her empty glass on a side table, she headed for the door. As Millie drew near to the bevy of men gathered around the glamorous woman in a red dress, the Countessa turned and regarded Millie steadily as she walked past.

Finding herself back in the corridor Millie wandered along looking at the larger than life portraits of the great and the good whose names she could only vaguely remember from Miss Drake's history lessons. She stopped in front of a very stern looking Victorian gentleman with great bushy side whiskers who was posed holding firmly on to his jacket lapels.

'That's a Landseer,' said a cultured voice behind her.

Millie turned to see the man in a dark suit with

a red sash across it standing behind her. He regarded her with the same condescending expression as many of the portraits.

Millie studied the picture again. 'I think I prefer his animal portraits,' she announced.

The man raised a grizzled eyebrow in surprise.

'I went to his exhibition of Highland works in the National Gallery a few years back,' Millie replied, feeling the dull ache that memories of happy times she had spent with Alex always induced.

Not wanting to stir more painful recollections, Millie turned from the artwork and headed for one of the ante-chambers running off the main hall in the hope that this would bring her back to the main party.

She turned the brass handle and the door opened on well-oiled hinges without a sound.

Millie slipped into a small side room lined with tall bookcases. There were a dozen or so people standing around between the old leather armchairs and side tables. Millie was just about to close the door when something scarlet flickered across her vision. She looked across and her heart lurched. Tucked in behind a bust on a plinth were Jim and the Countessa.

A knot of misery twisted in Millie's stomach as she remembered that Jim had once told her that he preferred blondes – and they didn't come much blonder that the woman currently very close to his side.

The Countessa was standing with her hips thrust provocatively towards Jim with an expression of invitation on her face. She arched her neck and her painted lips curled into a seductive smile. She gave a throaty laugh and said something. Jim shook his head and stepped back.

A sulky look flitted across the Countessa's beautiful face, but then her languid expression returned. She moved forward and with a sinuous movement, ran her hand up Jim's arm. He shrugged her off, side-stepped and tried to pass her, but she blocked his way.

Jim looked impassively down at her and his mouth pulled into a hard line.

A flush coloured the Countessa's throat and for one moment Millie thought she was going to stamp her foot. But instead she gave him a withering look and, with her silk gown swishing around her legs, swept out of the room.

An amused smile played across Jim's lips as he watched her go, then he threw back the last of his drink and walked back into the main hall.

Millie waited for a couple of seconds and then slipped out the way she'd come. Using the main door this time, she returned to the hall.

Millie cast her gaze around the hall. The Countessa was standing at the far end of the room waving a glass of champagne around in one hand and talking excitedly, apparently to the delight of her entourage.

Then Millie saw Jim was standing where he said he would be, by the statue of William Pitt. He spotted her and smiled warmly.

A feeling of happiness rose up in Millie. She smiled back and, with a slight spring in her step, made her way towards him.

'There you are, sweetheart,' Jim said as she reached him. 'I thought you'd got lost.'

'Sorry. I took a wrong turn from the ladies.'

'Never mind.' Jim slipped his arm around Millie's waist and drew her close. 'And are you enjoying yourself?'

Over Jim's shoulder she caught a glimpse of the Countessa. Millie's eyes locked with those of the woman in red for a moment, and then she looked back at Jim with a bright smile.

'Yes, I'm having a wonderful evening.'

Chapter Thirty One

Millie dropped the flannel into the enamel bowl, picked up the towel and dabbed it softly along Mrs Mundey's forearm.

For someone with cancer clogging up both lungs, the old woman had remained surprisingly stable since Millie first visited her three months ago. However, over the past couple of weeks she had started to deteriorate and had gone from three visits a week to one a day.

Millie placed Mrs Mundey's wasted arm by her side, and she repositioned the bath towel draped over her patient to expose the other arm. Retrieving the flannel from the soapy water, Millie gently washed and dried her patient's other arm, combed her hair and took her dentures from the pot on the side table and, after brushing them, popped them tenderly into her mouth.

'That's lovely Sister,' Mrs Mundey said, pushing her false teeth into place with her tongue. 'I don't know how I would have managed without you and the other angels from Munroe House looking after me all these weeks.'

Millie smiled politely. 'Before I move you to put on your fresh night clothes, do you want me to give you another dose of medicine?'

Mrs Mundey nodded. 'Thank you, sister,' she wheezed.

Millie's knees clicked as she stood up. She collected the bottle of morphine and spoon from the mantelshelf and returned to her patient. She held a generous spoonful to her colourless lips.

Mrs Mundey gulped it down and then relaxed back. Her hand stretched out from under her covering towel and groped on the side table.

'And can you let me have me fags?' she asked in a rasping voice.

Millie picked up the packet of Senior Service and handed them to her patient. With shaking hands Mrs Mundey took out a cigarette. Millie flipped open the lighter cap, rolled the flint and then held out the flame. The old woman took a long inward breath and closed her eyes.

The door opened and Joy came in. 'Do you feel a bit better after your wash, Mother?'

'What do you care?' Mrs Mundey said. 'I know you can't wait until I'm dead.'

'You know that's not true,' Joy replied mildly.

'Don't lie,' rasped Mrs Mundey. 'You can't wait until I'm six feet under so you can find yourself some other worthless darkie to take up with.'

Millie averted her eyes and made a play of putting her patient's things in order.

'I'll go and get supper soon. Do you want a bit of haddock if the fishmonger has any?' Joy asked pleasantly.

Mrs Mundey's flint-like eyes hardened further. 'It'd have to be some coon 'cause no respectable man would look at you now,' she sneered. 'To think that my own daughter let one of those nigger boys put his hands all over her makes me feel—'

'I can hear Ginnie,' Joy cut in. She walked to the door and opened it.

534

Mrs Mundey slumped back and lay unmoving while Millie straightened the bedclothes.

'Nurse Byrne will wash you tomorrow,' Millie said, picking up the bowl of soapy water from the side table.

'Thank you, Sister,' Mrs Mundey whispered, without opening her eyes.

Millie left the room.

As she entered the kitchen at the back of the house, Joy was talking to Ginnie. The toddler was sitting in the highchair at one end of the scrubbed kitchen table, chewing on a Bickiepeg teething biscuit attached to her cardigan by a pink ribbon. As Millie walked in, the baby offered it to her and smiled.

'No thank you, Ginnie,' Millie laughed. 'You eat it.'

The toddler stuck the peg-shaped biscuit back in her mouth and Millie went over to the sink.

'She's such a pretty baby,' Millie said, emptying the bowl into the sink.

Joy's expression softened. 'I think so,' she said, twisting one of her daughter's springy black curls in her finger. 'She was dancing along with the radio and bobbing to the rhythm. She gets more and more like her dad every day.'

Millie smiled politely and stared blindly out of the scullery window.

'I know what you're thinking, Sister,' said Joy. 'You're thinking I'm a fool like all the other girls left with a baby.'

Millie turned and looked at her. 'I can't say that thought hasn't crossed my mind, Joy. But just now I'm actually thinking, how in God's name do you put up with it?'

'My mother?'

'How on earth can you suffer all the abuse and still be so, so ... pleasant?' asked Millie.

'Because,' Joy tickled Ginnie under the chin and the child giggled, 'I have this little poppet, and when Marvin returns I have my whole life in front of me. And what has my mother got to look forward to?'

'Even so.'

'And when all's said and done,' continued Joy. 'She's my mum and it's my job to look after her. After all, Sister, I'm only doing what you did for your mum when she was sick.'

Jim brought his new MG Midget Roadster to a halt just in front of the house, sending chips of gravel shooting out in different directions. He yanked on the brake and switched off the engine.

'Here we are,' he said, beaming like a schoolboy. 'The ancestral ruin.'

Millie looked up at the impressive red-brick house. Her heart sank.

Tollshunt Manor wasn't actually very old, probably early Victorian at most, but with its well-proportioned wings and the white stone windows fringed with lilac wisteria, it was exceedingly grand.

The long drive to the front door had already alerted Millie to the fact that Jim's home was set in the midst of acres of rolling Essex countryside, but when they turned though the wrought-iron gates and into the enclosed area at the front of the house she seriously questioned if meeting

Jim's family for the first time on their own turf was such a good idea.

Jim unfolded himself from his seat and came around to her side of the car. 'Come on,' he said, opening her door. 'I can't wait for you to meet Mother.'

Millie climbed out. 'Do I look all right?' she said, straightening her skirt, which she felt now looked more like a rag than a garment after the two-and-a-half-hour drive from Stepney.

Jim gave her a peck on the cheek. 'Perfect.'

He took her hand and led her up the steps to the front door. He pulled on a brass stopper to the right of the door and a bell echoed inside. After a few moments the door was opened.

An old man wearing a baggy charcoal suit and weary expression opened the door. The folds of his aged brow lifted a notch when he saw Jim.

'Master James,' he said, his jaw wobbling back and forth as he spoke. 'What a pleasure to see you.'

'And you, Paget,' Jim replied, striding in and taking Millie with him. 'This is Miss Sullivan, our guest for the weekend.'

'Good afternoon, Miss,' said the butler. 'Is the luggage in the car, sir?'

'Yes, but I'll fetch it in a while.' Jim grinned at the old retainer.

'Very good sir,' replied Paget. He closed the door. 'Madam's in the drawing room.'

'James, darling, you're here!' a posh female voice exclaimed.

Millie turned. In the doorway opposite the sweeping stairs stood a willowy woman, with

537

short-cropped white-grey hair who was wearing an expensively tailored amethyst-coloured suit Ruby would give her eye-teeth, and her right arm, to own.

'Mummy,' called Jim, racing towards her and kissing the offered cheek. He hooked his arm in hers. 'And this is Amelia Sullivan. Millie to her friends.'

A charming smile very like Jim's lifted his mother's face. 'Miss Sullivan, how delightful,' she said, gliding over to Millie and offering a hand.

'Nice to meet you too,' Millie replied.

As the flat tones of her London twang echoed around the cavernous hallway, Jim's mother blanched ever so slightly before her genial expression returned.

'Please come into the sitting room.' She glanced at the butler. 'Take Miss Sullivan's luggage to the yellow room, Paget.'

'I've told him I'll take the luggage upstairs later,' said Jim, looking challengingly at his mother.

For a moment she looked as if she would argue the point but then waved a finely boned hand dismissively. 'Very well, but make sure you tell Judy we want tea immediately, Paget.'

'Very good, madam,' he said, shuffling away and disappearing down the stairs at the far end of the hall.

Jim's mother led them into a light, airy room tastefully decorated in pale floral wallpaper. There were deeply folded drapes at the window, which looked out on to the manicured garden, and delicate porcelain figurines dotted around the table and cabinets.

'I suppose all that nonsense about not letting Paget fetch the luggage is part of this new Socialist Utopia you and your friends are trying to build, James,' his mother said when the door closed.

'We're not trying, Mother. We are,' Jim replied.

Lady Tollshunt gave her son a sweet smile. 'Well, I'm sure that when all the old loyal servants like Paget are out of a job, they'll be very grateful to you for driving them to the workhouse.'

'As I've told you repeatedly, Mother, under Labour's welfare state no old person need fear poverty in their declining years,' Jim replied.

'If you say so, James.' She turned to Millie. 'Please make yourself comfortable, Miss Sullivan.'

'Thank you,' said Millie, tucking her skirt underneath her and sinking into the soft upholstery of the huge sofa. 'And please call me Millie.'

'Very well, Millie,' said Lady Tollshunt, sitting opposite her. 'James tells me you're a district nurse in East London, Millie, but tell me where it is you actually work?'

'Down by the London docks,' Millie replied, as Jim sat down next to her. 'I work in Munroe House.' And as the tea arrived and was drunk, she told Jim's mother about her work as a district nurse.

'How absolutely fascinating,' Lady Tollshunt said when Millie had finished. 'I'm so pleased James has brought you to visit us this weekend, as it means you can come to the church summer fair tomorrow.'

'That sounds fun,' said Millie.

Lady Tollshunt took the last sip of her tea and

put her cup and saucer back on the tray. 'I'm sure you must want to freshen up after such a long journey. Paget will get Judy to show you to the yellow room.'

She stared benignly at Millie.

Jim took Millie's hand. 'I'll meet you on the terrace in an hour,' he said, squeezing her hand.

'Of course.' Millie finished her tea and returned it to the tray.

She stood up and walked to the door. After an hour of being scrutinised by Jim's mother, Millie was quite glad to escape, but as she closed the door she heard Lady Tollshunt's clipped tones ask her son. 'Sullivan is an Irish name, isn't it, James?'

Millie wrote her name and '234' on a small square of paper and popped it into the tin.

'What number did you put, Millie?' James asked, his pencil poised over his own ticket.

'I'm not telling,' Millie laughed. 'It's for you to guess how many buttons there are.'

Jim gave her a pretend scowl and his eyes returned to his task.

They were standing in the St Laurence's rectory garden surrounded by stalls of all kinds, from bric-a-brac to homemade cakes. The whole village had turned out for the main summer event, and children with balloons and toffee apples dashed between bent-backed pensioners shuffling across the lawn.

The village of Tollshunt nestled in the lush Essex countryside as it had for a thousand years. The high street was a mismatch of low-slung

Tudor shops with dark vertical beams with well-proportioned Georgian town houses and square Victorian offices. The rectory itself was tucked away behind the Medieval church, as if hiding from its patron and benefactor, the baron, who lived in Tollshunt Hall at the top end of the village.

'Right, that's it, Mrs Gurney,' Jim said, flourishing his piece of paper. 'I have made my choice, based on scientific analysis, the laws of probability and my own gut instinct. I have concluded that there are three hundred and nineteen buttons in that receptacle.' He pointed at the sweet jar filled to the brim with buttons of all shapes and sizes. 'And as a freeborn Englishman I shall not be moved from my decision.'

'Master James, you always were one for fancy talking,' the woman behind the trellis table giggled. 'No wonder you've a mind to take up that politicking lark.'

Millie laughed, and Jim slipped his arm around her as they strolled on to the next stall.

'Are you enjoying yourself, sweetheart?' he asked, looking down at her lovingly.

Millie nodded. She was certainly enjoying his attention. 'It's lovely, just as I've always imagined a village fête to be. And Tollshunt is so pretty, just like the lid of a chocolate box.'

'Yes it is,' Jim replied.

He guided her out of the blazing July sunlight and into the cool shade of the refreshment tent. As they entered, the woman manning the tea and cake table curtsied to him.

'Although I do find all this deference a little

541

hard to take,' Jim said, acknowledging the ladies of the village with a benevolent smile. 'Let's get ourselves a cuppa.'

'Good afternoon, Mrs Kripps,' Jim said as they stopped in front of the red-faced woman in charge of the tea urn.

'Good afternoon, Master James,' Mrs Kripps responded, listing heavily to the right as she attempted to genuflect. 'I take it you want a nice cup of tea for you and your young lady,' she said, looking bashfully at him.

'That would be lovely,' Millie replied.

The woman handed her a cup of tea and then looked at Jim. 'I see going up to London ain't changed you none, 'cos you always did like to have the prettiest girl around and about on your arm.'

Millie blushed and stirred her tea.

Jim took his cup and turned to Millie. 'I think the band's just about to strike up and so shall we take our tea outside?'

He held the tent flap aside. Millie walked back into the afternoon sunlight.

Jim followed. 'There's a space on the bench under the elm tree. Let's–'

'Hello, Master James,' a woman's voice said from behind them.

Jim and Millie turned towards a young woman in her early twenties wearing a flowery cream and apricot dress. Her rich, chestnut-coloured hair was swept back and rested in rounded curls on her shoulders. Other than dark pink lipstick, she wore no make-up and although the warm colour of her hair was echoed in her hazel eyes, as they

542

looked up at Jim they were cool.

'Beth,' Jim said, looking a tad uneasy, 'I thought you moved to Whitehedge's Chase.'

'I did, but Tom, my husband, 'e brought me over so I could see my ma and come to the fête,' she said. 'I wondered if you might be here.' Her eyes flickered over Millie.

'This is Miss Sullivan,' said Jim. 'She's come up from London to spend the weekend with the family.'

'Hello,' said Millie smiling at her. 'You're so lucky to come from such a beautiful part of the country. Have your family been here long?'

'Aye, we Bassetts have been in Tollshunt for nigh on three centuries. Got one in the graveyard goes back to 1720.'

'How amazing,' said Millie.

'We ain't nothing special, mind. Just field workers mostly, 'cept for some of us, like me, who worked up at the big house,' she said, as her gaze returned to Jim.

Jim stretched his neck out of his collar. 'Well, it's jolly nice to see you, Beth.'

'Joe! Come here, boy,' Beth called.

A little lad untangled himself from half-a-dozen others swinging on a low branch and dashed over.

'This is my Joe,' she said, resting her hand lightly on her son's shoulder. 'You've never seen him, have you, Master James?'

'No,' Jim replied flatly.

Millie crouched down. 'Hello, Joe,' she said smiling at the boy. 'And how old are you?'

'Four,' the boy replied, his clear blue eyes regarding Millie in wonder.

'Well, your mum must feed you very well because you're a big strong boy for four years old,' she said.

Beth's reserved expression softened. 'Our Joe's tall for his age, but then he takes after his father.' Her eyes flickered briefly on to Jim.

Millie stood up.

'Well, it's good to see you again, Beth,' Jim said. 'And to meet this little chap.' He ruffled Joe's hair awkwardly.

Beth hugged the boy to her leg fiercely. 'He's bright, too, and quick with his letters. I hope as how when he's grown I might get him into some good school like...' She stopped and stared in horror at a point just over Millie's shoulder for a second, then bobbed a hurried curtsey.

'Good afternoon, Ma'am,' Beth said, lowering her eyes to the ground.

Jim's mother, resplendent in a pale apricot chiffon gown and feathered hat wider than her shoulders, swept into view.

'And to you, Mrs Scarrop,' she said, in an imperious tone. 'I believe I saw your mother by the nearly new stall.'

'Yes, Ma'am. I'll go and find her.' Beth grabbed Joe's hand and dashed off.

Lady Tollshunt contemplated her departure. 'Is that her boy?'

'Yes,' Jim replied.

'He's called Joe,' Millie said, watching the mother and child walking across the lawn.

'Indeed.' Lady Tollshunt turned to her son. 'I'm afraid there's been a disaster. Your father has had a run-in with the vicar about last Sunday's sermon, and now he's taken his gun and gone to shoot something.'

'Not the vicar, I hope,' quipped Millie.

Lady Tollshunt's glacial stare swept over Millie, and returned to Jim. 'But it means you'll have to judge the flowers and vegetables, James.'

Dread transfixed Jim's face. 'The flowers I don't mind but, for the love of God, not the vegetables!'

'I'm sorry, James. It has to be done,' his mother replied in a tone reminiscent of a particularly terrifying matron Millie had once known. 'It starts in ten minutes, so you'd better get over to the tent.' She turned to stroll off but then turned back. 'Oh, and one more thing.' She smiled sweetly at them both. 'Lionel telephoned earlier and will be joining us for dinner.'

'Thank you,' said Millie, as the maid, a fresh-faced girl in her mid-teens, set a plate of queen's pudding and pale custard in front of her.

The maid stepped back and Millie glanced at Jim sitting beside her. He gave her a reassuring smile, which did nothing to alleviate her terror. She adjusted the napkin on her lap and picked up her spoon, then glanced around at Jim's family.

Lord Tollshunt, a bluff, tweed-wearing man who stomped around the house muttering, was single-mindedly tucking into his pudding at the head of the table, while his wife pushed morsels of hers around with her spoon at the other. Millie and Jim sat on his father's left opposite Jim's brother Lionel, who'd arrived with a squeal of brakes and shrieks of maternal delight just after five.

There was no doubting that Jim and Lionel were brothers and, given that there was only eleven months between them, if she had been told they were twins Millie wouldn't have queried it. And it wasn't just their blond hair and startlingly blue eyes that marked them as siblings, but their self-assured gestures and mannerisms showed their common parentage at every opportunity.

Sensing her scrutiny, Lionel looked up.

'Is the pudding to your liking, Miss Sullivan?' he asked, regarding her with the same cynical amusement he'd adopted since they were introduced.

'Yes,' Millie replied. 'It's delicious. I wouldn't mind the recipe.'

Lionel looked artlessly at her. 'I'm sure Cook will be happy to let you have a copy, don't you think, Mummy?'

Lady Tollshunt smiled noncommittally.

Jim's brother turned his attention back to Millie. 'That's a very pretty dress.'

'Thank you,' said Millie. 'I made it for my friend's wedding at Easter.'

Lionel looked amazed. 'That's astonishing. You cook *and* sew.'

Millie gave him a measured look. 'And me mum taught me to knit, too.'

'Touché, Miss Sullivan.' Lionel turned his languid eyes toward his sibling. 'And what have you been up to, brother dear?'

'Nothing you'd have the slightest interest in,' Jim said feistily.

Lionel looked aggrieved. 'Come, come, James,

that's a little harsh. Haven't I always taken a keen interest in whatever you've been up to?'

'Only so you could interfere,' Jim replied.

'Well, if you're talking about this Socialist, workers-throw-off-your-chains nonsense, then be assured I wouldn't touch it with a barge pole.' Lionel's eyes ran over Millie again. 'But if you're taking about other activities, that's quite a different matter.'

'Take no notice of my brother, Millie,' Jim said, smiling at her. 'He can mock all he likes, but even Lionel and his Tory cronies are just running scared in the wave of radical changes sweeping the country.'

'Radical changes?' Lionel scoffed. 'If you mean confiscating property, assets and land from their rightful owners, then I wish I could. Nationalisation is just another name for thievery.'

Lord Tollshunt grunted as his contribution to the conversation and then poked his spoon into his bowl again.

'It's the factory and mine owners, along with the bankers, who are the real thieves,' Jim replied, jabbing his finger at his brother. 'Robbing the honest working man of this country of the fruits of his labours.'

'James!' Lady Tollshunt said, frostily. 'You know that I will not have politics discussed at the table.'

'But he started it,' Jim said, glaring across the table at his brother.

His mother waved his words aside. 'I've told you before, it upsets your father's digestion,' she said, looking up the table at her husband energetically scraping the last of his pudding out of

547

the bowl.

Jim pressed his lips together and frowned furiously at his brother, who countered it with a smug smile.

Millie popped the last mouthful of her dessert in her mouth and rested her spoon on the side plate. 'You have a lovely house, Lady Tollshunt.'

'Thank you, Millie,' Jim's mother replied. 'Are you comfortable in the yellow room?'

'Yes, very much. I have a beautiful view of the rose garden.'

Jim threw his napkin down beside his empty plate. 'So how have you been amusing yourself since I last saw you, Lionel?' he asked. 'Drinking, gambling and idling away your time at the Carlton Club as usual, I expect,' Jim said before Lionel had a chance to answer.

'Pretty much,' replied Lionel, quite unabashed. 'Although I saw Edwina Winkworth at the theatre last week. She asked after you and seemed surprised that you were in London and hadn't looked her up, what with you and her being such close chums at one time.' Lionel's eyes slid slyly back to Millie. 'Of course, having met your plucky little Cockney, I can understand you've been very busy.'

'I'm warning you, Lionel,' Jim said in a threatening tone.

Lionel smiled indolently. 'Is she helping you to get your accent right for when you stand on your soapbox and address the masses, James? Is she your Cockney Professor Higgins in a sort of Marxist version of *Pygmalion*?

Jim jumped to his feet. 'Leave Millie out of this,'

he barked at his brother.

Lionel put his index finger on his lower lip and his eyes rolled upwards. 'Didn't we once have a maid called Millie, Mummy? Or perhaps I should ask my dear brother?'

'If you'd excuse me,' said Millie, rising to her feet. 'I think I need a bit of air.'

Letting her napkin fall to the floor, she hurried from the room, down the corridor and out into the conservatory. She tucked herself behind a large fern in the corner and rested her forehead on the cool glass and took a deep breath. She heard a door slam and footsteps sound on the hall tiles. She turned to see Jim standing in the doorway, scanning the dark foliage anxiously.

'Millie, where are you?'

'Here,' she said, moving a long leaf aside.

'I'm so sorry,' he said, crossing the floor in three strides.

He tried to take her in his arms but Millie backed away. 'I don't know why I let you talk me into coming here this weekend,' she said with feeling.

Jim slammed his hand against the window frame. 'That bloody brother of mine gets more insufferable every time I see him. He's been the same since we were in the nursery. I wanted a pony, so then he wanted one, and because he was the eldest Mummy got one for him while I had to wait. I wanted a model aeroplane and so he wanted one too, and when Nanny brought us down on Christmas morning so we could open our presents he'd got a beautiful Sopwith Cuckoo biplane, complete with every detail, while I had to make do with a tin motor car. He's lucky that tonight I didn't drag him across the table.' Jim reached for her again and this time Millie let him gather her into his arms. 'Take no notice of Lionel as he's just trying to rile me and cause an argument,' Jim said, holding her close and kissing her forehead. 'You mustn't let him upset you.'

Millie slipped her arms around him and rested her head on his chest. 'But it's not just your brother, Jim. It's everything. My clothes are homemade, I don't know the difference between a butter knife and a fruit knife, and every time I open my mouth your mother cringes.'

'Mother's just a bit old-fashioned, that's all, but she was telling me how she admires the work you're doing for the less fortunate,' Jim said as he hooked his finger under Millie's chin and lifted her head. 'And I don't actually care what my family or anyone else thinks of you. I think you're just perfect.'

An emotion moved into in his eyes that sent a warm feeling pulsing through her. 'In fact, Millie, I think you're so perfect for me that there's something I want to say.' Jim took her hand and knelt down. 'Millie Sullivan, will you marry me?'

An image of Alex in the same attitude flashed into Millie's mind, opening once again the barely healed scar of his loss. 'Jim.' She didn't know what else to say.

'I know it's sudden, darling,' he said, reaching inside his jacket and pulling out a small box. 'But I've never felt like this about anyone.' He opened the box. 'It was my grandmother's.'

Millie stared down at the oval emerald flanked

by two sparkling diamonds. 'It's beautiful.'

'Let me put it on your finger.' Jim pulled the ring out of its mount.

Millie withdrew her hand before he could go further. 'After Lionel, your mum and everything this weekend, Jim, I'm a little unsure. Will you give me some time?'

'Of course, my sweetheart.' Jim pressed his lips on to her hand. 'I can't blame you for hesitating. But just because my family are members of the inbred, outdated ruling-class, don't hold that against me, please.'

Chapter Thirty-Two

Connie's pretty face formed itself into a sympathetic expression. 'My goodness, the whole weekend sounds an absolute nightmare.'

'It was. And worse,' Millie replied, taking another large gulp of tea.

She was propped up against the footboard of her friend's bed with her shoes kicked off, opposite Connie, who was resting back against the headboard. They were in Connie's third-floor room in Fry House.

Like Munroe House, the Spitalfields nurses' home had once been a family house, but it was at least a century older. While the rooms at Munroe House had echoed to the sound of a Victorian family's laughter, number eighteen Dorset Street had been a doss house in one of the most squalid streets in Spitalfields. In daylight you could still see the faint inscription 'Moody's Common Lodging House' painted over the main entrance. It had been leased to the Association at a peppercorn rent by the Sir John Cass Foundation Trust and had been restored to some of its former glory. But with winding staircases and dark corners, it wasn't a house anyone could feel comfortable in if they believed in ghosts. Thankfully, Connie had no time for such nonsense and had, with the help of her embroidered cushions, family photos and various china knick-knacks, turned her east-facing room that had once housed a silk loom into a snug retreat.

'I'm surprised Jim didn't give his brother a black eye for talking to you like that,' Connie said indignantly.

'He nearly did over Sunday dinner when Lionel started on about Atlee and his cabinet being like the Nazis,' said Millie. 'Lionel was only doing it to goad Jim, something he seems to have been perfecting since they were in the nursery together.'

'Jim's brother sounds like a nasty piece of work,' Connie said. 'No wonder you had such a horrible time of it.'

'To be fair, we had a nice evening on Friday down at the Shepherd and Dog in the village. I tell you, Connie, this pub was so old even I had to duck to get through the door. And I thought my sides would split listening to the locals tell endless stories about how "Master James" got into one scrape or another. And the church fair was great fun too, although Jim nearly started the Third World War by awarding Best Cabbage in Show to some old boy from a neighbouring village.' Millie laughed. 'It's like stepping fifty years back in time. Everyone knows everyone else, and they're all related to each other.'

'A bit like Wapping then,' said Connie.

'It is, except thankfully we haven't got to bow and scrape to someone like Jim's mother as we go about our business,' said Millie. 'And it must be very odd to walk past your great-great-great grandfather's grave when you go to the Sunday service.'

'It still sounds idyllic, with its rolling hills and quaint cottages,' said Connie. 'And a far cry from the brothels and sweatshops we have for neighbours.'

'It is.' Millie smiled. 'But it's not something I'm sure I'll easily fit into.'

Connie scoffed. 'Why do you have to...' her eyes flew open. 'Oh, Millie – he never!'

Millie nodded.

'Oh! Congratulations,' her friend squealed, bouncing up the bed to hug her. 'I'm so pleased for you.'

'I didn't say yes.'

Connie was flabbergasted. 'You never turned him down, did you?'

'I said I needed to think about it,' Millie replied.

Connie looked puzzled. 'But I thought you loved Jim.'

Millie untangled herself from her friend's embrace. 'He's a lovely man, so kind, generous and so considerate. But it's not as simple as that. There are things I need to take into account before I accept.'

'Like what?'

'Well, for a start, his family thinks I'm a grubby little commoner who can't speak properly,' explained Millie. 'Added to which, now that I've come to an amicable working relationship with Miss Dutton, things are settling down at Munroe House and I'm not sure I want to do anything to upset that. Plus me and Mum have only just got the house sorted out, and so I'm thinking it would be nice to catch my breath for a while.'

'It's Alex, isn't it?' Connie said astutely.

Millie let out a deep sigh. 'I know I should forget about Alex, but I just can't,' she said, feeling the familiar lump in her throat as she spoke his name. 'And although I do really care for Jim, and I think I might love him, it's just not in the same wild way that I loved Alex.'

Connie took her hand. 'You could no more compare Jim to Alex than chalk to cheese.'

'I know,' Millie hugged herself as memories of Alex's passionate embraces flashed into her mind. 'But I used to wake up thinking about Alex and drift off to sleep counting the hours until I could see him again. And I don't feel like that about Jim.'

Connie put on her displeased-matron's face. 'Look, Millie, Alex was your heady first love that burns your soul. But he's gone and is thousands of miles away.' Connie looked meaningfully into Millie's eyes. 'You have to forget Alex, like I've had to forget Charlie, and you need to look to the future. I think you know that. Don't you want a home of your own and a family?'

'You know I do,' replied Millie.

'Well then, if you accept Jim's proposal, you can have them, and with a man most of us would love to be married to,' Connie said, squeezing Millie's hand.

Millie bit her lip. 'Perhaps you're right, but then there's the other matter, you know, with me and Alex.'

'Jim's a good man and clearly he loves you, so I'm sure he'll be able to take that in his stride. After all, it was only Alex, and you *were* engaged to be married.' Connie laughed. 'And you can't tell me Jim hasn't had the odd fling or two.'

'Three or four or more, I shouldn't wonder,' replied Millie. 'But you know how men can be funny about such things. I couldn't bear it if he thought I was that sort of girl.'

'Don't be daft,' reassured Connie. 'People only have to look at you to know that you're not.' She squeezed Millie's hand. 'Don't throw away a chance of a home and family because of an impossible dream. And you can tell his snooty mother, boring father and idiot brother to stick it up their chimney if they don't like it. They will be lucky to have you as part of the family!'

Millie laughed. 'I'd like to see their faces if I did.'

There was a knock.

'Come in,' called Connie.

A young nurse with swept-back light-brown hair and freckles popped her head around the door. 'Sorry to disturb you, Connie, but it's Miss Sullivan I'm after.' She looked at Millie. 'I've just had a telephone call from Nurse Topping at Munroe House. There's been a fire in Stebbins House and she said you would want to know.'

With the vapour from the jars of Jeyes fluid and formaldehyde irritating her nose, Millie gazed down at Mickey Walters lying dead on the stark metal trolley in the London Hospital morgue. Millie only knew it was the lively six-year-old because the clipboard hanging from the crossbar had his name written across it. The charred, swollen face and singed hair made him look like a china doll that had been left too near the fire. He was totally unrecognisable. The staff on the children's ward had done their best to make his last offices as dignified as possible, but his spare frame was swamped by the sheet they'd wound around him, making him look all the more alone and vulnerable.

The door opened and Georgie Tugman, Alex's friend, walked in. Surprise registered on his face when he saw Millie, but he collected himself together and marched over, his size-ten boots echoing in the white-tiled room.

'Do you know the boy?' he asked, taking his policeman's helmet off respectfully as he stopped on the other side of the trolley.

'Yes, I've been visiting the family for a year and a half,' Millie replied bleakly, unable to take her eyes from Mickey's charred face. 'What happened?'

'As far as we can tell, the children were in the flat alone when a spark or cinder ignited some magazines on the floor. The whole place went up like a tinderbox, but this little chap,' Georgie's Adam's apple wobbled up and down a couple of times as he looked at the small corpse, 'was smart enough to slip the latch so the older two kids could get out, but he went back for the toddler. He was fetching her out when the gas cooker exploded.'

'Susie's dead, too?' cried Millie, thinking of the little girl she'd sung 'Ring-a-Roses' to only the week before.

Georgie shook his head. 'She's badly burnt as the boy had the presence of mind to shove her behind the upturned kitchen table and it shielded her from the worst. But he copped the lot. Poor little bugger didn't stand a chance, God rest him.'

'What about Mrs Walters?' Millie asked.

Georgie's expression hardened. 'We found her down the pub drinking with a bunch of bloody dagoes. She's sobering up now in the women's cell under Arbour Square and will be up before the Beak tomorrow. The Creeping Insect Department are prosecuting the case so I'm sure they'll want to talk to you about the family. Are you still at Munroe House?'

'You can get me there, although I'm living with my mother around the corner now,' Millie replied.

Georgie looked uncomfortable.

'I ought to go,' said Millie.

'Right you are,' said Georgie. 'I've got to hang around for the reporting doctor, and so I'll see you around. Probably at the inquest.' He looked at the dead child. 'Some people don't bloody well deserve to have kiddies.'

Millie reached out and tenderly smoothed the sheet tucked around Mickey's jaw, and then turned away.

'Bye, Georgie,' she said with a break in her voice, hurrying out.

Letting the door swing behind her, Millie took a deep breath to clear the choking smell of the mortuary out of her nose, then she started along the basement corridor towards the stairs.

'Millie!'

She turned to see Georgie striding after her.

He stopped in front of her and shifted his

weight from one foot to the other. 'Look, Millie, I want to say sorry for the way I treated you and your mum the last time we met.'

'That's all right – you were angry,' Millie replied.

'I was, but when Alex wrote and told me the whole story I knew I'd been in the wrong. Well, I'm sorry,' he said.

Millie stared at Georgie. 'You're in touch with Alex? Is he all right? I mean, you hear such dreadful goings-on – bombs and kidnapping. He's not been injured badly or anything?'

'He's had a couple of scrapes and had a piece of shrapnel lodge in his body armour, but he was fine and dandy when he wrote a week ago. He's got a couple of weeks in Cyprus at the end of the month and I'm flying over to see him,' Georgie said. 'I'm going again in December to be his best man.'

Something like a bass drum thumped in her head. Had Georgie said best man? Yes, he had!

'That's nice,' Millie said, her voice sounding to her as if it came from far away. She gathered her wits, and after a pause managed to force a smile. 'I really ought to go; I'm meeting someone.'

'Right you are,' Georgie said. 'And I'll see you in court.'

He turned and headed back to the mortuary.

Millie gripped the wooden banister worn smooth by decades of hands and very slowly climbed the stone stairs to the main part of the hospital. People brushed past her as she made her way in a daze towards the main exit. Stepping out into the fresh air, she walked under the neoclassical portico and on to the top of the marble steps.

'Millie!'

She stared blindly at the busy market on the other side of Whitechapel Road, before spotting a tall figure weaving his way through the stalls.

'Millie!' he shouted, waving as he dashed across the street and up the steps. 'I rang Munroe House and they told me where you were.'

'Jim! Oh Jim.' Millie threw herself at him, buried her face in his chest and sobbed helplessly.

'There you go, my love,' Jim said as he handed her a large gin and tonic. 'That should do the trick.'

Millie gave him a small grateful smile. 'Thank you, Jim,' she whispered, taking the drink in a shaky hand. 'I'm sorry,' she said, as she started crying again.

In fact, she hadn't actually stopped weeping since she'd run into his arms ten minutes before. They had planned to catch a taxi into the City for supper that night, but the best Jim could manage now was to guide her across the road into the Grave Maurice, the run-down pub opposite the hospital. The cloth-capped regulars had given them the once-over when they'd stumbled in, and then turned back to their pints.

'There, there,' Jim said, putting his glass down and slipping into the seat beside her. 'Your friend Eva said something about a fire?'

Millie told Jim what had happened to Mickey. 'He was such a bright little boy and so loving. I've been to the Welfare Department four times begging them to intervene, but they wouldn't.' She couldn't control her tears.

Jim's arms encircled her and he held her close, kissing her hair. Millie bawled until her ribs ached. He handed her a folded handkerchief and Millie wiped her eyes.

'I'm sorry,' she said, mustering a brave little smile from somewhere. 'Whatever must you think of me, weeping all over your jacket like that?'

He moved a damp curl from her forehead. 'I think you wouldn't be the Millie I love if you didn't shed a tear for a poor, neglected child.' Jim took her hand. 'I promised myself I wouldn't rush you, Millie, but now you're here with me like this, I just can't stop imagining us together in a little house with a garden and our own children playing in it.'

Yearning rose up in Millie too, and lodged in her throat. 'Oh, Jim,' she said, breathlessly.

He looked at her with tenderness darkening his blue eyes. 'Just say yes, sweetheart.'

Millie studied his eager face. Connie was right. She was risking throwing away the chance of happiness because of a ridiculously impossible dream.

She withdrew her hand. 'Before I do, Jim, I need to tell you something.'

He pulled a worried face. 'This sounds serious.'

Millie took a large gulp of her G & T. 'You know I was engaged before.'

'Yes, to that chap who shipped out to Palestine,' Jim said. 'What of it?'

'Well,' Millie twisted her fingers together. 'The thing is,' she took another mouthful of drink, 'we did what we really should have waited to do on our wedding night.'

Jim stared at her in surprise. 'You and Alex.'

'I don't want you to think I'm that sort of girl,' Millie said, 'because I'm not. We were to be married in a matter of months.'

'And he deserted you, the bastard,' Jim said angrily.

'It wasn't like that,' said Millie. 'But I'd understand if you now change your mind about wanting me as your wife.'

'Change my mind?' he said incredulously. 'Why would I do that?'

'Some men would,' Millie commented grimly.

'Well, I'm not some men,' said Jim. 'I stand by my word, not like that worthless rogue who skipped off once he'd got what he was after.'

'But–'

'You don't have to explain.' The expression in Jim's eyes changed. 'And I promise never to mention the matter again.' He smiled, and Millie's battered heart rallied. 'Now give me your answer.'

Millie shoved all her doubts aside. 'Yes.'

He grinned. 'Yes what?'

'Yes, I'll marry you,' Millie replied, smiling shyly up at him. Jim put his hand in his pocket and pulled out the small box. He opened it and took out the ring.

This time Millie let him slip it on her finger. She gazed down at the lovely emerald and diamond engagement ring.

'It's beautiful,' she said, twisting it to make it sparkle.

'And so are you.' Jim pulled her closer. 'I thought perhaps a Christmas wedding?'

Millie's eyes opened wide in surprise. 'That's

just four months away. I don't know how we're going to organise everything.'

'I know it will be hard work,' said Jim regretfully. 'But I want you to stand beside me as my wife when I'm adopted as the Labour Party's candidate for Leytonstone and Wanstead. And I'd rather have a quiet wedding. You know, just a few close friends and family.'

Millie nodded. 'Yes, without too much fuss.'

Jim pressed his lips on hers in a long passionate kiss that left her head reeling and pulse racing. A couple of the locals wolf-whistled, as Millie pushed him away.

Jim stood up and bowed. 'Thank you, gentlemen, and I'd like to announce that this young lady,' he indicated Millie with a flourish of his hand, 'has just consented to be my wife.'

The men at the bar raised their glasses and cheered. Jim acknowledged their good wishes and then resumed his seat.

'Drink up, and we can go and have dinner,' he said, downing the last of his beer.

Millie did just that and stood up. Jim tucked her hand in the crook of his arm and they walked out.

As he opened the door to the street he leaned towards her. 'I also thought we might take a spin out in the MG to Suffolk this weekend. There's a nice little hotel I know just outside Dedham.'

Millie sat on the edge of the chair and sipped her tea. 'I'm so sorry to hear about your mum, Joy,' said Millie. 'I've been off for the weekend or I would have come sooner.'

Joy gave a sad smile. 'Sister Topping said you were away, but I'm glad you popped in so I can say thank you for all you did for Mum. You know, getting the doctor in to give her the stronger medicine and letting me have the loan of the rubber cover for the mattress.'

'There's no need to thank me – it's my job,' said Millie.

'I know. But thanks all the same.'

Millie took another mouthful of tea. 'I understand it was quite quick in the end.'

Joy nodded. 'She was her old self up until teatime on Friday, you know, working her way through a pack of twenty and calling me all the time,' she glanced at her daughter stacking wooden bricks on the floor at her feet, 'but by the time I'd given Ginnie her tea at five, she was in a lot of pain. I did as you showed me and gave her two tablespoons of her medicine. By the time I came back down after putting Ginnie to bed she was asleep, and so I made myself a cocoa, put my feet up and listened to *Twenty Questions* on the wireless. I must have nodded off because I woke up to the radio fizzing at ten past eleven.' Joy's lower lip quivered a little. 'It's funny, but I knew as soon as I opened my eyes she'd gone.' She glanced slowly around the front room with its swept carpet, dusted surfaces and a vase of flowers on the coffee table instead of an over-spilling ashtray. 'The room seems so different without Mum.'

It was: the air was fresher, for a start, and Ginnie could play with her toys on the rug without fear of her grandmother taking a swipe at her with her stick or having to listen to her own mother being shouted at.

'People always feel that familiar places seem odd after a bereavement,' Millie said in a tactful tone. 'And it will take a bit of time for you to adjust. But at least you have Ginnie to cheer you up.'

She reached out and tickled the toddler under the chin. Ginnie tucked her neck in and giggled.

Joy looked fondly at her daughter and then tears sprang into her eyes.

'I'm so sorry, Sister,' she said, covering her face with her hands as she began sobbing.

Millie stood up and went over to her. 'Don't be silly, Joy, it's good to let it out and have a good cry. I know she wasn't always the cheeriest of people, but she was your mum, and it's only natural you should grieve for her.'

'It's not her I'm crying about, it's me. Me and Ginnie.' Joy pulled a crumpled handkerchief from her sleeve and blew her nose. 'The landlord wanted us out months ago so that he can rent the house out to half-a-dozen families, but even he, coldhearted old bugger that he is, wouldn't evict a dying woman. But now,' Joy started crying again, 'I can't work because I've got to look after Ginnie, and now Mum's gone Dad's pension will stop. I've got a little bit put by and that might help me keep a roof over me and Ginnie for a month or two. But if Marvin don't come back soon we'll be on the street by Christmas.' Joy looked forlornly at Millie. 'I wish there was some way I could get hold of Marvin because if he knew the trouble we were in he'd be on the next ship.'

Millie gave her a sympathetic smile. 'I'm sure

he would. But if he doesn't, maybe you could think of something else, like going to the council welfare officer for help.'

Joy shook her head. 'They'll take a look at this,' she held up her left hand devoid of a ring of any sort, 'and then try to make me give up Ginnie. That's what happened to Lou Wilson around the corner. They told her that if she really loved her baby, she'd sign him over to someone who'd give him a better chance in life. And like an idiot she did.' Joy scooped up her daughter from the floor and stood her on her lap. 'But I won't have to give up my little darling,' she said, pulling a happy face at her daughter, 'cause Daddy's going to be coming back for us any day now. Isn't he?'

Ginnie giggled. 'Yes Mummy. Daddy come home, Daddy come home!'

If she were being brutally honest, Millie thought Joy had seen the last of this GI when he shipped out. But as she watched mother and child laugh together, Millie hoped against hope that she was wrong.

Following Connie, Sally and Annie, Millie side-stepped along the row of chairs and sat down on the end one. Beattie, Eva, Pat and Joyce did the same in the row behind.

Although there was still ten minutes to go until the start of the meeting York Hall was already two-thirds full and people were now streaming in to take up the remaining seats.

The main hall, which was more used to seeing boxers slug it out than a political debate, had been spruced up by the local Labour party with posters proclaiming Labour for the Future and The Dawn of a Bright New Era for Workers. There were also tables set up at the back of the hall where earnest looking men and women enticed you to join the Women's Education Co-operative or the Friends of the Soviet Workers.

'Goodness,' said Connie as she tucked her skirt underneath her and sat down. 'I didn't think it would be so packed.'

'That's because everyone wants to hear about this new health service,' Sally said, making herself comfortable.

Someone tapped Millie's shoulder and she looked around.

'I bet your Jim's having kittens,' said Pat.

'I shouldn't think so,' Millie replied. 'He's used to addressing meetings, and he seems to enjoy speaking in public.'

'Well, I'd rather him than me on that platform, I can tell you,' added Joyce. 'There must be two hundred people in here, not to mention those in the gallery.'

Millie gave a wan smile and turned back to look at the stage at the end of the hall. The show curtains were drawn back and there was a long trestle set up with a dark brown chenille tablecloth covering it and three chairs behind. To the side was a large poster on an easel stating in bold red letters that the guest speaker was Mr Jim Smith. But what drew Millie's eye most was the podium with a microphone in front of it, from where in a few moments Jim would address the meeting.

The drapes at the side of the stage moved. Jim slipped out and stood on the corner of the stage.

He was sombrely dressed in a double-breasted navy suit that accentuated his broad shoulders. Millie's heart gave a little double step. She waved. Jim spotted her and hurried down. Millie stood up as he drew near.

'There you are, sweetheart,' he said.

'Hello,' Millie said, suddenly very flustered at the sight of him.

'And I'm always enchanted to meet your friends from Munroe House,' he said, casting his gaze over them.

Eva blushed to her roots, Sally giggled and Joyce stared in silence as she twiddled a lock of hair around her finger. All of them smiled approvingly up at him like a bunch of love-struck schoolgirls.

'And of course you remember my friend Connie, who lives in Fry House,' Millie concluded.

'Lovely to see you again, Connie,' Jim said.

'Likewise,' Connie replied.

'Is that a Distinguished Flying Cross?' Annie asked, pointing at the diagonal blue and white ribbon amongst the others pinned to his left lapel.

'Well, yes, but ... you know,' he shrugged artlessly.

Millie's friends gave a faint collective sigh.

Jim glanced at the stage and then back to Millie. 'I'd better go and get ready. Wish me luck?'

'Good luck.'

He slipped his arm around her and kissed her before hurrying back to the stage.

Feeling a little light-headed, Millie stared after him for a moment and then resumed her seat with feigned composure. She'd only just settled back in her place when Jim stepped out from the side of the stage following behind a rotund chap in a baggy grey suit, and Mrs Harper, who was dressed in a bottle-green gabardine suit with astrakhan trim. She and Jim took their seats.

As the noise in the hall abated the chap in the grey suit took his place on the podium.

'One two.' He tapped the microphone. 'Can you hear me at the back?'

'More's the pity,' some wag called from the rear of the hall.

The man in grey cleared his throat. 'Well then. Good evening everyone, and welcome to the meeting. There can't be many of you who don't know me, but for those who don't, I'm Sid Wheeler, chairman of the Stepney and Mile End Labour party. Now unfortunately, due to circumstances beyond his control, Mr Shottington, the president of our local district nursing association, can't be with us tonight–'

'Probably out boozing with his opera chums,' whispered Joyce from behind.

Connie half-covered her mouth with her hand. 'Or knocking back a whiskey at the nineteenth hole.'

'And so I'm extremely thankful to Mrs Harper, the chairwoman of the association, for stepping in at very short notice,' said Mr Wheeler, with a deferential nod in her direction. 'But our main speaker tonight is Mr Jim Smith.'

Jim uncrossed his legs and stood up.

'Comrade Smith,' continued the chairman, 'is not only the man who negotiated the recent settlement between our brothers in the Stevedore's Union and the Port of London management, but he is destined for great things in the Labour Party.'

'Great things, eh?' said Joyce.

'Well, I'd vote for him,' replied Annie in a dreamy voice.

'And he was one of Churchill's "few",' continued Mr Wheeler, 'who, with great bravery fought to keep the sky free from the Luftwaffe in 1940.'

There was a burst of applause. Jim acknowledged with a self-effacing smile.

'But tonight he's not here to tell us how he blasted the Jerries out of the sky, but to explain the new health service that we've all been reading about in the papers, and how it is going to work.'

'Well, let him get on with it then, Sid,' called a man from the gallery. 'Or they'll be calling last orders before we're done.'

There was a ripple of laugher.

Mr Wheeler shot an irritated look at the heckler and then turned to Jim. 'I give you Mr Smith!'

Everyone clapped as Jim stepped forward.

'Thank you, Mr Wheeler and Mrs Harper.' Jim glanced over the audience. 'Thank you all, too, for taking the trouble of coming out to listen to me after a long day at work. And,' he looked up at the gallery, 'I'll be needing a pint myself, after this, and so I'll be sure and finish before closing time.'

The audience laughed again and relaxed.

'Let me explain first how the new system will work.'

For the next twenty minutes Jim went through the various health and hospital boards that were to be set up to administer the new system, the reason why people needed to register for an NHS card, and how the health system wouldn't just cover nurses, doctors and hospitals, but also dentists, opticians and other services such as those that provided surgical appliances for special shoes or false limbs.

'And so you see,' Jim concluded, 'you will still be able to see your usual doctor as you do now; but his fee and any medicine he prescribes for you will be paid for by the government. You will no longer need to root around in your purses and wallets to pay for any health care you need.' Jim lifted his chin, showing his strong jaw line. 'Are there any questions?'

There was a bit of whispering and then a woman with an orange scarf covering her curlers stood up. 'What's going to happen to the nurses at Munroe House?'

'Perhaps Mrs Harper would like to answer that,' said Mr Wheeler, looking at the association's chairwoman.

Jim stood aside, and Mrs Harper took the microphone.

'The nurses will continue to work and live in Munroe House,' she explained. 'The committee decided that once we've handed over the day-to-day running of the nursing services to the health board, our association will become the Friends of Munroe House. Although we will no longer have to pay the nurses' wages or for the upkeep of Munroe House, as the Government will step in to pay these expenses, we plan to continue fund-raising activities to support the nursing service in the area. But for anyone being visited by a district nurse or a midwife, the only change they will notice is that the nurses will no longer assess the patient's ability to pay or collect money each week.'

'Alleluia,' said Connie.

'I'll second that,' agreed Millie. 'I've always hated taking money from patients. Made me feel like the tally man.'

The crowd muttered again and then another woman, dressed in a work-a-day wraparound overall, stood up.

'I'm not too sure about this free doctoring,' she said, folding her arms emphatically across her full bosom. 'I've always paid my way and I won't take no charity from no one.'

Several people around her nodded in agreement.

'This new health service don't sound much different from the poorhouse,' added another woman in an old checked coat and battered hat. 'Instead of the welfare inspectors picking over your business, it'll be some bloke from Whitehall. And how is Whitehall going to be able to foot the bill anyway?'

The hubbub in the hall started to rise, but Jim held up his hands and the room fell silent.

'I understand your fears, Madam,' he said, looking at the woman with a sincere expression on his face. 'But I can assure you that Labour's vision of the Welfare State, which will look after you from cradle to grave, is very different in every way from the old system, and it will be paid for through the income tax system. The National Health Service is for the ordinary working people of this—'

'You don't sound like no ordinary worker to me, chum,' shouted out a chap in a loud suit who was lounging against a pillar at the back.

'I can't deny it,' Jim replied in his well-modulated tones, looking around candidly. 'In truth I've never known a day of want in my whole life. In fact, I might as well tell you that my full name is the Honourable James Woodville Smith, although I never mention it because when I look into the faces of the men and women such as yourselves whose honest toil built this country, I'm deeply ashamed as I am in your shadow.' Jim gripped the podium with sincerity. 'And that's why I'm determined to do everything I can to improve the plight of the ordinary working people of this great country.'

'Your fiancé's got a very nice way of putting things,' whispered Eva in Millie's right ear. 'He's got strong hands, too.'

Millie's eyes widened as she stared across the heads of the audience at Jim. Standing tall in his perfectly fitted navy suit, Royal Air Force tie and medal ribbons on his chest, Jim was the very image of a hero. And judging by the expressions on the faces around her, Millie could see that most of them thought so too.

'Ordinary working people,' Jim continued, 'who often have gone hungry so they can find a couple of coins to pay the doctor to visit their sick child.' He paused and surveyed the now rapt and silent audience. 'Ordinary people who may have lost a little one because, already hungry and cold, they couldn't spare a sixpence,' he added in a softer tone.

A shiver ran down Millie's spine, and several women in front of her searched for handkerchiefs.

'But never again!' Jim punched hard the palm of his left hand with his right fist, making the audience gasp. 'From next July, every man, woman and child in this country will be treated according to their medical needs, and not their ability to pay.' His mouth pulled into a firm line, and he stood proud. 'That is the principle on which the new National Health Service will be built.'

There was a moment of silence. And then the hall erupted in raucous applause and a tumultuous standing ovation. With eyes shining brightly, Millie and her friends rose to their feet and clapped as enthusiastically as everyone else.

Mr Wheeler, clapping like a clockwork monkey bashing two cymbals together, made his way to where Jim stood. 'Thank you, Comrade Smith, for giving us such a full explanation of the new health service.'

The applause grew louder and Jim smiled. His gaze travelled slowly over the enthusiastic audience until it alighted on Millie. The implacable glint in his eye softened and a hint of a smile lifted the corners of his mouth.

And, in that instant, all the niggling misgivings and vague doubts that had been weighing Millie down since she'd accepted Jim's proposal simply vanished. She smiled warmly at him.

'And if there are no further questions?' Mr Wheeler asked. No one spoke. 'Then I'll declare this meeting closed.'

Jim shook Mr Wheeler's and Mrs Harper's hands, and then jumped off the stage.

'I tell you Millie,' said Joyce, as she finally stopped clapping, 'your Jim's a right cracker on all counts.'

'Yes, he is,' said Millie, her heart feeling full. 'And I'm going to marry him.'

Jim made his way towards Millie but was halted at every second step by someone wanting to shake him by the hand or slap him heartily on the back.

Millie left her seat and squeezed her way though the milling crowd.

As she reached him, a confident and unruffled expression warmed Jim's blue eyes.

'How did I do, darling?' he asked,

'Jim, you were marvellous,' Millie replied, staring proudly up at him.

He hooked an arm around her waist. 'Was I really okay?'

She nodded, enjoying the feel of his body pressed against hers. He smiled and dipped his head.

As Jim's mouth pressed into her lips, Millie closed her eyes and locked away forever her foolish regret at not becoming a policeman's wife, and imagined instead the exciting prospect of becoming a politician's wife.

Chapter Thirty-Three

Ruby scratched through another item on her list. 'Right, so that's the hymns sorted out. Now to arrange where everyone is sitting.'

'I thought we did that last week,' Doris said, pouring them all another cup of tea.

'That was before we knew that Jim's mother was definitely coming,' Ruby replied.

Millie groaned inwardly. Connie caught her eye and gave her a sympathetic look.

They were sitting around Ruby's dining-room table, overlooking the garden on a frosty late November day, as her aunt once again went through the plans for Millie's big day. In fact, Millie was a little surprised that her aunt hadn't made little models of herself and Jim, the guests, cake, flowers and church to push around a table mapped with a seating plan with a stick to make sure the configuration was just right.

'But surely all we have to do is shunt everyone on the top table down a bit,' Millie said.

Ruby looked at Millie as if she'd suggested that they all attend the wedding breakfast stark naked. 'Shunt everyone down! What, and have Jim's mother suffer Martha's chatter about budgies all though the meal? Amelia, I don't think so!' Ruby pulled the table plan closer. 'Anthony and I will have to swap sides in order that Lady Tollshunt can sit by me. At least I know how to converse properly with the upper crust. It's a pity none of the rest of Jim's family can make it.'

'Yes, isn't it?' replied Millie. 'But his father rarely leaves the estate and meanwhile his brother's in Monte Carlo for the winter with friends.'

Her mother and Ruby looked impressed.

In fact, Millie was heartily relieved that only Jim's mother planned to come to their wedding. She suspected, too, that even this was only after much persuading on Jim's part, and was only under tremendous sufferance. And as they were having a quiet wedding, it saved his many aunts, uncles and cousins the trouble of concocting excuses as to why they couldn't be there. Other than his mother, his best man Tim Braithwaite from the Ministry of Health, and a handful of Air Force chums, most of the twenty-five people at the reception would be from Millie's side.

'Now, your dress, Connie,' Ruby said, moving on to the next item on her agenda.

'I've finished it,' said Connie. 'And I'm having it pressed at the cleaner's a day or two before.'

'Good,' said Ruby, marking that line off as she took a quick mouthful of tea. 'Doris, have you organised the flowers?'

Millie's mum nodded. 'I've told Hattie in the market that you want yellow tea-roses for Millie's bouquet and Connie's posy, and carnation button-holes, preferably red although pink will do if the red are more than sixpence apiece.'

Ruby struck the floral requirements off her list.

She looked at Millie. 'The cake?' Ruby said, her pen hovering over the notebook.

'I've given the extra coupons from the food

office to Mrs Pierce and she's going to start soaking the fruit next week,' replied Millie.

'And the cover?'

'I'm afraid the best plaster cover from Hoffman's is out that day,' Millie said.

'Damn it,' said Ruby, as if being told the POW escape tunnel had just collapsed. She lit a cigarette and blew the smoke out of the side of her mouth. 'I know. Madge Finch at church is chummy with the manager of that fancy foreign cake shop on the Broadway. She owes me a favour after the fiasco of the Harvest supper; I'll have a word with her.' Ruby looked down at her list again. 'I'm sorting out a suit for Bill so he doesn't show us all up when he walks you into the church. Anthony's in charge of the cars, and we've covered the table wine for the toast. And so I think this only leaves your outfit, Amelia,' she said, smiling fondly at Millie. 'I rang Maurice at the factory and his sample machinist will have it ready for the final fitting on Friday morning. Are you free to meet me and your mother there at eleven?'

'I'm on a half-day, so could we make it at three?' Millie replied.

'As long as you're prompt,' Ruby replied. 'Anthony and I are invited to a drinks reception at the town hall that night, and so I'll have to catch the four-ten from Stratford.'

Doris sighed. 'I wish you were having a proper wedding, Millie,' she said, not for the first time.

'It is a proper wedding,' Millie said.

'You know what I mean, Millie,' said Doris. 'I thought you always wanted a white wedding.'

An image of herself dressed in Connie's beau-

578

tiful wedding dress walking down the aisle on Alex's arm flashed across Millie's mind.

'No,' she said, forcing a light laugh. 'I'll be just as married when I walk out of the church with this ceremony.'

Ruby closed her notebook and flicked ash into the half-filled ashtray at her elbow. 'You know Anthony's coming to move your stuff to the house next Saturday?'

'Yes,' Millie replied. 'And I'll have it packed and ready for him when he turns up.'

Ruby gave a satisfied nod.

As they couldn't live in the Boatman after they were married, Jim had found a terraced house in Leytonstone just off the High Street, convenient for the shops and a short walk from the train station. As he had been busy with the dockers' union business for the past months, Millie had spent all her spare time cleaning, decorating and hanging curtains. Jim had used his savings to buy Utility furniture for the downstairs and a new bed, while Millie had scraped together the money for a second-hand wardrobe as well as the household crockery and linen.

'I don't know why you have to move to Leytonstone,' said Doris with a sigh. 'Surely there were nice houses you could have rented in Bow or Stratford.'

'There were, but Jim thinks if he lives in the constituency he's more likely to be adopted as the prospective candidate,' Millie explained. She reached out and covered her mother's hand with her own. 'I'll still be working around the corner in Munroe House and I promise that I will pop in after work a couple of times a week.'

Her mother smiled. 'I'm not worried about me – I'm thinking of you cycling all that way to Wapping before you've even started your day.'

Ruby looked shocked. 'But surely, Doris, Amelia will be giving up work to look after the house for Jim?'

Millie laughed. 'Not just yet, Aunt Ruby. In fact, we're so short of nurses that Mrs Archer came to Munroe House and practically begged me to stay on after I got married.'

Ruby pursed her lips. 'These modern ways! But I don't suppose it will be for long anyhow, and once you've fallen in the family way, you'll have to give up. But your mother's got a point: it must be almost four miles from Leytonstone to Munroe House.'

Connie looked at Millie and raised an eyebrow.

Millie laughed. 'I had wanted to see your face when I just turned up on it, but I'll have to tell you.' She beamed at her mother and aunt. 'Jim's bought me a Swallow Gadabout.'

'A what?' asked Ruby.

'A motor scooter,' said Millie. She reached down and pulled the showroom brochure from her handbag. She handed it to her mother. 'It does over a hundred miles a gallon and the seat lifts up so I can stow my nurses' bag. It's being delivered next week. Of course I'll have to have L plates until I've passed my test, but it will save my aching legs.'

Doris and Ruby looked up from the leaflet in astonishment.

'What a lucky girl you are to be marrying such

a caring, considerate man,' said Ruby. 'When I think who you could have had.'

Doris glared at her sister.

Ruby reached across the table and covered Millie's hand with hers. 'And it's no more than you deserve, you know.'

'Thank you, Aunt Ruby,' Millie replied stiffly.

Ruby glanced at the mantelshelf where the jolly china pixie displayed the twenty-first of November on his wheelbarrow. 'Just think, four weeks tomorrow you'll become the Honourable Mrs James Woodville Smith,' she said, with a misty look in her eye.

'No, I won't, because firstly, according to Jim, you never use the Honourable and secondly, Jim doesn't agree with titles so I'll be plain Mrs Jim Smith. And very happy I'll be, too.'

As Jim paid off the taxi, Millie made her way up the steps to the Leytonstone and Wanstead Labour Party offices. Her hand went for the umpteenth time to check that her close-fitting hat was straight. The cabbie flipped up the For Hire sign on his meter and drove off.

'Are you sure I look all right?' Millie asked, as Jim trotted up the steps to join her.

He smiled. 'Perfect.'

Millie wasn't so sure. She'd spent hours in Boardman's in Stratford trying on different outfits with Connie, before settling on a square-shouldered aubergine suit with a straight skirt, but now she wondered if she would have been better off with the russet and black dogtooth-check one.

'I mean, is it grand enough for a constituency

reception?' she persisted, as she took his arm.

'It's impeccable. And when the executive panel see you on my arm they'll make me the prospective candidate for the Leytonstone and Wanstead constituency on the spot,' Jim joked, opening the heavy front door and guiding her through.

As she walked into the reception hall Millie wasn't so sure.

The 1930s bold block-designed interior was abuzz with people. The men, nearly all large prosperous types dressed in dark suits, seemed to be bellowing rather than talking to each other, while the women at their sides were either fussing with the jewellery at their throats or preening the furs draped around their shoulders.

Millie fervently wished she'd taken up Ruby's offer and borrowed her fox stole to give her a bit more 'class', as her aunt put it.

Jim's arm slipped around her waist. 'Let's get a drink and then we can mingle.'

They walked over to the improvised bar next to the Bakelite telephone switchboard at the back of the room. Jim handed Millie a dry sherry and had just taken the froth off the top of his pint of brown ale when a man with a face like a gargoyle, dressed in a double-breasted suit two sizes too small and a florid neck-tie, puffed towards them.

'Oi! Jimmy boy,' he shouted, as a strand of grey hair oiled flat across his bald head slid forward.

Irritation flitted briefly across Jim's face, but then he turned and smiled. 'Mr Kirby, what a pleasure.' He offered his hand.

'Good to see you, comrade,' Mr Kirby replied, pumping Jim's hand enthusiastically. 'And we're all equals now, so it's Ted.' His piggy eyes slid on to Millie. 'And who's this pretty little thing?'

'This is my fiancée, Miss Sullivan. Millie, this is Mr Kirby, the chairman of the candidate selection committee.'

'It's very nice to meet you, Mr Kirby,' Millie said, smiling pleasantly at him.

Ted grabbed Millie's hand in his sweaty one. 'Likewise I'm sure, love.'

'Millie's a district nurse with the St George's and St Dunstan's District Nursing Association,' Jim added.

Ted looked impressed.

'Can I get you a beer, Mr Kirby?' Jim asked.

Ted patted his considerable belly. 'Perhaps a whisky.'

Jim put down his pint and strolled back to the bar.

Ted turned to Millie. 'Sullivan,' he said thoughtfully. 'Your family Micks then?'

For Jim's sake Millie smiled sweetly. 'Like most people in East London, I have some Irish in me, but my mother's family came from Bethnal Green and my father was from Bow,' she replied in an even tone, 'and that's where I was born.' She gave Ted the brief history of her family.

'Good,' said Ted approvingly when she'd finished. 'I told Jim lad he needed to find himself a local girl with solid working-class roots to have a hope in hell's chance of winning over the Commie-lovers on the selection committee, and it looks like he's done just that.'

Millie stared past him at her fiancé chatting to a thin man in a baggy hopsack suit with spec-

583

tacles wedged on to the end of his nose. Sensing her eyes on him, Jim turned and looked at her with concern. He finished his conversation and strolled back.

'There you go, Mr Kirby,' Jim said, handing him a cut-glass tumbler. 'I got you a double.'

'Trying to get me in trouble with 'er in doors, are you?' Ted asked cheerfully.

'It's a Ballantine's single malt,' Jim replied.

A crafty expression spread across the committee chairman's face. 'But then again, what the eye don't see, the 'eart won't grieve over.'

Ted Kirby threw his drink back and slammed the glass down on the table beside them.

'I'd better put my face around, but I'll be seeing you at the meeting next week, lad,' he said, touching the side of his nose with his finger and winking.

'You most certainly will,' Jim said. 'And thank you for all your support. I won't forget it, Mr Kirby.'

Ted beamed benevolently at him and then turned to Millie. 'It's been a pleasure meeting you too, and,' his chubby hand slipped around behind and patted her behind, 'you can come and give me a bed bath anytime, sweetheart.'

He ambled off. Millie stared incredulously at him for a moment, and then swung angrily around.

'Did you see that?' she muttered through gritted teeth.

'He's just being affectionate, that's all,' Jim replied.

'Aren't you going to say something to him?'

584

Jim glanced around. 'Keep your voice down, Millie, please. You're making a scene.'

Millie glared at him. 'I'm not now, but I will when I march over there and slap Comrade Randy across his fat face.'

Jim grabbed her elbow and ushered her into a quiet corner. 'Ted's got a lot of clout in the selection committee, remember. Or are you deliberately trying to ruin my chances of being selected?'

'If I let him put his hand down my knickers will he recommend you for a place in the Cabinet?' Millie snapped.

'Now you're just being ridiculous!' Jim replied.

'Well then. Perhaps you ought to get yourself another "local girl with solid working-class roots" who doesn't mind having Comrade Ted's sweaty hands all over her,' Millie suggested.

'What are you talking about?'

'Didn't he tell you to hook up with a local girl with solid working-class roots?'

Jim gave her a puzzled look. 'I recall he said some such nonsense a while back. But surely you can't really think...? Oh, Millie!' Jim gathered her into his arms, and Millie's humiliation subsided a little. 'I didn't ask you to marry me on Ted's recommendation. I did it because I love you, and I want you to be my wife.'

'Do you?'

He ran his index finger along her jaw and kissed her. 'How can you doubt it? I'd like nothing more than to march over there and beat Comrade Ted to a pulp, but if I do it will destroy everything I've been working towards for the past ten years. With Ted backing me, I'm certain to be accepted as the prospective Labour candidate, and then our future and,' he kissed her lips this time, slowly and deeply, 'our children's future, is assured.' He looked lovingly down at her. 'How many did you say you wanted?'

'Three or four,' she replied, feeling a maternal ache at the thought of them.

'Well then, do you understand why I'm suppressing my chivalrous inclination to knock Ted Kirby's block off, Millie?'

'I suppose so,' she replied dubiously.

A satisfied smile spread over Jim's well-proportioned features. 'Good. Now let's get another drink and mingle.'

As she hadn't quite mastered the brakes, Millie's new scooter jolted to a halt outside Mrs Mundey's house. She was immediately surrounded by children muffled to the cheeks against the chilly weather, jostling for a better view. They weren't the only ones who were mesmerised by Jim's gift. Annie and Sally's eyes had all but popped out of their heads when they saw Millie putt-putt into the back yard of Munroe House that morning, and she'd been the centre of attention in every street she'd visited since.

Millie switched off the engine and pulled her bright blue Gadabout on to its central stand. After rubbing her hands to bring some warmth back into them, she removed her bag from under the seat.

Stepping between two lads holding on to invisible handlebars and making 'vroom vroom' sounds, Millie knocked on the door. After a few moments Joy opened it.

'Sister Sullivan, what a surprise,' she said, her warm breath escaping in little puffs as she spoke.

'I thought I'd pop by and see how you were keeping,' Millie said, noting that the young woman looked drawn and puffy-eyed. She also noticed that Joy was wearing a coat and open-fingered gloves.

Joy smiled. 'Come in. We're in the front room.'

Millie stepped into the house and then went through to the parlour. Ginnie was playing with a rag doll in front of the hearth. She, too, was in her outdoor clothes and although the safety guard was in front of the fire, it wasn't alight.

Millie noticed, too, that whereas the last time she'd been in the room eight weeks before it had been crammed full of fixtures and fittings, now there was a small extendable table and two hardback chairs pulled up close to the fire and very little else, although there was a single bed and a small chest of drawers against the far wall where the sofa had been.

'What on earth happened to your mother's furniture?' Millie asked, gazing at the flimsy cotton curtains hanging now where the plush chenille drapes had been.

'The welfare man,' Joy replied, indicating for Millie to sit.

Millie put her bag on the bare-board floor and pulled out one of the chairs from the table. Joy sat on the other.

'I had to go to the council after my savings ran out two weeks back,' Joy said. 'They sent the pigging welfare officer around to poke his long nose

587

into everything. After an hour of wanting to know the inside and out of a cat's arse, he told me that as there was only me and Ginnie, I needed two chairs, a table and a bed, and I'd have to sell the rest before the assistance board would consider helping me. I did exactly what they told me to, along with selling half of my clothes and a couple of pairs of shoes also. But now I've given the landlord his money, I've only got enough for milk, bread, a couple of pounds of spuds and a bit of scrag-end to tide us through until Monday.'

'What about coal and electric?' Millie said, already feeling the cold even through her winter coat.

'Sadie next door gave me a bucket of coal yesterday and I'll eke that out for as long as I can,' Joy replied. 'She brought in a bit of stew for me and Ginnie, too, and said she'd save me a bit of supper tonight. But she's got five young 'uns to feed so I can't keep taking from 'er, or Winnie across the road, who gave me a couple of shovelfuls and fed us the day before.'

'But you can't live without proper heating,' said Millie. 'If Ginnie gets cold she could become sick.'

'I know,' said Joy, lifting Ginnie up and kissing her forehead. 'That's why I light the fire when it gets dark for an hour or two and give her the best bits of meat. Once the bed's warmed up I wrap her up and we turn in for the night and keep each other warm.' She pressed her lips on to her daughter's curly black hair. 'If I'm careful with the pennies and if it don't get much colder we might be all right for another week.'

'You must go back to the council, Joy,' said Millie. 'And tell them you've got no light and heating, and a child to care for.'

'What, and have them take her away from me? If they put her into a kiddies' home I'll never get her back,' cried Joy, holding Ginnie fiercely to her.

Millie regarded Joy sadly for a moment and then looked at the little girl with the big, brown eyes and sunny disposition. A spectre of her sitting alone and unloved in a dormitory in a stark children's home rose unbidden.

Millie put her hand in her pocket and dug out all the money she had.

'Here, take this,' Millie said, thrusting two green pound notes and a handful of loose silver at Joy.

She looked shocked. 'It's so good of you, Sister, but I can't take that.'

'I'm not giving it to you,' Millie said, pushing it into her hand. 'I'm giving it to Ginnie. It might keep you going another week or two until–'

'Marvin gets back,' Joy cut in, as her hand closed around the money.

Millie was about to tell Joy that she should do as Millie had had to do, and accept that her lost love wasn't coming back. But as she stared at Joy's eager face the warning words died on Millie's lips.

She smiled instead. 'Yes,' Millie said, 'until Marvin gets back.'

Chapter Thirty-Four

'Doesn't she look a picture, Ruby?' Doris said, standing back and staring fondly at Millie.

An almost maternal expression spread across Ruby's carefully made-up face. 'Straight out of a society magazine,' she agreed.

Millie ought to look her best. After all, they'd all been up since six to get preened and powdered ready for the big day. Millie had taken advantage of one of the baths in Munroe House the night before for a good scrub and so, after a full strip-wash in the kitchen, she, her mother and aunt had all dashed to Mona's Salon in Chapman Street for an eight-thirty appointment to style their hair. Connie had met them there and after two hours with her hair in curlers under the dryer, Millie sat for another hour while the hair-dresser pinned her hair up, Rita Hayworth-style. The whole creation was then topped off with her pill-box hat with a half-veil, which was secured into place without disturbing her looped auburn curls.

They'd come back to find Aunts Martha and Edie and Uncle Bill in their best clothes, drinking tea in the front room. The flowers had arrived just then and, as there was a mix-up with the button-holes, Ruby had to go around to the stall to sort it out. This gave everyone a little peace and Connie a chance to discharge her chief bridesmaid's duties without Ruby's directions. By the time her aunt had returned, Millie was already dressed in her powder-blue box-shouldered wedding suit.

'Turn around again,' said Doris. 'Let's have a proper look at you.'

Millie did, and stared at her reflection in the long mirror. Her mother came around and stood beside it. 'You look an absolute treat,' she said, with a tremble of emotion in her voice.

Millie craned her head back. 'Are my seams straight, Connie?' she asked, lifting her skirt to adjust her suspenders.

'As a die,' Connie replied. 'Although you've still got the price on the bottom of your shoe.'

'For goodness sake,' said Millie, hopping on her left foot and snatching at the other.

Connie caught her and removed the label. They looked at each other and grinned.

'Any second thoughts?' asked Connie.

'No, just collywobbles,' Millie replied. 'What's the time?'

'Nearly eleven. You've got a quarter of an hour yet before we have to go,' replied Connie, glancing at her watch. 'It's only five minutes to the church.'

'Let's make sure we have everything,' said Ruby, going over to the open suitcase lying on Millie's bed. 'Are you sure you've got enough?' she asked, looking dubiously at the modest number of neatly folded clothes.

'Yes,' Millie replied. 'Jim has an important meeting at Congress House on Thursday, and so we're only away for three days, and luckily the Grand at Eastbourne has a laundry facility.'

'Oh, the Grand,' Connie said in a pretend

plummy voice. 'How grand!'

'Of course Jim's booked somewhere exclusive for the honeymoon,' said Ruby. 'It's what he's been brought up to. After all, you wouldn't expect him to stay in a guesthouse on the Prom, would you?'

'In my day,' said Doris. 'The bride didn't know where she was being whisked off to until after the wedding.'

'He had to tell me because they dress for dinner and he wanted to make sure I packed something suitable,' replied Millie.

'What about your,' Ruby leaned forward conspiratorially, 'wedding lingerie,' she mouthed.

'Tucked in the bottom,' Millie whispered back.

Ruby nodded. 'Good, you'll be nervous enough when you get to the room without having to search for your nightclothes.'

Millie's cheeks grew warm as she caught Connie's eye.

'I'll go and check the flowers are all right in the sink, Mrs Harris,' Connie said and left the bedroom.

'Have you spoken to Amelia, Doris?' Ruby asked as the door clicked shut.

Doris looked puzzled. 'About what?'

Ruby jerked her head. 'You know. The wedding night.'

Doris laughed. 'For goodness sake, Ruby, Millie's a nurse.'

Ruby looked sceptical. 'Studying ... you know what ... in books is one thing, Doris, but it's a different matter having,' although there were only the three of them in the room, she glanced surreptitiously over her shoulder, 'a male wotsit coming at you. I remember the shock I had when dear Bertram, God rest him, got into bed on our first night all...' Ruby raised her index finger.

Millie suppressed a smile. 'I've given bed baths on a men's surgical ward, Aunt Ruby, so I know what an erect penis looks like.'

Ruby blanched. 'You may have, Amelia,' she said, tucking an imaginary curl back under her hat. 'But that still doesn't prepare you for what it will be like.'

'Thank you, Aunt Ruby,' cut in Millie.

Doris glanced at her wristwatch with a smile. 'Is that the time? Do you think Tony's arrived with the car yet, Ruby?'

'I'd better go and see,' replied Ruby. She left the room and her heels could be heard clip-clopping down the stairs.

Millie and her mother stared at each other for a moment, then they burst out laughing. 'Oh, Millie,' her mother said, wiping her eyes.

'I know,' replied Millie, carefully dabbing a tear from her lower lids before it smudged her mascara.

Her mother's expression became serious and she took Millie's hand. 'You're not worried are you?'

Millie smiled. 'No, Mum.'

'Because there's nothing to be–'

'I know.'

Her mother gave her a thoughtful look and then smiled. 'You do look so beautiful, Millie. I only wish your dad could see you.'

'So do I,' replied Millie.

A car tooted in the street outside.

'That sounds like Tony,' her mother said. 'Are you ready?'

Millie's heart thumped a couple of times and then galloped away. 'Can you give me a few moments?'

Doris drew her towards her and kissed her on her cheek. 'I'll wait downstairs.'

Her mother left and Millie sat down at her dressing table. She stared through the mesh of her veil at herself in the mirror for a couple of seconds and then pulled open the top drawer. Reaching in, she rummaged through her handkerchiefs and trinkets until she found her white leather confirmation Bible at the back. Opening it, she took out the photograph of her and Alex with their heads poking through the comical seaside screen. A wistful smile lifted the corners of Millie's lips as she gazed at Alex's laughing eyes and she remembered his hand resting lightly on her waist. Other images that a bride shouldn't think on her wedding morning started to form, but brusquely Millie pushed them aside.

'Goodbye, Alex,' she whispered, dropping the photo into her wicker basket containing discarded cotton wool and an empty jar of cold cream.

She picked up her lipstick, reapplied it, and then stood up and walked out of her bedroom to marry Jim.

Uncle Bill blinked rapidly and raised his pint. 'I give you my niece and her new husband Jim. Mr and Mrs Smith.'

The guests raised their glasses and repeated, 'Mr and Mrs Smith.'

Jim's mother, who in the absence of her husband, was sitting at Millie's left elbow, sniffed loudly.

The two dozen people in the grill room of the Minories Hotel resumed their seats. Jim's hand closed over Millie's.

'Happy, darling?' he asked, giving her the warmest of smiles.

In the ten months she'd known Jim, Millie had never seen him anything less than immaculately dressed, but he'd excelled himself for their wedding day. The understated dark suit was clearly made to measure and it fit him to perfection. With a crisp white shirt beneath and his navy, claret and white striped Air Force tie tied in a double Windsor knot at his throat, he looked exceptionally handsome.

'Yes, very,' Millie replied, enjoying the ripple of excitement running through her.

Millie had been a little worried after Jim had suggested a weekend away that he'd also expect that they would share a double room, but he hadn't. In fact, he'd never so much as hinted they might pre-empt their nuptials, which meant that their first night as a married couple would still be special.

As the formalities were over, people were leaving their places to chat with each other or replenish their drinks at the bar.

Jim squeezed Millie's hand. 'I'm just going to have a word with a couple of the chaps. Will you be all right until I get back, Mrs Smith?'

Millie giggled. 'I should think so, Mr Smith.'

Jim stood up and strolled off to greet some

guests and Millie's gaze travelled around the room.

Her mother had left her place next to Jim to speak to May and Wilf who were sitting on one of the other tables, while a couple of Jim's RAF friends were in deep conversation with Tony at the bar. Bill stood up and went to join them. Millie looked across at Jim's mother, who was sitting on the other side of Bill and talking to Jim's best man, Tim Braithwaite.

Lady Tollshunt had clearly decided to make the best of things and she had dressed for the occasion. She had removed her three-quarter length sable coat that had had Ruby's eyes out on stalks all through the ceremony to reveal a purple gown with bead trimmings. She had a long string of pearls hanging around her neck and diamonds dangling from her ears and right wrist. To complete the ensemble Lady Tollshunt wore a very broad hat with exotic feathers encircling the brim. Having finished her conversation with Tim on her left, Jim's mother turned to Millie.

'That's a pretty colour,' she said.

'Thank you,' replied Millie. 'Did you have a good journey down?'

'No, it was frightful,' Lady Tollshunt replied, her tetchy expression corroborating her story.

'I'm sorry to hear that,' replied Millie. 'It's a pity Jim's father couldn't come.'

Lady Tollshunt regarded her coolly for a second or two, and then spoke. 'I know James has these strange notions about equality between the classes, but can I ask, Millie, that from now on you call my son by the name he was christened with, at least within my hearing?'

'Of course,' Millie replied, feeling her cheeks flame with embarrassment.

Her mother-in-law gave her a chilly smile and then turned to study the far end of the room.

Millie looked across at her husband, who stood at the bar laughing and joking with two of his old flying friends, willing him to return. Out of the corner of her eye Millie spotted Aunt Ruby making her way towards them and she groaned inwardly.

'I thought I'd pop over and make sure everything is all right, Lady Tollshunt,' Ruby said, smiling deferentially at Millie's mother-in-law.

'My lady,' said Jim's mother.

Ruby looked confused. 'I'm sorry?'

'You address me as Lady Tollshunt the first time you speak to me, after which you can address me as "my lady",' Jim's mother said with a condescending smile. 'And other than I would have preferred to have had my son and his wife acclaimed as Mr and Mrs Woodville Smith, I'm quite all right thank you.'

Ruby put her hand on her chest and let out a long breath. 'Thank goodness. Because I know my brother Bill can appear a bit strange if you don't know him, but he's got a heart of gold and is no bother unless something flusters him. I do hope you've enjoyed the day.'

'I can't ever remember attending such an extraordinary wedding.' Lady Tollshunt's benevolent lady-of-the-manor smile spread across her face.

Ruby positively beamed. 'Why, that's very kind of you to say so, my lady.'

'But I'm a bit surprised it's legal to marry a couple in a hut.'

Millie gave her mother-in-law the sweetest smile. 'St George's suffered a direct hit in 1941, so they put the hut inside and the bishop re-dedicated it a year later.'

'How very plucky,' Lady Smith replied.

Ruby smiled uncertainly, and there was an uncomfortable silence.

Jim strolled back and put his arm around Millie. 'Don't you think, Mother, that Millie is the loveliest of brides?'

'Indeed,' his mother replied, as her eyes flickered over Millie once more. She unfastened her handbag and took out her gloves. 'Don't forget, James, you have at least a three-hour drive to Eastbourne and that it will be getting dark soon.'

Jim looked at his watch and then turned to Millie. 'Mother's right. Perhaps we should cut the cake?'

Lady Tollshunt smiled to show her agreement.

Jim took his wife's hand and tucked it in the crook of his arm. He led Millie over to the table in the corner where the cake was set up. They took their places behind it and Ruby handed Jim the cake knife.

'Fill your glasses for the toast,' shouted Tony over the noise.

There was a scramble as people topped up the drinks. Ruby took off the plaster cover to reveal the square fruit cake beneath. Jim handed Millie the knife, the photographer came over, and Millie and Jim smiled. There was a pop as the flash fired and then, with lights bursting in her vision, Millie gripped the knife handle and Jim's hands closed over hers. Laughing, they sliced though the cake and a cheer went up. Jim slipped his arm around Millie and pulled her closer. He leaned forward until his mouth was next to her ear.

'If we leave by half-two we can be booked into the Grand by five,' he said in a low voice. His arm tightened around her waist. 'And we don't have to go down for dinner until eight.'

Millie looked up into Jim's ardent blue eyes and smiled. 'Well, we'd better chop up this cake and get going then.'

Under a shower of rice and holding tight to Jim's arm, Millie hurried down the front steps of the Minories Hotel with the guests in hot pursuit.

'Bye, Millie!' shouted Connie, Beattie and Sally, bobbing up and down with excitement.

'Good luck, old man!' bellowed Jim's RAF friends, raising their pints in salute.

'Your bouquet!' screamed Annie.

Millie turned and handed the collection of wooden spoons tied in ribbon, cardboard horse-shoes and black cats to Jim.

'Ready?' she laughed, raising her flowers above her head.

Swinging her arm in an arc, Millie hurled her yellow roses in the air as Connie, Beattie and Sally laughed and jostled to catch them. Connie stretched up but a last-minute leap by Annie meant it was she who secured the prize.

A cheer went up, and Martha and Edie dabbed their eyes while Doris and Ruby stood with their arms looped together and wearing the same sentimental expression in the hotel doorway. Jim's mother was standing by herself on the extreme right with a somewhat censorious look on her face.

Jim put his arm around Millie. 'I ought to put you in to bowl for the Tollshunt first eleven.'

Millie laughed as he guided her towards the car. He opened the door and she climbed in. He went around to the other side and got in behind the wheel.

Gathering her into his arms, he kissed her. 'I love you, Mrs Smith.'

A cheer went up outside and Jim started the engine.

Millie wound her window down. 'Bye!' she shouted, waving furiously as the car pulled away from the kerb.

Suddenly there was a loud clattering and clanging behind them. The guests roared with glee as the trail of tin cans, saucepan lids and bent ladles tied to the back of the car clattered over the cobbles.

Jim pulled a face and Millie giggled. Passers-by pointed and laughed as they drove along with what sounded like half the kitchen dragging and banging behind them.

'I can't drive all the way to Eastbourne like this,' Jim said as he veered past the Tower of London towards Tower Bridge.

He turned into East Smithfield and pulled up. 'I'll only be a few moments.'

'While you're doing that, I'll shake some of this rice off,' Millie replied.

They climbed out of the car and Jim went around the back. Millie brushed off her jacket and flicked her veil to release the grains lodged in it.

'Excuse me, Ma'am,' a deep voice said from behind her.

Millie turned and found herself staring up at a tall black man wearing a square-shouldered brown striped jacket with matching wide-kneed trousers. He touched the front of his broad-brimmed fedora with a long index finger.

'It's been a while since I've been around these parts, and I seem to have lost my bearings. I was hoping, Ma'am, you might do me the kindness of putting me on the right road for Clementine Street.'

Millie stared at him, feeling slightly light-headed. 'Clementine Street?'

'If it's no trouble,' he said respectfully.

'You're American!'

He smiled and his teeth cut a sharp white curve across his face. 'I am. From Detroit in the good old U.S. of A.'

Millie blinked and gathered her thoughts. 'Follow the road for half a mile until you get to the church,' she said, indicating towards the Highway. 'Cross over the road and then, keeping the Old Rose pub on your right, walk down Gravel Lane and head towards the river. Clementine Road is the second on your left.'

The young man touched the brim of his hat again. 'I'm much obliged, ma'am.' He turned and strolled down the road, whistling a lazy tune.

'Who was that?' asked Jim, as he came around

601

from the back of the car.

'Marvin,' Millie replied, watching him heading down the road.

Jim gave her a questioning look. Millie laughed and threw herself into his arms.

She kissed him deeply and he hugged her closer. He released her lips and Millie ran her fingers through his hair.

'I'll explain on the way,' Millie said, taking in every detail of her husband's finely chiselled features. She kissed him again. 'Now, get back in the car and put your foot down all the way to Eastbourne, Jim.'

Acknowledgements

Call Nurse Millie has been quite a leap forward in time for me and unlike my previous four Victorian East London books this story is set within living memory. From a research point of view it has been a double endeavour as not only am I trying to capture the austere post-war period but also my own profession (I'm a qualified District and Queen's Nurse) at a time before the NHS and most of the medications and treatments we take for granted today had been developed.

As always, I would like to mention a few books, authors and people, to whom I am particularly indebted:

For Millie's nursing background I used a number of nursing biographies, including Lucilla Andrews', *No Time for Romance*, Edith Cotterill's *Nurse on Call, Yes, Sister, no, Sister,* by Jennifer Craig, which although set in Leeds gives much of the flavour of post-war nurse training and culture as does *Of Sluices and Sister*, by Alison Collin. I garnered a couple of self-published gems in my travels including *My Life and Nursing Memories (from 1914–2008)* by Nurse Corbishley and *'Nurse' 'Yes, Sister'* by Dorothy Gill. I, of course, read Jennifer Worth's accounts of 1950s East London in her popular books *Call the Midwife* and

Shadows of the Workhouse, but the most detailed account of a pre-NHS Nursing Association came from Irene Sankey's biography, *Thank you Miss Hunter*, (unpublished manuscript). Ms Sankey became the Superintendent at the East London Nursing Society in 1946 and it's her detailed accounts of that time which helped me bring the Munroe House nurses to life.

I've also drawn on *Learning to Care, A history of nursing and midwifery education at the Royal London Hospital, 1740–1993*, by Parker and Collins (1998) in, association with the London Hospital Museum, and *The London Volume II 1840–1948*, Clark-Kennedy 1963.

For Millie's professional life I have used several text books of the period including *Handbook of Queen's Nurses* (1943); a 1940 edition of Faber's *Nurse's Pocket Encyclopaedia and Diary and Guide; Parenthood, Design or Accident*, Fielding 4th edition (1943); *Psychiatry and Mental Health*, Rathbone-Oliver (1950); *Nursing and Disease of Sick Children*, Moncrieff 4th ed 1943 and *A Short Text Book of Midwifery*, Gibberd (1951), which has a number of medical illustrations that are not for the faint hearted.

For general background of the period I used *Our Hidden Lives*, Simon Garfield (2005), *Nella Last's Peace*, ed. P & R Malcomson (2008), *Austerity Britain 1945–51* by David Kynaston (2007) and although I can vividly remember the warmth and neighbourliness of the old streets I re-read the seminal research study into post-war East London by Young and Wilmott, *Family and Kinship in East London* (1957), to make sure I captured the true spirit of the dockside communities.

I also used several post-war photographic books including *'Couldn't afford Eels' Memories of Wapping 1900–1960*, Leigh (2010), *The Wartime Scrapbook*, Opie (2010) and *The Forties, Good Times Just Around the Corner*, Maloney (2005) and, although it is slightly later than the period Millie's story is set in, *London's East End, A 1960s Album*, Lewis (2010) which documents the sights and sounds I remember as a child.

I'm grateful to the team at the Queen's Nursing Institute who allowed me access to their archives and supplied me with tea while I sifted my way through their treasure trove of documents. There is a fascinating insight into their history on their website http://www.districtnursing150.org.uk/

My thanks to Doreen Bates, who was nursing the people of East London as a Queen's Nurse while I was sitting in my pram. Doreen and I spent many a pleasant hour putting the nursing world to rights, while I gleaned priceless first-hand knowledge of what it was like to nurse in East London in the early 1950s.

I've also used many family stories such as Aunt Ruby's house in Ilford which was really my Aunt Nell's, Alex's war service was taken from my father's war experiences in the 8th Army and Doris's time in St Mungo's is drawn from my mother's treatment in a 1960s mental hospital. There are many other instances and details which can be found on my website. www.jeanfullerton. com

I would also like to thank a few more people.

Firstly my very own Hero-at-Home, Kelvin, for his unwavering support and my three daughters, Janet, Fiona and Amy, for not minding too much that they are literary orphans sometimes. My fellow author and chum Fenella Miller and my brilliant critique partners and friends Elizabeth Hawksley and Jenny Haddon. Once again my lovely agent Laura Longrigg, whose encouragement and incisive editorial mind helped me to see the wood for the trees. Lastly, but by no means least, a big thank you once again to the editorial team at Orion, especially Kate Mills and Laura Gerrard, for once again turning my 400+ page manuscript into a beautiful book.

The publishers hope that this book has given you enjoyable reading. Large Print Books are especially designed to be as easy to see and hold as possible. If you wish a complete list of our books please ask at your local library or write directly to:

Magna Large Print Books
Magna House, Long Preston,
Skipton, North Yorkshire.
BD23 4ND

This Large Print Book for the partially sighted, who cannot read normal print, is published under the auspices of

THE ULVERSCROFT FOUNDATION

THE ULVERSCROFT FOUNDATION

... we hope that you have enjoyed this Large Print Book. Please think for a moment about those people who have worse eyesight problems than you ... and are unable to even read or enjoy Large Print, without great difficulty.

You can help them by sending a donation, large or small to:

**The Ulverscroft Foundation,
1, The Green, Bradgate Road,
Anstey, Leicestershire, LE7 7FU,
England.**
or request a copy of our brochure for more details.

The Foundation will use all your help to assist those people who are handicapped by various sight problems and need special attention.

Thank you very much for your help.